Praise for *The Aardvark Is Ready for War*

"A mad, dark comedy of war and the American penchant for self-absorption. A funny, raunchy novel, written in the secret language of electronic warfare and media overload. Comparison's to *Catch 22* will be commonplace—and earned."
—Stewart O'Nan, author of *Snow Angels*

"Along the way to this spectacular debut, Blinn appears to have digested the 20th century's most fiery fictional voices and come roaring through with an individual style to match the dirtiest, angriest and wittiest prose of his generation. . . . Since Thomas Pynchon we've been waiting for a writer who could rhapsodize our paranoid century with the same sick glee and pyrotechnic imagination, and here he is at last."—Carey Harrison, *San Francisco Chronicle*

"Every war has its books, and this certainly is one that will outlive the memory of the Persian Gulf fiasco. . . . A joy to read."
—Hubert Selby Jr., author of *Last Exit to Brooklyn* and *Requiem for a Dream*

"Imagine Irvine Welsh, with an American accent, in the Gulf War. Blinn's shipmates are J.D. Salinger and Joseph Heller. *The Aardvark Is Ready for War* is a novel of men behaving so badly you have to read it twice to believe it."
—Tibor Fischer, author of *The Thought Gang*

"One part *McHale's Navy*, one part *Apocalypse Now*, and one part *Neuromancer*. [Blinn] shows that while war may be hell, virtual war is a heck of a lot weirder, and no less deadly."
—Phil Patton, *Wired*

"Absolutely authentic."
—Robert Stone, author of *Outerbridge Reach*

"If *The Aardvark is Ready for War* is what the new navy's all about, then William S. Burroughs must be the new chief of naval operations and Charles Bukowski is the captain of Blinn's ship." —Lawrence Naumoff, author of *Silk Hope, N.C.*

"James Blinn has taken up Heller's satirical baton and produced a richly textured and insightful novel about the Gulf War. . . . It was our first virtual war, largely fought out on television screens, with CNN providing a commentary more appropriate to a baseball match. . . . Blinn spent nine years in the US Navy where he gathered the inside information that makes the book so persuasive. His outstanding novel deserves a place on the same shelf as the war stories of Heller and Evelyn Waugh." —Andrew Biswell, *London Daily Telegraph*

THE AARDVARK IS READY FOR WAR

James W. Blinn

Thunder's Mouth Press
New York

BLINN, JULIA
BORDEN, STUART
BUMPUS, JERRY
C.H., EXEMPLAR AND MENTOR
ISAAKS, ANNE
LUVAAS, WILLIAM
MATSON, PETER
MAULE, MICHAEL
MOTHER AND FATHER
PIETSCH, MICHAEL
YANNUZZI, DOROTHY

deep gratitude, all.

———————⦿———————

THE AARDVARK IS READY FOR WAR

Published by
Thunder's Mouth Press
An Imprint of Avalon Publishing Group Incorporated
161 William St., 16th Floor
New York, NY 10038

First Thunder's Mouth Press edition 2003

The characters and events in this book are fictitious. Any similarity to real persons, living or dead, is coincidental and not intended by the author.

Library of Congress Control Number is available.

ISBN 1-56025-546-3

9 8 7 6 5 4 3 2 1

Printed in the United States of America
Distributed by Publishers Group West

Obscene is that which eliminates the gaze, the image and every representation.

— Jean Baudrillard

ONE

Aardvark

Day Forty

I'M EATING A POT PIE and CNN's on the tube.

It's almost dark. I got my binoculars at the ready.

More missiles slam Tel Aviv. No gas. At least that's what they claim. But there's gas, all right. Aardvark gas. Changing everyone into aardvarks.

Tape of the CNN guy giving his report when the sirens go off. Man, he drops that mike and yanks on that aardvark mask like nobody's business. Cut to the Jerusalem bureau — whole room full of aardvarks and some woman talking head (talking AARDVARK head) yells into the mike, practically goes ballistic. What a hoot! I spit out a pea when I see THAT.

I fetch a brew. I leave the kitchen dark so the babe across the way can't see me clear. I'm just a shadow. Less than a shadow. She'd have to look hard to spot me.

Her place is all lit up real nice. I can see red lights on her stereo, a-blinking and a-flashing. I know she's home. But there's no action. Not yet. Must be around back. Hiding from me.

Another war expert. These guys bust my gut. Half the time they can't tell an F-18 from an F-16 from an M-16. They think Hawkeyes and AWACs are the same birds just because they both have flying saucers. What a maroon. This guy's telling me about some bombed-out comm center but it doesn't have a single goddam antenna on it and could just as well be some raghat sheep-banger 7-Eleven for all anybody knows.

She's doing her bit now. It's MTV since she moved in. Thinks she's safe behind those bamboo shades. Thinks my eyes can't touch her in her taped-up room. Behind those shades. But they're transparent at night. Leak like a screen door. Radiate like a CRT.

She cranks that stereo and jams around all hot and sexy. Thinks she's

Madonna or something. Pretty good bod. Ass be a little gangly but fairly humongous boobs. No '55 Buick, mind you, but not droopy AT ALL. Hard as rubber. Hard as bullets.

I'm going over her totally with the trusty Bushnells. It's funny. I mean I'm crouching here in my kitchen spying on this obviously hot babe and I'm not even all turned on or anything. Like I don't even think about fucking her or anything. I just get off surveilling her.

Every night it's like this. Me all hiding out in this dark kitchen, peeping with my binocs, scoping out this moderately awesome babe, just surveilling the living shit out of her, and I don't even get hot over it. At least not THAT way.

Day Thirty-nine

WHEN I GET HOME from the base I got a sixer and five Budget Gourmets and my aardvark mask over my shoulder. There's the fat chick from downstairs at the mailbox. She's some kind of artsy thing — always in black and has this unreal black hair that's whacked off on one side like she does her 'do in a paper cutter. Says she hears I'm shipping out.

I just say, Yup.

Her eyes kind of flick to the mask all nervous-like. You can't tell what it is — just says *Mark 1 Mod O* on the canvas bag. It doesn't like broadcast, *hey I'm a fucking gas mask yabba-dabba-do!*

Says I should take care of myself over there. Even though she says it nicely I can tell she's trying for an opening. Wants to dazzle me with her impressive war thoughts that fly so good down at the leather bar. I don't want to hear it. I just say, You bet, and walk upstairs pretending to sort my junk mail.

Plug the Budget Gourmet in to zap. Then I undo the computer and move it to the living room. I set the monitor on the blue director's chair beside the TV and run the keyboard over to the coffee table. The cord's too short so I push the table up close. I stack up the disks I smuggled from the shop today. Each one has SECRET stamped in red at the top and the CMC inventory code felt-tipped underneath. I'd get hammered if I got caught with these. But the Chief says anybody that doesn't ace the tac-bombing test is up for a seabag inspection. That guy's so ate up.

Dumping the tac-training program on the hard disk. It's four full disks but that's okay. I got forty megs.

We HAVE the technology.

The zapper beeps and I fetch my dinner, Chicken Cordon Bleu in a plastic tray. Glazed carrots and apple wedges.

I pop a brew and cop a shot at the babe's window. Catch a little action behind the blinds. She's there but it's still too light to see. She's just smoke. No detail. No depth. Not a person yet.

I get the mirror off the door to the head. I prop it on the kitchen stool, angle it so it reflects out the window to her living room. HER window in MY room. I have to go sit on the sofa twice before I get it all set up just right. Early warning.

Then I clear off the coffee table and arrange everything just so: the taste-tempting frozen dinner, my brew, computer keyboard in front of that, the mouse run out to its black neoprene pad, TV remote on the right, binoculars on the left. Then I snap on the web belt the aardvark mask hangs from.

I punch in *TACPRO*. When the menu pops up I run the cursor down to *MK 82 Bomb Run*. While that's loading I punch the channel flipper to CNN. It's a story about Israeli kids decorating their gas masks with finger paints — flags and missiles and jets. I check the mirror on the stool. All's quiet on the awesome-babe front. I'm all set. Shit. Forgot my fork. Gotta have a fork. A fork.

Day Thirty-eight

WORK'S A DRAG. Work's always a drag. Makes my shitty little apartment look like a pleasure palace. Finally it's dark and I hunker down. It's Miller time.

Jackpot! There she goes. She's gonna do it. I knew if I waited . . . Yes! Fingers sweaty on the focus knob. But I'm steady. Elbows tucked tight. That oily rubber sucked snug to my face, sucking at my eyeballs with each breath, tugging at my sinuses like there's hooks in 'em. Refine. That's the ticket. Yeah. Focus fine as a cunthair, finer than froghair. And . . . Off . . . It . . . Comes! RIGHT over her head. FULL frontal exposure. Look at her shake 'em. She likes that. Yes. The straps dig in behind my ears. YES! My breath wheezing through the filter, through the diaphragm, loud, like I'm on a respirator, like I'm goddam Darth Vader, like AARDVARK Vader. Gotta like that! And those awesome tits, those awesome, awesome titties. Oh yes.

Lights out.

End of show.

I should get me one of those night scopes — like the helo guys have.

Day Thirty-seven

THE CAMCORDER'S GOT A TEN-TO-ONE ZOOM so I ace right in on her window, pierce her defenses. I crack the shade just enough for the lens to poke out and make contact. I go out and check. You can't tell what it is.

I set up the new monitor on a stack of magazines by the other monitor and the TV, all three in a row. Sex, war, television. Looks like a network control room in here. A network of control in my room.

The target's a hardened ammo bunker. We're at transit altitude, busters at four hundred knots. I bring up the radar and pick up the bloop-bloop of the target, pass the pilot a vector of three-two-zero at forty. Throttles max. Drop to angels two. I punch in two weapons fly-to-points on top the radar fixes then transfer downrange-travel circles up front. We're a little off the vector so I give the pilot an easy left, then an easy right — on the nose twenty miles.

Larry King's talking all heavy-handed blah-blah-blah about fuel-air-explosives. They implode your eyeballs, pop your eardrums. Do they have them? Do we have them? Does SHE have them?

I bring up the radar again and give it two sweeps — superimpose the tactical plot, all the glowing symbols: x's, circles with numbers inside, vectors with range counters ticking down, the airplane bug jittering and scooting. Egyptian Nintendo. FTPs are still good. I'm a-gonna JAM these suckers right down that guy's throat. ESM picks up two emitters — both air friendlies. I inhibit them so they don't clutter the scope.

On the nose for ten.

Drop to angels one.

She enters the bedroom. She's wearing a short, silk bathrobe. Looks blue on the monitor. Poses at the mirror. Screws with her hair. Walks out.

The downrange-travel circles shrink up like little assholes a-puckering.

I crank up the radar again for a final check. Under range-fifteen radar's *verboten*. Emitter silence. You bet it's risky. But if the TACNAV dumps the whole run-in goes to shit. You shoot your wad on some dicklick orphanage or something.

She's back. She messes with the stereo. Back to the mirror. She looks this way then that, likes what she sees. Makes a couple moves. Pulls a little something from the closet. Lays it on the bed. Walks out.

I fix the targets one last time. Leave the radar in standby. On the nose for two. I double click the mouse and the pilot arms the weapons.

Standby for drop on my third *NOW*.

I keep down-scaling and the downrange-travel circles choke shit outta the fixes.

She's back. She's scoping her face in the mirror.

We're just about there. . . . I wait till the nose of the bug just nibbles at the fix.

Now. . . .

She unties the belt of her robe. It falls open.

Now. . . .

Ready to release. Two more clicks and the bug's there. Grease up them rug merchant butts!

The robe drops down over her shoulders. A peek at a peak.

Standby.

Standby . . . *a-a-a-a-and*. . . .

Then, there it is just like a big dog — *Emitter Alert*. Abort! Abort! Abort! I do an auto-class and sure as shit it's a Russkie AA-8. We go full evasive.

Kiss off the bomb run.

I flop back on the sofa. The screen goes red and says:

Aphid Up The Tailpipe!
Drop Your Socks And Grab Your Cocks!

Those software guys. What a fucking sense of humor.

Little Miss Madonna Babe drops her robe. Holds up the blouse and looks in the mirror. Drops the blouse. TOTALLY stark. Turns to the window, looking right at the lens, right through it and right at me. Like she sees it, sees ME. But she can't see through that bamboo shade. I know it. I know it. But she keeps standing there, firing that look my way, through video lines, pixels, and I want to gawk at her boobs, g-get my load of that bodacious bod. Make some memories from those mammaries. But that look's got me pinned down.

I crawl over to the monitor — 'bows and toes — looking for eyes. There's some light on her face and I'm looking for eyes. My nose against the cool glass. But no eyes, just dark holes, like peering down a shotgun's business end. And all I can do is gape into them holes and think how she's got me, she's got me balls down.

Then her face detonates in a fireball.

I jump back, slamming the table. I'm clawing at the bag till I get the thing out and I yank the straps over and a buckle about rips my ear off and it DOES tear out a glob of hair but I got the thing on and maybe I'm okay and maybe it's too late and for sure my heart's leaping out of my chest and my drawers are THOROUGHLY crapped.

I'm sitting there all shaking and I'm afraid to look but I do and I see it's just a cigarette. She's puffing on a goddam cigarette.

Larry King's at the phones. *Hello, America!*

Day Thirty-six

AFTER WORK ME and Rudy hit the Forty-Niner Club and Rudy buys a pitcher. There's this skanky old stripper, waist thicker than her hips. Rudy's creaming his jeans. He says, "How'd you like to get a little of them sweetcakes?" I say, "I wouldn't touch that clapdog with YOUR dick."

We down a couple more pitchers and shoot the shit about everything except the only thing we're REALLY thinking about.

There's a table full of jarheads all dressed up like bushes and they're getting real loud. One of them catches this big old cockroach and stands on the table and yells out that he'll eat the thing for twenty bucks. A hat goes around and we all throw in. This zitty little guy says the roach has to be chewed and not just swallowed whole. The jarhead on the table agrees. He's got the roach crawling from hand to hand so we can all see how big it is. He says he's calling it Esther after his mother.

We're all cluster-fucked around the table. Even the stripper stops dancing and comes over to watch, leaning over the edge of the stage so her big belly dangles like a third tit. The jarheads start chanting, ooh-RAH! ooh-RAH!

He pinches the roach, holding it high above his mouth. From over Rudy's shoulder I see the thing squirming. Rudy joins in on the ooh-RAH chant. So does the stripper, shaking her G-stringed butt with each ooh and RAH.

"Say goodbye, Esther!"

He pops that thing in like it was a Cheeto and makes like he's chewing but you can't really be sure because his mouth is shut tight. He's got this big yum-yum grin on his face and his jaw's pumping away. The skanky stripper says, "Let's see! Let's see you really eat that bug!" The jarhead looks over at her and his whole expression slumps into something different and ugly. He opens up and slides out that tongue all covered with legs and mashed-up wings and shell and this white goo. The stripper about gags but she keeps looking. The jarhead rolls back his tongue and leans into her face. You can tell she's about sick with it but she doesn't flinch or turn away. The jarhead gets his face right into hers and blows that junk all over her. Just fires on her. Hoses her with spit and roach parts.

She lets out a howl like a banshee. Two bouncers show up and start pounding on the jarhead. Somebody flings a pitcher and a bouncer catches it in his ear. There's blood everywhere. Then the jarhead's buds jump in and the whole place erupts.

We beat feet out of there. WARP drive. In the parking lot I'm blinded for a minute and that shit back inside's pounding around in my head. We both got a good buzz on and Rudy's got his big old arm around me and calling me his buddy. He invites me over for dinner — says his old lady makes this killer lasagna. I figure, why not?

I'm following behind Rudy's Blazer — he's doing okay. A little weavy, maybe, but no major bust. We stop at a light and I see this dynamite babe in a Jap ragtop. She's wearing these thick-framed Ray-Bans. I put on my own shades and keep watching her. She's got some tremendous fat red lips and I think about kissing her and I especially think of the clicky sound our sunglasses make while we're kissing. In fact maybe I don't kiss her at all. Maybe we're just rubbing lenses. That's what does it for me, the sound of our shades bumping and grinding. I would never let her take them off.

We down a bottle of Chianti with the lasagna. Rudy's wife, Anita, puts the wine away pretty good. She's a partier. I'm surprised how pretty she is, I mean considering what an ape Rudy is. I can tell she kind of likes me since every time Rudy says something stupid she gives me this what-a-dink look.

Rudy bought the dining table in the Philippines. It's made of that monkeypod wood and under a glass top is all these demon masks. So every time you take a bite of food this crazy face that's all teeth and feathers is gawking at you. I keep seeing that jarhead's face right before he creamed the stripper. Finally I have to lay my napkin over it.

Anita puts away the dishes and Rudy cracks open a bottle of this Mexican brandy. When Anita takes my plate I get a little cleavage shot down her blouse. I look up and she gives me a grin and I don't know if it means *bad boy!* or *Merry Christmas!*

Rudy says, "Hope you got your fill."

I say, "What?"

"You ain't getting nothing like that when we're haze-grey and underway."

I think of this big ape pounding my dick into the dirt and I just say, Nope, real cautious like.

Then he says, "Shit's got three different cheeses in it. I got a lactose intolerance, makes me squirt like a motherfucker. But I don't care. I'll put that shit away till doomsday."

He pours me a brandy in this little mug that says *Hang Loose* on it. Anita comes back and says she isn't drinking from some stupid souvenir and pours hers into a wineglass. We shoot the shit for a while then Rudy starts telling about his first fuck. Anita gives me one of her looks. Rudy goes on with this typical gross Rudy-story about this whore he hooks up with in TJ and how he smears toothpaste all over her chest because he wants to tit-fuck her and how the spearmint or whatever burns his dick so he dumps a Coke all over both of them to get the toothpaste off and she gets pissed and stuff and it's all going round and round in my head and I look over at Anita; she's just staring real bored like she's heard it about a million times, only moving to hit off the brandy which she is like PUTTING away.

So it's my turn. I tell about when I was fifteen and getting it on with my cousin in the carport lockers and how when I'm fumbling around trying to get it in she says, "If the goal here is buttfucking you're doing great." They both get a big hoot out of that so I pour it on thick. I say when I finally found the right place it was like jamming a marshmallow into a piggybank. Well that about puts Anita on the floor. Rudy thinks it's funny but not *that* funny. Anita's holding her gut and saying over and over, *Marshmallow in a piggybank!*

I say, "Okay, Anita. Your turn."

Through her gagging she says, "My turn what?"

"First sex story. Gotta pay to play. No peso, no *beso.*"

"Oh Jeez. Do I have to?" But that was for Rudy's benefit. You could tell there was no keeping her back.

I give Rudy a quick one but he's busy pouring more brandy. He skips Anita.

When Anita stops laughing she grabs for the bottle but Rudy stops her. She shakes him off and says, "Screw off, hon. I need some fortifying for this."

"You look plenty fortified," Rudy says. I see Rudy's big face carved into the tabletop. I'm surprised how natural he looks in feathers. Or maybe I'm not.

Anita ignores Rudy and starts telling her story which, it turns out, is about her first old man. It's all this sentimental stuff about champagne on the beach and a roaring fire and sleeping bags zipped together and *tender* this and *sweetly* that — but I can see she's really into it so I slap on my sincere face like when the Chief's babbling on. About halfway through she does this weird thing. She reaches over and touches my hand. Just taps it like you do when you're making a point. And it's so warm it shocks me. There's my hand laying there like a clam and she touches me and it's like a sonofabitching soldering iron. I think I flinched.

I'm pouring brandy like it's going out of style and she's going on and on and I pretty much forget Rudy is even there till he gets up and walks out. Anita just shakes her head like *don't worry about him* and goes on with the story. I just figure he's off to the shitter till I hear the TV.

Anita checks on him. When she comes back she says I should go. I ask why. She says not to worry, that Rudy'll be okay in the morning. I figure the night's over and I'll just say goodbye to Rudy. But Anita says, no, just GO. There's this edge to her voice and I'm not sure if she's mad at me or if Rudy's mad at her or what. While I'm trying to figure it out Rudy comes storming in bellowing, GET THE FUCK OUT! YOU JIVE SHITHEAD! GET OUT!

The next thing I'm coldcocked — on the deck flailing around, trying to get untangled from the chair, still holding that damned *Hang Loose* mug, flubbering around trying to get out some words. Anita's all screaming bloody murder and old Rudy snatches me up and I'm out the door and bouncing my head off his concrete drive.

Driving home freezing off my gonads for having the window down so I can spit out the blood. I'm trying not to fall asleep or be a bust so I'm concentrating real hard on what Anita was yelling. I think it was, *I'm glad you're going.*

Day Thirty-five

SPENT THE WHOLE DAY running my ass off. Putting my shit in storage, haggling with the apartment manager over my security deposit — last-minute stuff. Now I'm lying on the floor biting hunks of dead skin from inside my cheek and spitting them at the ceiling. My whole jaw is yellow and swollen on that side and there's a chipped tooth I can't keep my tongue away from. Maybe I should go see dental.

I get another three aspirins and a beer to chase them. The lights are out across the way. Maybe she's sitting in her dark room watching. For a second I think she knows and she's laughing. But that's stupid.

Just then the lights come on. I take a step back. There's my Madonna. But she's not alone. Some longhair guy is with her. I touch my cheek. Still tender.

I go in the bathroom and run water in the sink. I think of washing my hands but I don't. Instead I stare at the mirror, at my fat yellow jaw and cracked lip. I need a hit off my beer — hell, maybe I want to pour the whole thing over my damn head. But I left it back in the kitchen.

She's doing her act for him. He's out of the picture — on the floor or the bed or I don't know. I roll the cold bottle across my forehead. When she gets to her panties she rolls them down her legs then twirls them over her head and flings them across the room. The guy stands up and nuzzles in between her jugs. My awesome titties. She holds him tight then looks right at me. I reach over and drop my shades. I just can't take that shit.

I finish packing my seabag and put it by the door with my aardvark mask. Liberty won't expire until 0600 but I'm thinking maybe I'll just spend the night on board. Why put it off? I mean let's face it. I'm ready for war.

TWO

Boat Time

Day Thirty-five

CAB TO THE SHIP and tip the guy a fiver, which is too much but he's pretty friendly. Some twenty-year shitcanned first-class boiler tech, arms covered with blobby tattoos. Retread written all over him. Got back my security deposit so what the hell.

He hauls my shit to the afterbrow, gives me a sarcastic salute and says, "Kick some A-rab ass, Ace." I don't say anything, or maybe a Yeah, sure. I got my camcorder so I video him hulking to his cab. Then I grab all my gear and stagger up the brow.

They got tables set up on the sponson and MAAs searching everything. Even got a dope dog. Don't want any nasty unnatural stimulants getting on board. No guns or knives. Nothing threatening, God forbid. Meanwhile they're craning on pallets of thousand-pounders and Sidewinders and torps and Sparrows and twenty mike-mike ack-ack belts and Harpoons and cluster bombs and Phoenixes and Tomahawks and who knows what all.

While waiting for the MAA to finish tearing up my seabag I do some more video, panning around the bay and base. Establishment shots. Parting shots. Suddenly I remember the tac-training disks. A flood of hot fluid. What'd I do with them? I panic. My mind's hauling ass, trying to figure where they are and what'll happen if they find them. Look cool. Still videoing while monitoring the MAA with my other eye. Seabag drooping, clothes strewn across the table. He's got the stroke books I brought for the smut locker. Calls his buddy over to ogle some greased-up *Hustler* booty.

I figure these guys being dumbshit blackshoes, they see a big red SECRET stamped on those disks they'll go BALLISTIC. Think they're

Stallone saving the collective ass of the free world — Mom, apple pie and Microsoft. And the chance to stick it to an uppity prima donna airedale like me — they'll get off bigtime. Little swabby dicks'll be harder'n Chinese math.

Mind's racing. Fear. The grip of fear. What'd I do with them? Hoping they're at the U-Lock-It place.

Planning lies for the Chief. A rigger found the disks in a JG's helmet bag, entrusted to me for safe conduct to the SDO.

But that won't fly. I signed for them, affixed my mark. Fuck it. What can they do? Yank my clearance? Down me? Bust me? (Naw.) Revoke my birthday?

Bored with booty the MAAs are back digging through my bag. I think, Oh Shit.

A shuttle bus pulls up at the foot of the brow and a gaggle of boots comes rolling off. Fresh from NTC, clean scrubbed and gawky as fresh-hatched turkeys. Hauling seabags, suitcases, ghetto blasters and heading up the brow. Must be scared shitless. I'd be. I waste some tape, stay safe behind the viewfinder. Keeping down the panic.

When the MAAs spot the herd of cue balls rolling up the brow they drop everything, forget about my bag and wave me off. I'm shit-grinning all the time I'm stuffing my skivvies back in.

I'm halfway across the hangar bay, just starting to savor my re-lief, when I hear this voice from behind yelling, *Stop! Stop!* My gut re-clenches. This dumpy Filipino chief's waddling toward me, flailing his arms. His big old T.J. Hooker MAA badge flapping from a breast pocket and I'm thinking ain't THIS the shits.

He comes rolling up with this fry pan face, bloated gut about to blow khaki buttons from here to Basra, eyeballs my name tag.

"Hey shipmate, you wit da Fightin' Redcocks?"

"Fighting Red*tails*. The Redcocks are VA-22. We're VS-21. They're attack, we're anti-submarine warfare. S-3s."

"Focking Hoovers," he says. "You got dose birds sound like focking vacuum cleaners."

The standard line. S-3s have these turbofans that make this whoop-whoop sound kinda sorta like a vacuum cleaner. Since we're not fighters or attack jets we're low on the flight deck pecking order, just above helos and E-2s, so people like to give us shit. Like we're not REALLY jet jerkeys or something. The other endearing term for S-3s, which the chief here is too polite to use, is *whistling shit cans.*

"That's us," I say all quasi-normal.

"I like dat Redcock motto, *You can't beat a Redcock!* Focking fonny."

"That's them, not us."

"I know. You're Hoovers. Still it's focking fonny."

"Yeah, I guess."

Turns out all he wants is access to our smut locker, do a little smut-swapping. He's got a Coke mess he's running down in the MAA shack, says he can guarantee cold sodas for the duration. It sounds dumb but when you're out on Gonzo and it's so hot the non-skid sticks to your flight boots and you haven't seen an ice cube in sixty days — it'd be a tough choice between a cold Dr Pepper and a blow job from Michelle Pfeiffer. Kinda tough.

He points to my camcorder. "You got focking tapes, too?"

"Naw, but my chief's got a shitload."

Goes wide-eyed, amazed. "You don't make your own focking tapes?"

"Probably nothing you'd like."

"You take dat ting to P.I. You get so much sockie-fockie it'll curl your focking toes. I got a shitload of tapes. TWO focking shitloads. Enough to sink dis focking ship. *Debbie Does Dallas, Debbie Does Detroit,* Debbie does every focking city in North Focking America. I got John Holmes, you know, Long Dong Silver?" He makes like he's holding a twenty-incher. "Boy, dat focking guy! He bust open dose poosies like focking cantaloupes, man. Too bad he got himself murdered . . . or, or . . . he murdered some odda guy or . . ."

"Wasn't that Johnny Wad?"

"Yeah, Yeah, whatever da fock." Then he gets a little misty-eyed. "Shame to shitcan a focking good acting career."

And I'm thinking, what's he going on about? But he's a chief so I try looking like I care. "Damn shame," I say.

"I got eight hundred and ninety focking fock tapes. You talk a focking shitload. I got everyting but . . ." Pauses all tragic like he's telling me his kid's got leukemia. "But dey're all on focking Beta."

A major crisis. Caught behind the T&A technology curve. Raw deal. If he wasn't a chief I'd laugh in his face. Or maybe I'd cry. But why's he telling ME about it? Why are people always trying to get close up and personal with ME? A total stranger? Go tell it to a priest. Go tell it to your mother. Go tell it to your friends. Don't people have FRIENDS anymore? And on top of all that my sore jaw's starting up again. I'd kill for an aspirin.

I'm about across the hangar bay, the buzz and chaos of onload. Dodging forklifts right and left, roar and exhaust stink of zooming yellow gear. Almost get knocked flat by an A-6 under tow. Bunch of recruit types sweaty and filthy and about worked to death humping five-gallon milk cartons down a hole. POWs on a chain gang. I think of collaring those newbies back at the brow, showing them what they're in for. Like it says on the San Diego buses, ¡Bienvenidos!

I video, head up the ladder.

Rounding the ladder on O-2, something painted on a wiring box catches my eye. Something red, out of place in these puke green passageways. I'd stop but I'm loaded down, sweating and struggling up these ladders, jaw aching. I just want to get to berthing.

Trudging down the O-3 passageway, seabag catching hatches and fire hose racks and every damn thing else, when I see another wiring box with another red blob. I crane around, smack my shin on a kneeknocker, sprawling. Camcorder, seabag, suit bag, everything. Some LCDR tippy-toes over me, "Throwed a shoe, Petty Officer?" Must be nice being so entertaining.

I rub my leg, check the camcorder. Skinned up my shin but the camera's okay. Then I notice the flurry in my gut. That same hot adrenaline ball of guilty fear bouncing and careening like back on the hangar bay when I thought I was snagged. I don't know why it's still there. I got away right? I'm safe right? But there it is and I start to remember. It comes like a forgotten dream brought crashing back by a detail, a smell. It's not there because of the MAAs or the disks or that chief — it's there because I'm on the ship.

This same feeling every time I come aboard.

I walk onto this thing, this ninety-thousand-ton thing, eighty high-tech warplanes, five thousand American Fighting Men, big as three football fields and tall as a twenty-story building, and I'm inside this thing and there's just not enough of me. I'm too dinky and fucked up for it all. Not like gung-ho, oh-gee-whiz, it's my responsibility to protect the High Value Unit from the dreaded silent menace from below or any of that ate-fucking-up Yankee Doodle crap. Nothing like that. But still. Like there's this hollow statue you can see through, this transparent hollow statue, and I'm supposed to fill it up but I don't and everybody's watching but there's not enough of me and every time I fill a gap there's another empty spot and the more I try filling up the thing the more I become like smoke, thin and drifty like smoke getting thinner and thinner till it's gone and the statue is empty again and I'm gone.

Suddenly I'm aware of the camcorder in my lap. I see my face reflected in the lens. My nose real big and the rest of my face dribbling away to the edge and behind it the matte black suggestion of steel shutter, tiny springs and gears, circuits and photo-sensitive cells.

I get up, brush off, square myself away, tuck in my shirt, straighten my gig line. Then I check out the thing on the wiring box. It's a stenciled mushroom cloud and underneath it says, *Nuke Em Till They GLOW!*

I video it.

In berthing I search out a rack. Middies are all snatched. I'm sure not sleeping in a top rack with A-6s pounding my head all night. Ditto a bottom rack and mornings with a face full of gungey feet and boot prints on my sheets and crawling around doggy style to get my shaving kit. No thanks. Reconnoiter a middie staked out with some AOAA's seabag. A baby BB stacker. Toss the ordy's shit on a bottom rack. Sorry, boot. Rank has its privileges.

I find the tac-tra disks tucked into one of my flight boots. Don't even remember putting them there. Spaced it out totally. Don't know where my head was at.

Unpack, hustle up a set of jack-off curtains and a rod. I make my rack with the least filthy sheets I can dig up, fluff my pillow (tie-dyed with drool and jism), fold my blanket nice and neat. I slap on a padlock and Ta-Dah! Be it ever so claustrophobic. . . . My rack, my bunker, my home.

Then it's down to the shop. Right by the ready room and the O-Board hanging there with all the officers' pictures in order of superiority so you can always tell who's stepping on who. My TACCO's picture toward the bottom, Mr. Dumchowski, replaced with a *Far Side* cartoon of a warthog and the caption, *I am Mister ASW.* Poor guy. I'd feel sorry for him if he wasn't such a douche bag.

The shop's padlocked and I forgot the combo. The NerdMan reset it with some shithead mnemonic. Something about the fundamental blade rates of three classes of Soviet diesel subs all making ten knots. Talk about ate-fucking-up. So I'm trying to remember the blade configurations and the *tpks* for all these boats and juggling the formulas around and nothing works. Then I spot some numbers discreetly penciled on the doorjamb. So much for security.

The shop already reeks of cigarettes and stinky flight suits. Imagine three months from now. But I won't care by then. Other things to worry about. I check off on the muster board. Chief's aboard, NerdMan, naturally, Buckethead. But no Rudy. Probably getting his wick dipped one last time. Anita bending over me and wiggling those tits. My tongue rolls across my jaw and hits that chipped tooth. I grab the Advil from the Chief's drawer.

Punch on the TV looming from its angle-iron rack. Still getting CNN, Bernard Shaw live from the El Rashid. Arcs of light in a black sky. Guess we're still wired up to shore. Or maybe they got a satellite dish. I heard talk. Dump the *Hustlers* in the smut drawer and hang my aardvark mask in the corner with the others. Strange fruit hanging from the hat tree. Then I crack open the big safe and stash the disks in my Secret folder like they've been there all along. I make a space in the bottom drawer, behind the Sound Velocity Profile Pubs, and tuck away my camcorder. But first I take out the tape.

There's a note taped to the VCR in NerdMan's psychotically neat, upwardly mobile hand: *Property of AW2 (NAC) (AWS) Nierman — No Askee, No Touchee!* Peel the note off careful. Wish I had a blowup sex doll (*Real Human Hair!*) to stick it to. Plug in my tape while figuring a good spot for the note. Channel changing (channeling, changeling) I pass the PLAT channel — quiet on the flight deck, vacant. Airwing'll fly on tomorrow. Like it's crawling with giant grasshoppers, like that old movie about the giant locust. *THEM!* Or was that the one with the giant ants?

There's my Madonna Babe. Won't be seeing her again. Too bad. Nice bod. Fast-forward. There's the cabdriver. *Kick some A-rab ass, Ace!* The sponson, the brow, dope dogs and the MAAs. I'm thinking maybe I'll record the whole cruise like this. Make a movie out of it. *What I Did on My Summer Vacation. What I Did on My Winter, Spring and Summer Vacation.* Too long. *Robo-Cop Does the Persian Gulf.* Like the sound of THAT. *Whistling Shitcans on Parade.* Whatever.

There's the guys humping milk. The POWs. Then there's the wiring

box with the red mushroom cloud. Pause it. Nuke Em Till They GLOW!
Wishing this queasy feeling would let up.

I'm kind of fuzzing when the 1MC crackles. *Taps, taps. Lights out. All hands turn into their own racks. Now taps.* Gotta love it, their OWN racks. Time to break up the pajama party. Stick NerdMan's note to the TV's radiating image — stencil of a mushroom cloud. *No Askee, No Touchee!*

¡Bienvenidos!

THREE

The Prime Mover

Day Thirty-four

BRYANT GUMBEL HOOKED LIVE TO RIYADH, counter-
parting with a reporter done up in a khaki safari jacket. Banana
Republic warwear. Static. Satellite problems. Safari Jacket's in a Saudi oil
field brain-jamming that earplug trying to hear. I'm watching a TV,
Bryant's talking to a TV, Safari Jacket's talking to a lens.

Patriot downed a Scud in Riyadh. Much hoopla. Rudy nudges me with
his knee-sized elbow.

"You believe that shit?"

NerdMan, pale, freckled, soft at the edges, jumps in.

"YES! That's it, boys! Shoot a bullet *with* a bullet." Slaps the desk, ju-
bilant. "Those dumbshit camel-jockeys don't know who they're messing
with! We'll wipe the floor with 'em!"

Siren goes off in Riyadh and Safari Jacket shits his pants. Head on a
swivel, boy. Doesn't know WHICH way to look. Gumbel's asking what's
happening and Safari Jacket is like, *Fuck you, Bryant,* clawing for his 'vark.

Rudy's all "Yeah, maybe it worked, maybe it was dumb luck. Either
way, the point is *we* don't have 'em. One of those Scuds'd grease your
fuzzy butt, Slick." I crack up at that. See old Nierman with an SS-1
shoved up his ass. *Yes sir, Please sir, May I have another, SIR!* He be liking
THAT shit.

Nerdy's off the deep end with a load of *We got Sparrows, We got
C-Whiz, We got layered defense,* blah, blah, blah.

Rudy kicks back. "Ever seen one of them Sparrows? I seen 'em on
the Shitty Kitty. Turds. High-tech turds. Safest place was in the target
drone."

Camera sweeping the Riyadh sky, blue screen with oil derricks, air raid sirens. I imagine plunging my fingers into hot desert sand, fiery granules. Rudy and Nierman aren't watching.

"What're you talking, Rudeman?" Nerdy sneers.

Rudy leans forward, story mode. "We're all on the flight deck. Big shit Sparrow test. Flag's there, staff, everybody. Big dog-and-pony for SURFPAC. Gonna be bitchen, right." Rudy reaches up, mutes the volume. "Here comes the drone. Supposed to be an incoming missile. Nothing happens. No Sparrow. Drone just flies on by, happy as can be. We're all up there in the hot sun going, *What the fuck, over?* It was a real missile we'd all be Crispy Critters. Drone flies by again, this time low and slow. More nothing. Drone flies by *again,* lower and slower. Coulda spit on it. It's about to the horizon and *finally* they get off the Sparrow. Real pretty missile — all white and shiny, like a wet cock. Maybe like your little white cock, Nierman. Except big, very big."

"Fuck you." Nerdy.

"And not circumcised," says Bucket.

"Fuck you too."

"Gets a little altitude and just stops — hovers there sniffing around. Everyone's going like this is gonna be *BADASS.*"

Safari Jacket's back. Now he's aardvark disguised. Mike pressed to his snout, rutting creature licking a black Popsicle.

Rudy's going on. "Some little rocket fires and the thing goes cartwheeling, totally out of control. The whole place goes crazy, running, diving into catwalks. Meanwhile the fucking Sparrow does a water smashdown port of one of the escorts, almost takes out the oiler." Rudy snorts. "Be safer giving those things to the ragheads."

Shop door flies open. The Chief jumps in and bellows (acting all real chiefly like he does) "NBC attack is imminent! GO!"

Jeez.

Talk about a dog-and-pony. We're yanking on 'varks, tucking pants in boots, buttoning up cuffs and simulating slamming our thighs with atropine. Chief's counting off the seconds.

"One thousand THREE!"

While scrambling with my mask I glimpse Safari Jacket in HIS 'vark still talking away silently. Almost like he's one of us here in the shop. Sitting up there watching us, trying to tell us something. But nobody's listening. Nobody except me and I can't hear. But I know it's something critical because of the fear. Can't see his face but his body's all wrapped up tight. Wants to keep checking his six but he doesn't. Maybe because he's afraid of looking afraid or maybe because he's afraid of what he might see. Maybe he just has to get out what he's trying to say and he's worried he won't have time.

"One thousand SEVEN!"

I think of Rudy's story and how we're always simulating stuff. Missile attacks, gas attacks, sub-hunting. Everything is simulation. Hits me how my whole shit-ass life is spent simulating. My shit-ass JOB is simulation. We fly simulated missions in these big old Singer-Link flight simulators against computer-generated simulated targets. We fake up simulated environments for fighting these simulated battles. But Safari Jacket's telling me something REAL. If I could just get past this drill, if I could just hear it.

"One thousand TEN!"

Or else we fly real airplanes, tactical jets, against simulated targets that are real submarines simulating Russkie badboys. Drop torps with simulated charges. Track noisemakers that simulate the props, gears, and auxiliary equipment noises from Soviet subs (which are much noisier than ours because they can't simulate our technology). And now I'm simulating getting microwaved, toasted, infected or poisoned by a missile full of real nasties I can't see, smell, feel or taste. I'm simulating getting dead.

"One thousand *THIRRRRR-TEEN!*"

Got a 'vark on, just like Safari Jacket. A real 'vark just like his. (I can tell it's real because it's giving my sore jaw a lot of hell.) But he's not simulating. Or maybe he is. *He* doesn't know. *I* don't know. Ain't that a kick. The guy on TV is real and I'M the slope-oid simulation. The TV guy is more for real than me. Trying to tell me something about the difference between where I am and where he is.

"One thousand FIFTEEN. *TIME!*"

I'm all squared away. So's Nerdy and Bucket, happy as pigs in shit. Rudy's a tangle of thumbs and hair and ears and straps. Gotta get this over with so I can un-mute the TV.

Chief says fifteen ain't good enough. JOs got it down to twelve in the last AOM. He's not having us make fools of *him* if a GQ goes off while we're briefing. He makes a fucking contest out of EVERYthing, like *MY dogs are trained better than YOUR dogs.* But it's not just the Chief, department heads are just as bad. Skipper's worst of all. Must be all that cocksucking.

Help Rudy straighten out his mess. Show him how to stow the 'vark so it goes on easy. You gotta roll the straps over the face, secure them under the respirator. Then sink your face in snug and suck it tight. Pull the straps over slow and easy. You get all frantic and ham-handed you're heading for pain city. But if you just take it slow, you'll make it.

I go for the volume just as Safari Jacket vanishes, replaced by a dancing teddy bear selling fabric softener.

Day Thirty-three

JUST AFTER MUSTER and I'm checking the weekly, surprised to see ASW events every day. Why practice anti-submarine warfare when the bad guys don't have subs?

"Hey, Nerdy," I ask. "Iraq got any subs?"

Nerdy's kneeling at the door in a litter of reflector tape bits, scissors, X-acto blades, straight edges. Yesterday he painted the door blood red and now he's sticking up cutouts of S-3s and lightning bolts and torps and blown-up submarines, all beneath the motivational rubric Death From Above.

"Look it up."

"C'mon, I know you know."

Rolls back on his haunches, lets out this massive sigh like I'm interrupting this project of earth-shaking importance. "The Iraqi order of battle includes Soviet missiles, tanks and fighters, including the top of the line MiG-29 Fulcrum. Chinese anti-ship missiles, armored personnel carriers and T-59 and 69 tanks as well as Chinese F-6s which are copies of Soviet MiG-19 fuselages packed with off-the-shelf Western avionics. They have French Mirage fighters, Exocets and APCs. Soviet SA-7s which are copies of U.S. FIM-43As. A smattering of U.S. artillery donated during their righteous struggle against the evil Iran. Swiss turbo-prop trainers. Canadian 155 mike-mike guns, South African G-5 guns, Austrian GHN-45 guns, Brazilian Astros-II multiple-rocket launchers, and Czech OT-64 APCs."

The smug shit. "Gimme a straight answer. Subs or no subs?"

"Though estimates vary their naval forces seem to consist of five Italian frigates, four Soviet guided missile corvettes, ten Bulgarian missile carriers, six torpedo boats of unspecified Eastern Bloc origin, eight mine warfare ships, six amphibious assault craft and two presidential yachts. Your basic international Salvation Army mix. But no subs. Still, you can't be too sure since countries don't advertise submarine transfers. Chinese sell their old Whiskeys to anybody. The Soviets or the Russians or whatever they are these days hand out diesel boats like ballpoint pens. But why am I telling *you*? You are, are you not, an anti-submarine warfare subject matter expert."

"So if they don't have subs, why fly all these sub ops?"

He smooths air bubbles from a ruptured ballistic missile boat with the edge of a nickel.

"What else we gonna do?"

Just then Rudy pokes his big head in, looming over kneeling Nerdy.

"You're late for muster, Esperanza," whines Nerdy.

"Go back to your arts and crafts."

"Eval time's coming up. Better do something 'bout that attitude."

"Wipe your chin, Nierman. You got a little jism on it." Then to me, "Let's get some chow before the Chief volunteers us for some lame-ass working party."

Down the ladders where the mushroom clouds are stenciled. I point one out. Rudy just grunts like, *Yeah, that's typical.*

On the hangar bay the one-wires are running up the APU on 702. I plug my ears against the deafening onslaught. It's the high-frequency stuff that gets you. Stuff you can't hear. Beyond human range. Should be wearing my earplugs but it just seems like you spend so much time protecting your senses out here it's like why have them at all. Earplugs, Nomex flightsuits, steel-toe aircraft-fuel-resistant boots, safety goggles, flight helmets, cranial helmets, mickey-mouse ears, tinted visors. Even my forgodsake long underwear is flash retardant. Sometimes I feel like that kid in the plastic bubble, like EVERYTHING'S lethal, so you keep padding and blunting your senses until the self-inflicted stuff is worse than if you dropped your guard totally. Except nothing's worse than being dead. I guess.

It's pretty late so no chowline. We grab trays and while I'm trying to figure if the white goo is Cream of Wheat, which I'll eat, or grits, which I won't eat, Rudy's already piled up and ordering two omelets. I ask what the goo is and the mess kid shrugs and mumbles to push my tray up. Probably about the bazillionth time he's been asked and at first I feel like

34

giving him shit. But then I see his pimply face all greased up like a sausage (and about as lively) and the sweat-soaked paper hairnet they make these schmucks wear. Probably been up since oh-dark-thirty, every spare second plotting his recruiter's assassination. I pass on the goo settling for shriveled-up ham and spuds and a big old cinnamon roll which is one thing they really do decent.

Rudy's already scarfing down at a four-topper that looks like surplus from Jack-In-The-Box. He says, "You can't beLIEVE the fucking juices they got." Three glasses in front of him, plus coffee. "Fucking ice machine even works." All amazed like it's shooting out diamonds.

The sign on the milk machine reads, White Cow, Brown Cow, Diet Cow. Pour a glass of chocolate milk. Then another, figuring this won't last. A week out of Pearl and we'll be on mystery milk and bug juice. NOT to die for.

Rudy's already polished off one omelet and showing no mercy on the second. "Fucking Nierman." Language traveling through egg medium. "That guy gets on my case."

Looks like the Rudeman is adopting me for the cruise. I don't mind. Rudy's no violin prodigy but at least you know where he's coming from. Could be worse. Some of these guys are so ate up with making rank you don't know if they're saying hello or greasing your butt.

"Don't let Nerdy get to you," I say. "Just wound too tight. See the weekly? ASW hops from here to Pearl."

"Great," he groans. "Just what I fucking need. I catch any?" Rudy hates flying ASW. He's no good at acoustics so he's no good at sub tracking. For him an ASW mission is just a chance for looking like a rock. I know this but pretend otherwise.

"We all did," I say. "Round-the-clock ops. You, big fella, fly tomorrow . . ." I hesitate a little since this next factoid will REALLY make his day. But then I rub my tongue over my chipped tooth and I don't mind so much. ". . . with the Skipper."

"Shit." His fork clatters in his tray.

"Least you know you'll get a good bird. 711's been holding together."

"Yeah. Master Chief's not sticking the Skipper with no sled. That's a fact."

Rudy's chewing on this and I'm just watching him but making like all my attention's lavished on this cinnamon roll. After about a minute of looking off at nothing he drops his head, starts talking to his tray.

"706 is *my* bird," he says real soft. "I can *wish* that thing down." I'm not sure what he means and I tell him so. He drains his tomato juice with one long glug then belches big and long. What a pig.

"Done it three times in a row," he confides real secret-like. "I swear to God. All during my preflight I'm wishing the hop won't go. By the time they're pulling the chocks something breaks, an engine, hydraulics, something. And that baby's down — *hard*! Three goddam times." Wagging beefy fingers. "I'm telling you, she's so shaky you can *wish* her down."

This chocolate milk is great. I'll really miss it when it's gone.

Day Thirty-two

THE TARGET is a Los Angeles Class fast attack sub playing a Soviet Echo II guided missile boat. A stretch. Like a Nissan NSX simulating a pathetic rusted-out Datsun B210. With missiles. The Echo II is a
Khrushchev-era, first-generation nuke. Max speed twenty knots. Noisy
as a freight train. A total piece of shit. Thing has to surface to salvo if you
can believe that. Soviets honed their reactor shielding technology after
crews came back glowing. Still lose about one a year to reactor fires. Or
rust. I could track a real Echo II five miles off, ten miles in good water.
Not that I've ever SEEN a real-world Echo II. Not that I'm ever LIKELY
to see one.

The L.A. Class on the other hand is our newest, fastest, quietest, mega-
bitchenest attack boat. Max speed is top secret. The coy reference in *Jane's
Fighting Ships* says thirty knots *plus*. This boat I'll be lucky to hear from
two thousand yards. Plus I got Dumchowski sitting TACCO, my tactical
coordinator who couldn't coordinate a sneak attack on a dead dog. That
drops my detection range another kiloyard.

While transiting to the op-area the front-seaters talk war stuff,
buzzing voices in my headphones. The muffled roar of the engines. I
adjust my lumbar pad. Pilot says he wants to get in on this Baghdad
bombing before it's all over. He's an academy dildo — they ALL think
like that. At least they all TALK like they think like that.

Lieutenant Commander Whitman, flying COTAC, says he doesn't see
any use for a low-and-slow ASW platform in a land war. Even though
we *can* carry ordnance, every other swinging dick on the flight deck
does it better and the Air Force does it better than anybody. He sees us
pulling mail runs to Diego Garcia, tanking and surface plotting. Maybe

some charity bombing after it's all over — just so everybody gets an air medal.

Dumchowski pipes up, "I'd give my left nut to stick it to some of those sheep-bangers and bag me a couple air medals."

A rush of bleed air fills the cabin. A smell like bread baking but sickening sweet.

I cough a *shit* into my boom mike.

"Whassa matter, SENSO," Dumchowski asks, "I suppose *you* don't want any air medals?"

What I WANT to say is, *Well, sir, with an air medal and a wallet full of peso-nality, I guess even YOU could get your dick licked in Olongapo.* Not smart in front of the Ops Boss. Whitman would love it but he'd be obliged to annihilate me for form. "I guess I've got enough rating exam points without putting my ass in a sling for two more," I say. Dumchowski looks at me like *You're really out of it, bud.*

The pilot says all swaggering, "You can't be too buff or have too many medals, right Commander?" That academy — must start right off with Knob-Polishing 101.

Our primary mission is search and destroy. Secondary is to keep him down, prevent him from surfacing and getting a fire-control solution on the carrier, the high-value unit. The HVU. Mother. We're on-station. A perfect blue day. COTAC calls up the sub on secure voice. They do their secret code-of-the-day crypto-comm wojo-mojo and pretty soon the sub surfaces. We yank around for a mark-on-top and he pulls the plug. *Deposit twenty-five cents and press* START.

Dumchowski deploys a DIFAR buoy on the swirl. On my scope the aircraft bug φ shits a buoy symbol δ. Codes of the tactical plot.

Ten seconds later Dumchowski asks if I have contact. I tell him the buoy hasn't even hit the water yet, SIR, and I'll pass a point soon as I can, SIR. Whitman tells him to hang on till he gets the plot stabilized. Whitman's the mission commander thank God. He's pretty normal.

Assign the buoy to my left headphone.

In my right headphone electronic imitations of the pilot and Whitman chat about Hawaii. The JOs got a suite in Waikiki. Guess they'll be simulating their wild and crazy college days. Maybe even have a toga party. Groovy. I tune them out and get down to it.

The hydrophone crackling, falling through the water, descending on its wire tether. Falling, falling. My ear in the cold ocean. I forget about everything else and do what I do best. I listen. Liquid sounds, biological sounds, current and sway. Noise. Not what I'm looking for. I press the helmet to my ear, an aural coupling with the tiny speaker. The plane banks suddenly. "Vox," someone says. "Check your vox." Muffled engine roar. Green back-lit function switches on my tray. The time-code-generator pulsing Zulu time in red LED. Dumchowski peeling an egg. Sun arcing past scratched Plexiglas. Tongue tip explores the boom mike, ridged plastic. All noise. Compartmentalize, I think. Compartmentalize. Stay in the medium. I filter out the random, the arbitrary, the single event in favor of repetition, rhythm, rotation, revolution. Then I hear it. A clanking, metal on metal. Machinery. A casual chopping laces in, almost lazy. The propeller, it's the prop. Adrenaline, noradrenaline. Then a high whine, a cyclical thing, a spinning thing. Generator maybe, the turbine I hope, the prime mover, fat with propulsion data. The voice is layering, thickening. Target language. I have him.

"Aural contact on the target of interest."

A voice, Dumchowski. "Gimme a pointer."

"Standby."

Aural data, analog data, raw, unprocessed, vague. I hear him with my ears, gratifying but useless. I check the upper display, the ALIs, automatic line integration — frequency versus amplitude, the voice digitized, processed, linearized, disassembled and re-integrated into a quantifiable form. Spiking action, the voice broken into a mountain range of constituents. Peaks and valleys. Collectively the submarine's signature, an aural photograph, its sonic image. The tallest mountain, the loudest source, falls at sixty hertz, the ship's service turbo-generator. SSTG. I form it with my lips. I measure other frequencies, assign them sources in the computer's notepad or annotate the mysterious with *unk*. Building my case, defining the evidence. Select up a grams/b-scan display below on the MPD, the multi-purpose display. Frequency versus time. Frequency versus bearing. Just a taste of contact. I have him. Lines breaking out of the static, standing out black and narrow, discrete frequencies against a background of ambient noise, chaos, clutter. I wait for enough data to generate a pointer. Pixel by pixel it builds.

I move the crosshairs over a processing cell full of submarine, hook and enter. Computer displays the relative bearing from the hydrophone, other useful information. Intelligence. Now's when I share what I know, what I see and hear. I hesitate. So private this act between me and the sub, a secret relationship, an intimate thing. Subject and object. Viewer and viewed. Agressor and victim. I'm expected to be a team player. I don't see it that way.

I call contact, Poss Sub Level Two, and pass the bearing to Dumchowski. Peripherally I see the vector appear on his scope, a line of light beaming from the buoy symbol into infinity. The target is somewhere on that line.

The tactical coordinator must now make a decision. Dumchowski decides to go ballistic. Radios in like he accomplished something dropping a buoy on a viz. What he SHOULD do is punch out another buoy. Priorities. His priorities are fucked up. I mull over whether to tell him. There's the etiquette thing, protocol. They like the enlisteds spunky but not cowboys. The hierarchy must be respected.

Whitman's on the ball. Tells Dumchowski to get his shit together and drop some buoys.

Still got contact but it's fading. Target's getting out of range. The ALI spikes are processing out, flattening, disintegrating. The gram lines breaking up, diffusing. Accumulated contact time might be a whopping one minute, two max. In my ear the prop is slipping into murk. The SSTG whine is barely audible. I'll be losing contact REAL soon. What's taking Dumchowski?

I announce darkly, "Target is departing the buoy at a high rate of speed, sir."

"Roger," he mumbles.

Then Whitman, irritated, "You listening to your SENSO, TACCO?"

Dumchowski's punching in fly-to-points like they're going out of style.

"Yessir. Just about got it."

But it's already too late.

I update the bearing, the last time from this buoy.

The propeller's chop-chop attenuated to a weak throb, then gone.

The last bearing dot disappears, a burnt-out celestial body. And like a celestial event, an echo, a binary light image of the past. Historical data.

"Lost contact."

Dumchowski yells *Shit!* and bangs his tray. The pilot asks what the noise was. I say, *TACCO tantrum.* Dumchowski's shooting eye missiles at me. The pilot and Whitman go back to chatting about the Milli

Vanilli/Madonna lip-synching controversy. Is it a *live* concert if the singer's not really singing?

Next buoy deploys. I feel the kick. This one misses we're out of the ballgame.

Dead time waiting on the buoy. I won't look at Dumchowski. Let him sweat.

I imagine the ARU and the MPD underneath as two TVs. Only instead of pictures they're showing me acoustic data, sound. (You can get pictures, too. IR camera in the nose. Goes for the hot spots. Useful for anatomy lessons on female ground crew.) Two monitors radiating what's behind the shades. The object. The story of the object.

I wonder what she'd look like on a gram. What frequencies she'd give off, what kind of amplitude, how many harmonics of each discrete tone. Sound IS vibration. Rhythm. Pulses per second. Hertz. How many hertz is her heart rate? What's the frequency of her breath? Her eyelids blinking? Her clit all a-tingle? What's the Doppler as she approaches orgasm? Peaks out? Departs the buoy? Opens the gap between her taped-up room and those surveilling things leaking in? I think of her moaning. First up-Doppler, then down-Doppler — like a car jamming by, the tone compressed, frantic and squealing, heading straight for you:

ᴀᴀᴀᴀᴀAAAAAᴀAAHH!

Then it passes by, intensity dribbling away:

...aaaaaaaᴀᴀᴀᴀᴀʜ.

The tones all stretched out and lazy, relaxed. Spent.

Dumchowski smacks my shoulder. I hate that and almost smack him back without thinking. "I *asked* you what buoy eleven looks like!" Dumchowski's eyes are BUZZING and I realize the buoy's not even tuned and the LOD's already at three. Fuck me in the heart.

The buoy is way behind. But there's contact. Dumchowski's managed to pull his tit from the wringer. I manage a point.

"I have regained contact."

Dumchowski is elated.

One more hot buoy and I can cross-fix. But even that won't be enough. With the processing time, the bearing lag, we'll always be two minutes behind him.

What I REALLY need is a buoy in *front* of the guy. Then I can see what he sounds like up-Doppler. Crucial data. I can watch the woman-ish backward curve of frequencies as he passes my hydrophone, shifting from up-Doppler to down-Doppler, that drop in register, a vocal inflection that gives away his position, his motion relative to the receiver, his needs and desires. His intentions. I will know him completely, not just where he was or where he is but where he will be. This is what it is to know the target.

Up-Doppler, down-Doppler — sound like dog commands, sound like the in and out thump-thump rhythm of sex, sound like sound weaving in and out of my eyes. I SEE the sound of a button, a zipper, the whisper-slither of silk and elastic just like I SEE the blades cavitating, SEE the buzz of the turbines, SEE a hatch slam, SEE the hum of the fan that blows air into the berthing compartment where men lie on their racks reading or listening to Anthrax or Guns N' Roses on yellow Walkmans or pounding their puds dreaming of Madonnas real or simulated, shining their shoes, doing everything but thinking about me up here, six thousand feet above them, listening, listening hard, with my eyes.

I can SEE the scream of a torpedo, too. I've seen that. A Mark 48 wipes out the gram, maxes out the ALIs. You can see THAT godawful scream forever. I'm always seeing it.

Another buoy and I'm listening. Still behind but closing. A stern aspect. Whoosh-woosh of the prop, his soft spot, tilling the water. That's what the torp goes for. Circling, circling, listening for that prop, big lazy circles, a meat-eating bird. That big brass prop churning with so much torque it plows the gases from the water, makes bubbles, millions, and the bubbles burst and the torp hears them (*I* hear them) and it's full bore, Mark 48 screaming up that black ass.

But that's in the real world. Wherever that is.

He knows I'm up here but not where, not how close. He's wondering if maybe he's safe.

Two buoys in contact. Multiple aspects simultaneously. Like ears at oblique ends of the playing field. Looking at his voice like those cubist paintings. Combined perspectives, multiple aspects. Moisture skims my window. We fly through clouds.

Hook and enter. A new bearing. It intersects the old bearing and he's *fixed*.

Another buoy launches. The kick. Select it up to the headphones. While waiting for some aural action I update the two points. Looking good. If this badboy lights off quick enough he'll run it over. Triangulation city. Killer, Killer, KILLER.

Bring up the new buoy. Beautiful up-Doppler all over. Textbook perfect. My heart swells.

I study the gram, waiting for the pass by my buoy, CPA — the closest point of approach, the Doppler-shift that'll tell me what I need to know. He's bearing down on the buoy, loud, louder than I've heard him. Amplitude is proximity. He's close. I pick up his turbine rate. I use the computer to divide that by the step-down gearing ratio to his prop shaft. Once I have the shaft rate I multiply it by sixty for the shaft rpm which I then divide by the turns-per-knot ratio for this class of sub and *Presto-Change-o!* I've got his speed. Twenty knots. Max speed for the Soviet boat, an evening stroll for the stand-in. Looks like he's playing by the rules. I tell the crew. They are properly dazzled, reminded that I am the hub about which the mission revolves.

But something's wrong. The Doppler never shifts. No CPA. Proximity to the buoy remains steady. He's right on top of it. Right on top but isn't passing it. I'm getting antsy. I hear mechanical things, maybe dive planes, an up-tick in the turbine whine, changes that haven't shown up on the gram yet.

He's turned.

Bastard's turned, going evasive. I tell Dumchowski and he screams, "Which way? Which way's he fucking turning?" I can't figure it out. Just when his Doppler should shift down, nothing happens, all the frequencies hold steady. As if he's hovering, hovering but doing twenty knots at the same time. It's impossible. The whine in my ear is higher than ever, piercing, like he's right beside me. I know it's the turbine and he's moving out but the data's not showing yet. What I hear doesn't match what I see.

Then it starts coming. The turbine frequency's bending up, a steep incline. Twenty-five knots, thirty, thirty-five, thirty-eight. I'll lose him. Gnawing in my belly. Then I realize. I kick the console. He circled the buoy. The shithead circled my buoy. He knew exactly where I was all along. And now he's bulleting. Worst of all he's heading right back to the battle group. He knows if he closes the BG before we nail him he'll vanish into the surface ship noise.

And that's just what happens. Next buoy's way behind. So's the one after. My grams are clobbered with surface blade rates and loud gearing, masking the whole bottom spectrum. Bearings point all over. Some to him, some back to the carrier, other ships. Nothing correlates. There's nothing I can do. Except maybe call up Mother and request the whole battle group go dead in the water. Not too likely.

Of course that's JUST what we'd do in a real war. In a real war with real submarines and real people dying I could tell the Admiral to shut down his ships and he'd do it. In a heartbeat. But this isn't real war. It's practice for real war. But even the real war we're practicing for isn't a real war yet. Not that any of us knows what a real war is like. Except maybe some of the old farts who caught the tail end of Nam.

He's done his act for me and now he's finished. He let me see what he wanted and now the show's over. Lights out. Headphones roaring with surface ships. Like isolating a whisper in a room full of screaming. If I lose him now, it's my fault. It's not REALLY my fault but it'll look like it is. They don't understand the difficulties, the variables, the complexities and subtleties. They'll always believe a better SENSO could have pulled it off.

Finally I lose all trace of contact. I cycle the buoys over and over, hunting for a sniff. Nothing. My face is burning. I hesitate before telling the crew. There must be something I can do. The humiliation. The disappointment. The fear.

I know what I'll do. I know. After all, simulation is my business.

Bring up the Systems Status Tableau, select line thirty-three, the acoustic tape recorder which records all the in-flight acoustic data. The evidence. Punch in *Disable.* The *ATR DEFECT* alert pops up. Delete it before anyone sees. They won't suspect. It's a big, gunky old twenty-eight-track reel-to-reel. Ancient technology. Unreliable equipment. There's already enough data recorded to prove we had contact and tracked the shit out of him. The module guys just won't have any aural on the kill. They'll give it to us — and even if they don't, it's mechanical error. Nobody's to blame.

As for my crew they only know what I tell them. If I say there's a sub down there it's gospel. They can't see or hear what I see and hear. When we drop a torp it's an act of faith. ASW's a religion and the

SENSO's the high priest. They drop it because I say there's a badboy down below.

I'm the one doing the acoustic magic. But, like a priest, even I don't KNOW there's something down there. All I know is the lines on the grams, noise in my ears. Encoded messages. Indications. Probabilities. It's probably a sub but it could just as well be a Jap freighter twenty miles away, or a tuna seiner. It might be the carrier for all I know. Natural phenomenon, unnatural phenomenon. It's all in the interpretation. You just never know for certain what's down there. Maybe you're chasing a sub, maybe you're just boring holes in the sky. You drop a torpedo on a probability, a collection of indications and signs. On faith. Faith in what I hear and how I see what I hear.

I call a turn on the sub. Dumchowski eats it up. Manufacture some fake bearings to verify. Dumchowski doesn't hesitate. He's dropping buoys and I'm calling contact and speed and up-Doppler and down-Doppler and shooting bearings and they all think we're just closing in on the sucker and really it's air, all air. A simulation of a simulation.

Why not? What's the loss? All anybody really cares about is NOT looking bad. Let's face it. It's not like anybody gives a fat flying fuck about finding the sub or not finding it. It's just a matter of LOOKING like you found that big bad old sub — found it and tracked it and bombed it. You made IT look bad and not the other way around. That's what it's really all about. What it looks like is what it is. Just like Madonna and Milli Vanilli. What's for real and what's not for real? Who cares? I mean it's not like I'd pull anything like this in real life.

We need three attacks before we hand-off to the next crew. We've tracked plenty long enough but need another sensor in contact for attack criteria. Dumchowski wants to call in the H-3 for a coordinated attack. My skin crawls. One ping off their dipping sonar and the whole world knows there's nothing there but water. The helo's equipment isn't sophisticated. They can't always tell WHAT'S down there, can't distinguish a sea-mount from a sub, but they can sure tell when there's zilch. I can fake contact all day but if there's nothing for that ping to bounce off, no three-hundred-foot-long seven-thousand-ton chunk of iron and steel in the very near vicinity, then I am one very dead piece of meat.

But fortunately for me Dumchowski's idea, besides being bad for my little scam, is also dumbshit tactics. Whitman nixes it. No active acoustics. Why alert the target for nothing? He wants to stay passive, corroborate with the magnetic anomaly detector.

I announce another turn.

Whitman extends the MAD boom and we set up to fly down the non-existent simulated badboy's simulated track. Vibration through my boot soles. The fifteen-foot boom cranking out the tail, isolating the magnetometer head from the plane's aura of magnetic influence. We drop down low, a hundred feet, cherubs one, to accommodate the MAD's short range. Turbulence, air pockets, details of the ocean surface, a sense of great speed.

I load up the tacplot with pointers and trackers to keep Dumchowski busy. I can see Whitman up front hunched over the MAD display, the line slithering down his scope like a lie detector's trace. His left hand at the armament control panel, middle fingertip beneath the plastic idiot shield, poised to pickle the mock torp. I bring up the tactical plot and watch the aircraft bug scooting toward the fix symbol. Whitman says, "Standby for MADman. Standby. *Sta-a-a-ndby.*" The bug's about to on-top the fix. I check Dumchowski — he's lost in his scope. My mouth forms the word *now*. I reach over and cycle the MAD power switch. When the power surge hits Whitman's display it makes a textbook perfect MADman, a seismic pin-banger, as if we just on-topped a giant chunk of ferrous metal.

Whitman calls out, "MADman! MADman! MADman!"

Ⓜ appears at the intersection of two bogus bearings.

"Standby for weapon drop on my third now," he says. "Now . . . Now . . . *NOW!* Weapon away."

A weapon symbol pops up adjacent the mad symbol. Ⓜ⊗ Climax of the tactical plot.

"That looks good," Whitman says. "Very damn good. Let's come round for another."

Dumchowski's screeching and doing the Arsenio Hall crank and jumping around in his ejection seat like a little kid. If he wasn't strapped in he'd be bouncing off the bulkhead. "YES!" he squeals. "YESYESYES, *YES!* Eat my hot, squirting lead you commie fuck!"

I can't help but grin myself. But it's not for getting off the attack. And it's not for getting away with the whole other thing either. It's seeing

Dumchowski all wriggling and squiggling that makes me smile. For once I could almost like Dumchowski. All that college and AOTC and a year of ASW training, all that education, all that cocksucking, and he can still act like a kid hitting his first home run. It's kind of nice when you think about it. Sort of, I don't know, real.

Day Thirty-one

I WHISPER INTO THE CAT'S EAR, testicles and testosterone. These are the words I wake up to. I'm REM-ing all over the place when the bos'n's whistle blows me out of my dream. That's all I remember while I jump up and struggle against and around the other guys rolling out of their racks, wiping their eyes, groaning and moaning and blinking in the sudden mean light, whining *Shit* and *What the Fuck.* I drag on my stinky flight suit — the Nomex cold from the air conditioning, still damp with mission sweat. A hairy foot pops out from the top rack, brushes my nose. I yelp and backhand it. Tug on my boots, not bothering with socks or even considering lacing the damn things up. I'm still motherfucking asleep.

I whisper into the cat's ear, testicles and testosterone. This is what I keep hearing as I stumble through berthing, rubbing up against a mass of naked, simmering, sleep-sweaty bodies. The air is thick and hot and would reek of bad breath and farts if I wasn't used to it from breathing it all night. I climb through these bodies to the door and into the passage-way which is just as jammed up and I'm bouncing and pushing and being pushed against the bulkheads and it's like this all the way but instead of kicking back and waiting for the rush to thin out I keep shoving, thinking the sooner I get to the shop the sooner I'm back in my rack. And all the time I'm thinking of that line from my dream and trying to remember the dream and why I or anybody else would say such a thing. But all I remember is the line and nothing bigger to put it into that would make some kind of sense.

I go rolling into the shop and it's all dark except for blue TV light. When I get focused I see Buckethead there all kicked back. He's wearing his flight gear and zoning on the tube. I guess I surprise him because he jerks back his head all guilty like and he's fucking around with something in his lap. But when he sees it's me he relaxes.

"Greg, baby. What's shakin'? Hey, you gotta check this out."

But I'm still not together enough to know where I am. "What fucking TIME is it? Is this a drill or what?"

He cranes his big old head back. Something unsteady about it, puppetish, distorted. *Elephant Man.* How did they ever get a helmet to fit him?

"You look like dogshit warmed over," he says. "It's just a man-overboard drill. You're mustered. Hey, but don't jam till you check this out."

I really don't want to focus on anything for fear I'll get too waked up and won't be able to get back to sleep. I hate that. But he keeps insisting so I scope at what's so fascinating on TV. I tell right away by the cheap, contrasty, home-video look that it's smut. A woman's face covered with jism, grinning and slurping and rubbing this cock all over and I'm thinking — no, I'm SAYING — "Neato, Bucket. Real neato," and I'm about to leave but Buckethead stops me. "Wait. Just watch." So I do and it's all slo-mo and it DOES look a little weird but it takes a second to click just what it is that's different. It's that the jiz is coming OFF her face, like she's vacuuming it up with the cock as she rubs that big jerking head all over her cheeks and nose and eyes and lips and tongue.

Buckethead's all laughing and giggling and squealing, "Look at how the cum all jumps back into that dude's love-hammer! Check it out, man! Is that cool or what?!" And I see his hand kinda twitching back toward his lap and the outline of his little boner beneath the flame-retardant Nomex and I'm like, *Damn, Buckethead, get a life.*

I don't say anything but just stumble out the door, back into the throng of bodies. A hand falls on my shoulder. I try to ignore it, keep going, but it doesn't let go. I give in and look up. It's Rudy. Dressed in skivvies and flight boots. People are pushing all around us in the passageway and I don't want to give up my momentum so I just yell back, "Buckethead's taking muster. I had a late debrief. Tell the Chief I'll be in at eleven."

"Whoa, wait a minute," says Rudy. The 1MC comes over with *Time is zero plus six minutes.* "Nierman just got back and he's gunning for you."

"What are you talking about?" I'm really in no mood to stand out here and chat.

"He's pissed, man. Was all crying that you passed him a bogus hot-swap."

I don't need this BS. I just give him a wave-off, like *Fuck that turd and the horse that rode in on him* and head back to my rack. Rudy's yelling after me over the mob, "Watch your ass, Bro. He's a real weasel!" I'm fighting to get back, swimming upstream through all these sleep-walking bodies and all I want is to get back to my rack. Above it all the 1MC crackles, *Time is zero plus seven minutes.* I just want to get back to sleep.

Next time I wake up it's to the electronic throb of the alarm in my watch dangling from my racklight. The watch is a Casio in a black plastic case. It's got an analog display with a sweep-second hand and a digital display showing two other time zones, the day and date. It has two alarms, a stopwatch and a light. I use the analog display for local time, have one of the digitals set to Zulu time and the other on San Diego time. I use the alarm for wake-ups and for brief times. The stopwatch I use for turn-counting props and figuring speed, also for bomb runs, timing CPAs, and taking my heartrate when I'm working out. The black, plastic band is both silent and nonreflective which makes it a helluva good watch to wear when shot down behind enemy lines. And it's waterproof to thirty meters. It cost twenty-four dollars at the May Company at the Mission Valley Mall. I adore this watch.

I'm waiting for my morning hard-on to wilt. I remember a guy in boot camp who was scared to death the chow was spiked with salt-peter. Thought it would make him impotent. He was a spidery black dude and walked like a spastic. But the walk was a put-on. An attitude walk he got from the Crips or some other L.A. gang. It probably looked real bad down on Manchester but it just looked fruity there in the barracks.

One morning at reveille he's strut-limping up and down the bar-racks screaming that he doesn't have a hard-on. He's had a *muhfucking* hard-on every *muhfucking* day of his *muhfucking* life and now he doesn't have one and there's gonna be hell to pay from these jive mess cranks who poisoned him and messed with his *appaRATus* and he's gonna sue the U.S. government and the navy and President Ray-gun and the company commanders and who he doesn't sue he's gonna plain kickass on.

I don't think I ever thought about that guy since. It was pretty funny at the time but now I'm thinking maybe he had a point. Only it's not my hard-ons they're dicking with, it's something else. Something I can't quite put my finger on but it's easily as important as getting it up. It sounds stupid to say that and then say, yeah, but I can't say what that thing is that's being dicked around with. But all the same something's missing and even if I can't remember having that thing I know it's gone in me.

After I shit, shower and shave I head to the shop. Nobody's there so I have to search out the combo again. When it's twenty-four-hour ops like this everybody's always either flying or sleeping or getting ready for one or the other.

While twirling the lock dial I'm looking at that stupid S-3 and the lightning bolts and I think of Nierman and what Rudy said this morning. A bogus hot-swap. It WOULD be Nerdy in the relief bird last night. I press my forehead to the slick, red enamel. He's about the only one on-the-ball enough to catch me. Him and maybe the Chief. I lose my place and have to spin the dial three times and start over.

Inside I check in on the muster board. There's a note there to see the Chief when he gets back from flying. I'm not up to this. I'll dodge him all day — hang out in the gym, maybe the library. Those are two places he'll NEVER look. Hell, he doesn't even know where they ARE. Tomorrow we'll be at Pearl and he'll be so hot to get off the boat he'll forget about the whole thing.

Light's on at the sludge pot, thank God. Something's different about the shop but I can't tell what it is. Still stinks like tobacco smoke and floor wax, same WWII-vintage steel desks jammed together like dominoes so there's hardly room for chairs, gunmetal grey hatrack draped with lifeless zoombags and 'varks in their canvas pouches, blackboard, four-drawer safes lined up like halfbacks, red LOCKED sign displayed on each, fan buzzing away in its overhead-mounted cage, TV on its angle-iron rack with Nierman's VCR jury-rigged underneath, bookcase full of thick blue NATOPS manuals and submarine books and three volumes of *Jane's Fighting Ships* and PQS pubs bungee-corded up so they aren't "missile hazards," overhead crammed with pipes and ducts and wiring harnesses, each one stenciled with *compressed air,* or *steam,* or *salt water,* or *hydraulic,* or *1MC,* or *3JG.* And like the bulkheads, paint so thick you'd think it was applied with a firehose.

Then I spot it. The grey duct tape stands out against the nicotine yellow pipes. All around where the steam pipes and water pipes and wire harnesses pierce the bulkhead. And all around the insulation seams. Tape. All sealed up tight as a tick. Somebody's been busy.

I turn on TV, energize it, initiate television. Some army guy says he's not fighting unless we *utilize our nuclear arsenal* on Iraq. This brain surgeon figures there'll be too many casualties otherwise. They're court-martialing him, natch.

I switch to the PLAT, the flight deck observation channel. An A-6 on the ball, making his approach. Pour a cup of sludge and hear the whistle, then the smashdown. The whole shop lurches and trembles. A steel box slammed. But there's no arresting gear screech. Bolter. I look up and sure as shit he's off the pointy end, headed for another come-around.

The coffee's soupy thick, oily JP-5 slick shimmering on top.

I unlock the safe and liberate my camcorder from the bottom drawer. Flop the LOCKED sign to the green, OPEN side. Check the battery meter. Then I spin slow on my heel videoing the duct-taped bulkheads. I rotate that way three, four, five times till I get a little dizzy, plop into a chair and shut my eyes, still sensing motion, waving cilia. Then I'm gazing at the rack of 'varks, like sacks of small heads, oscillating from the blood pounding in my eyes.

After I get my 'vark on I settle in with the Plan of the Day, theme-decorated with hula girls and pineapples. I check the inport watchbill. Caught me a shore patrol. Bitchen. Three days inport and I catch the duty. Forget *that.* I got other plans.

The 'vark feels lopsided. I let out the left strap and tighten up the other side. Dine and fandy. It's not so bad once you get used to it.

A notice for a college class. They do that occasionally. Get some loser prof with a degree from Nowhere U. and offer credit in some bumfuck city college in North Dakota or something. Who'd teach out here if he had a choice? It's a religion course. I'm not hot on religion but I'll probably sign up. I take all the courses I can find. Been doing it since I got in. Three junior colleges, Navy Campus For Achievement classes, correspondence courses, CLEP tests — you name it. Might have a year of units. Figure I'll declare a major about the turn of the century. Have a diploma in time for retirement.

No use putting it off. I hang up the POD and head for the ready room.

A crew brief's going on so everything's hush-hush. I figure to just sneak in and grab the message boards. The watch nods, gives me this weird look. I take the yellow confidential message board from the desk. He leans over and whispers, "Why you wearing that mask?"

I hold the snout up to his ear and whisper back, "Practice."

Up front the crews are watching our intel officer Mister Simpson on the CVIC monitor doing the weather brief. All the squadron spooks take turns reporting weather and intel updates. Simpson's all decked out in luau garb, ugly Hawaiian shirt with a big old ALOHA necklace, one of those dumb souvenir straw sombreros and a pair of Ray-Bans. I can't hear him but I can tell he's cutting up. He's ALWAYS cutting up.

The watch looks a little confused, leans in and whispers, "Practice for what?"

I say, "Practice for Practice" and walk out, closing the door real quiet behind me.

Back in the shop I leaf through the outgoing messages for mission summaries. The summary Whitman wrote up on our flight reports three good attacks on target of interest (SSN 688) generated by passive acoustic sensors and corroborated by magnetic anomaly detection equipment. Hot contact swap to Beefsteak 702 — that's when we handed off the target to Nerdy's crew. Buoys in contact: pointers 7, 14, 22.

Of course I didn't have ANY contact at the hand-off. But I had to give them something.

Two of those buoys were just about down when I had Dumchowski pass them. The other had *beaucoup* artifacts and surface noise — you could make any kind of target you wanted with it. I was hoping the other crew would just think they dropped the ball and lost contact. I check for Nerdy's mission summary but it's not here. Must not have gone out yet. I'll need to see it before the Chief collars me. Get my ducks in a row.

Suddenly there's a huge BANG! and the whole shop jolts like it got whacked with a giant baseball bat. I jump. Then this horrible screech, deafening, metal-on-metal. I about spit up my heart. The coffee sludge, which I can't drink because of my 'vark, is sloshing all over. The fan cage is still resonating as I check out the TV. That A-6 finally got down. Damn. I must be on edge or something.

FOUR

Pineapple

Day Thirty

PULLING INTO PEARL the airwing's tasked with manning the rails. We all dress up like Popeye and cluster-fuck on the flight deck. Oh seven hundred and it's cold as shit. Tropical paradise my lily white shivering ass.

We finally get formed up. Me and Rudy parade resting while creeping through the harbor. Rudy's beside me going on about what a kickass time we'll have ashore. Two arm lengths apart but that doesn't stop old Rudy from yammering away. No sir. I told him I wasn't hanging out but he won't listen.

"We'll get us some that good Hawaiian skull," he says. "And a little brown-eye for dessert. I'm cutting loose, bro. Just get me off this fucking grey thing and watch me tear."

Skull. How touching.

I don't feel like tearing. "Maybe I'll catch up tomorrow."

"Don't shine me on, man. Could be the last go-round for all of us. You know what I mean. Look at this thing." He's getting excited. Waves an arm around the deck. Some blackshoe first class yells to stay in ranks. Rudy ignores him. "It's the death ship, man. We all got the bad ju-ju. I can smell it."

"You're crazy," I say.

"Yeah, I'm crazy. But I ain't blowin' off my last chance. I'm getting me a six-pack of hookers. And one of those Samoan water buffaloes. Roll her in flour and dick the wet spot. I'm getting me fucked sixteen ways to kingdom come. Could be our last gasp."

"What are you talking about?" I say. "There's still P.I. And maybe Singapore. And besides, we're NOT gonna die."

"Singapore's out," he says, and I know he's right. Singapore was on before the war. Now we'll be lucky snagging three days in the P.I. "And P.I. don't take Mastercard."

The shore crawls by. Undulating land colors. Cold wind infiltrates my protective layer of thin gabardine. The runways at Hickam and the giant Quonset hut hangars, then all the ships, lined up like game pieces: destroyers, frigates, tenders, relic-looking minesweeepers with plank hulls, cruisers and amphibs, guided-missile ships, hydrofoil patrol boats, roll-on roll-off tank boats, oilers. Very inspiring. If you're inspired by that sort of thing.

A big billboard facing the channel says, *We Support Our Heroes!* What's THAT supposed to mean? Last week we were all just scummy squids but now we're heroes?

Rudy starts in again. Just to shut him up I agree to meet for a beer at the monkey bar. He's a decent guy and all but he just doesn't get it. What's the use in getting off the boat if you just hang with a bunch of squids? I mean *heroes.*

The Arizona Memorial rises like a stretched-out greasy-spoon napkin holder. Last time here I got seriously bored and took the ride over. It really is like a ride, too. You start out in this gift shop where they sell paperweights and bumper stickers and T-shirts, the usual geedunk. (I bought a flag that flew from the wreck's mainmast. Came with a certificate that says on blah-blah date this flag was raised over the blah-blah. Must be a guy who does nothing but run these souvenir flags up and down. Imagine. It's somebody's JOB.) Then you pile onto a boat and cross over to the napkin holder. About two-thirds of the other tourists are Japanese. Guess they can't resist it. Like those mutts in Japan who wear T-shirts that say, *My Daddy Flew B-29s.* Ambassadors of goodwill.

In the napkin holder they show this film about the attack and all that. I think there's a bunch of shit cut in from the movie *Midway.* Clips of Jap planes coming in guns all blazing and dropping torps all over. Explosions, fire, sirens. A real turkey shoot. Those Japs must have had a blast.

Guys out there in their skivvies pounding away on ack-ack guns. Giving it right back to those Japs. I mean DAMN! WAKE-UP CALL! Planes and strafing and explosions and just a world of shit and these guys don't care. They're getting them a Jap. They're pissed.

One old chief took a destroyer out by himself. Practically alone. He was the seniorest guy left on the whole ship and, man, he took charge. Kicked ass and took names. Fired that tub up and drove it right out the harbor. THOSE guys are heroes. I can respect that. But us? Program a Tomahawk from two hundred miles away and let her loose. Drop a torp from a thousand feet up on a sub a thousand feet under. Where's the heroics? THOSE guys fought eye-to-eye. They SAW who they were shooting at. Close up and personal. I don't want to sound like some gung-ho kill-crazy jarhead or something, but there's a difference. There's got to be a difference.

It just seems like as long as you're gonna kill people there ought to be some etiquette about the whole thing.

After we're secured I go below and change into civvies, pack a bag, then head down to the shop. If the Chief's there I'll just . . . I don't know but I sure don't want to see him yet.

When I get there the door's unlocked and I hear voices. There's a little hole in the bulkhead I caught the Chief using once to spy on "my men." That's his butt-sucking term for us. Like, "Don't worry, Skipper, if 1st Looey can't get a handle on buffing out that deck *my men* sure will." I try peeking in. But somebody taped it over from inside.

I cruise over to the ready room.

Nobody's in there but the watch, this goofus non-rate with a hook of hair plastered to his forehead like Napoleon. He's busy rewinding last night's movie. I'm about to say something but it's taboo to hang out here in civvies. So I snag the message boards and slink into a chair in back where nobody can see me.

I'm scoping the mission summaries for Nerdy's. It's my last chance to concoct a story for the Chief. I know I can't get ashore without bumping into him so I better have my shit in one sock.

Napoleon's still screwing with the projector. He's not really rewinding, though, like I thought. He rewinds some, stops it, then pulls out a bunch of film and holds it to the light. Then he wraps it back on and rewinds some more. I figure, dumbshit airman, some dirt-scratcher from Gimcrack, Iowa, probably never seen film up close and wondering where the little people come from. It sounds dumb to think like that, like people that stupid exist anywhere outside movies but they DO, and the navy's got them. Hell, the navy's MADE for them.

I'm flipping through the outgoing messages and there she is. Nerdy's mission summary. I can't believe what I'm reading. I drop the board in my lap, blindsided, when I see Napoleon again with another strip of film he's all eyeballing like it's the plans to the Deathstar or something.

He scissors out a single frame from the film and scotch tapes the two ends back together. Then he heads to the desk, all the time holding this frame of film up to the light and still not seeing me back here yet.

Schizzy behavior. I watch, collect details.

He pushpins the film to the desk blotter. Then he starts scraping at it with a pocket knife. What the fuck, over? Then I see he's scraping off the emulsion. He's real methodical, draws the blade down shaving off a curl of emulsion, then again, over and over until it's all scraped off and nothing's left on the celluloid.

And I'm thinking, shit, now I'll never know what was on the frame, which I really want to know since he's treating it so weirdly.

He pushes all the emulsion into a neat little pile, then leans back and stretches, pretty proud of himself. He brushes away his Napoleon lock and it snaps right back.

I slink down, remain covert.

The door opens and Lieutenant Dumchowski pokes in. Napoleon about leaps out of his skin trying for military bearing. Dumchowski asks, "Everything all right?" He's wearing the SDO badge.

Napoleon says, "Roger, sir. Everything's copacetic."

Dumchowski nods. "Great. I'll be in the jungle if anything happens. And . . ." He puts his hand on the kid's shoulder like old Uncle Dumchowski, "You don't need to call me sir when nobody's around."

What a guy. Only a dumb JO would say something like that. Fresh out of college and full of that liberal, everybody's-equal bullshit. Generally, they're about over it by the time they make lieutenant but Dumchowski's a little slow on the uptake. And when they make commander they're all magically transformed into fucking Nazis.

Dumchowski says, "Hasta la bye-bye," and ducks out.

I see the message board but can't remember why it's there, like somebody just plopped it there when I wasn't looking. I re-read it and get knocked on my ass all over again. Says they tracked the sub for three solid hours without interruption. Got off three clean attacks before going off-station. It says, and this is the part that REALLY gets me, they gained initial contact off a hot swap from Beefsteak aircraft 700 — me and Dumchowski in double nuts. Then it lists the buoys I passed them, which I know full well weren't within ten miles of the target.

Napoleon gets a cup of water from the scuttlebutt. Spoons in a deadly dose of white processed sugar. He scoops up his pile of emulsion, real careful to get every little bit, and dumps it into the sugar water. Stirs vigorously. Then he drinks it all down in a swallow. One shot — GONE! Wipes with a finger getting all the yum-yums and sucks it clean. Straightens his gigline and walks out.

I need to work fast.

I'm checking out the frames around where he spliced but I can't see a thing. Nothing but figures all tangled up. Investigate the movie box for evidence, telltale information, corroborating data. Nada. He left his scissors and tape, though, so snip-snip — I got my very own souvenir. Tuck it in my wallet and I'm out of there.

Nerdy's alone in the shop. Spitshined and military creased and squirting Pledge on his devastatingly shiny pair of Corfams. He even shines the lace tips.

"What's up, bonehead?" I ask all fake jolly.

He finishes with the shoe and starts in on his belt buckle. "Fuck off," he says. "You're not allowed in here with civvies."

"Who died and made you LPO?" I ask.

"If you came around more often instead of rack-hounding or whatever you do you'd know I *AM* the LPO — least till we get a first class in here."

I look around at the muster board and sure enough the seniority order's all screwed with so Nerdy tops the second classes. His billet slot says ALPO.

"Alpo, huh. What's an Alpo?"

"It's A-L-P-O. ACTING leading petty officer."

"Don't get your bowels in an uproar. Just giving you shit. You know anybody wants to take my duty tomorrow? I'm paying forty bucks."

"Nobody in here."

I can't say ANYTHING right to Nerdy. He's just one of those guys. He's not all that bad; I've gotten along with a lot worse. But even when I'm trying to be nice it blows up in my face. Like people are preset with polarities, either plus or minus, and I'm a plus and Nierman's a plus and every time we get too close there's all this friction pushing us apart. Which is really weird. Some people seem attracted to me. Hell, I can't keep them away half the time. And then others just hate me for no reason. And then there's guys like Nerdy who seem like they're trying to like me — but not trying TOO hard today — and somehow just can't pull it off.

My coffee cup's all gooked up so just for a needle I ask Nerdy to borrow his shine rag. He looks up from his belt buckle where he's immersed in making that crow sparkle. He gives me the eye and says, "Get real."

Fuck him. I ask if he knows what tonight's movie is, get him off-guard before I pounce.

"*Apocalypse Now*, 1979. Martin Sheen, Marlon Brando, Robert Duvall, Dennis Hopper. Francis Ford Coppola's 40-million-dollar epic adaptation of Joseph Conrad's novella *Heart of Darkness*. Coppola's vision of war is manic, surreal, and overwrought in this lily white, pinkosympathizer mockery of the manly act of halting the dreaded march of communism. Color, 153 minutes, rated R."

"I hear you're pissed at me," I say.

"Where'd you hear that?" he asks, acting all blasé.

"Rudy," I say and start screwing with the safe dial being all blasé like him.

"Consider the source."

"He gave me this story how you were all upset about the swap the other night. Said you were gunning for me." Then I decide to really open the safe since my camcorder's in there. So I pull out this little wad of paper towel I have all the combos written on.

"Gunning for you, huh." Nerdy says *gunning* like it's the stupidest word he ever heard. All of his movements are careful, planned. I know I pushed a button. Nerdy's not the kind to let on anything. Tries to keeps it all bottled up. He's Mister Perfect. A real serial-killer type. Or TV evangelist — take your pick.

"Said you were complaining my buoys didn't have contact. Which of course they did. Right?" He's ignoring me, puts away the Pledge and screws around in the desk drawer.

I'm getting a little pissed. That kind of pissed I really hate. I hate it because I don't know what it's about. Why should I be pissed at Nerdy? I know what he did, know he faked a whole mission, just like me, so he didn't look like the one who lost the contact. I know it all. That ought to be enough. But it's not. I just have to push it. He's trying to ignore me because he knows there's nothing to say. He's giving us both a chance out of this but I won't, or can't, leave it alone.

"I mean there was sub contact all over, right? There had to be, right, since I saw your mission summary and APPARENTLY you tracked that badboy all over the godforsaken ocean for three hours and all and got off those really splendid kills and everything, right? Isn't that right, Nierman?"

"You're in deep shit the Chief catches you with those combos written down."

That's one thing I really respect about Nerdy. Here I think I got him backed in a corner and he just slithers right out slick as snot. Somebody asks me a tough question'all I can think is to answer or freeze up or lie. But not the Nerdman. No wonder he's the ALPO. He oughta be fucking president.

"Nier*ma-a-a-n . . .*" I whine like to a little brother. He pulls out these two long things wrapped in purple velvet. They look heavy. Then he pulls out this book and I can tell by all the gilt and the black cover that it's a Bible. He sets it by the long things and padlocks his drawer.

I grab my camcorder and slip into a chair.

"And you're not supposed to keep personal gear in the safes, either," he says.

"You can eat shit and die you think I'm leaving this in berthing with THOSE dirtballs."

He unwraps one of the tall things and it's this really big, really ugly, brass crucifix. Something you'd see in *The Omen* or *The Exorcist,* one of those movies about crazed Catholics. He starts in polishing with the same manic intent he showed his shoes. Which makes a kind of sense. A guy ate up by the navy might as well be ate up by God, too.

"You having a revival meeting or something?"

"Helping out the chaplain with services," he says.

Twerp. I start messing with the camcorder, pointing it at the crucifix and zooming in and out on Jesus' brass face, which looks more Japanese than Jewish or Arab or whatever he's supposed to be. It's kind of twisted watching Nerdy's cloth-wrapped finger rubbing on the arms, shining up that bony chest, like some giant giving the little brass Jap-looking guy a sponge bath.

But I got it all in the viewfinder now so I feel better, cockier. "Helping out the chaplain, huh? That's pretty damn nice of you. You're a hell of a guy, you know that, Nierman. TWO hells of a guy."

He grins like the sap he is. "I know it," he says.

"Good for a bullet in the old evals, huh."

"You bet."

Liberty's called away over the 1MC. I video Nerdy shining up Jesus.

"Time for you liberty hounds to hit the beach," he says.

"Yeah, sounds like the brow's up." Nerdy, black and white, vibrating, video-ized.

"You better get before the Chief catches you in here," he says.

"Yep."

The whir and hum. The tiny display. Contact on the target of interest.

"I won't narc on'you for the combo thing. Just don't do it again," he says.

"Appreciate it, shipmate." Zoom in. Eyebrows knitting a sweater. He's concentrating way too hard on polishing. You'd think it was a bomb about to blow up in his hands, those hands which I just know are soft and wet and cold like Ann Felton's hands in square-dancing class in sixth grade.

"You know," I say, locked and loaded. Ready to zing. "Shame about that tape recorder of yours."

"What tape recorder?" he says all innocent.

"The *acoustic* tape recorder, dip. The ATR didn't record a thing, right? I mean, that's what I heard. Down the whole flight. Right? It's just tough is all. All that mission data wasted — could have made up some juicy training tapes."

He swaps one crucifix for the other and starts rubbing old Jesus all over again.

"Keep it still," I say, "I can't focus when you're jacking him all over like that."

"You must have heard wrong," he says, "I didn't have any ATR problems."

Pow! Right in my gut. I look up from the viewfinder.

Nerdy's a smiling dildo.

"I thought I heard for sure your ATR went down."

"Nope, not mine. Had some half-system problems, but the ATR was hunky-dory."

Nerdy pulls another one out his ass. You gotta admire the guy.

"Look," he says, that all-American face smug as a pawnbroker, "I'll take your duty, but it'll cost you fifty bucks."

On the shuttle into town I'm going crazy trying to figure that Nerdy thing. How could he pull it off without faking a down ATR? No way. Unless he REALLY had contact, unless he REALLY had a sub on those buoys

I gave him. Except that I'm an ASW expert and things like that don't happen to us experts.

Like that Ticonderoga class cruiser shooting down an Iranian airliner a couple years back. I can just see the scene, boy. Dead of night. Little third class gets an emitter alert on some radar blip. *Air Hostile* says the computer. Kid doesn't know what to do. Doesn't know the system can't tell an F-14 from a 747 from a MiG-29. Best technology money can buy. No reason to think when you got a system like this baby. *Ten Years in Development! A Bazillion Dollars in R & D! A Cast of One Thousand MIT Grads! It's Big! It's Complicated! And Nobody Knows How to Work It!*

The Skipper's yanked out of his rack and he's breathing fire down that kid's neck. The whole ship's at GQ. Is it a bad guy? It better be, pup, or you can color yourself Cheez Whiz. They measure the scan rate, the pulse repetition frequency, the pulse width — the *emitter fingerprint* they call it, trying to make it sound like SCIENCE. Ha! It's for certain. They don't know WHAT it is. But it COULD be a bad guy. Or it could be a hundred other things that go Blip in the night. Who knows? Nobody knows. What's real? Who cares? Time for a command decision.

When in doubt, take it out.

Two minutes later there's a cloudburst over the Arabian Sea. It's raining Iranians. Pitter patter. Just thank God they weren't REAL people.

It happens.

What those guys needed was one of those synthetic inverse aperture radars. At least they could've seen how big the thing was.

The shuttle drops me in Chinatown and I find a hotel. A real dump. Rooms by the month, week, day or hour. TV in every room. Perfect.

I drop off my gear and wander down to a Chinese market. Get some rice crackers and a six-pack of sake in dinky cans like tomato juice. The meat counter has roasted ducks strung up by their feet. I buy one. They roll the duck in paper so the feet stick out. I'm gonna look real dufus hauling this down the street.

In front of the hotel there's this hardbody with a stack of brochures. Bikini top and tight little shorts, sliver of ass. Kickass tan. Big shades. She glances over and I look away, monitor her kind of peripherally. Remain passive.

She's not passing out the brochures. Plenty of people walking by but she doesn't move on any of them. But then this isn't exactly the touristy part of town anyway so what's she doing here?

"Wanna go to luau, sailor?" she says, all crinkly cleavage nod-nod wink-wink.

I get it.

I'm ready to push on by but she shoves this brochure right up my face.

"C'mon, sailor, you need to go to luau. Hot meat." She slaps her rump, leers over her glasses. Nice eyes. Usually the eyes give it away, all hagged out and dead looking. But she looks okay. Fresh and clean.

"Kahlua pig," she says. "Very juicy. Very [rump slap] *hot.*"

I glance at the brochure, turn it over, and hand it back.

"I don't think so," I say and start for the door.

"You going in there?" she asks. "How come? You staying here? You want some company?"

Point to the duck with my chin. "Got company, thanks."

"What is that thing? That a chicken or what?"

"It's a duck."

"Ohhhhh, a *duck.*" She rolls her head. "Fuck . . . a duck. Much better to have pig." She slaps her rump again. "You don't like Kahlua pig? That's okay. Better to have pig *in a blanket.* A pig in a blanket's worth two fuck-a-ducks. Double money-back guarantee."

On the way upstairs I keep seeing that sliver of butt. Inside I jam to the window but she's not there. Then I see her up the block leaning into a Honda, rolling back and forth on a tall heel. What an ass. I look around wildly for the camcorder and rush back to the window. But it's too late. She's gone.

Pound down one of the sakes. Tastes like nail-polish remover mixed with tequila. Pop open another and plop on the bed for a little tubing. They're bombing the oil slicks in the Gulf. Oil blazing away on the water. A water inferno. That's a new one. Smoked halibut for everyone!

A panel on whether it's ethical to assassinate Saddam Hussein. What's ethics got to do with anything? Like these guys are gonna give their blessings. *Yeah, it's okay to knock him off, you can sleep easy.* Do the bomber guys have that option? Can they call back and say, *Hey, I'm ready to dump some thousand-pounders on this building here and I think it's a command bunker but it might be an elementary school — requesting ethics check, over?* Is that how it works?

Then a story about tattoo parlors. Business is booming. Eagles and

American flags are very hot. As is the pithy *Mess with the best, die like the rest.* A shot of that hooker's very bitchen butt comes to mind and I think about pounding my pud for a while. Instead I just roll over and nod off.

When I wake up I'm late for meeting Rudy at the monkey bar. Just enough time to rig my surveillance nest and scoot.

The coconut-faced monkeys gape from behind Plexiglas. The way Rudy's hunched over the bar you could easily mistake him for a steroided-up relative.

Rudy's maudlin. And a little lit. He's been calling Anita but she's never home.

"I'm gonna kill that cunt," he rumbles.

He's radiating deadly doses of negative energy, lethal enough to zap a fly. My tongue's running all over that chipped tooth and I'm wondering how I can get the hell away. But at the same time I'm sorry for the guy and wish I could put it back together with him and the old lady. But as soon as I think that, there's this picture of Anita's jugs all wangling in my eyes. A moth flutters in my crotch. Then my tongue's back on that damn tooth again and the moth is zapped good as if it buzzed into Rudy's sphere of influence. I don't know whether to shit, go blind or fall off my barstool.

Sometimes I think it'd be better to be put in a little box, just stuck in a box and left alone forever.

"Little early to sweat it," I say. "I mean so what she's not home?"

"She knew we'd be in. I told her I'd call, the bitch. She's yanking me around. She does this shit."

"I wouldn't worry."

"She hasn't written either. Not once." Like it's the last nail in her coffin.

"Look," I say, screwing up my courage, "you're not gonna hit me again, are you? Because if you are I'll just be scooting. I don't mind a little violence now and then — probably good for the soul or something — but when you get in these weird moods . . . I mean, you could turn my face into dog food and I'm not really into that."

Rudy downs his beer and orders up another with a tequila shooter. "I'm real sorry about that," he says. "Didn't mean nothing. Just the booze . . . and that fucking Anita. She makes me so goddam crazy sometimes I just wanna. . . . Yeah, why sweat it?"

He shoots the tequila and stares at the monkeys. One's trying for a hump off another when this big white one comes along and knocks him off. Teeth baring, monkey noises. The little guy finally sulks off. Rudy grunts. "Used to they didn't lock 'em up like that. They ran around loose and you could play with 'em. My old man told me about it. They had one that'd steal shots of whiskey if you didn't watch him. Now they lock 'em all up. Probably some stupid health code."

"Fine with me," I say. "I don't want those things crawling all over me — touching me and shitting and whatnot. My third-grade teacher had one. It'd climb up your back and sit on your head and steal stuff from your pockets. The things are kleptos, every one of them. And they bite, too."

"Ain't natural not to touch things. Everything's like this, wrapped in plastic or stashed behind glass. Sanitized. I gotta feel things for myself, get my hands on it so I know it's real. This kind of bullshit, it's just not normal."

Looks like Rudy's calming down, the tension rolling off. He's still depressed looking but that's status quo for Rudy. Least that's what I'm hoping. Then he grabs the empty shooter and squeezes. I think of Superman squishing a lump of coal into a diamond.

"When I got back from last cruise you know what that bitch did? She made me wear a rubber. My own wife. Like my seed is poison, she's gonna die if it gets on her. For a month I had to wear rubbers with my own wife. Said she couldn't be sure where my dick had been. Believe that shit?"

That's it. I'm out of here. Never did get around to eating my duck. Should've stayed in my nice, safe room.

Rudy's going on and on like he's talking to somebody but it's not me, all the time squishing on that shot glass. "I ain't poison, man. Treating me like I'm cumming toxic waste. That's too shitty."

While I plan how to slip out of these surly bonds I'm watching the monkeys. You don't want to make eye contact when somebody's whacking out. The white monkey's having his way with the little Madonna monkey. Her ex is off in a corner taking a dump in his tiny black hand. I didn't know that was a big thing for monkeys, shitting in their hands. I guess if you're locked up long enough you'll do about ANYTHING for entertainment. I can relate.

Rudy's not the type to let a party end without a struggle. Escaping with my life will take serious tact. The little guy with the handful of shit hops around on driftwood branches till he gets right above where the white monkey's getting off bigtime. Whiteboy's going at it like a jackhammer, and the chimpette all pinned down so you can't tell if she likes it or not, which I guess is not a factor. Then the little guy drops down from his limb and lands right on whiteboy's back. Takes that handful of shit and smears it all over whiteboy's face. I bust out laughing and look over to see if Rudy caught the action when I see he's all novocaine-faced, like his whole skull was flash-frozen.

I check my Casio all dramatic like I've got some urgent appointment. I can't get over the dufus stuff I do when the heat's on. Grace under pressure, boy.

Rudy's just staring, then says real low, "It's a real fucked up world when your wife thinks you're poison."

He heaves that shooter into the Plexiglas, a left-handed looper — BAM! A crack snakes from top to bottom. Reminds me of a wind-screen crack from a bird-strike, the way the Plexiglas just sort of parts without shattering. The whole bar gets quiet and everybody freezes, me included — except the monkeys, they're going nuts, running and screeching and throwing shit.

Rudy drags me off my stool snapping, "Beat feet!" Like I have any choice. Bartender's going, *Hey! Hey!* and I'm just shrugging like *sorry, shit happens.* Rudy screams out at the top of his lungs, "This place sucks!" and we're out the door. I can hear the monkeys screeching till it swings shut.

We're jamming full speed down the block. The bartender and a couple other guys rush out and they're yelling at us, calling us motherfuckers and I'm thinking as we duck around a corner how we're not motherfuckers at all. So I yell it out loud as I can, "We're goddam HEROES you COCK-suckers!" But I keep pumping because if those dudes catch us they'll beat our hero dicks into the dirt.

Old Rudy moves good for a porker. When we finally stop, my heart's pounding and we're both huffing and puffing. Rudy's bent over, choking and laughing. I guess I feel a little better, too, like the excitement and the run shook off some rust.

"Well, that was fun," I say. "Waddayawannadonow?"

"Night's young," he pants, squatting, leather mitt hands gripping his knees. Rudy wheezes, "Let's go get us some pooh-see." He slaps me on the back and starts off. Feels like I got slapped with a damn pot roast. But I follow him. Don't ask why. He's charging along chanting, *Pooh-SEE, pooh-SEE, pooh-SEE!*

*　　*　　*

It's a long ride back to Hotel Street. Every bar we pass, Rudy stops the cab so we can run in for a shooter. After three times I bribe the cabbie to get us on the highway. He swings onto Kamehameha. Rudy's pissed.

"Hey, stay on the streets, man, I'm a thirsty *cabrón*."

The cabbie stares ahead. "No can do, bra. Got to take highway."

Rudy glares at me.

I shrug, "Got to take highway, bra."

The tequila slithers into my blood. Things are softening up. Twenty minutes ago I'd be crazy to be in this cab with Whacko Rudy. So why am I here? Careening around Honolulu with this sociopathic primate whose brain is nothing but a handy carrying case for a pint of testosterone? I'm not sure. Except for this. Rudy can be scary but at least he's solid. Rudy's a genuine thing. You know what he's about, what he wants. Rudy wants a drink. Rudy wants to get laid. Rudy wants to pound your face. He's primal that way. Maybe it's how I want to be. How I want everything to be. Solid all the way through. No wiggle room. No doubt.

The strip club's so big and so dark and the music blasting about a million decibels it's like wading into a thick aural pudding. Sensory trauma. Three stages, each one square and lit up like a boxing ring so all the light is trapped inside the ring and you can't see anything around it, no audience or tables or anything else but these cubes of colored light, quadravision TVs hovering in space, each with some mostly naked babe bumping and grinding and thumping the deck, puppety, isolated in her cube of gyrating spots and flashing kliegs and strobes and lasers that slash the cigarette smoke, marble the atmosphere. I'm floating, suspended in murky solution. It's probably just the tequila but while Rudy chats up the Tom Selleck look-alike checking I.D.s ("chatting," that is, by screaming into each other's ear) it's like the floor falls away and I'm drifting in blackest space, wishing to God I had something to anchor me and wishing too that I could knock the volume down a couple notches so they might hear me if I scream. Just me and these three porn light-cube asteroids suspended in a SurroundSound pudding.

We cadge stools ringside. More beer and shooters. Rudy's yelling at me but I can't hear a thing. The signal attenuated. I know it's just stripper critique of the object of interest, this skinny white girl moving slo-mo, trying for sultry but looking medicated, eyes posted with a DEFINITE vacancy sign.

I fake like I hear Rudy. Nod and laugh. Then I make a game of it. Point out a cocktail tech done up like Elvira and move my lips, laying on a big leer.

Rudy brays, "*Wha-a-at?*"

I move my lips again, hike my thumb and laugh.

"*WHA-AT?*" he brays again.

I do it again acting impatient. Finally he gives in, nods like he hears me. Then he yells something else and I pretend to hear *that* and pretend to answer and he pretends to hear *that.* This goes on until we get bored and both return to our isolation, each gazing into the Jell-O cube asteroid at the white-girl-of-the-living-dead. She's slipping into a new song which is an old song called "Radar Love." By a never-was band whose name I can't quite get at.

She comes up with this weird looking gun which she rubs up and down her belly and into her top, all over her tits. She dances over and I see it's a cop radar gun.

Lip-synching and rubbing that radar gun all over her thighs and up her crotch like she's hot as hell for it.

Then from nowhere, the sky or the rafters or whatever's up in the black beyond above the top of the cube, above all those blinding candy-colored lights and strobes and the mirror ball, above the blasting, howling, pounding source of "Radar Love" falls, light and graceful as an acrobat, a tire, a big old truck tire.

The skinny stripper, as zoned as she is, catches it on the first bounce, straddles it. Off comes her top and skirt and she's down to French-cut panties — almost cute if you squint and ignore the dead eyes. Twisting and writhing on that tire, waving that gun all over, lip-synching for all she's worth. She arches back, delineating every rib, every line of muscle, tits stretched flat so she looks like a little boy, like maybe I used to look, scrawny, skin white as a maggot, almost transparent so you can see the green veins lacing her chest together and tracking the insides of her thighs.

> *No more speed I'm almost there*
> *Gotta keep cool now, gotta take ca-are . . .*

Rudy's completely mezzed. Guitar riffs buzzing like bugs, a beer puddle echoing concentric rings. She points the gun at each seat making like she's blowing us away one at a time. Boom! Boom! Those deadened eyes suddenly lit up by things exploding behind them.

I know she can't see us out here, outside her cube — she must be blind with all those lights — but she KNOWS we're here, out here in the dark, watching, gawking, surveilling — whatever the fuck we're doing.

Then, from hidden nozzles, the smoke comes crawling over the stage. My hands react, clench, move with purpose, somehow independent of me, reaching for my hip where it's supposed to be at all times but it's NOT THERE, the one goddam time I need it and it's not there and I watch my hands fumbling, searching, powerless, hearing the seconds tick by, panicking, knowing this is crazy so I look up, blinking, fearful, and there she is pointing that stupid gun RIGHT AT ME, right at my chest and right at ME, those eyes lit red like flash pictures of dogs, then, BOOM!

A-A-A-AHHHHHHH, One More Radar Lover's GONE!!!!!!!!!!!

It's like this pillow wallops me in the chest and I go down. Right off the stool and plop on my candy ass.

By the time I'm back up the song's over. Rudy's so locked-on to the skinny babe he doesn't miss me.

The music's replaced by this horrible voice screeching over everything. I strain around like Safari Jacket, crazy, trying to localize the source of this howl busting through my skull and finally I find a dark window looming from beyond the cube, a sinister face hovering over a glowing control board, adjusting knobs, watching. It's the DJ strafing us with machine gun patter, boosting drink specials, reminding us to tip heavy.

The stripper's cruising ringside snagging tips. Phantom hands poke from the dark perching folded bills on the ledge. She plucks them up like birdseed, moves along.

Rudy drops a five on the ledge and yells what I think is, "Bait."

I yell back, "What?" He gives me a *watch this* look.

She bends for the five and Rudy reaches out, piercing the boundary, invading her space. He grabs her elbow.

He yanks her close and pulls out the waist of her thong, stuffing the bill deep into her crotch and copping a muff-grab that brings her up on tippy-toes. Her eyes bulge like she just swallowed a football, teetering from foot to foot, straddling his hand like a bike.

Everything comes to a screeching halt. The air pressure changes. I figure death is imminent.

But while waiting for Tom Selleck and the cast from *American Gladiators* to drop on our heads like a brick house I suddenly remember the name of the "Radar Love" band. Golden Earring. And everything is okay. The binary *zero* to fear's *one*. I don't care if we get bounced. Everything is fine just for remembering the name of some stupid one-hit band.

Waiting for the blitz. I don't care about it any more but I'm waiting anyway. But nothing happens. No hairy hand clamping down on me. No head-beating, no ass-kicking.

Rudy's got her up there see-sawing on his palm like straddling a catapult. I can see he's weighing whether to launch her off the stage into his Barcalounger lap. He could do it, too. Flipping a nut in his mouth. And he WANTS to do it. Maybe he will, maybe he won't. Set her down nice and gentle or drag her off into his cave and have at her with all the crazy juice boiling up inside him.

The only thing stopping him is that little bit of brain, that brain that's like a toothpick propping up a crumbling dam, that brain that's never done him any favors, that's afraid of death and can't hold back life. And now it's the only thing between his lust and a whole bloody, fighting, fist-fucking world of shit.

But the brain is, predictably, losing ground. I see it in those sloshy root beer eyes and the quick breaths and the flaring nostrils. I know that oversized heart of his is pounding out a flood of wild animal blood and Rudy's peanut brain is slipping and is maybe already washed away.

A new song revs up and the pounding, blasting, annihilating noise thickens the air back into pudding, suspending the instant. Freeze frame. From somewhere there's a scream. At first I think it's her, but it's not. Then I think it's the song but it's not that either. Finally I get it located. It's coming from my head. I mean it's inside my head I hear this screaming, and not from outside (pudding's a lousy transmission medium) and the screaming is words, and it's me screaming, *Let her go, Rudy, let her fucking go!*

But I know he can't hear me. Nobody can hear me. I can't even HEAR me. My ears don't hear me, only my head and my throat where the words are torn out with razorblades. I hear me with the pain ripping my throat and my lungs, but that's all, so I scream again, *LET — HER — FUCK — ING — GO — MAN!*

Where are the bouncers? Where's Tom Selleck and the *American Gladiators* come charging in to keep this crazy ape from doing what he's about to do?

And the others, the audience; they watch. I can't see them but I know. All along the rim of the stage they see that oak branch arm piercing her cube, gripping her from the outside, about to pull her down to their bleak territory. And they're waiting. They're waiting for something *REAL* to happen. They're waiting for some second-hand, full-contact, real life to happen, the bastards.

And they're waiting for me, too. *I* can be real life here.

I can hit him.

I can haul off and slam old Rudy. I can MAKE him hear me, punch through the dark and the light and the wall of noise. I can make him hear me with my fist. No thinking, no planning. This is what you do. Just hit him. That's action. That's real.

Should I pound his shoulder? Will that be enough? Maybe he wouldn't even notice. I'm thinking how my fist looks so puny and impotent. Like hitting him with a Nerf ball. How the pudding atmosphere will slow me down. In his hormone stupor he'll never even notice. Unless I blind-side him. That'll at least get his attention. If I don't just whiff off that greasy face. One throw's all I get. He don't go down and I'm eating a dogtag for sure.

Hit him! Just hit him for chrissake!

And I WILL hit him. That's certain. It's a good feeling, better than remembering the name of that band. I WILL hit him. It's like I've already done it, like I'm the hero and everybody loves me. Which is a stupid way to think. I used to think that way about babes I wanted to ask out, plan the whole thing out and get all cocky and feeling as good as if I'd already had my way with them and all of a sudden it was like a done deal and I lost all my desire and never even got around to calling or anything.

But I WILL hit him.

If I kick him he'd go down quicker, one of those Steven-Seagal-Special roundhouse kicks. Plant some shoe leather in his temple. Lodge my size nine in his ear. Compact some earwax.

But just then that skinny little girl, all weak and sickly looking in her near-nakedness and zombie skin, all teetering and tottering and hardly touching the ground, she reaches right out and smacks old Rudy, stretches out of her cube into the dark pudding-thick emptiness and slaps Rudy upside the head. I hear it with my eyes, WHAP.

Rudy drops her and she kind of wobbles on her heels like maybe she's going down. But she doesn't. She pulls back together, arranges her thong, continues down the line plucking her bucks like nothing happened. Not even looking back. Putting on that canned grin for the next sucker in the dark.

Rudy's laughing and slapping his knees. Then he's holding his finger under his nose, whiffing like crazy, laughing some more.

He sticks that fat finger under MY nose, vise-locks my head and screams in my ear, so right-on-top-of-me his breath is like steam, "UP FOR SOME *STINKY?*"

Then there's the old pot roast slam on the back and he's haw-hawing like a madman. Like a goddam madman.

Day Twenty-nine

WOKE UP with a bad case of hangover stupids. Saw that duck still lying there in its body bag of greasy butcher paper and knew I had to get out. So I ended up at the Royal Hawaiian sucking up some hair of the dog.

Normally I hate Waikiki, it's so hokey, like a cheap movie set. But the Royal Hawaiian's okay. It's hokey, too, but it's SUPPOSED to be all hoked up — this humongous pink monster with potted palms all over and those murals of Hawaiian royalty that all sold out to the wide-eyes, and the fakey thatched-roof barefoot bar where all the grey-skinned chain-smoking Japs run around in baggy bathing suits that look Woolworth's circa 1955. . . .

I really get into this place.

So I'm at the plasticky bamboo bar suckin' up my Missionary's Down-fall and humming the theme to *Magnum P.I.* Then I switch to *Hawaii Five-O.* The bartender gives me this another-dumbfuck-tourist look so I hum louder just to annoy him. Then I switch to "Blue Hawaii," doing my shoulders real Elvisy and snapping my fingers all retro-cornbally. What's the guy expect working in some aloha-hooey dump?

I'm about to pay up and jam (my gut's calmed enough for some chow) when this voice ratchets through me.

"Hey! Dere is my Redcock shipmate."

I squint over my Ray-Bans. Sun's a killer.

It's that Filipino MAA chief with the format-thwarted porn flicks. He's all done up in a huge luau shirt which instead of hiding his beergut makes him look like a big flowery bell with two skinny clapper legs. I guess he wants to blend in, which he does. He could easy be a busboy here.

Looks happy to see me as he mounts the pink Naugahyde stool.

Chuckling like some overbred yap-yap dog. "You can't beat a Redcock. Boy, dat's focking fonny, you know?"

"How's it hanging, Chief?" I ask in a voice designed to say goodnight.

"I can't get over dat Redcock ting. At least once every day I tink about dat and I chuckle to myself." More yap-yaps.

"Yeah, who doesn't? But I'm a Red*tail*, remember? VS-21? Fighting Redtails?"

"Sure, dat's right. Focking hoovers. Whoop-whoop."

"Yeah, whoop-whoop. Look, I was just jamming . . ."

"No, man. Don't go yet. I'm waiting for my girl. You gotta meet her. She'll knock your focking socks off." Gives me this big I-Love-Lucy wink. No shit. He actually winks.

I figure, okey-dokey. I'll hang out a few and make his day. Can't hurt to have a bud in the MAA shack.

"Hey, how come you don't come by?" he asks. "Cokes only fifty cents. We got all de flavors," he counts off on his fingers, "regular, diet, no caffeine, Classic, cherry. De whole nine yards. No shit. De real ting. Cold as focking ice. And we got de movies going all de time."

"Sorry, Chief. Been going to the ASW module. They're up on O-3 like us. Don't have to screw with all the ladders."

"Oh-h-h-h, the Module got a mess, huh," he acts all offended like I betrayed him. "All you airedale types stick together."

I shrug.

"Dey got a reefer?"

"Dunno. Not like they need one. All those computers, they keep the whole place about forty degrees."

"Oh yeah, dot's right. De whole muddahfocker's a reefer." The way he rolls back and chews on this it must be a juicy morsel of intelligence. Guess Coke-messing's a cutthroat biz. "Dey got no capital outlay. Profit right from de start. . . . How much dey charge?"

"Same-o."

"Same-o, same-o?" He's shocked.

"Yep."

"Shit! An' I bet it's not a legal mess," he moans. "I betcha dey're bootlegging. So dey don't give de rec committee nuttin'."

I shrug again.

He gets all self-righteous. "My mess is *legal*. Ten-percent to de rec committee, right off de muddahfock top. So dey buy volleyballs and shit, barbecues on Grande Island, all dat. We gotta pay dat AND we gotta buy de reefer, too. We got overhead. But it's all *legal*, got de mess chit right on de muddahfock reefer." He throws up his hands all disgusted. "How can you compete wit dese bootleggers?"

"Guess it's tough."

"You bet it's tough. And all you airedales up on O-3, you don't want to hike all'a way down to de messdecks. Who can blame you? I don't like running up and down focking ladders. Who does?"

Another shrug.

"Nobody, dat's who. So how do I get you airedales to buy Cokes from me and not from dose module bootleggers who got no overhead?"

"I give."

"I got to offer a better product, dat's what."

"Guess so."

"And I GOT a better product. I got movies. I got movies running all de time. Dose module guys got movies?"

"Not that I know of."

"Fock-movies twenty-four hours a focking day, man. Dey got anyting like dat?"

I fake like I'm seriously considering this. "There's a tape library of acoustic grams, but you gotta have a clearance for that."

"Acoustic glands? What's dat? Like snuff flicks?"

"Kinda. Secret stuff, and a little TS. I could tell you about it but then I'd have to kill you."

His little eyes get big as knobs. Blackshoes are such suckers. Then he grins. "Focking fonny guy. You Redcocks kill me."

"Red*tails*."

"Right," he says.

I start easing off my stool, "Good seeing you, Chief. I gotta be getting."

"No, man. She'll be here any time. Hey, you hear about dose marines got killed?"

That gets my attention. "What marines?"

"You didn't hear?! A dozen of 'em, man. Oh, shit yeah, some big muddahfocking battle up by the Kuwaiti border. Dose Iraqis, man, like focking gangbusters. Dey had der turrets turned backwards so dey look like dey're surrendering, den *BLAM!* Focking raghats, man."

"Dozen jarheads, huh."

"Dat's what dey're *saying*. Who knows how many. Dose focking Republican Guards, man. Tough sons of bitches, you bet. Dey been fighting dose crazy-fock Iranians for years. Dey know how to kill. We don't know shit about killing. Not shit." He swivels around. "How do you get a focking drink around here?"

"You know the *Magnum P.I.* theme?"

I'm seeing that jarhead downing the cockroach, picturing him with his head blown apart. Thick blood oozing, staining sand cammies. Then concussion bombs and the shockwaves rolling up to you and smashing your bones and your lungs and your flesh, or those fuel-air explosive things and suddenly your eardrums and your eyeballs go blooey like stomped-on ketchup packets. Or nerve agents and your body going all twitchy and jerky and your brain like a transformer hit by lightning. Or chemical junk burning through the skin and muscle and tendon and bone, boiling your marrow, just eating you away so your flesh peels off while you're watching like some damn Freddy Krueger movie. Or good old HE and one second you're standing there and a nano-second later you're a cloud of pink vapor. Or maybe it doesn't hit so close and you're just cut in half looking at your guts spilled on the sand and thinking, *So that's what my liver looks like and those, why those must be kidneys, by golly!* and you reach to shove 'em all back in but there's no arms to reach with and you think (because you have TIME to think before the last blood in your brain dribbles out) you finally realize, hey, I guess I'm dead. I'm a fucking dead man. Used to I was a sailor, I used to be a naval aircrewman, an Anti-Submarine Warfare Specialist Second Class, I used to be a technician, a Madonna-watcher, an ace sub-chaser, an American, a cynical young man, a good little boy, a consumer, a TV junkie, an alcohol abuser, a jogger, an air-guitar master, a slacker, a smart-ass, a target audience, a high school dropout, a juvenile delinquent, a partier, a video-drone, a surveiller, a prick, a sailor, an asshole, and a helluvaguy. . . .

But now I am a dead man. Mangled meat. Cut to black. *Click!*

But even while I'm thinking all this it's not me I see all bloated and burned and vaporized and dismembered and dead. It's not MY body it's all happening to. It's somebody else's. It's that cockroach-chomping jarhead. It's him I see and not me at all. HE's the fucking victim. I thought he was the badguy, I thought he was the aggressor, the way he hosed down that sleazeball dancer. SHE was the victim. But no. It's not that way at all anymore. It's all turned around. It's not the dancer and it's not my Madonna-babe.

The jarhead's the catcher.

And if that's true then what about me?

It's ALMOST like real people are dying, now. Before, it wasn't real people. It was Iraqis, strangers, paper people you hear about but never see, touch or feel. But A-FUCKING-MERICANS . . .

Almost like real people but not quite, thank God, not quite YET real people. Just closer to what I know, closer to something like maybe my Madonna-babe back home. Not real yet but a shadow of real. And a shadow's closer than I want to hear about.

But then again it's just *hearing*. There's no dead marines here. It's just words I'm hearing rolling from this tubby Chief. This isn't the danger zone. It's a schmaltzy hotel bar on a white sand beach packed with live bodies sweating and playing and drinking and snoozing.

We got sunscreen, we got Ray-Bans.

We're all taped up here. We're safe.

The Chief's babbling on about god-knows-what. War talk. I can't understand him anymore. It's all blurred together. It's just words, that's all, just words. Sound. Acoustic energy. Vibrations gen'd in the Chief's froggy throat. Waves vibrating air molecules in a zillion vectors, one of which just happens to be a straight line to my eardrum which vibrates sympathetically making a little imitation dipstick Chief's voice in my head. That's all it is. Words are nothing. Nothing. No thing.

They're not even NEW words, not HIS words at all. Just words he's repeating from some other source, only not *even* a source but a re-lay — radio or TV or the papers, pulled in by an antenna, bounced off a satellite in geo-synchronous orbit, maybe two, maybe more, from where? From never-never land. Just a chief saying what a newscaster read from what a reporter copied from a CRT wired to a modem that's hooked up with a news service where an inputter copied it from a memo from an-other reporter who got the words from a phone call with ANOTHER reporter who got it from some military press briefer who read it from the message put out by some unit commander — who MAYBE saw it (whatever IT really was) happen.

My gut's giving me hell again, like when I first got on the boat. I'm not thinking about this any more. Try and fucking make me. Just try. I order another drink.

Suddenly the Chief jumps up going, "Here she is! Here she is!" He's hugging on this really decent looker all done up in a sarong thing, a big floppy straw hat and spikes that give her six inches on the Chief. Legs and cleavage. Smells like coconuts. He's on tippy-toes cadging air kisses when something about her yanks my attention.

The Chief's all giving her the moon eyes and introducing us like I'm his oldest bestest buddy in the world and I'm trying to figure what about her looks so familiar because that's what grabbed my notice. I've seen her before.

The Chief sees me gawking and says, "I told you she's beautiful, man. Didn't I tell you?"

She whines in this fake-cutesy voice, "Ben-*neeee.*"

"But you *are* beautiful, baby," he says. "Just seeing you makes my dick so hard it's gonna break."

She rolls her eyes and touches my arm. I flinch. She notices but pretends not to.

"Benny's such a turd. I don't know how you put up with him."

"A turd, hah? I better send back dese drinks I just bought, hah?" The Chief tries to out-cute her. They're having a cute-out.

She grabs her strawberry margarita or whatever it is. A big, red concoction.

"Not on your life," she squeaks. "I need this drink. Besides, you're a cute turd." A cheek tweak. "I don't mind a drink from a turd so long as he's a cute turd."

Then she rubs his big gut like wishing on a Buddha. He's eating it up, swallowing it whole and raw. Must be paying MAJOR bucks to swag treatment THIS sickening.

Then she does this little thing with her foot, rolling back and forth on that spike heel.

And I remember.

"Remember ME?" I ask.

That fake grin disappears. She peeks out under the hat brim, kind of suspicious.

"You guys know each odder?" the Chief asks looking even more confused than normal.

Her gaze hangs on me, like she's running my face through a mega-heavy database. Probably got more personnel files than the CIA, the KGB, and TRW combined.

"At the hotel yesterday. I'm the guy with the duck."

I consider pulling off my shades. Nah. In fact I'm wishing for my camcorder. She looks at me real level and icy.

"I don't know you," she says.

"Sure," I say. "You were handing out those fake luau folders. Remember?"

She's still gaping at me but talking to the Chief whose mouth is kind of hanging. "What's the matter with your friend, Benny? What's he been drinking?"

"I don't know," he says. "What's focking up wit you, shipmate?"

"Sure, *Pig in a blanket,*" I say all cool. "Remember? She use that line on you, too, Chief? It's a great line. Really cracked me up."

The poor Chief is getting a little hot. "What is dis? You guys focking know each odder or what? What's dis *duck* shit? What's dis *pig* shit?"

So I tell him. What the fuck. "Your hooker was hitting on me yesterday, that's all. No biggee."

The Chief about FLIES off his stool. "Whadda fock, man! Don't you call my lady a focking hooker, man!"

You'd figure I'd have that red drink of hers all over me by now. But she fools me. She's real calm. A real calm liar.

"I don't know this guy from dogshit, Benny. He's crazy."

"Let's get another shot of that caboose," I say. "Turn around. Let's have a gander at some of that *hot meat* you rent out."

Chief's flushed out like a tomato. "She's got a great ass," I say. "I commend your taste in rump roast. She parting with any of it yet?"

Then he goes ballistic. Jabbing at me with his pudgy finger. "You focking guy!" he screams. "Whassa matter wit you?! You get your focking ass outta here before I focking pop you. You airedale FOCK!"

"I'm going. Glad to." My leg gives out when I slip off the stool. I smack my knee on the deck. But I recover before anybody notices.

"See, Benny," the bitch whines. "The shithead's drunk. I told you he's fucked up."

I'm so sick of her and her bullshit. I'm just so goddam sick of ALL this bullshit. I grab her arm to calm her down. I say real cool so she knows I mean business, "Look, bitch, the Chief here is a friend of mine. I'd hate to see some bloodsucker like you leech him dry. You be careful. You just be very careful."

I let her go and I'm about out of there but I forgot something. "And I

82

don't want to hear about your dead marines anymore." Her mouth twists up like she doesn't know what I'm saying. "Don't play dumb with me. No more dead marines. None." The Chief's about to say something but I know it's bullshit so I cut him off. "You neither, Chief. And I don't mean maybe."

Then I get the red drink.

On my way back my shirt's all soaked and clingy but I don't care. I keep thinking about her arm when I grabbed it. It was so . . . solid. Don't ask why but I expected my fingers to just slip through like grabbing at vapor. The things you think.

When I get back to the hotel the desk guy asks what happened to my shirt. The strawberry pulp's coagulated into clumps. I just say, "Drive-by shooting." Head up the stairs.

While the tape's rewinding I pop open a sake and chew on some dried-out duck. Duck skin in my teeth. Plaque. Gingivitis. It's pretty awful but I'm so hungry I scarf the whole thing. Even gnaw the fatty stuff on the tailbone. But I leave the head and feet.

Finally I go to sleep. I wake up once from a dream that's me throwing myself against a brick wall. Slamming myself over and over, stopping just long enough to pick myself up and do it again. The wall never budges and I'm almost glad about it. In fact I AM glad about it. It's good to have something sturdy to trash yourself against. Dependable.

I want to scan my surveillance tape but I need a cable to wire into the TV. I could watch it with the viewfinder but I feel the need for living color. The desk guy suggests the Ala Moana Shopping Center.

Even after dozing all afternoon I'm not feeling so great. But at least I'm with it enough to bring the camcorder.

I'm cruising the merchandise while the guy fixes up the cable. The Mega-Giant Discount Home Electronics Audio/Video Bonanza Super-Plex Warehouse. I finger remotes, initiate sound, images, touch cool glass, gentle plastic pushpads. A fifty-yard wall of TVs, hundreds. All tuned to the same station. Some local show with this Don Ho type crooning meli-kalikimaka music. In fact it IS Don Ho. Whoa! My old lady got off on him when I was a kid, way back in the seventies. Must be pushing a hundred and fifty by now.

Two definitely-not-local old ladies are watching and you can tell they're sweating up their panties, boy. Wrinkled old hearts a-throbbing.

"Wouldn't you just adore seeing him? Ben can get tickets," says one.

"Oh, I don't know, Melba. We've got that video thing now. Why see him live when he's right there on tape whenever I want?"

The guy comes back with my cable and when I go for my wallet I see Napoleon's film frame. I ask the guy if there's some way to get a look-see. He's not real keen at first but I tell him it's a hot sex scene from some movie and suddenly he's motivated. We go over to the photo department where he drops it into a slide projector. Primitive technology. I mean you can see how it works just by looking at it. But then he gets called away by another customer.

I'm about to fire up the thing when those two old ladies come moseying up. They're really horrible looking, gargoyle faces all painted up like Halloween masks, basketball bouffants, overdressed as two Dallas Episcopalians. I wait hoping they'll shuffle off before I splat some Technicolor porn in their faces. One starts playing with a tiny TV.

"My grandson's been plying me for one of these," says Melba's friend.

I figure these two are SO gruesome it's my duty to preserve them for posterity. I real casual turn the camcorder their way and hit the record button. Very sly. Thank God for auto focus.

"Speaking of which," says Melba. "Did you hear about that mass murderer they caught in Atlanta?"

"The one who dressed like a clown and buried the kids under the gazebo?"

"No. I know who you're thinking of though. He was in Kentucky."

"Then you mean the one who went after co-eds who wore bicycle pants and mary-janes?"

"*Asiatic* coeds. I didn't know about the bicycle pants and mary-janes. But that's not him anyway."

"Denver, you say?"

"At*lan*ta. Teenage boys was his specialty. Your grandson reminded me."

"He kept the toes in baby food jars?"

"No, that one was in Anchorage. *He* wasn't really a mass murderer, just more of an occasional rapist-torturer. I'm talking about the one who kept the skulls in his living room."

"Oh, yes. And he whacked off the hands, too, as I recall. So the bodies couldn't be identified."

"Melba, be *serious* will you. That was in *Tuc*son and it was a *cult* for godsake. Where is your head?"

"Texas?"

"Pardon?"

"Wasn't the cult one in Texas?"

"That was a different cult. They barbecued theirs."

"Oh."

"This one kept the skulls for knickknacks. He spray-painted them so they would look artificial. Is that precious? Like having Waterford and pretending it's dimestore."

Finally the gargoyles toddle off. I shut off the camcorder. Then I light off the projector. Blur. When I finally get it all straightened up and focused the store guy comes back.

He takes a look and snorts real sarcastic, "Hardcore, huh. Maybe for jockeys. They sell you that on the dock, sailor?"

He's laughing pretty good as he leaves. But I don't care. I'm gazing real hard at this image of two horses fighting. They're in this beautiful green pasture and they're both reared up on their hind legs, striking with their hooves. Wild eyes, spit and froth everywhere. Sweat-polished fur glistens. On the white horse an ear is busted, hanging twisted and gnarled, blood gushing down his long white jaw.

That's a keeper.

I video it.

Day Twenty-eight

AFTER BREAKFAST I'm tooling up Kapiolani by the college when I feel the weather shifting. Smells like cloudburst. That's how it is here; barometer nosedives quick as the pressure chamber at aviation physiology where they teach you to Valsalva your ears. One second it's postcard breezy blue then suddenly some howling monsoon unloads on you.

Diamond Head's black with clouds.

I'm feeling pretty up. Don't ask why but I am. Something about that whole thing with Napoleon and the image of the fighting horses yesterday. Makes me feel like I'm getting, I don't know, NEARER. To what I can't say but I know I just got a notch closer and it feels like a helium bubble swelling warm and pink behind my sternum. Funny how the good things register in your chest and the bad things in your stomach. And the REALLY bad things vector straight to your asshole.

But at the same time I'm antsy. Last port-day jitters. Like I'm never coming back and I should make every second count. Like I ought to do something, something big, desperate. Bungee-jump a volcano, wrestle a great white. Something.

Gumball-size drops start spattering the sidewalk. I duck under an awning, dry the lens with my shirt tail.

There's a newspaper rack so I scan the headlines: *WAR'S EFFECT ON SPORTS.* Something about airtime pro games are losing to the war. Reminds me of this cryptologic technician I knew, a real sports freak, said football was a substitute for warfare. He thought all men had a need for combat, for killing, and football was a way of working it out vicariously, all that stuff about taking territory and the touchdown like planting a flag on a fresh-taken hill. Said it was twentieth-century war technology that made football so popular, since there aren't many opportunities for real combat anymore. Used to you could count on a war for every generation so everybody got a chance to work out their aggression cookies at least once a lifetime. Attain hero status. The wars are still here but stand-off ranges have gone from the distance between the rifle stock and the bayonet to hundreds of miles. The psychic charge just isn't the same. So, in its place there's football, a kind of warfare masturbation — the uniforms, the anthems, the regional fervor, teams like armies, the forward pass like primitive airpower insurgence, cheerleaders on the sidelines like some caramelized myth of the good woman on the homefront.

Sounded reasonable at the time but now I think about it maybe he got it ass backwards. All these people watching the war on TV, the color commentary by the guys in Riyadh, the generals doing the play by play, endless instant replays. *Scud! Scud! Down a Scud! Go-o-o-o-oh* Patriot!

I think this war is a substitute for football.

Another item about Harriers blasting an Iraqi tank convoy. One pilot says, *That was very much a fun mission because you could see the parts of the trucks flying.* Must grow these guys in petri dishes.

Just then this jeep screeches up to the curb. One of those tourist rent-a-jeeps, no top and painted up in sunset colors. A girl jumps out all mega-pissed and screaming at the guy who's humped over the wheel, cringing from the rain — or her. Both I guess. She's yelling every obscenity I ever heard of as he peels out. "My shit, you scumhole! What about my *shit*!?" The jeep screeches again and things come flying: shoes, a bundle of cards or brochures that go blowing all over and some shapeless bag that splashes into the gutter.

It's coming down like a waterfall. I watch her through a water screen pouring from the awning. She's leaning against a white-painted palm trunk, pulling on her shoes slow and easy like she's not being slammed by this cloudburst. Even drenched and dripping you can tell she's a looker. Not so tall but leggy, meaty enough for comfort.

I buy a newspaper and wrap up the camcorder nice and safe. What I SHOULD do is help her out. Rush around in the pelting rain gathering those pamphlets blowing all over, water-glued to the sidewalk like gaudy flagstones. Hand them to her and tip my white hat. *'Twarn't nothin', ma'am.* Saunter into the palm-lined sunset whistling away like one of the Sons of the Pioneers. But that's not what I do. Something holds me back, tells me that's not right even while my brain says it IS right. I just watch.

She takes off down the street. A brochure, wet, windblown, lands by my foot. Some hotel pamphlet. I turn it with my toe. Something clicks. More than just clicks, it fucking FIRES on me. So I give that butt of hers a high resolution ogle; it's a winner, no doubt, but is it the same one? For certain this isn't the Chief's hooker but maybe SHE wasn't the right one after all. Maybe I just thought she was and I was too drunk or stupid or whatever to tell the difference. I'm confused and kind of panicked. I'm trying to remember exactly what she DID look like. This COULD be the one. But I don't know. All I remember is parts and pieces, disconnected jigsaw pieces that don't assemble into a whole: the curve of thigh where it blooms into asskick ass, an ankle rolling on a tall heel, eyes that are lively but could be brown or green or yellow for all I know. Is this her?

I track her. The rain lets up. Wet street smell, like the flight deck. I think of the boat and Nerdy and the shit with the fake hot-swap. But I push it away, compartmentalize, concentrate on my mission.

After a block I'm certain it's her. I don't know if it's wish-fulfillment or what but I'm certain. Cert-slut — highest level of contact-probability. The evidence mounts: that back-end wiggle, the pamphlets. And the way she swings her arms, a little too *Hey-Look-At-Me*. A major attitude. That one had attitude too. Sure. *Fuck a duck.* That qualifies.

Contact on the target of interest. Bearing three-six-zero, relative. On the nose twenty yards.

She's moving out of range, slipping into a crowd. I fire up the camcorder.

I jog to catch up, holding it waist level so I'm not so obvious. *Lookdown shootdown.* Hard as hell to maneuver like this but I'm a pro. Electronic surveillance is my life.

Struggling to keep up. A real power walker this one, dodging through crowds and shit. Finally she stops at some ugly government building, one of those places with block-wide concrete stairs. She stands there looking around. For what? Then her gaze lands right on me, locked on, and I think I'm busted. But then I realize I got the zoom on so even though it looks like she's peering right at me all up close and personal, really to her I'm a long ways off, a blur in the sidewalk action. She climbs a few steps then plops down, calmly eyeballing the scenery.

I take a seat on a bench trying to look like a potted plant. I keep the camcorder in my lap and my body turned away from her so I can watch her like with one of those see-around-corners spy-scopes they used to sell in comic books. Right next to the ads for X-ray-vision glasses which were real rip-offs and didn't work at all and one of the major disappointments of my life contributing significantly to the cynical smegma I turned out to be.

Something cold is slithering up the back of my thigh. I realize I'm sitting in a puddle. Pretend like I don't care.

Target's doing a bunch of nothing, fucking with her bag and yanking on her bra straps. (Talk show segment: Why women ALWAYS screw with their underwear.) Finally she heads off. We go on for a couple blocks like this. Twice she looks back. At first I flinch but then I maintain so as not to draw attention. Funny how if you just act like you know what you're doing you can get away with the weirdest stuff and nobody even notices.

It's turning nice. Warm, humid but not too humid, I'm tracking a handsome babe in a tropical paradise. Life is sweet.

The target goes dead in the water, waiting for the light to change. I pretend to check out a frozen yogurt stand, mill around smartly till she gets underway again. A crowd builds around her at the corner and I lose sight of her in the clutter of the surface traffic. But I know she's there.

The light changes and the crowd spills into the street. I take off after but I'm not looking where I'm going and smack into some giant Samoan galoot in a hardhat. He's got this tiny cup of frozen yogurt he's eating with one of those little wooden spoons. Looks like Godzilla holding a teacup all nicey-nice and dainty. "Hey, wassa matta wit you?" He makes this move like he's gonna smack me. But then he sees the wet blotch on my pants and takes a step back. "Wha-a-at, you piss yo-self, man. Get outta he-ah wit you." I stutter apologies and rush off. Piss power. Gotta remember that.

But when I bumped him I must have smacked the lens. The auto-focus is zooming in and out like mad and I can't see a thing. I look around all frantic for the target but she's gone. I rush up to the corner like a crazy guy. Nothing. Then across the street, almost killed by a tourist bus. Nothing again. Lost contact.

I cross back. I don't know what to do. All the helium's leaking out of my chest and my general daily panic is taking over.

I stop to fix the auto-focus. I'll be really pissed if that yogurt-guzzling grizzly did major damage. I cycle the power a couple times, aim at these three wiener dog puppies in the window of a pet store. Zoom in, zoom out. Looks okeefenokee. So I scan around inside the shop some and then — Whoa!

Up at the counter. My target. She's paying for something in one of those Chinese take-out boxes. The hair raises on the back of my neck. The helium's pumping back in. Must be love. But then I realize I'm out in the open, exposed. First instinct's to run and hide. But it's too late so I get a grip and pretend to still be watching the puppies gnawing at their shredded newspaper bedding.

She's coming out and I'm watching those damn puppies like my life depends on it. The door beside me swishes open and it's her. I feel her shape pass by. I hold my breath until I figure she's on her way then real slow I aim the lens while still making like all my attention's on those pups. The sidewalk spans out in the viewfinder but I can't localize her. So I try the other direction, still trying to be cool, but just more nothing. I'll have to risk being overt and just hope she's not someplace looking right at me. So I pull my eye from the viewfinder and try reconnoitering the reflection in the window glass. Still no contact. Then I just make like I'm bored looking at the pups and wondering where to head next. But when I turn, my goddam balls jump up into my belly and my heart comes to a screeching halt and if I could crawl out of my skin I would and from about an inch away from my face, shades glinting, teeth wet and white and wrapped in colored lips, angular and tight and hardly lined at all comes the whistling buzzing siren of a locked-on target acquisition radar, the last thing you hear before the missile rips through the belly of the airplane bringing the whole game to a seriously abrupt and non-refundable end.

She asks, "Do I, like, *know* you?"

At least I think that's what she says. It's hard to tell since my brain is going like a Cray II on crank and for every image that flies by there's a question and it's the same question each time looking for an answer I'll be needing in about ten giga-seconds, searching, searching, searching for that answer that'll solve all my problems if I could just locate it in time, if I could just answer the question, the simple little question, *Why am I watching?*

Having your asshole feel like it just took a hit from a Tomahawk doesn't help much either, I can tell you.

So finally I deploy a brilliant time-buying tactic.

"Sorry?"

And she's still right in my face and waving that Chinese food carton around going, "I mean you've been following me since the college and I just thought I had a right to know whether you're some whacked-out stalker type or a *Candid Camera* scout or just some halfwit voyeur getting cheap thrills."

She's pretty held-together but pretty irate, too. I figure I'll just try the truth. That ALWAYS surprises people.

"I guess I'm mostly just the cheap thrills type," I say. "I thought we met before."

She looks me over. "Yeah? You go to U of H?"

A student. Oh boy. I really missed the mark here.

"Look," I say. "I'll level with you. I don't mean to insult you or anything but I thought you were a hooker I met at my hotel the other day. Obviously I'm all screwed up. I don't want to insult you but that's the god's honest truth."

But she doesn't mind being mistaken for a whore. Instead she snaps back like a reflex, "There's no such thing as truth."

"Okay," I say, unsettled by this weird rejoinder. "Whatever. Just trying to be honest."

"*Trying, honesty* — too slippery for meaning. You thought I was a hooker? Like a prostitute? Now *that* is interesting. This woman you thought I was, she performs sex for you and you give her money?"

Jeez, what the hell have I got here?

"I never went with her. I just met her is all."

But she's not listening. She's nodding like she is but her eyes are checked into a different hotel. "So she's like this reified sexual commodity whose personness you subvert economically on an overt level and then covertly by following her with this, this — what is that, a camera?"

"It's a camcorder for, you know, video."

"Video! Perfect! You thought I was a whore and you videotaped me, right? You *did* videotape me, right?"

I guess I shouldn't feel guilty about it. I mean it's not like I took her soul or anything. Still, I hedge, "Ummmm . . ."

But she's not only NOT pissed but all jazzed about it, like she just won Miss Sugar Cane Queen and being all ironic.

"That is *too* perfect. So I'm on this videotape and for all intents and purposes I'm a whore. Right? You've got the camera and you think, you *impose* that I'm a whore so when you watch this with your buddies or whatever kind of sickness you indulge in, you say, *That's this whore I was following.* Right? And because you say it, because the preconception is there, it's good as true. I *am* a hooker. At least insofar as your videotape-mediated reality is concerned."

"But there is no truth." I'm catching on.

Boy, she likes THAT. "Ex*act*ly. And because of that I *could* be a hooker. I really could be. In *fact* —" and she makes like there's quotation marks around the word. "In *fact* I *am* a hooker. I mean, virtually. I am virtually a hooker via my defacto collaboration with the simulacrum, the videoscape I've unwittingly become accomplice to. You've made me a hooker. Will my mom ever be pissed."

I guess I'm looking pretty dumbshitty since she gives me this snap-to face and says, "That's a joke. Ha-ha."

Normally I'd be bugging out from some artsy-fartsy lunatic jabbering all this bullshit-of-the-overeducated nonsense but there's something about her. She's got this enthusiasm that seems really genuine. I mean I don't know half of what she's talking about but it's a real kick watching her get off on it, whatever it is.

And she DOES have a great ass.

Her name is Tamara. We end up walking and talking. I ask her what she does at the university. Says she studies literature, says she's a writer, fiction and poetry. So I figure, okay, literature, I can deal with that. *Huck Finn*, Stephen King, *The Red Pony*. I did my time. Even read Dostoyevsky once for a mail-order class. "That whacked-out Raskolnikov guy," I say. "He was all right, plotting to murder that old woman just to prove he was living his philosophy. I respect that. Murder's not such a great idea, but at least he really believed in something, had the courage of his convictions."

"I wouldn't know. I don't read DWMs."

"Pardon?"

"Dead White Males."

So I explain the story to her. "Sure, he ended up losing it but it seems to me like we're all so twisted anyway — you get away with it as long as you look normal from outside. It's only when you make noise that people figure how dicked up you really are and put you away. Shit, if they ever looked into *my* head when I wasn't looking I'd be locked up in a green flash."

"Yes, I'm afraid there's precious little tolerance for camcorder-toting voyeurs stalking prostitutes."

You can tell she's eating this up. Before you know it we're getting along dandy. I'm thinking it'd be nice to take her to lunch or a movie. "You seen *Dances With Wolves* yet?"

"Kevin Costner, Mary McDonnell, Graham Greene, Floyd Red Crow Westerman, Nathan Lee Chasing His Horse. U.S. cavalry soldier, sickened by western white male bluster, ignorance and murderous ways, joins a village of Lakota Sioux where he finds peace, serenity and spiritual and political balance. Color, 181 minutes. Saw it." Then she gets this weird, spacey look. "I'm heading home now."

I figure she's trying to dump me. "Oh, okay, I just thought it'd be nice. I gotta check out of my room, anyway."

But she locks her eyes onto mine and says, "You misunderstand. You have to come with me. You absolutely *have* to come with me."

She lives in this high-rise concrete thing that could easy be another government building. It takes a key to use the elevator.

Her apartment looks like it's under construction — or demolition. The walls are all torn out like somebody went at them with a sledge-hammer, raggedy plaster hanging all over and the studs and wiring and plumbing all exposed. The place is gutted.

"Jeez, what happened here?"

"Like it? I did it myself."

"On purpose?"

"It's a de-centering of the male-dominant architectural status-quo which privileges smooth white walls over the aesthetic of infrastructure. I've foregrounded the infrastructure. Took me two weeks to smuggle the debris down the trash chute."

What do you say to something like that?

"Bet your landlord'll be pissed."

"Fuck him. He's a fascist."

"Lotta that going around."

She dumps her stuff and heads for the kitchen with the white carton, but since the walls are de-centered or whatever we keep chatting through the studs.

"What is that thing anyway?" I point at the carton.

She opens it and lifts out a green lizard by its neck. "It's a gecko. They eat cockroaches." She lets it loose and it scampers off the counter and halfway up a stud where it freezes.

"I hope this guy has an appetite." She shitcans the carton.

"Yeah, for your sake I hope he's a real pesticidal maniac."

I guess she de-centered the furniture, too, since everything is upside down or sawed in two or otherwise mutilated. I flop onto a cushion spray-painted graffiti-style, FUCK THE DOMINANT PARADIGM. It's situated behind the sofa it must have come from which is now upended and supported by books so it serves as a kind of table. Along where a wall used to be there's a bunch of TVs stacked willy-nilly into a lopsided pyramid. Must be nine, ten of them, some sideways, some inverted, all of them tuned to different stations but with the sound off. I like it. I video it.

"So you're a writer," I say. "Ever sell anything?"

She snorts. "I won't have my work appropriated and/or commodified in this degenerate capital-driven market. As a passive pro-active defense I don't write anything."

"Nothing?"

"It's the essential subversive stance."

"Kind of tough making a living."

"Oh, I'll probably teach. If your politics are right you can get along on grants and fellowships." She tosses back hair like wet hemp. "I'm a mess, a soggy cornflake."

"I think you look okay."

"I better change. Just be a sec. If you're hungry there's gorp in the raku."

From her bathroom she keeps talking. I settle back and watch all the TVs. It's really a very cool set-up. There's so much on.

"I used to be a gibber-poet." At first I think it's Oprah, but it's just Tamara from the bathroom where the walls are unfortunately not de-centered all the way down but instead just punched through in a few spots so she looks like another talking head. ". . . assemblages of appropriated text from cereal box side panels. I'd spell every third word backwards to foreground the slipping signification of say, *riboflavin, dextrose,* whatever — the arbitrariness of the act is what charges the work with politically subversive anti-hegemonic gender inspecificity. Once you implode the ingredients hierarchy you've eradicated the implicit privileging of the phallocentric socio-economic taxonomy. The whole banana to *slip,*" more finger quotes, "into pro-metaphoric usage is so de-centered you can bet your boots they won't be recon-deconstructing Sugar-Frosted Flakes again till the cows come home to roost."

"Damn. You're a serious jargon junkie, you know that?"

"Sorry."

But you can tell she's not. In fact she's really smug about it, like she's a member of some exclusive club, like she's on the inside and I'm on the outside, an attitude which normally would turn me off quick, but there's something about her. Sincerity I guess. She really believes what she says, whatever the hell she's saying.

"It's the lingua franca of progressive theory," she says. "It's convoluted, even obstreperous, but mandatory for a certain level of dis —" The blow dryer snatches the rest.

You see a lot of jargon junkies in the navy. Usually means they don't know their ass from a hole in the ground. The rallying cry is *If you can't dazzle 'em with genius, baffle 'em with bullshit.* But she's not bullshitting. At least she doesn't know she is. I'm thinking maybe she's an idiot savant or something.

She comes out looking Nakamichi in a punky short skirt over black leggings, silk top and army boots the purple of a fueler's jersey.

"That was my last phase that left any textual residue. Committing words to paper just leaves one too vulnerable, too open."

"You got a beer?"

"In the oven. Help yourself."

She asks what I do and I'm tempted to give her a dose of some acoustic techno-wizardry airborne anti-submarine warfare jargon. Initiate a little battle of the jargonauts. Lay on some acronyms and abbreviations: ASW, FASOTRAGRUPAC, ECS, MK-82, ADP, INCOS, SENSO, TACCO, COMNAVAIRPAC, ECP, NATOPS, ESM, MAD, SAP, ACLS, AN/ALR-47, ASWWINGPAC. Or just gab along in navpubspeak: *The mission of the Sierra-3 Viking fixed wing, carrier-based, all-weather, tactical anti-submarine warfare aircraft is to utilize its suite of active and passive computer-assisted detection sensors to localize, track and terminally engage surface and sub-surface hostile contacts in electromagnetically charged combat environments.*

But then I'd be as dippy as Tamara here. I don't see why people can't just talk straight. We've got this language we spend our whole lives learning so we can talk to each other. But communication isn't good enough.

They have to turn it into something secret and snobby. Why? Don't people WANT to talk to each other?

Instead I just say, "I'm in the navy."

And she naturally gives me that *Oh-the-military* look. No details required. People always do that. Especially, it seems like, people who are supposed to be smart in every other way and who should know better than to slap labels on people. Yet when it comes to us "heroes" they're perfectly willing to think we're all a bunch of morons and baby-killers and each of us personally participated in the My-Lai massacre that probably happened when I was about three years old and that just because we all dress the same we must all BE the same underneath, there's no possibility for individuality or personality or, god forbid, original thoughts or anything else they'd give credit for as a matter of course to the lowliest most ignorant dust-squatting aborigine.

But I'm being touchy. I don't know for sure she's thinking like that and I guess by ME thinking I know what SHE'S thinking I'm just as judgmental and ignorant as the people I'm accusing.

But I tell you, it's the shits. Either you're a hero or a war-mongering dickhead, there's hardly any in-between. Hardly any chance to be just a standard-issue HUMAN doing some BEING.

Tamara downs about half of this really warm beer, jumps up and says, "Well, let's get to it."

"To what?"

"How does it normally go?"

"How does WHAT normally go?"

"You're the male and you have the money so you're the empowered one. The first move is yours, right?"

"First move?"

"Or maybe not. Maybe since *I* have what *you* want, I should call the shots. If it were me *I* would certainly insist on retaining control. And since this *is* me I should act like myself and not appropriate an alien stance."

I'm just gawking.

"It's funny but I always posited the woman's body as commodity, that the man *bought* the vagina. But that's not necessarily accurate is it? The vagina can be looked upon as the *means* of production, which works on many levels, ha-ha, but for the present the product might be considered male erotic pleasure, more specifically, the male orgasm. If that's the case then I as possessor of the means of production, as elementary Marxist dogma tells us, am in the position of power. I control the market." She crosses her legs, controlling her market. Looks real pleased with her little herd of babble. "Well, let's get to it. You have fifty bucks?"

And she slips out of her silk top and now she's all black lace bra and plump creamy skin. "This is what you want, isn't it?" she asks. "I'm a whore, right? You made me a whore and here I am. All yours."

I don't want this to happen. I DO but I don't. I mean I just can't keep up. The way she's doing this I'm totally intimidated. I couldn't get it up with a crane. She moves over to the Fuck The Dominant Paradigm cushion with me and starts nuzzling up all coy like and rubbing on my thigh and that helps some, no doubt, but still I'm thinking all kinds of weird things like whether she shaves her armpits or her legs like some of these intellect types don't, even though I can see she does, and how much I really want to reach out and cup one of those lace-wrapped breasts in my hand and squeeze real tight but my hands just feel like dead fish tied to my arms and her hand is roaming my thigh and teasing my crotch and a bra strap slips down and I'm wishing it down some more, wishing I could bite at that little pink rose holding together the two cups, bite off that rose and watch the cups fall away and she's talking now, talking low so she sounds more like a woman than she has and this voice surprises me.

"This is what you want, right? This is what you want me to be, you want a whore and I am a whore. I want you in my mouth I want all of you in every part of me, I want you to fuck me everywhere, in my mouth and my pussy and my ass, I want you all the way up my ass, all the way and more until all of you is up me, I want all of you inside me, breathing inside me, waiting and stretching and reaching inside me. I want penetration, invasion, colonization." Which SOUNDS good but what it FEELS like is she really wants to pack one of those purple boots up my ass until you'd have to reach through my nose to tie the laces.

Then she kisses me, hard, practically choking me with her tongue which is long and hot and sweet. But her cheek is rough against my face, so rough it's like she's got whisker stubble and when she pulls back I look but don't see anything. She kisses me again, pulling me to her, pressing, like she wants me to feel it, and I do, coarse, scratching, like kissing a guy, but I've never kissed a guy so how do I know? And then I remember Dad coming home late from the old Top Hat Tavern and kissing me whiskey breath sloppy and rough with his scratchy stubble.

She sits up and reaches behind her back. She says, "You want to see my tits?" And when I don't say anything she demands, "You want to see my tits?" like she's talking to a dog, and I guess I probably look like a dog, too. She's grinning kind of half YES and half mean, posed there arms in back like they're lopped off. "You want to see them now?"

"Sure, Tamara, if that's what you want."

"No, if that's what *you* want."

"Okay."

"No!" she snaps. "Say you want to see my tits."

"All right. I want to."

"No. Say it better. Say, let me see your fucking tits, you whore."

And her whole face gets huge and distorted, lips red, inflated, teeth like bathroom tiles, spitting and hissing out the words *say it, say it, SAY IT!*

"That's not how I want to say it."

"But that's what you want."

"Yes."

She unsnaps the bra letting it slide away. "Here they are. Here are the whore's tits. How you like, sailor boy?"

And even before I can see how nice they are, how round and lightly freckled and nipples pink and wrinkled, even before I can enjoy any of that I see the scars. Two thick death-white gashes tracing the curve under each breast.

"This is what you want, right? My beautiful whore's tits? Just like Mama's?"

The room is quiet and I can just sense faces on the TVs watching us here like we're in a department store window and all these faces, Oprah, and Geraldo, and some pretty, well-dressed soap opera types and a newsguy in sand cammies and a toy rabbit wearing Ray-Bans beating a drum and Saddam Hussein and Lee Iacocca all of them, faces inverted, sideways, pressed up against the glass, watching us act out this weirdness in this upturned bombed-out high-rise, Tamara's beautiful and damaged breasts heaving, mocking, scars like grins, her hands fumbling with my belt and me remembering suddenly that I DID kiss a guy once, goddammit, it all flashes on me like a photograph, like when you eat a Baby Ruth bar and you remember another time when you were eating a Baby Ruth bar, something you maybe never remembered since it happened, and that's how I remember this: It was just after boot camp and I was out slumming downtown holes with Buddy Vandergrift, a really freaky guy, and I don't know what I was doing with him but we were really drunk and he says he knows where there's a party, a place where there's always a party, every night, and we go to this old house downtown and Buddy lets himself in and we walk through a long dark room toward music and go through a door and it's this big wood-paneled room with an old-fashioned pool table in the middle, everything in this room is brown, the paneled walls, the wood floors, all this antique furniture with carved snakes and lion's heads and gargoyles and there's this expanse of beautiful green felt and it's like this perfect miniature meadow in this dark, stale museum, and the pool table is surrounded by all these pretty, slim teenage boys wearing nothing but white skivvies, all standing around holding pool cues and beers or stretching over for shots.

That's the picture. This green pool table surrounded by boys in white bunhuggers.

And there's this fat queen with one eye pointing off crazily, he's installed in this throne-like chair going, "Welcome, welcome. Take off your pants and get a stick. Go ahead, take off your pants. . . ." I'm about ready to cut and run when weird old Vandergrift drops his drawers and gets right into it like he's a regular old rump-bumping fool and does this every night, and maybe he does for all I know, probably a scout for this wall-eyed ogre queen and gets a commission for bringing in fresh meat like me. So I'm about to book but I'm so drunk I don't know how to get out and I end up in this dark room with nothing in it but a cold fireplace and a sofa and I'm trying the doors but they're all staircases or closets and then a hand drops on my arm and when I turn around it's one of the underwear guys in the shadows and I'm about to push him out of my way when he steps out of the shadow and I see his face.

He looks like me.

He looks just like me except younger and prettier and with long blond hair. He doesn't say anything and I say, "You look like me, you know that?" And he still doesn't say anything but walks over and settles into the sofa, and I remember remembering — Gawd, I can't believe how these things come back to you — I remember remembering how some punker said in an interview that he always had a fantasy about fucking himself and that's why he married his wife because she looked so much like him. I tell this kid that and he doesn't say anything but just looks at me like I walked out of a spaceship and then I say, "You ever thought about fucking yourself?" and I lean over and give him a kiss on the lips and feel that little milk whisker stubble and he's real passive and lets me do it but he doesn't kiss back any. We part and he looks me right in the eye, even his fucking EYES are the same as mine, green and kind of dull but always on the edge of motion, he looks at me and says, "No." Then he wipes his hand across his bare, hairless chest and says, "You want me to suck you?" I shake my head. I like the kid and feel kind of protective like he's my son or something and I try like some dipshit to warn him, to give him some advice. He's pretty but his eyes are sad like an old circus animal. I don't want this kid to turn out sad. But that's not what I say to him. What I say is, "You should be careful, all that AIDS shit going around. . . ." And he looks off in that passive way and says, "Do I *look* like I have HIV?" I just shrug and he shrugs, too, and drifts out.

And now here's Tamara with my pants all undone and me in her hand and her saying, "You want a blow job? Would you like me to perform fellatio?"

Silicone. That's what I think staring down at her and her gnarled breasts. Silicone. Even though I know no surgeon would leave such horrible scars. It's funny when you think about it. Here I thought she was the hooker with the brochures from the hotel and then I thought she was the chief's slut (who may or may not have been the first hooker) and now I'm not even sure she IS a girl at all.

And maybe the weirdest part is I'm not all that certain whether I even CARE about what she really is. All I know is she's got my cock in her hand and it's torpedo hard and I sure as hell want SOMETHING, but I don't think it's this that I want. Or maybe I just don't want it THIS way. Or maybe I'm so twisted up and out of tune, like being in crackle space between two radio stations, that I don't know what I want and in fact don't WANT anything and just think I do — because I'm an American and that's what I'm programmed to do, want.

And now that she's slurping away pretty good I'm CERTAIN this isn't the way I want it, here with Oprah and the gang watching and that damned gecko that just pounced on a moth or some wiggly wingy thing it's got broken and tangled in its jaws. We go on like this, her working her lips and tongue to the bone on this erection of mine that's about as sensitive right now as an assassin on Xanax.

I KNOW nothing is going to happen but she's so worked up on this project I don't want to disappoint her so I start all my old fantasizing tricks to maybe get me going, which is another funny thing since what I do is fantasize about other women I've been with. Funny because when I was with THEM I was fantasizing about OTHER women and on and on and on. It's like I'm never there at the moment it's happening. It's not real until I remember it and play it back. So I guess someday I'll be fantasizing about what a great time I'm having here with Tamara but until then, until I run her through the old memory machine, this . . . isn't . . . real . . . enough.

But the thing I'm really thinking about is what's under her skirt. And how it's better if I don't know. If there's a big old throbbing wanger down there I'll probably get sick and puke. And if there's what's supposed to be down there then I'll probably lose what little buzz I've got by taking the edge off the mystery. I mean I'm not getting off here or anything but at least I've got a hard-on and with a few well-timed grunts and Ohmigods at least she thinks I'm having a good time which I would like to think contributes to her having a good time. No matter what she's got down there, unless there's some third option I haven't considered that's going to turn me on like a faucet, the show will be over in a seriously unsatisfactory manner.

But she was talking about a vagina, talking like a person who had one. And she looks like a woman. I mean you can put tits on a guy and cut off his wanger but that doesn't make him look like a woman. Tamara looks like a woman. So I know I'm thinking irrationally, thinking like a crazy guy with all this worry I'm just making up. OF COURSE she's a woman, she's just got some wicked scars and some weird rash or something that makes her skin rough.

But I've seen benny-boys in the Philippines who you couldn't tell from a beautiful young girl. And the stuff they do with hormones. . . .

And what about the fight with the guy in the jeep? What made him so happy to get rid of her? What did he find out?

"Are you going to war?"

I'm surprised to see Tamara scrutinizing me.

"Are you thinking about the war? Or my breasts?" she asks. "Guess they're both hot topics right now."

"I guess I'm not thinking of much of anything," I lie.

"Maybe you're thinking of death. You thinking of dying? That's what I think of when I see myself in the mirror. I'm like war that way. Two things that make you think of death."

"You want to tell me what happened?"

Her gaze drops to where she's still holding me. "Look, you're all wilted. Shriveled. Detumescent. A natural reaction. There'll be a lot of that where you're going."

"Imagine so."

She tucks me away and sits up. Then she lifts her breasts exposing the scars. When she talks it's like she's talking to them. "My two smiles. My two sardonic smiles." Her voice drops, takes on a metallic edge. "The word *sardonic*," she says, "means a mirthless grin. It comes from a myth about a poisonous plant from Sardinia which when eaten sends the victim into convulsions of laughter from which they ultimately die. Sweet, no?"

"I guess."

"Do you feel convulsive laughter coming on?"

"No."

"You don't talk much do you?"

"Sometimes I do. But mostly I just like to listen. Hope I'm not too boring."

"No. That's fine. I trust a quiet man."

"You do?"

"Why so incredulous?"

"Just seems to me you don't trust much of anything."

"The trust issue. A central theme." She thinks. "You know, prior to gassing herself in the oven Sylvia Plath taped up the door to the nursery where her children slept. She left them bread and milk. That's what I know about trust."

I nod, pretending like I get it.

A gesture to her cradled breasts. "So, you want to hear it?"

"If you want to tell me."

She drops one breast and traces the other's white, furrowed scar line with her finger like someone trying to remember when it was new, or maybe when it didn't exist.

I'm feeling antsy, embarrassed, so I grab the camcorder and start fiddling.

"I suppose you'd like to videotape this."

"That's not what I meant. I'm just screwing around."

"I think you *should* tape it."

"No thanks."

"I want you to tape it. But I want it so we're both in it. Can you do that?"

"Sure, I can do it but . . ."

"Can you make it so we're on TV?"

"Sure. I can just cut in between your cable box and your split-ter. . . ."

"Do it."

"But . . ."

"Just do it."

So I set it all up. There's just enough slack in the cable so I can perch the camcorder on one of the TVs. I put it on wide angle.

"There."

"Is it recording?"

"We're on."

I sit back down and that whole wall is covered with me and Tamara, inverted, sideways, in living color. Her with her purple boots kicked up and those sad breasts. There's a shadow falling across the hollow of her throat and that really gets me. I'm suddenly overcome by this incredible desire rising up in me. I go to one of the screens, careful not to block the camera, and put my hand on Tamara's face, trace the glass across her sharp nose and full lips down past the hollow and around a breast. It's wonderful.

"Get back here. Let's get going."

I sit beside her but I can't look at her, can't get my eyes off those screens where Tamara is in profile looking at me but my face is straight on looking at her (and ME) video-ized, MORE real — as real as Oprah and Geraldo and Stormin' Norman.

"Look at me," she says.

"No, look at ME," I say pointing to the camera atop the TVs.

She turns so we're both full face now. "Yes, you're right. That's better isn't it? Should I start? First I need to know something, something from you."

"Okay."

"You're going to the Persian Gulf, you're on an aircraft carrier, isn't that what you told me?"

"Pull out in the morning."

"And they've got those missiles, and that nerve gas."

"That's what they say."

"And we're bombing their city, slaughtering civilians. They'll probably throw everything they've got at you, especially an aircraft carrier. Sinking one of those would be a real treat, wouldn't it?"

"In the trade we call it the High-Value Unit."

"So you might die."

"I guess there's a chance."

"You just said you're on the High-Value Unit, you're a prime target. They want that aircraft carrier more than anything. They'll launch suicide missions to get you."

"What are you trying to say?"

"That not only might you die but that you'll *likely* die. I wouldn't tell what I'm about to tell you to anybody except maybe somebody I thought would die soon. I've never told anyone about this. It's the most personal secret I have. So before I tell you I really must be assured of your impending death."

Her face on the screen (third from the right, second from the bottom) is bigger. Even though it's smaller it's bigger, more forceful, like God is talking at me. I'm totally mezzed.

"So, what, you want me to SAY it?"

Her eyes do this *afraid-so* thing and I know I should resist because I'll be watching me say this, say that I'm good as dead. It's one thing to say it, to form the words and let them loose into your world. That's a dangerous thing all by itself but to WATCH yourself say it, to not just hear it but to SEE IT, see it on the screen where the world's divided into two categories: targets or friendlies, combatants or noncombatants, victims or aggressors. It seems so simple, so clear-cut but it's not. It's NOT. White hats and black hats, who's to know the difference. Iranian vacationers can turn into aggressors (read victims) at the muted click of a keyset switch — hook the contact, press Target Designation, choose option: 1. Air friendly 2. Air hostile 3. Surface friendly 4. Surface hostile 5. Sub-surface friendly 6. Sub-surface hostile 7. Unknown. Tamara's an unknown. I thought I had her designated, thought she was a hooker, thought she was a woman, thought she was a man, thought she was a woman again — *female friendly*. But my designations won't hold, classifications keep slipping out from under me. Every time I get a lock-on, the target swaps skins so I can never take action. Can't take it out, can't pass it up. Stasis. And now here's Tamara wanting me to classify myself, wanting me to fix myself and designate me. *Victim, surface hostile.* A target ripe for terminal engagement. Another symbol on the screen where things go blip in the night. Tamara here like the stripper aiming her radar gun at me, locked-on, ready to zap. And me needing to know where those ugly smily scars came from, needing to know so I can extrapolate the truth, figure what's between her legs. But I don't even care about that anymore. It doesn't matter. Doesn't matter except insofar as I can use that intel for a firm classification. I can designate this potential target. But in order to do it I have to designate MYSELF a target first.

"You're going to die out there, aren't you." She practically hisses it.

I can't resist it, the face on the screen, the talking head, the talking hissing head and, counting the one on her face, Tamara's three mirthless grins.

"Yeah, I'll probably die."

"You *will* die. There's really no doubt. There's no way to avoid it. They will kill you good, my friend."

I give in. "Yes, I will be killed, I will die."

And the sound's boiling up in me again so I feel the words before I hear them, but then I DO hear them, like there's some three-second delay wired in, but worse, I SEE my face saying those words, designating me a victim, "YES. I WILL DIE. THEY'RE ON THEIR WAY TO KILL ME WITH GUNS AND BOMBS AND MISSILES AND TORPS AND GAS AND FUEL-FUCKING-AIR-EXPLOSIVES I'M ON THEIR SCOPES IN THEIR DARK WHIRRING BUNKERS AND THE ORDER'S BEEN GIVEN AND I'M DEADDEADDEADDEAD*DEAD*."

Suddenly I feel volcanic, explosive. I grab the camcorder and yank off the cable, pulling down the mountain of TVs that go crashing and smashing in a splintering, shattering heap. Tamara's yelling and squealing and chasing me out the door of her bombed-out bunker but before I'm out I stop for just a second by the counter where that gecko's still munching away on what used to be a bug. I squash him with the camcorder while Tamara screams at me, calling me a motherfucker and can't wait till I die die *DIE*, can't wait till all of us DIEDIE*DIE* and she's out the door ahead of me still screaming DIEDIE*DIE*, still topless bounding through the hall to the elevator and still screaming DIEDIE*DIE* while unlocking the elevator, still screaming when I get in and there's blood running down her lip and chin and I don't know if I did it or she did it but suddenly she stops screaming and the silence is profound like when a tree full of screeching birds all stop at once and the silence is louder than any screeching could be and I see the blood and the tears and her face twisted up worse than her mangled heaving breasts and I try to get some control because I have to know, I don't know why but I have to know so I say to her, trying for calm, I ask her, "Just tell me if you're really a woman."

That twisted contorted face melts like wax, wet and teary and bloody and blurry, lips stretching exposing those white tile teeth, the third grisly grin and just as the doors are closing she says in this voice I recognize but not one that came from her today, but one I know from not long ago, she says, "Fuck a duck, sailor boy." Then she howls, "*Fuck . . . A . . . Du-u-u-uck!*"

Even after the door closes and the floor tries to drop out from under my feet, the chrome walls reverberate with her howl, like the fan in the shop when an A-6 catches the one-wire. I can feel it. And I do, with my fingertips, touch the last feeble energy of Tamara's hate and fear resonating through the polished metal, a fine tone, cram packed with harmonics that come back to me, seep into me, through my fingertips, where molecules bang molecules that bang other molecules, numberless billiard balls all set into a dance that mimics Tamara's howl, infecting me, infesting me with that horrible howl so everything in me is displaced by it, all my strength is gone, chased out, so all I can do is slump down in the corner and tuck my head between my legs and cover up with my hands and stay that way, remembering those hotel pamphlets and how now I'll never know, that this is a kind of knowing that I will never have, that can't be had. The betrayal of information.

I don't know how long. I stay that way until a custodian kicks at me and tells me to get out. I have to get my ass outside.

FIVE

Cruising

Day Twenty-seven

I DON'T KNOW how I get back but I do. I crawl right into my rack and stay there. It's all I've been thinking about since Tamara's. To be back in my rack. I sleep bad. The noise, constant shit going on outside the rack curtains, last-minute drunks and dips stumbling in all night, booze-stinking rowdy. Outside stuff leaking in, grabbing at me.

My rack is almost perfect. A perfect box. Six feet long, two and a half feet tall, enclosed on five sides. Stale warm security of my sheet wrapping, scratchy wool blanket. *Natural fibers breathe.* Except for the curtains. Wedges of red night light slip in, slivers of outside, stray foul odors. I only want my own stink, nobody else's.

When I can't take it anymore I crawl out and slip down to the paraloft. I steal a roll of Velcro and rubber cement. While gluing Velcro strips to my curtains the watch tells me to turn off my rack light. Can't I see people are trying to sleep? I'm almost done and I tell him so, but without so much as looking at him. You don't want them thinking they have the least little effect on your life. I'm waiting for him to shove off but he doesn't. I tear off another strip, daub glue. Then he asks, "Hey, aren't you that crazy AW always wearing his gas mask around?"

Slowly I turn.

In the red shadows I see it's old Napoleon, the picture-eating ready room watch, that same hook of hair plastered to his forehead. He's wearing the wrinkliest most wadded-up set of dungarees I've ever seen.

I utilize a whisper version of my command voice. "They got a new invention now called an iron. Ever hear of it?"

He crumples easy. "Aw, jeez, c'mon," he whimpers. "The section leader wrote me up, laundry's down since we pulled in, and I wasn't even supposed to *have* a watch tonight."

I feel kind of sorry for the kid. I remember what it was like being a dirtball airman and every dicklick with a crow always sharpening their shitty self-esteem on you. Besides I'm curious about that act back in the ready room with the film frame. I've been wondering about it since the stereo store. But I don't know what to say. How do you bring up something like that?

He's about to move on when I blurt out, "You like horses?"

He glances up surprised, then a cloud of caution passes over his face. "I guess I do. How'd you know?"

"Just a guess. Been around them much?"

"Guess I about cut my teeth on saddle leather." He's still a little hesitant but I give him my Sally Jessy Raphael *I really want to hear more* look and he falls for it. "Uncle raised trotters in Kentucky. Did my growing up there on his place. I'd give anything in the world to be there right now."

"Why aren't you?"

"Went tits up. The A-rabs. Ran the thoroughbred market sky high. Then blooey, they all bailed and prices ate shit. Lot of breeders bit it. Then Uncle got sick. When they opened him up the cancer was all over." He brushes away that fishhook of hair and it snaps right back. "You know horses?"

"Mister Ed, Trigger, Scout."

"You're kidding me. Man ain't a man till he's rode." Dropping his eyes, "No offense."

"That's okay."

"You get to fly, though. That's pretty kickass."

"I guess. I mean, yeah, it's okay. You going back after you get out?"

"No place to go back *to*. I'm saving up though. I'll be getting m'own place."

"Forty acres and a trotter, huh?"

"You got that right. Except thoroughbreds. *Big* difference."

Just then the stinky-footed ordie in the bottom rack pokes out his bleary head, bellows to shut up and let him sleep. Napoleon, spooked, stumbles back into the red darkness.

"I better go," he says.

"Yeah, see you shipmate."

But I stop him. There's something I have to ask and old Napoleon here's as good as anyone. Maybe better.

"You ever think about dying?"

I can't really see his face too clear but I can tell he's thinking seriously and not just being nice because I'm psychotic and likely dangerous. "Not much," he finally says. "I guess mostly I just think about horses."

The Velcro works perfectly. It's practically airtight in here. I'm hermetically sealed. Vacuum-packed. Shrink-wrapped. Tattoo an expiration code on my haunch. *Best if annihilated before . . .*

Don't get much sleep before reveille. Drag on a flightsuit and go muster, then skulk back to my rack. I sleep in fits, trying like a son-of-a-bitch to think about horses. But I don't know anything about horses and mostly just think about the other thing. And about Tamara all scarred up outside and inside. About mutilated marines, charred, smoking human meat. About eating cockroaches. That stripper, BOTH those strippers, the one the marine unloaded on and then the skinny one with the radar gun, and Rudy holding her fate in his big old mitt. And what Rudy said about the bad ju-ju. And fuck a duck. And the girl I used to surveil from my apartment. And Rudy's old lady screaming *I'm glad you're going* and I still don't know if she was talking to Rudy or to me. That gecko crunching that bug. Shit keeps rolling around so I don't even know the difference between sleep and wakefulness, can't tell time is passing except for some cues from outside. Lights doused for the day sleepers. The boat's rocking sway meaning we're out of the harbor and back at sea. Four bells, eight bells; I never did learn how to tell time that way. 1MC announcements for duty section musters and working party musters and securing the special sea-and-anchor detail. A speech from the captain about battle-readiness followed by the XO's post-portcall piss-test schedule, then a prayer from the chaplain beseeching The Man At Angels One Hundred to help us liberate the peace-loving Kuwaitis (who I saw on *60 Minutes* are sitting out the war in Paris discos) from the clutches of the evil invaders. But I don't hear anything, really, just kind of sense it, like you sense somebody hiding in your room. The only thing I really HEAR is the hum of the berthing compartment fan and I wonder who else is listening to that hum, who else ten thousand feet above me or hundreds of feet below me or a thousand miles away is listening to that hum coming from a little hieroglyph of green light on a scope in a dark, cold, buzzing space.

Day Twenty-six

IT'S NERDY that brings me out of it. Nerdy and that mission I know he faked. You just can't think about those big things, can't dwell on the stuff that's out there, out there coming at you all the time whether you know it or not. That'll always be there, invisible, ticking, scanning, watching. You have to find other things to worry about, smaller things, controllable, manageable, something, like Rudy said, you can get your fingers around.

Nerdy.

Day Twenty-five

IF NERDY'S ACOUSTIC TAPE RECORDER really did work like he said then the ASWMOD still has the tape. Those guys aren't particle physicists but even THEY should be able to ID a nuke sub when they see one on a gram. Sure, ASWMOD duty's a shitcan job, a hole of a billet where they stick retread AWs who can't hack it anywhere else. But even so, they still have to verify contact and there ain't a snake's butt of a reason for them to do Nerdy any favors — especially since they hate all us prima donna, flight-suited, spit-shined aircrew types and would just as soon see our asses sucked up an S-3 intake as say good morning.

The Module door looks a lot like ours, glossy red with pretty reflector tape cutouts of blown-up submarines. Except for this: where ASWMOD is stenciled in big international-*help!-help!*-orange block letters some joker's taped a square of thermal imagery paper so it covers up the ASW part. On the paper is scrawled OZ. OZMOD.

Being a super-secret bastion of highly sensitive information there's an electronic combination door lock and a sliding peepdoor. I endow my knock with authority. The peepdoor slides back.

"State your business." It's Maeterlink, a hyper little second-class with a shape-shifter face that never looks the same way twice. Chief tagged him Lon, for Lon Chaney, and it stuck.

"I need to review a tape," I say.

"The Acoustic Wizard's not seeing anyone."

"C'mon, Lon."

"Don't call me that." The peepdoor slams. I want to get pissed but I know better. That's just what Maeterlink wants.

I knock again. The trick with these clowns is you got to make them feel human, even though they're not.

From behind the door comes, "Who is it?"

"It's still me, *Maeterlink*. I really have to get this done, okay."

The peepdoor slides back.

"FTA's powered down. Come back later."

"I'm qual'ed on it. I can power it up. Only takes a minute."

"We're closed for field day. Come back tomorrow."

"Sure. Just let me in, *pleeeeeez*."

"We're all naked in here. Can't be disturbed. Top secret, NOFORN, for-our-eyes-only naked stuff." He starts moaning and slamming up against the door like he's taking it up the back end, then the peepdoor slams.

I'm thinking of giving it up. I mean what am I doing here? All I want is to prove Nerdy didn't have any damn contact when he said he did. It's just revenge on Nerdy. Who needs it? I got away with it, HE got away with it. Except I know that's not all there is to it. I have to know HOW he got away with it. I'm about the only guy around who knows that equipment as well as Nerdy. There's no way he could fake contact without disabling the acoustic tape recorder, no way he would risk bringing a tape back here for post-flight analysis. That's the evidence. That's firm. That's solid. Unfakable. Either the sub's on the tape or there wasn't a sub at all. And I KNOW there wasn't a sub, so how could the tape show there was? And why did Nerdy tell Rudy I burned him on the hot swap, then change his story?

But even THAT's not what it's about. In the big scheme of things who cares if a couple anti-submarine-warfare analysts faked a training mission? Nothing's at stake. Nobody's in danger, no impending capital D death looming. And death is what really matters. What it always comes down to — books, movies, stories, always about dying, somewhere down the line it's about death. Stories are a kind of theme park of mortality. Deadnyland. Someone, someBODY, needs to die. Nobody's paying admission unless someone dies. And nobody's dying over this. No mini-series, no book. It's not like we're all steaming for Midway and Nerdy sold the Pac Fleet battle plan to Yamamoto. No. This ain't squat. It's not even a story. It's just inconsequential ho-hum reality.

There are other things that might kill us, that might make a story out of us. But this isn't one of them.

So why make a big deal? Who gives a rat's ass?

But my brain can't answer me. It's not a brain thing, it's a gut thing. And my gut says it IS about death, MY death, in a way that's too squirrelly to get hold of, like Maeterlink's face, rubbery and shifting and never the same way twice.

I knock again, cajole through the door. "Hey Maeterlink. *Petty officer* Maeterlink. It's for a report, straight from COMASWWINGPAC," I lie. "Flag level stuff. Crucial."

The peepdoor snaps back. It's Maeterlink again but his face is totally different. You'd never know it was the same guy.

"I get credit?"

"Sure. I'll cite the module for their usual generous support and ultra-professional demeanor and exemplification of the highest blahbedy-blah of esprit de corps or whatever."

"Not the module. *Me.*"

"Even spell your name right."

"Brownie points. Dig it. Ain't that a horse's ass of a different color." The lock buzzes and the door unlatches loosing a blast of cold, sterile-smelling AC. The electronics like it chilly.

Maeterlink tosses me a parka like the one he's wearing.

"This way, Dorothy," waving me to follow. "And stay on the yellow brick road or I'll drop a house on your ass. I'll turn you into a *bee-e-e-e-*hive."

We follow a path of yellow linoleum winding through the dim, cold, claustrophobic module, between the icy glass plotting boards and the humming processor banks and the green-lit scopes peeking out over a thousand-mile radius of ocean. All those glowing symbols, all those contacts. Boats, ships, planes, helicopters, submarines. Us watching them, them watching us. Microwaves bouncing all over, an electromagnetic mat. But not a mat, a shroud, shrouding everything. You'd think we'd all be suffocating in it. Or at least going sterile — which we probably are.

"Got an event number?"

I give him Nerdy's event number and he sorts through shelves of fifteen-inch glass reels.

"You're lucky we haven't de-gaussed these yet."

"I'm feeling lucky." My nose and fingers and toes are already numbing. I blow into my hands, shove them deep in the parka pockets where a fingertip meets something slippery and disgusting. "It's a wonder you guys don't keel over from hypothermia."

"Unusual weather we're having, ain't it? We like it. We're cold-blooded killers." He settles on a reel. "Here we go." My heart shifts gears and I bite my lip. He pulls it down, slips off the protective band. "I'll have one of the Munchkins load 'er up."

"I can do it." I try to sound routine. You can't let these guys know if you want something. You can't let ANYONE know if you want something.

"No, no. These things must be done delicately, or you'll hurt the spell."

Maeterlink passes the reel to a techie who unloops some tape before locking it onto the fast-time-analyzer. My stomach's doing flip-flops. Finally I'll know. As he threads it through chrome spools and ratchets and onto the take-up reel, I notice a sign over the equipment: The Miracle Wonderland Carnival Company.

"Really maxing out your new motif here."

"I'll take that as a compliment. My own personal vision. Something to get us through this hazardous and technically unexplainable journey. The div-off came up with a billet for morale petty officer. Times being what they were, I accepted the job."

The techie gets the paper threaded onto those four big old thermal printers they're still using. I give Maeterlink the list of Nerdy's hot-contact RFs. "Well," he says. "Let's get this collection of caliginous junk rolling."

He powers up and the printers all fire at once, the buzzing and clanking making the space seem somehow even colder. Maeterlink's obviously very into his new billet. Figure I might as well get some goodwill points while the grams come up. Even at four times real-time they take forever to build.

"Morale petty officer, huh. Sounds pretty highfalutin."

"The chipmunks genuflect to me. Isn't that so, Munchkin?"

The techie nods. Maeterlink dismisses him with a wave. He turns and his face shifts into something sharp-cornered and mean.

"So, looks like you aircrew types are done for the duration."

"What do you mean?"

"Didn't you hear?"

"Hear what?"

"Well, bust my buttons. The elite-of-the-fleet fighting-fucking-

Viking-jet-crewman the last to know all the sub-ops have been CAN-Xed."

Something plummets in my gut. "No way. We're flying submarine missions from here to the Philippines. I saw the flight plan."

"Not no*body,* not no*how.*"

"Where'd you hear this?"

"New flight plan. It's all revised. They swapped around everything. I'm surprised you didn't hear. Not much use for sub-hunters in a war without no *Unterseeboots.*"

He's waiting for the effect, the jerk.

"Yeah, that could make a guy feel a little like — "

"Tits on a boar hog? Looks like that's you all over."

"They'll need recon, surface plotting."

"Mail runs. Anyone can do that. Doesn't take an acoustic wizard like you."

"Makes a guy wonder why he's here."

"Joke's on you."

"Ha. Ha."

"Hold onto your heart, hold onto your hope."

About thirty minutes of gram-time has built up. Enough to work with. I ask Maeterlink to show me the contact he verified. He spreads his harmonic dividers, looking for related frequencies. He locates a source at sixty hertz with harmonics at one-twenty, one-eighty, and some upper spectrum clusters well over a thousand. I don't know why he's screwing with it. Just auxes and artifacts — no more a submarine than I am. He marks the lines with a red marker.

"Okay, here's your basic L.A. Class." I quick-check if he's straight-faced, whatever straight-faced would look like on Maeterlink. Straight as a fish. Cold as my nose. "This line here's the main coolant pump reinforced by the ship's service turbo-generator. That's why it's so dark and stable. This up here is the main saltwater coolant pump which runs at twice the fundamental of the SSTG that powers it. This way up here at three hundred hertz is a cluster of, um, electronics sources, probably fire control stuff and, you know, various compressor motors and such."

I can't believe what I'm hearing. I'm just gaping. I scoot up close so we're huddled over the gram. The printer gives off a sulfury smell as the thermal pin skitters across the paper, the paper ratchets a millimeter, the pin skitters back, etching the sounds picked up by Nerdy's hydrophone a week back. My 'vark holster brushes against Maeterlink's. We're wearing them all the time, now. I pull away quick and notice the hand holding the harmonic dividers to the gram, Maeterlink's hand, pink and white-knuckled with the cold. It's trembling.

"Okay." I try to act normal. "So you've got a sixty hertz family. Anything that's made in the United States runs off sixty hertz power. Everything on this ship runs off sixty hertz power. My forshitsake VCR runs off sixty hertz power. What's there to corroborate?"

His cockiness vanishes.

"Right. Corroboration. Just, um, stand by one moment." Then all bullshit-confident, "The Wizard will explain it. I'll get my debrief notes."

After Maeterlink rustles off I check another printer, a different gram. Nothing. Then another. More nothing. And another. They're all the same. Nothing but surface traffic and biologics. Junk.

He comes back shuffling through wadded notes and clutching an armful of open pubs, fold-out demo-grams trailing behind like a tail. His whole head's shrunk into something small and pink and cartoonish poking from the lumpy parka. Mousy Maeterlink.

"Up here around eighteen hundred," ref'ing his notes, his neck and cheeks flushing red as a push-pin. "All this broad-spectrum noise is, uh, flow noise, like here in the *Characteristics of U.S. Nukes* pub. That's what really cinches it as a U.S. nuke. But there's more. This Lloyd's Mirror effect back about five minutes is a close-aboard CPA and you get a little hint of blade rates at forty-five hertz which puts his speed at about . . ." working it out on his calculator. "About sixteen knots."

Lon or Maeterlink or Petty Officer Maeterlink or Dorothy or however he wants to be designated is suffering. I got to put him/her/them out of his/her/their misery.

"What's your background?"

His face pulls tight like every muscle just went to general quarters. He knows that the jig — whatever a jig is — is up.

"VP. I was at VP-40 for five years."

Now I understand.

"P-3s, huh. *Non*-acoustics?"

"Primary radar operator, electronic countermeasures. I was the best airborne emitter guy they'd ever seen."

Figures. The goofus was a NON-acoustic sensor operator. Never saw a gram, never listened to a sub in his life. They take a guy with jackshit acoustics experience, push him through a kindergarten-of-acoustics course and plop him second-in-command of an acoustics-analysis module. All because he needs sea time to make rate and nobody with two neuro-transmitters to rub together wants a haze-grey-and-underway lifestyle. The sad part is he probably *was* a hot emitter analyst. Should've left him where he was. Better for him, better for the Big Picture. But it doesn't work that way. The navy is like a socialist country. Efficiency isn't part of the jargon. If we're beating down the dreaded red menace I swear I don't know how.

I gesture to the techie at his console.

"Doesn't he have a working party to get to?"

The color drains from Maeterlink's face. The muscles slacken so the features droop into whatever gravity wants to make of them. I think it's his real face. A wax hound dog set too close to the furnace. He sends the techie to chow.

With the techie gone Maeterlink sinks onto a stool, pulling at his drippy face. "I'm a very good man, just a very bad acoustic wizard," he says. "Guess it shows."

"You got no finesse. You don't speak the language. Or barely. Your language skills are rudimentary, like an autistic person. And even if you did speak the language, which you don't, you got to listen, listen with your ears, not just your eyes. You weren't listening." I rewind the tape. "There's your flow noise, right? Flow noise is a phenomenon specific to certain U.S. nuclear subs, including this mission's target-du-jour, the Los Angeles Class. There are baffles in the hull and when the boat gets to a certain speed the water rushing across the baffles creates a resonance, like a kazoo. A seven thousand ton kazoo. You get this broadband noise on the gram here, all this blurby looking stuff you pointed out."

"Okay, so what? There it is all over the place. I've got nuke grams in the pubs that look just like that."

"Right. They *look* just like that. Just exactly like that. But the difference is *they're* flow noise and this isn't. Look, each line, each event on a gram is a sign. It's trying to tell you something, impart information. But signs are multidimensional, you have to read the whole thing, not just one aspect. What if you were driving along and you saw a sign that said stop on it. That'd be a stop sign, right?

"So what?"

"And you'd stop, right? Cause you're a good little traffic Nazi, right?"

"So?"

"So now I tell you this alleged stop sign is green. And on the left side of the street."

"Could be a one-way street. Could be in another country."

"But it's not. You're in the U.S. and it's a two-way street and the sign is green and on the wrong side and it's scrawled on a piece of cardboard and nailed to a tree. And hey, guess what? It's *not* a stop sign. Who knows what it is but it's definitely not a stop sign. But you were perfectly willing to make it a stop sign from the two lousy bits of data I gave you. You didn't know the whole story, didn't know the *context,* didn't ask about the environment, the circumstances that brought you to this sign, didn't use your other senses, didn't know the perspective, where you're standing in relation to it. There are a *thousand* things. Tens of thousands. Signs are everything. *Everything.* That's all we got. And they're nothing. But that's okay, 'cause that's all we got, too. Nothing." I can see I'm ranting and starting to lose him. The thought of losing him, of the connection breaking down, sends my right hand toying with the icy latch on my 'vark holster. A nice feeling. A bad sign.

"How do you init the audio on this thing?"

Maeterlink hits a retro-tech single-function keyset switch. The aural environment is radically altered. The electronic hums and the clack and buzz of the printers, fan-whirs, all the steady-stream modulated frequencies, constant, unvarying, relentless in their fidelity to the sixty-cycle god, all that vanishes behind a cascading wave of liquid biological sound. Sound from a thousand feet down in the sea where Nerdy's eavesdropping hydrophone hung from its wire tether. Silent. Listening. Surveilling the medium.

Gurgling sounds and long, looping wails layering, twining round each other. Clicking, snapping, popping sounds. Sizzling bacon sounds. Sounds that are anything but the lock-step hum and buzz of resonating technology. The module's swimming in it, suspended.

And under and around and through all the ambient biologics come deep rumbling moans. Rolling through the ocean like thunder lumbering across a valley — sourceless, pathless, from everywhere and nowhere. Long, low, mournful howls, sad but not sad. Ghostly. A kind of moaning you can't tell is from crazy passion or deadly pain.

It's funny, standing here, listening. Usually I think of biologics as noise, so much interference between me and my target's telltale buzz and hum and clank and grind. That's what they tell you noise is, random energy, chaotic energy that comes between the source and the receiver. It's the stuff that's not data, that's not information, that's not REAL. A thing that's what it's NOT and not what it IS. Noise is chaos, terrible chaos. But chaos is continuity. I know this in my gut. In a broad sample noise is static and static is consistent, always the same across years and distance, an even distribution of energy, homogeneous, democratic. Static on my grandmother's black-and-white Dumont in 1951 looks and sounds like static on my 1990 Sharp Lynitron. I watch static on a dead channel and know it's talking to me. On a spectrum analyzer the characteristics are predictable within boundaries — the wave height won't be above this or below that, the frequencies dwell inside a fixed range. It's a voice. A million voices. Babble. I just don't know the language, the code. Yet. Chaos is untranslated order. Noise is communication. If you've got the code, if you see the pattern. If you talk that talk and walk that walk. There are stories in the noise. I know it. I know it because that's what I do.

I make stories from the noise.

Isolate the target, pull it from the clutter. Then keep it isolated, discrete. Follow it. Listen when it turns, when it dives or ascends. Listen for the clues to its intentions: a turn pattern, hatches slamming, sensors deployed, noisemakers launched, geckos purchased, a red light on the stereo. A sequence, a line, a trace, a yarn. To the untrained ear it's all noise. But I know different.

But THIS noise, these moans and wails and whoops and clicks, put me into another place. Spherical, nonlinear. All of a sudden I think of Napoleon and his horses and that image of the two horses rearing up under black skies, fighting, trying to kill each other. Blood and spit and hair and eyes.

"Jeez, what *is* that shit?" asks Maeterlink.

I'm feeling a little stupid but Maeterlink's voice makes me shake it off, even though it's a good kind of stupid and I wouldn't mind hanging on awhile longer.

I know I should preach more, tell how if he'd listened he'd have known it wasn't a sub, how there's a thousand ways of telling when sound is NOT a sub and almost no way of telling for sure when it IS a sub, and that his job is to prove me wrong when I say *sub,* to keep reading the signs from different angles and perspectives, with different sensors and senses until he finds the weak spot in my case. That he's the science guy and I'm the illusionist. That my job is just to organize a sequence of traces, data, EVIDENCE (whatever *that* is) to construct a semblance of certainty, to make him think what I want him to think. But I don't preach. I don't say anything. I just keep listening, mezzed by sound that's not sound, noise that's not noise.

Finally Maeterlink drops the volume. The sixty-cycle god, the buzz and hum, is back in charge.

"Whales," I say, distracted, trying to clear my head while running my finger in a slow circle around the blurby representation on the gram. "They migrate down the coast this time of year. It's just whales."

Day Twenty-four

STARTED OUR CLASS TODAY. Me and Rudy. Religions of the World. Classroom's an airless old ammunition void you crawl through this tiny hatch to get to. It's bisected by a fat hot water pipe emitting heat like a radiator. Or radiating heat like an emitter. Dizzying, claustrophobic, like some underground cell where self-flagellation and human sacrifice take place. Bloodletting and secret handshakes. We pile the chairs in the corner, squat on the deck where it's only about a hundred and ten.

The class can't go as long as scheduled because of the war or the bombing or the blitzkrieg or whatever it is. All the noncombatants are off-loading in the Philippines, so class is compressed to a week which isn't a problem since all the sub ops are canc'ed anyway making my sub-hunting expertise, and me in general, a case of total superfluousness.

Our professor, who wants us to call him Mel, is a bundle of flicking nerves as he stacks and restacks, sorts and resorts, shuffles, unshuffles, and reshuffles this sad-looking mound of textbooks, dog-eared manuals hairy with yellow Post-its, loose papers, ratty folders and a cube of food-looking stuff wrapped in a beige paper towel. While turning this disorder into different disorder he chats us up, lets us know he's a lapsed Orthodox Jew from some strict New York sect. A dropout from a sort of rabbinical seminary. Seminary. I crack to Rudy that it sounds like a high-end sperm bank. We snap to when a book slams to the deck, a refugee from Mel's stack. Mel about has a stroke. He's got this woolly beard where sweat collects in beads and girlish lips, flushed and wet. His wiry hair is out of control and recently lopped to earlobe length, likely a prerequisite for this wonderful job. His pinball eyes zoom all over and his left nostril tics. He's scared, you can tell. Which I could understand if he was going where we're going, but he's not. Then I realize that it's US he's scared of. Get that. Like a gaggle of bored, overworked and underachieving enlisted pukes is threatening. But he's measuring every word, every gesture, like he's tripped into a nest of barbarian rapists and pillagers or Nazi interrogators or Turkish exterminators or crazed Right-to-Lifers or Islamic author-hunters or Khmer Rouge re-educators or Argentine *generales* or Tijuana cops or Maoist Shining Path assassins or Hezbollah terrorists or CIA hit squad guys or serial killers or Christian missionaries or Portuguese explorers or IRA bomb-lobbers or Spanish Inquisitioners or glassy-eyed Idaho survivalists or musketed New World settlers or screaming Mongols or Skinheads in Doc Martens or evangelistic fundies or name your bloodthirsty savage. Like we're just waiting for him to say something suspicious so we can gouge his eyes and whack off his head or pump him full of hot lead.

But when you think about it maybe he should be afraid. I mean we ARE people. And people DO slaughter people for what they say. Grunts and squawks, lines scrawled in deadly patterns. No meaning without a receiver, an organizer and decoder like me to interpret hostile intent. Lines on a gram. The right frequencies in the right patterns and it's weapon-away time. A screaming torp chasing down a tin can village packed with people designated baddies.

I don't really do that, though. I only simulate it. I don't really DO anything.

This ectomorph yeoman type asks about grades. Mel's pinball eyes careen around various points in space like searching out a voice from nowhere then, giving up, he answers as if talking to himself. "Grades? Sure. You want grades? Let's play nostalgia-mode didacticism. Grades for everybody." He turns his back to rummage through papers. From the pile he extracts a stack of books. "Read these or don't. It's up to you."

Then he launches into this stupid story about a fish which I guess is supposed to be like a parable you tell to little kids and morons. Rudy looks at me like what the fuck and I can't blame him. I mean we're sailors, not retards.

So there was this fish in Fishworld who is obviously the symbol for some bullshit god-knows-what and he's swimming around and everybody in Fishworld knows the three boundaries no fish can ever cross are the bottom, the surface, and where they meet which ectomorph-suck-up correctly identifies as the shoreline. So there's all this blah-blah and the upshot is the fish-hero is naturally a flying fish and when he leaps out of the water he sees this whole other world exists, sun and sky and sand and all, where everyone thought was just monsters and death. And when he comes back to report this golly-gee discovery all the other fish turn on him and amputate his wingy fins and leave him to die.

So what's the point?

Then he goes on about how this is a story about perception and reality and how we're all stuck in these little boxes of perception and how we don't even know we're in them unless we get outside for a look. And how most people never get outside their little boxes. And how those who do are visionaries and seers and by the way he's going on all televangelicalized you can be certain he thinks he's a member of this holier-than-wow group. Rudy does like he's jacking off.

Then Mel launches into this thing about the Machine. How the Machine is the sum total of all these boxes within boxes and how inside the Machine is violence and insanity and death but outside is all this wonderful knowledge and wisdom, self-knowledge and other-knowledge which is somehow the same thing, like if you can see the Machine you can see your own reflection in it.

Mel cocks his head, relishing his words, or just lost in them. Me and Rudy look at each other. Rudy's dripping with sweat. But old Mel here must be reassured that no one's leaped up to rip out his throat. He's warmed to his subject, hitting stride. An energetic delivery, eyes glisteny and fishy but still pinbally.

"Two sides of the same perceptual coin. Enlightenment, self-realization, Buddhahood, Nirvana, the unified field, Heaven, Kavvanah, Satori, Valhalla, Bliss — call it what you will, it's all the same thing. Perspective, vision. Seeing.

"But reality is relative. Ever hear of the Uncertainty Principle? Viewing an action is altering it. If you're on the inside, it alters you. If you're on the outside, you alter it." For a nanosecond his eyes, fiery like an F-14 afterburner, light onto mine, jolting me with a current that makes me sit up straight even though my thighs ache from squatting on the steel deck. "Watching," he announces jabbing at air, "is participating.

"No objectivity. To *be* is to be inside of. To *see* is to be an accomplice. There is no meaning, only shades of meaning, slippery hues of truthishness. The absolute is dead. Death is the last absolute. Maybe." The 1MC crackles but no voice comes out.

"Particle physics is a quest for quantum angels. Smash particles into particles, then smash those particles and keep smashing on and on until . . . until what? Until you hit the irreducible particle, right? That's what they thought. That's what Western thought was based on. That's logic. It's Newtonian. An ordered universe. We can parse it with reason, logic, assail all problems, mechanical and spiritual, with the grammar of deductive and inductive reasoning. The collective Western mind speaks in if/then statements. What if there were no *then*? What if there is only *if*? What is the sound of one quark colliding?" Mel's forehead collides with a low pipe. He pretends like he doesn't notice.

"The *what if* happened. The particles don't behave. Their deportment is not up to scratch. Subatomic chimeras shifting from mass to energy and back to mass again. Two electrons spin off in opposite directions — one into the past, one into the future. Time is bent so we see both at the same moment — temporal dimensions experienced as perceptual layers, so many glass slides wedged together, all of time existing at once, all instants in one instant. David Byrne says stop making sense. Let's all *stop making sense*."

I think, sense, cents, scents, sinse, since.

Mel pauses, squeezing his hands. The afterburner light fades, fuel starved. He's spent. "Questions so far? Comments? Criticism?"

Rudy pulls up from his sweaty slump and bellows, "I thought we were learning about religions. All I'm hearing is New Age Star Trekkie weird science."

Mel paces between sprawled bodies. "A valid question. Let me see if I can impose structure on this willy-nilliness." He moves cautiously, dodging all glances. Rehearsed gestures designed to put us at ease, lip pinching. "Since Thomas Aquinas religion and science have been converging." His fingers trace two converging vectors. "Since Heisenberg the disciplines are inseparable." Fingers snake together. "Locked in elegant embrace like the double helix of DNA. The chalk lines are fading. Art, Science, Philosophy — the new holy trinity." He tries adding a third finger but it doesn't work and he gives up, dropping his hands and addressing the air, or maybe the hot water pipe over my head. "Convergence. Collage. It's all in the interdisciplinary mix. Painters talk like astrophysicists, holy men talk like social scientists, quantum theorists talk like Eastern mystics. All points accelerate into the vanishing point — not coincidentally the breakthrough discovery in the visual arts which solved in a fell swoop the age old problem of . . ." Dramatic pause. "*Perspective.*" He pauses, glancing around like he just woke up and unexpectedly recognizes a face, which is Rudy's. "Have I answered your question, Mister," reading Rudy's shirt stencil. "Esperanza?"

Rudy, arms crossed, head listing, mouth gaping, says flatly, "Nope."

Mel tries a good-sport chuckle but it comes out more like a titter. "Esperanza. It means hope, eh? *¿Habla Español?*"

Bad move. Rudy hates being called a Mexican, hates if you just imply it. Not exactly a pride-of-heritage type. "Little *cholo* Spanish," he grunts.

Mel knows he fucked up but not how, and he doesn't know how to recover.

"From the verb *esperar,* which also means to wait. Well I *hope* that if we *wait* long enough we'll get around to religion. Or maybe I've been talking religion all along." The way he says it you know he really doesn't know.

I find myself raising my hand. His eyes glance off two bulkheads, rebound from a third and land on me, or in my vicinity.

"I wonder," I ask. "Could you talk some more about what you said about watching? About how watching is participating? About how you can change something just by looking at it?"

Day Twenty-three

I GET UP BEFORE REVEILLE to prepare for today's project. Grab the camcorder, flick on the power, check the auto-focus to be sure it'll stay focused on me at arm's length. I'm off. First head I check is vacant and I'm thinking yahoo. But the plumbing's backed up and the showers are full of brown water, an *Exxon Valdez* layer of soap scum, shitpaper bits and shredded tobacco floating on top. Check the other local heads — no water; no hot water; secured for field day; flooded; filthy. Finally I sneak into an out-of-the-way officer's head I know up on O-3. Prop the camcorder on the sheetmetal shelf. Nobody's around so I take my time, shaving real careful, popping all my blackheads which just go crazy in this steamy clabber boat air.

Back in berthing reveille's gone off so the lights are on. Don a new T-shirt right from the package, collar snug and white, not grey and baggy like from the laundry. I take out my best dungarees. The denim's blue, crisp, new. My name embroidered on, not just stenciled with a laundry pen. Buff my boots. Shine the fittings on my 'vark belt, stow everything and lock up. As the stinky-footed ordie rolls from his rack I'm cinching the 'vark straps, getting it settled and centered on my face.

I video myself cruising down to the shop. Inside I do shots of me checking in on the muster board, scanning the POD and flight schedule, watching a little three-day-old Willard Scott doing old folks' birthdays and the weather for a part of the world I won't be seeing for a long time and possibly never.

The ready room. Still early so nobody's here but Napoleon straightening chairs and the duty officer on the phone, cramped up with military bearing.

"Yessir . . . Yes*sir* . . . Comsec inventory's complete, boards updated, first brief's at oh-seven-hundred . . . Roger . . . Roger that, sir . . . Uh-huh . . . *Thirty-six Hours of Hell.* A troop of marines battle Japanese forces in the South Pacific during World War II. Richard Harrison, Pamela Tudor, directed by Robert Marrtero. Dubbed. 1977. Ninety-five minutes. Color . . ."

Napoleon sidles over and asks what I'm doing.

"Self-surveillance," I mumble through the 'vark.

"Oh."

I move around the room, get me in front of the white board, the ops map, then the CVIC monitor where an A-6 bombing brief is going on hosted by a Tom Cruise look-alike with a retractable chrome pointer. The SDO yells at me. I can't video in here. It's a security breach.

"This room is classified confidential." Swilling from a mug grafted to the end of his arm.

"But sir," I ask. "Isn't everything on the ship classified confidential?"

"Right."

"So everyone onboard is cleared for confidential, right?"

"That may be so but that doesn't mean they have a need-to-know."

"What if I promise not to show it to anyone without a need-to-know?"

"Get out of here."

I do me having eggs and flaccid bacon and cinnamon rolls in the chowhall. Gotta un-don my 'vark but that's okay. Then at the ship's library where I filch a computer magazine. Working out at the gym, first on the rowing machine where I vise the camcorder in my crotch, then doing bench presses with it locked between my knees. Pre-flighting my flight gear at the paraloft — checking the strobe, the flashlight, the flare pistol, all the junk in my survival vest, my helmet, the mike, the tinted visor which I replace with a clear one for night ops. The senior rigger, Waterman, pug-nosed, walrus-shaped, looks up from the video game he's hulked over but doesn't say anything.

Then up to the flight deck where I see Nerdy jogging. I fall in behind at a good surveillance distance, even though it's me I'm surveilling. Get looks from some red shirts loading up an A-6 but I don't care. Jumping over tie-down chains and thick greasy arresting wires, ducking under E-2 props, almost gored by an F-14 stabilizer. On the stern Nerdy circles around a parked huffer and catches me. Guess I look pretty stupid here with my 'vark and camcorder perched on my very tired outstretched arm so I'm not surprised when he just stops and gawks, jogging in place, not saying anything. He's wearing a Naval Aircrew Candidate School T-shirt and UCLA shorts. Very preppy. Always trying to pass. We do a little stare-down and any casual observer could tell something's come to a head between us. I lower my arm, pull off my 'vark. Nerdy's face is a blank gram, an empty RF.

"Whatcha doing?"

I smooth my hair and shrug. "Dunno. Just screwing around."

"Looking pretty weird."

Even though it's early the sun's already beating down, breeze hot and wet like breath, sky a gaping heartless blue.

"Guess so." Now's good as ever to lay it on him. "Hey, speaking of weird, I was in the module looking at tapes the other day."

"Glad to see your interest in ASW."

"Spare me the ALPO bullshit. I had Maeterlink replay the tapes from our last sub ops and you'll never guess what."

For the flight deck it's reasonably quiet. An APU's dying siren up forward, the wind gulping and gusting past my ears, Nerdy's running shoes scuffing the deck like rhythmic Velcro rips.

"Gee Beav, I dunno, what?"

"You'll never guess."

"Just tell me."

"Hard to believe."

"I'm outta here." He takes a couple paces up the deck.

"Where you going, Ahab?"

Nerdy stops, sighs. "If you want to make a point I wish you'd just do it."

"A point? Yeah, I do have a point. Did you know that on the subatomic level you can alter an action just by watching it?"

"You've been watching the Discovery Channel. I'm very impressed."

"Isn't that a kick? Just by watching something you can change it. You can have an effect on it."

"Could we get on with it. I want two more laps before they close the flight deck."

"Well, Ahab, it's just this. The whole world's watching. Everyone is watching everyone else. We're influenced by it all the time. We're different because of all this watching. We're molded." A glint on the deck, broadcasting from the black, lunar surface of nonskid. I squat to retrieve it. "Check it out." Displaying the bit of safety wire. "Potential foreign-object-damage. Where's a FOD bucket?"

Nerdy's face says who cares, but his voice says, "Nice work, eagle eye."

"Hard to believe this could bring down a high-tech warplane, huh?"

"Weren't you saying something?"

He's hooked now. Let him twist. "A jet mech showed me an engine after it sucked up a screw. You could see right on one of the fan blades this perfect impression of a tiny screw, threads and all, molded in the titanium like it was Play-Doh. Unreal. Said if they hadn't shut down, it would've blown like a fragmentation bomb. Tiny thing. Big effect."

"Amazing. You were saying?"

I pocket the wire. "You and me, we're ace sub-surveillers. We track a sub, we listen, we observe. We watch. And it's altered because of that. In some minuscule way we've changed its destiny. Subatomic particles deflected. Some balance of fate slightly shifted, askew. Like the screw hitting the fan blade, there's a wobble that wasn't there before."

"What's all this Ahab crap?"

"I used to be really frustrated because of all the simulating we do. All the exercises and wargames and computer models. It was like I'd never do anything *real*. But that's the nature of the peacetime military, right?"

"Maybe it's escaped your notice but this isn't peacetime."

"I mean you don't ever want to actually do what you're trained for because that would involve war and death and danger and mutilation. But if you *don't* do it then you're like an unproved resource, like some great violinist who never gets to play for an audience. Pretty soon you wonder what's the use? Why be so good at what I'm doing if nobody *knows* I'm so good at it? And that's what I was thinking when I lost that sub and handed off a tri-tac of dead buoys to you and your crew. And now I understand why *you* did what you did."

"Which was?"

"Why you turned a bunch of whale farts into a contact. You figured what the hell. Nobody knows the difference. Nobody cares. Nobody can see the reality. There's no reality to *see* for shitsake. Why not manufacture one, right? Crew gets the exercise points, you get your pat on the back. Life is good."

Nerdy's normal deadpan takes on a pinkish glow. "I don't know what you are and I sure don't know what you're talking about. If you're implying that I faked a sub contact on a mission, lied to my crew including the XO of the squadron, all I can say is you better talk to the flight surgeon or a shrink or get a piss test because your head is on crooked. I don't fake missions, got me?"

"Don't go having a cow on me, Nerdman. I'm not laying to sully your precious reputation. I'm trying to tell you something important."

He squints, suspicious. "Yeah?"

"Don't you get it? If you can change the target, object, whatever, just by watching it then surveillance is an *action*. It's not just something passive. It's an *action*. I mean like we're really *doing* something and not just jacking off doing *simulations* of something real, we *are* doing something real. I'm not expressing myself very clearly, am I?"

"I think I understand what you're trying to get at. I'm not sure I *care. . . .*"

"Soon as I figured that out I knew why it was wrong faking the mission like we both did."

"Like *you* did."

"Say what you want. I heard the tape. You were chasing whales, Ahab. Anyway, there's a principle. There's integrity."

"You know a lot about *that*."

I ignore him. "By surveilling something I change it. That's real. By letting that sub slip away I stopped affecting it. I was powerless, impotent. It beat me. And it knew it beat me. Doesn't matter what outsiders thought about the holy-as-hell mission. That doesn't count. It's about me and the sub. I let it beat me. That's real. I don't feel right about it and neither should you."

"You're right. You should be strung up by the balls. But don't try implicating me in your little fraud. It won't fly."

"You deaf, Nerdy? *I . . . heard . . . the . . . tape.* Whales. You know? Like Shamu?"

"I'll pretend I never heard any of this. Next time I won't be so generous."

"You're unreal, you know that?"

Nerdy waves and takes off. I pick up the camcorder and zoom him jogging off. "I'm watching you," I yell after him. "I'm watching!"

*   *   *

132

That night I have trouble sleeping. Stress, anxiety, whatever. After a while I switch on the racklight. Initiate light. The fluorescent tube emits an annoying buzz. Take down the camcorder from where it hangs on the towel rack. Replay the tape from earlier. It helps me relax. I fall asleep watching myself through the viewfinder. I'm in the gym. Rowing, rowing, rowing.

Day Twenty-two

I'M CROSSING THE HANGAR BAY back by the jet shop when I see Mel. His beard and wild hair make him stand out despite his civilian onboard disguise of khakis without insignia. But now he really stands out for the drop-jawed horror on his face.

"Yo, Mel. What's up?"

He flinches, looks at me blankly, gaping, then recognizes me. I think. Least he talks to me, or in my direction. "Do you know what this is? Do you know what these men are *doing*?"

The nuke-wep training team is practicing a load on an F/A-18. The plane's cordoned off by armed marines. The team leader drones checklist items to the bored team members huddled around the mock bomb, which is bright blue and very bomb-looking. Mel must be upset by the jarheads and their guns. It's rare to see guns on the ship, which is odd when you think about it. The world's largest warship you expect to see some wicked weaponry. But the low-tech stuff is locked away and the sexy stuff, Tomahawks, Sea Sparrows, C-Whiz, is camouflaged in bland low-slung boxes.

"I can't even say what they're doing. It's unspeakable."

"It's simulation," I tell him. "It's just practice."

"It's reality. Worse than reality, it's reality disguised as simulation. Geo-politics, coalitions, tyranny, liberation. *That's* simulation. Sophistry, propaganda dressed as a representation of some cohesive moral reality. The fallacy of a new world order implicit in which is the assumption of an old world order when all they're really talking about is cultural and political hegemony. Domination. Sacrifice the savages to the maw of capital. Should I be saying this? Will they shoot me?"

Jeez, I should fix this guy up with crazy Tamara. Mel's okay, though. I think he's got something I want. Or need.

"I don't think they're listening."

"Can I trust you? Will you turn me in?"

"For what? Talking's pretty harmless. I think it's allowed."

"But that, THAT," pointing to the blue BDU. "That's real. Real as it gets."

"It's just a practice bomb. They lock up the real stuff."

"You see. They *are* here. They're here with us."

"It is my government's policy," I drone, "to neither confirm nor deny the presence of . . ."

"You're not one of them, you know."

"Sorry?"

"I was watching you in class. Behind those stealthy eyes, beneath your meticulously pressed uniform, something goes on. I see these things."

"That's right. You're the little fish that could."

"The rest, the lambs, need assurances, parables. They believe in mythology, symbols, archetypes. It's how they relate to the world. They can't see straight, can't recognize what's before their eyes without mediation. They need it pre-digested, served up on a platter. That's what I'm saying.

"We talk about terror, " he says. *"Terrorists.* What do we mean? We mean brown people with bombs out to disrupt the order imposed by *Western Civilization.* But it's the West that invented terrorism. That right there is the first and biggest terrorist tool. You fuck around and it's headed down the chimney. We deliver, anywhere, overnight. Guaranteed."

Where does he think he is? What does he think we are? "I'm no terrorist. And that's just a practice device. There's nothing to it. It's hollow. I know a guy who stole one and put legs on it for his kids to play on like a hobby horse. It's not *real.*"

"I need a drink."

We head below. It's between meals so the chowhall's empty. We settle in with glasses of warm bug juice. Mel examines his like a beaker with some fascinating chemical reaction.

"What is this concoction?"

"Bug juice. It's really Kool-Aid. They call it bug juice because it attracts flies."

"Right. And it's purple so we know it's grape-flavored. A simulation, like your bomb."

"Not *my* bomb."

"An image of grape, a shade, a *trace*. But no longer even a trace. Not a hint of essence. Take a sip and what do you taste? Imitation grape flavoring. It has no relation to grapes, no *grapeness* to it. Likely it's a petro-chemical derivative. You're conditioned to suffer a grape-nostalgia even though it's lacking any element of its supposed model, a sentimentality for something that never existed."

"Because it doesn't taste like grapes?"

"Taste, smell, look, feel, sound — no sensory semblance whatever."

"What's a grape *sound* like?"

"Don't let's split hairs. It's beneath you." Pinball eyes roam the chowhall. Maybe it's frustration. Maybe boredom. Maybe attention deficit disorder. "There are no grapes and can't ever be again. The grape has vanished. It was gone before you were born. I'll put it country simple. In the beginning there were grapes, I think they were called Concord grapes. It's been so long I don't even know. I have an ornate recollection of my grandparents' place in Crown Heights, a broad porch vaulted by a trellis, an arbor, perfect dangling clusters of dew-kissed globes." His expression gets all dew-kissed. "Each globe mottled with a tender white dusting one scrubbed away with his pink child's tongue before popping it between tiny white teeth. A burst of flavor. Then there was Welch's grape juice, which was good and was the real thing, even though invented as an alcohol-free substitute for sacramental wine. Did you know that? Then a corporation — Nehi? Nesbitt's? Pepsi? — did what corporations do, they fabricated a cheap imitation, a washed-out simulation, the prime purpose of which was to ignite the market with desire, create a frenzy of cheap. There's no bucks in the authentic, so wean them off it.

"So there was grape juice, then *imitation* grape juice which tasted nothing like grape juice but people drank it to conserve capital, bucks, *dinero*, filthy lucre — in itself an abstraction with no basis or even counterpart in reality. Time passed. Memories faded. Imitation grape flavor became more grape than grapes, a dissimulation further aided by an unfortunate confluence of politics and phenomenology — the farm labor movement playing into the hands of the corporate imitation grape factions saw to it that Concord grapes vanished from our fruit bowls. There was nothing left but the *image* of grapeness which supplanted the reality of the grape which then became its own reality and now it's the only reality show in town. Plato's — or was it Socrates'? — concept of the simulacrum, a copy referencing no original. The grape is dead."

"The grape is dead?"

"More than dead. Or you could say less than dead. Deader than dead. Imitation grape flavoring is all there is. It's not an imitation of anything. It's all by itself; alone, discrete, an original. Nothing came before it and nothing exists independently of it. It is that it is."

"You don't sound much like what I imagine a rabbi would sound like, you know that?"

"That's what they said at yeshiva." He shoots down the bug juice and makes a face. "I told them God is a grape."

"Would you say that God is a fish?"

"No. I'm a fish. God is a grape. The distinctions are obvious. The scary blue thing is a grape, too."

"Does that mean the scary blue thing is God?"

"*Bingo!*"

"Then what's imitation grape flavoring?"

"So glad you asked. It's television."

"Boy, am I lost."

"You're a demi-god by virtue of your awareness. But wait, as they say, there's more." He leans in like he's about to tell where the Nazis stashed the Holy Grail. "Television is gone, too."

"Gone?"

He nods, a hand rakes scraggly hair. "Gone, assimilated, transmogrified, perceptually imploded."

"What's replaced it?"

"We don't know yet. Nobody's been able to get outside for a looksee."

"Not even the little fish that could."

Mel snorts. "Him? Mrs. Paul got him. He's battered and baked and microwave dished. Available in your grocer's freezer."

Out on the sponson I watch the shitcan detail heave trash. Bobbing line of Hefty bags receding to a point on the faded horizon. The monstrous churning of the boat's four huge, unstoppable props, the mind-boggling stink of this Mount Everest of trash and rotting chowhall slop, the rhythmic shotgun plop of each bag of our relentless shit punishing the face of the ocean. I aim at the horizon. Trail of bags, Morse code of receding dots and dashes, a run-on sentence talking-talking-talking us east across the Pacific back to a place called the West. I thumb the blistery red button in the grip. The word *record* appears in the viewfinder, itself a tiny black-and-white cathode ray tube — liquid crystal? — monitor. Micro gears shift, ratchet. Muffled motor hum. Voice-over. But I don't know what to say. I try like hell to think of something, something worth saying, that encompasses these weird feelings balking at word-capture, slithering around and through me, twisting and oozing and dribbling between my fingers. The only thing I can think of is *The Machine.* I whisper into the foam-covered mike. *The Machine. The Machine.*

Day Twenty-one

SLICK SWEAT between the rubber and my jawline. I keep smearing around, wiping away at this oily membrane and especially trying to dry a razor-burn patch stinging like a sonofabitch. Makes me crazy. Two hours at general quarters and even though it's just a drill, everyone in the shop's getting antsy. Energy waves. I can barely concentrate on the *Navy Times* in my lap.

Rudy tried sneaking out on a Coke run but got caught breaking a watertight hatch by a repair-party team leader. Now he's stretched out on the deck with his back against a safe. His voice sounds like he's talking through a paper towel tube.

"Fucker told me to call Damage Control Central." *Hucker tol me to hall dahage contro hentro.*

Buckethead asks, "What kinda hatch?" He's futzing around like playschool with scissors and paper and a jar of rubber cement. He's got these big paper eyelashes taped to the lens of his 'vark.

"Circle-zebra."

"You can break circle-zebras, can't you, Nerdy?"

Nerdy's at the Chief's desk going through lectures. He thinks we're doing some training while waiting for the all-clear.

"Doesn't matter if you can or not. Nobody's breaking watertights to go on a Coke run. The Chief'd shit." *Shiefa hit.*

Rudy mimics him all sarcastic, "*Chief'd shit. Chief'd shit a big fucking red brick.* Somebody get this boy a reality check."

A dead voice from the 1MC. *Incoming missile alert. Relative bearing One-Two-Zero at seventy. Multiple sub-sonic contacts. Mark time. Time is Zero plus fifteen seconds.*

A snorting sound comes from Buckethead's 'vark. The lens fogs. Guess he's cracking up. (Guess we're ALL cracking up.) His paper eyelashes twitch and jerk. He stops what he's doing which, now that I notice, is stuffing coffee filters into his shirt like fake boobs, even though we're all supposed to stay buttoned up to our necks.

Nerdy turns in his chair in an I'm-in-command way he must have been practicing when nobody was around, his back bulkhead straight, but with a turkey-shoot cock to his head.

"Still nothin' from the old lady, huh, Rudeman."

Rudy's 'vark-nose twitches like he got a whiff of predator. "What are you talking, little guy?"

Nerdy gives a shrug. "It's either that or you're menstruating. Something's got you on the rag. I figure it's fidelity worries which is nothing to be ashamed of. Pretty woman like Anita, I'd worry too."

Below where the straps dig in Rudy's thick neck muscles clinch like two ropes.

"Careful, twerp," he rumbles through his 'vark muzzle.

Nerdy swings back around like he's got better things to do. But he can't resist another poke at Rudy's hot button.

"Fine, Rudy. No reason *I* should give a shit who's hosing your old lady." *Ooth-hosah-eurolaly.*

Our whole taped-up world shifts into slo-mo like when movie tension gets thick as mud. Buckethead, boobs all stuffed and those dufus fake eyelashes, stops buttoning his shirt, freezes in mid button-holing. Eyes lock onto Rudy. But instead of leaping up and twisting Nerdy's head off and stuffing it down his throat like I expect, instead of that, he just slowly, carefully, deliberately, puts one of those ham-sized mitts of his on either side of his own head, squeezing real hard like someone with a migraine trying to squeeze out the most excruciating pain — but maybe not really a real pain, maybe more like the fear of pain, of a pain so horrible and so threatening and so potentially unbearable that you'd rather just be dead, rather give it all up and just die right now than risk suffering that pain for even a second. As soon as I think that, I realize it's a feeling I know, a feeling I've been living with all this time.

He squeezes hard. His head twists over. I'm half wishing to see his eyes and half glad I can't but I can hear him sucking air slow and deep, sucking in as much as the filter will let him. Sounds like he's swallowing the whole shop in one long inhalation, like the walls will buckle and all the duct-taped seams will split wide and my belly flops at the thought of what might come oozing in to claim us.

I can't see Nerdy's face but his posture says he's not the king of smug of a few moments ago. His life's probably flashing by — if he's got any sense at all.

Estimated time to impact, two plus zero zero minutes.

Finally Rudy lets go his head with a snap, shakes and snorts. He pushes his beefy body from the deck and hulks over beside Nerdy, looming. Nerdy's trying hard to look like he's concentrating on those lectures but his back's stiff as concrete and his shoulders hunched up to his ears.

Suddenly I'm talking, rattling on about this B-52 that went down after a bomb raid and how three crewmen were lost at sea and how they're saying it was mechanical problems and that the plane didn't take any hits over Baghdad or anything and as I'm saying this I'm surprised to see Rudy paying attention. But his hand, as if disconnected from his body, drifts over, settling ever-so-gently, gracefully, a helicopter touching down, on Nerdy's head. Beefy fingers wrap the skull over rubber straps that make Nerdy's hair poke out all over. I remember what it's like having that five-fingered vise latch onto you and wonder at the same time why Nerdy just sits there taking it, like he doesn't even feel it. Rudy chats on like nothing. "It's the fucking ju-ju, man. B-52s don't just fall outta the sky." As he's talking I see his other hand moving like a robot arm, settling over the air hole on Nerdy's 'vark filter then clamping tight. "First off, those things got like eight engines — they can probably fly on four — and who knows how many hydraulic systems backups. A bird like that don't just crash for no reason."

Standby for impact. Impact time thirty seconds. Mark. Brace for shock.

Oxygen deprivation's got Nerdy responding, jerking like a busted wind-up toy. But Rudy grips him tight, pulls his head in close so Nerdy's flailing arms can't get a grip. The rubber flesh sucks in like a bladder. A squeaking sound. "And second thing," Rudy says, "those Air Force mechs don't let that shit happen. They been doing that SAC shit for thirty years, keeping those birds in the air twenty-four hours a day, seven days a week. . . ."

Nerdy's neck is going the color of beef liver and part of me says Nerdy's dying and I better do something but part of me sees Rudy all calm and normal like nothing's happening and that visual reassurance makes me think there's something wrong with ME. Like I'm misreading the signs and actually everything's hunky-dory, nothing to get fragged about. I check Buckethead for a second opinion. He's staring with that bloated head and 'varky snout in drag eyelashes and stuffed boobs like some grotesque alien babe. But through the rubber and the paper there's an expression, almost like it's a real face with real feelings and right now that face is passive and calm and reminds me of the kid who wanted to blow me. Then, without saying anything, he gets up and I'm thinking, okay, now he'll do something to stop this. I was right, there IS a problem here and I'll just be leaping up and giving old Buckethead an assist peeling Rudy off Nerdy before Nerdy's oxygen-deprived brain drops a few of those precious IQ points of his. But Buckethead just slithers past Rudy, even mumbles an excuse me, opens the door, steps out, pulls it shut behind him.

Multiple bogie contacts bearing three-one-zero. Estimated engagement time — three mikes. Now launch the alert-five fighters.

I want to turn on TV, to point my eyes at television, at talking heads, be lulled by the soothing buzz of Uncle Dan, sucked in by the fake drama of a tabloid host, coddled and cooed in Oprah's big warm lap. I want lovin' from the oven. But there's no TV during a GQ. There's nothing on, a really scary phrase. There's nothing on. Just a test pattern. Nobody home at the Huxtables'. I can't have the one doctors recommend most. It's up to me if I want Rudy to leggo Nerdy's Eggo.

Then the taped-up airless shop is filled with a voice. It's me. I'm going on about these eight marines killed by friendly fire last week, seven when their LAV got zapped by an A-10 hot-dogger who couldn't tell good guys from bad and one other sand-pounder fragged by a cluster bomb. Another LAV was hit by Iraqis and four more jarheads bit it.

"So the score's eight to four, good guys leading." Rudy's bearing down on Nerdy, twisting the mask, wiping his face with it. Nerdy's gone limp, no resistance. "We'll show them ragheads. Nobody snuffs Americans better than Americans. We got experience on our side. Right, Nerdy?" With that he lets loose. Nerdy's head thumps to the desk like a helmet bag, a padded hollow sound.

I jump up to, I don't know what, check for a pulse maybe, when Nerdy's arm spasms up, ripping off the 'vark, exposing his face red and contorted and mask-creased. He's lying there gasping like a fish. Rudy's haw-hawing like back at the strip club except the mask makes it sound like some weird car alarm. Then he bends down close over Nerdy's convulsing body and growls, "Better not get caught with your mask off, sonny boy. Chief'd shit."

Now secure from general quarters.

I pull off my 'vark, loosen my collar, untuck my cuffs. The TV switches from the AFRTS test pattern to a long shot of a "woman on the move" in some New Yorky executroid office setting. Zoom on the boudoir blue box she slides from her designer bag. The soothing voice-over: "Now for you. Gyne-Lotrimin in the handy combination purse pack."

Rudy is transfixed by the images on the screen, tension draining from his bulk as if his fingers are spigots. Nerdy, head on the blotter, still heaving and gasping, gulps once, then again. Irises wide and black, pinned fatally on Rudy. But then, as if directed by some compelling force, his gaze shifts irresistably to the television, and stays there.

Day Twenty

MAIL CALL GOES OFF. When I get to the shop Buckethead's got it all sorted into neat stacks, already sniffing deep into a glossy porn rag called *Bounteous Babes*.

"Check out this one with the big birthmark on her boob. They call her Gorba-chest."

"There's writing in there, huh?"

"More than it needs."

Somebody once said carrier aviation is hours of tedium punctuated by moments of terror.

I flop into a chair, kick my boots on the desk in typical hero pose. Among bills and software catalogs is this strange-looking letter with no return address. But I don't even have time to wonder about it when the bos'n's pipe goes off long and shrill over the 1MC. We both freeze like deer in headlights waiting for the end of the whistle to see if it's an announcement from the Skipper, which would be okay since no effort's involved, or a fire drill, okay too since only the blackshoes would have to respond, or a man-overboard drill, just a muster and no biggie, or worst of all another general quarters, which under the best of circumstances is bad but after yesterday's near murder is an experience of particular loathing and dread.

"Damn, you'd think there was a war on," says Bucket over the GQ announcement which provokes a feeling in my stomach like the one you get hitting twelve and seeing Technicolor.

"Rudy get anything from his old lady yet?" I yell over the bells while grabbing my shit.

"The big *nada*."

"I'm heading for the ready room. You should, too."

"War War War," he chants. "Kill shoot sex fuck."

Generally the day before a portcall is like the day before Christmas vacation at school, all relaxed and everybody easy and just marking the hours to release. Not today. A full flight schedule, the Green Sheet's packed with drills of every flavor, tension thick and rubbery as chowhall Jell-O. There's that thing in the air wrapping us all up tight. Maybe it's just fear. But I'm thinking maybe it's more, something to do with that thing Mel was talking about, that thing we can't get outside of.

The ready room looks like an aardvark coffee klatch. All the O's in the squadron milling around smartly, mostly flight-suited, all gas-masked. Napoleon's fixing a pot of mud in the industrial ready-room hundred-cup percolator which looks like Robby the Robot from *Forbidden Planet*. I decide I like old Napoleon. He's nonthreatening. These days that's maybe enough to get on my A-list. And there's the horse thing which gets me in the gut in a way I don't understand. There's something real about it though and I'd like to have it for myself. Maybe I should start eating film emulsion. I give him a what's-up smack on the shoulder. He jerks like something awful touched him, spilling coffee grounds on the green tile deck. He's probably sensing that whacked-out manic craziness I'm still oozing from the shop scene yesterday. Or that other craziness I'm just oozing all the time. He's on his knees, scooping up coffee and whining *I'm-sorry-sirs* like some horse-whipped dog. He sees it's me and relaxes.

"You look good in a mask," I say. "Very natural."

"Damn, Petty Officer Bender. Ya scared holy hell outta me." *A cared oly ell outta me.*

"Why so twitchy?"

"Shoot." He rolls back on the balls of his feet, preface to a whinefest. "Everbody's down on me today. Must be Kick-an-Airman Day or something. Hold this?" I squat down making a dustpan from a flight schedule. "First thing, I come in this morning and the XO's on his knees sniffing the deck like a dog."

"I can't hear you. Hold your snout up."

He recons over his shoulder and leans in close. "I ask if there's something I could help out with. Thought he maybe lost something, I dunno. He goes bal*listic*. Gets me right down with him and jams my face right there in the deck and yelling all buggy that I waxed the deck with a sour swab, *smell that deck, sailor,* he says, *that's waxed with a sour swab.* What *is* a sour swab?" I shrug. Napoleon brushes grounds from his hand. "So now I have to stay after the movie tonight and strip the whole deck and rewax and buff."

"What's the movie?"

"*Flying Tigers*, 1942 — John Wayne skippers a squadron of misfit mercenary pilots against Japan in pre-WWII China. Paul Kelly, John Carroll, Anna Lee, Mae Clark. 101 minutes. Colorized."

I shitcan the grounds and redo the dustpan for the last of it.

"Big deal," I say. "So the XO's in a shitty mood. Tomorrow I'll buy you a beer at the Shark's Cove, salty old aircrewman den of vice and horror."

"Take you up on it. *If* I live that long. Been getting my ass bit at all day. The SDO, the CO, everyone's shitting on me. They're all crazy, this whole ship's gone crazy." He gets the last of it and we both straighten up. "Got back at the XO, though."

"Yeah, how?"

"Can I trust you?"

"No."

"When I was cleaning the coffee cups I wiped my dick inside his."

"Well done."

"Thanks. I creamed it really good. I mean *really* good."

I take a seat in the back to read my mail. A flight brief's going on down front and the crew is huddled at the CVIC monitor. Our intel officer Mister Simpson is giving one of his cut-up weather/intel briefs. He's done up like a Kuwaiti sheikh — white robe, white towel raghat, Ray-Bans on his 'vark with a little black mike taped to the snout. He points at a chart of the Middle East with an empty champagne bottle.

"Sheikh Omar reporting from my Bentley in front of the Sharper Image Disco on the beautiful Côte d'Azur. Baghdad's cooking tonight and our own four-star chef Norm the Storm's dishing it out. More storms — storms, hell — fiery, shattering blizzards of airborne savage death and mayhem cascading down all day with a front of B-52s hurtling in from the south followed by unending widowmaker waves of A-7s, F-18s, Harriers, and gashing, rending squalls of F-117As shredding in by early evening. Mutilation, immolation, purest bleakest horror plummeting from the vast desert sky and continuing through the burning harrowing night and the next night and the next until the cradle of civilization, Sumeria, Akkadia, Babylonia, Mesopotamia, home to Gilgamesh and Tammuz, Cyrus and Sargon the Great, is bombed into a smoldering pre-cuneiform Stone Age cinder. It's Armageddon, folks. Joy to the gas-guzzling Western world. I love the smell of napalm in the mosques. We should all thank our lucky stars and stripes to be part of it. More Tomahawks gusting, sweeping, marauding in from the Gulf. Tornado watch in effect for suburban areas, trailer parks and baby milk factories. This just in. Traveler and refugee alert: airfields socked in by Rockeye steel rain. Stay clear of anything with the mildest semblance of transportation. It could blow to searing quarklets any time: planes, tanks, trucks, minivans, skateboards, baby carriages. Watch your Middle Eastern asses. Highway advisories for anyone headed for Syria. Take along those white flags and flak jackets for the kiddies. Farther west in Israel, mild with the occasional Scud drizzle and a possibility of chemi-cal biological agents. Gives new meaning to the term acid rain. Ha-ha. Down south the folks in Riyadh can expect the same. Next up our special fashion report. Accessorizing your chemical retardant suit."

Down front the Skipper shifts his glance from the cadre of 'varked department heads and buttsuckers, including the Chief, gathered round his gaudy, lightning-bolted, ready room chair/throne to ask in his fake-folksy voice of no one in particular, "What, I ask you, *what* in blue quivering blazes is tickling the ass of our trusty intelligence officer now? XO?"

"Yes, Skipper."

"Let's schedule an attitude-readjustment talk with the good *Left*enant Simpson. Humor is one thing but moderation is a man's best friend. Moderation in all things. And a rack inspection. Handle that, XO. I'll want a full report on the material condition of his bedding."

"Photos, Skipper?"

"Photos may or may not be necessary. I'll leave that to your savvy dis-cretion. You can tell a lot about a man from his rack. The Chief here can back me on this one. Wouldn't you say that's true, Chief?"

"That's a-firm-titty, sir." Chief Mattick, gangly, smoker-skinned and baby-condor ugly. I always expect him to say yuk-yuk like some Looney Tunes hick parody. "Rack's a covert electronic all-weather infrared, laser-guided detector of a man's soul."

"Very colorful, Chief. We'll put that wisdom in the POD, share it with the men. Note that, Admin. How's it go again, Chief?"

"That's a-firm-titty."

"The other."

"A man's rack is a high-tech wire-guided stealth-delivered missile to his perfidious soul."

"You're the poet laureate of the squadron, Chief."

"Roger that, sir."

Suddenly I remember a dream I had last night where I checked out a video and kept it too long. I was terrified, so terrified I woke up covered in sweat, my sheets damp, hair slicked to my forehead, my skivvies so wet I couldn't tell if it was sweat or piss. I mean SCARED.

The mask is burning and itching so I know I'll be sprouting zits right on the edge of my chin or that crevice where my nostril hooks into my face. Just in time for portcall. I'm going through my mail again when I come across that letter, a pink envelope with doves on the flap. It's addressed to me at the FPO in this unfamiliar but very female-looking hand. Postmarked two weeks ago from San Diego. I'm about to open it when I hear this 'varky voice over my shoulder. ". . . I want dog-fucking and your sweaty loins against my ass. I want your hot, dirty breath in my ear hissing squirm bitch, Daddy's fat cock up your bloody animal whore cunt piss and shit and filth you slimy fuckwoman like that time in your Firebird and oooh! I'm so wet here on my bed with Jocko's paws on my ass and I have to touch myself thinking of you baby and your big swollen manly cock shooting my mouth full of your fishy spunk jism coconut milk. . . ."

I twist around and it's Dumchowski, I can tell by his potato sack girth, reading a letter to Buckethead. Dumchowski's arm is draped around Buckethead like old buddy. That's how you can tell a zero is on the skids, when he hangs with the enlisted types.

"She is *so* hot for my bod," he confides to Bucket in that dim braggy voice that is not improved by his 'vark.

"Yeah?" Bucket, lurid as all get out.

"Oh, man. She's bug crazy for flight suits. I wear my zoombag and she's on me like stink on shit."

"She give face? I love face."

"Mouth like buttered velvet."

"Got any pictures?"

"Yeah, shit yeah, boy." He pulls one from the envelope. "A new batch every letter. This isn't the best one but the rest are going around back at the jungle."

"Nice tah-tahs, sir." Bucket's practically licking the photo. "Can I keep it?" Then like Peter Lorre in a 'vark, "I wan' to have my way weeth eet." He sees me watching, rolls his eyes behind the lens like can-you-believe-this-sap. Dumchowski, in that excited pathetic show-offy way, just can't stop going on. "Yeah, sure, I don't care. I got hundreds, and video too."

"I really get off on pictures."

"I know what you mean, I like whipping it to a picture much as anyone."

"I like it better than real fucking. It's not so messy and you don't hafta give a shit about anyone but your own self."

"I hear you. I love Kelly here and everything. I mean I love the shit out of her. We're getting married after the cruise. But what you're saying. Sometimes I just like to put on one of our videos and pound it and let her watch. She really gets off on that. She loves watching."

"Me, too."

"I don't think anything heats her quicker than watching me jack off to a video."

"Any video?"

"It's gotta be her. She teaches grade school. You know, expects to be the center of attention."

"What's she doing in the video?"

"Which one?"

"The one she's watching you jack off to."

"*Jacking off,* man. That's the great part. Feeling herself up all over and sticking her finger in there and everything, man, just *everything.* We have videos of her watching me watch her on the video."

"Wow. Auto-eroticizing. I saw it in *Penthouse.* But I guess that'd be more like auto-auto-auto-eroticizing."

"Man, she goes crazy watching those, strumming that clit like a banjo. Probably had one on when she was writing me."

"I'd *kill* to see *that.*"

Old Dumchowski gives him the elbow. "I got a video. I'll bring it down. But only you, okay. I don't want a bunch of jerks getting off on my old lady."

"Wow, cool sir." Bucket strokes the photo like I'm afraid to imagine what. "Can I ask a personal question, sir?"

"Shoot."

"She ever do it with Jocko?"

The letter's got to be from a woman. But who? I hold the pink envelope to the filter and inhale deep. Nothing. I lift up my 'vark and tuck the envelope under my nose. ZOOM, I'm off the ship and someplace with overstuffed pillows and powders and those little bags of dry flowers women put in their drawers. The letter's on this old lady stationery with the same doves as the envelope. The writing is all flowery and loopy and like from another time. Then I realize it's because I never see anything handwritten anymore. The last page is signed by someone named Anita Esperanza. I have to think before realizing it's Rudy's old lady.

After we secure from general quarters I start walking. Up and down ladders, some steep as cliffs, some angled gentle like stairways in plush houses you only see on TV. I go through dozens maybe hundreds of hatches, chromed and sparkly or white and polished in Officer Country or black and dented and dirty down in the engineering spaces. I pace myself in long passageways, three steps and a high-stride over a kneeknocker, another three, another high-stride over a kneeknocker, polished steel, or painted red or blue or green or rusted brown, through Zebra fittings and Yoke fittings and X-ray fittings and Circle-William fittings, through ammunition spaces with yellow dollies stacked high with bright missiles or textured olive-drab five-hundred-pounders strapped to steel pallets, past the ship's store, our little hope chest of corporate logos, plastic-wrapped Fruit-of-the-Loom T-shirts and skivvies and colorful rows of cigarette cartons: Camel, Winston, Marlboro, Salem, Merit, a Hallmark rack of pathetic greeting cards, Cricket lighters, Polaroid film in sizes no existing camera uses, then past the chowhall where a guy in a grey T-shirt (Fruit-of-the-Loom?) and a white paper chef hat is sawing a block of fat-covered beef on a table saw, past medical where a sign on the door reads *STD test 0600-1000, line forms port,* the MarDet where another sign reads *Iraq, Iraq, We'll Bust Your Back,* up to the foc'sle cavernous and eerie in its spotlessness, ceremonial painted decks and bulkheads and anchor chain with links curled like frightened boys laid end to end. And everywhere the bulkheads crowded with pipes and wiring harnesses and red fire stations coiled with firehose, yellow boxy battle lanterns, mysterious bulging cabinets sprouting conduit, hand-crank valves, brass fittings, OBA lockers, greasy cable and cockeyed stanchions and plates and sprinklers, gauges measuring pressure or temperature or capacity in some unknowable vessel, a plastic trash bag hanging scrotum-like to catch condensation from a cold air duct, and more pipes, everywhere pipes, the veins and arteries of the ship moving critical fluids and gases up, around and through the steel body, skinny snaky ones and plump lumbering ones — chill water in, chill water out, auxiliary steam, AFFF, JP-5, fire, hydraulic, air exhaust, supply, salt water, and always, in every space onboard, the 1MC speaker hardwired in.

I'm trying to lose myself. I don't dwell anywhere. Keeping on the move till I figure I've gone about a mile which seems a good distance. Takes me a while what with all the ladders and the dead ends and backtracking. But finally I'm down somewhere on what I think is the sixth deck, under the waterline. I stop in this dead-end passageway somewhere near the evaporators — valves and pressure gauges galore. And pipes. I try picturing myself in relation to the ship. A game I play sometimes. I construct the ship in my mind — lay the centerline, the ribs and frames, the decks, then imagine where I am in that three-dimensional model rotating in my mind like those 3-D computer imaging systems. CAD.

But I can't stay focused. I reach for the letter. Suddenly I'm hypersensitized, like my fingertips grew eyes. I feel every muscle in my arm, every knuckle on my fingers. I rebutton the pocket, smooth it against my butt. I trace a water pipe, dimpled with enamel paint, cool and fleshy. I take out the sheets. Feel every fiber of the paper, the texture magnified a million times so it's like a relief map. That handwriting, the blue ink, curves and slopes and crosses. I sniff the letter and again I'm away. I want to keep sniffing, keep snorting up the delicious woman-scent like a drug but I'm afraid I'll suck up every molecule and there won't be any left.

She says she's sorry to bother me but I'm Rudy's best friend and she trusts I'll do the right thing. She's leaving Rudy and she doesn't want him to know where she's gone. She's got all his stuff in storage. He shouldn't bother her mother because Mom doesn't know where she is. She hates to do it this way but she's afraid. She's a coward and a bitch and all fucked up inside. Rudy probably won't care anyway but just get mad since that's all he knows how to do but that's not true he can be a big teddy bear when he wants but he just can't stay straight and his moods are all over and she can't deal with him anymore and hopes he understands she doesn't want anything bad to happen to him but she just can't be with him ever again no matter what and she can't write to him direct because she's too much of a chickenshit and she tried maybe twenty times and drunk or sober it just wasn't any good so she's doing it this way. She doesn't want forgiveness but just to be left alone and not bothered. And finally she's asking me to do this because I seemed nice and something about that story about my cousin in the carport lockers touched her and she remembers it every now and again.

I fold up the sheets, slip them into my pocket. Go back to locating myself on the ship. I lay the centerline again, the ribs, the frames, the decks. But it gets too complicated. I try to keep it simple but details pile up. A hundred eighty frames aft to fore, too many to picture. Three decks above the hangar bay and another six? in the superstructure. Is it nine decks below the hangar bay or nine decks below the waterline? I know where the chowhalls go, and the shop, and the ready room, and berthing, and the ASWMOD, and the paraloft, and maintenance control, but where's the library go? The gym? CVIC? Where's the void where Mel's class meets? The MAA shack with the porn chief bricked in by hardcore cassettes? I can't localize me until I localize them. It's too big. The patterns aren't clear enough.

Then there's the net (more like a web), my place in the electronic eyeball dimension — hundreds, thousands of microwave tethers hooking me to satellites, dishes, ships, airplanes, spy installations, submarines. Subjects and objects, targeters and targets, victims and aggressors — Dan Rather, Wolf Blitzer, my Madonna-babe, Nerdy's whale, the fat artsy chick from downstairs, the girl with the shades in her Jap ragtop, Tamara, the cabby in San Diego. And now Anita. Where am I relative? Vectoring threads bursting and reeling from my belly, arcing across oceans and continents and into space, monofilament ballistic trajectories tracking me through time and distance, through dimensions that don't even have names, like one of those telephone commercials with the worldwide global network map — *Reach out and touch someone.*

The impossibility of placement.

I think about tomorrow when we pull in. Our last port before we're off to the Gulf, to this thing which may or may not be a war. I list all the things I want to do: drink beer in a quiet place with pretty waitresses, snorkel out at Grande Island, see a movie in town at the ancient firetrap theater, maybe a massage, a real one, a steak dinner at the P.O. Club. . . .

But the thing that really gets me, that imposes over and over even though it's about dull as dirt but still the one thing I really truly in my heart of hearts desire: I want to have my laundry done. I want the stink of the boat steamed and soaped from my clothes. I want clean clothes pressed and folded and tied with white twine, bundled and wrapped in cellophane.

I want clean clothes.

SIX

Olongapo

Day Nineteen

BY THE TIME liberty's called away and I plod the long snaky hangar bay lines of fevery desperation, finally get my chance to ask permission to go ashore — which still knots me with authority resentment — salute the ensign and trudge down the steep slick brow, the Subic dock is a sizzling nest of franticness. Cranes and forklifts and overloaded pallets, scurrying Filipino Ship Repair Facility workers, liberty hounds like me, shore patrol initiates shoving, pushing, heaving in conflicting vectors. It's survival of the pushiest. And me loaded down and bulky with my bulgy laundry bag and camcorder smacking and getting smacked by everything and everyone.

Finally I get my laundry dropped off. I tell the girl extra bleach on the whites and my name embroidered on all my dungees. An extra buck apiece but I don't care. The sight of the laundry ticket fills my heart with joy.

I'm shooting some dock action when my sweep is arrested by a solitary figure standing out from the man-machine mayhem. Hunched, scruffy, manic, bent by a shapeless pack and shrunk into a faded fan T-shirt with a crucified Elvis and a spattered band name: *Immaculate Infection*. What makes him stand out in this calamity of intersecting lines is his directionlessness, his utter lack of momentum and trajectory. In this confab of forward motion he's not GOING anywhere, just slowly revolving on a worn sneaker, wearing this golly-gee look that'd translate to victim in any metro-center, fluorescent with sensory overload, eyes oscillating at max scan. Like a kid just off the bus, or no, what really comes to mind is a waltzing mouse, this kind of mutant mouse with a genetic inner-ear defect that makes him spend a lifetime on hind legs shuffling out a retarded dance. A hyper waltzing mouse.

"First time in the P.I., Mel?" Fearing he could fly into shock, like waking a sleepwalker. Those Ping-Pong ball eyes zooming and careening. But he's stopped revolving so I figure he knows I'm here.

"The air's density," he says all blissed. "So heavy, organic. And that aroma. Straight from the Pleistocenian sauce."

"Yeah, it's kinda generic to this side of the world. Cross between wood smoke, sewage and rotting fish heads."

"Delicious."

"'Sokay I guess."

He's headed townward. It'd be manslaughter to let him out there alone so I offer to show him around.

On our way to the main gate he gets to talking — or ranting or rhapsodizing or spontaneously combusting. Tells me he's cadging a hop from Hickam back to the States, prattling on like he thinks the Air Force is TWA, in-flight movies and drink carts. I try steering him right.

"Last time I tried getting a hop outta here I spent five days and nights on a waiting room bench with no place to wash and nothing to eat but stale Fritos. My reward was a fourteen-hour hop in a stretch C-131, canvas jumpseats, no heat and a dB level that'd deafen a heavy metal band. And there wasn't even a war on."

"Is this a war?"

I shrug. "Who knows?"

"Don't you?"

"Don't *you*?"

"Since you ask . . ." He looks around all covert like. "It's a diversion."

I look around, too. "From what?" I whisper.

"Diversion *from*?" He chews this while stubby fingers caress the anguished Elvis. "Yes. Well. What makes us long for something to be diverted *from*? A sweet implication of causality. An anachronistic and binary notion. We could discuss the fusion of subject and object. But the plain dirty fact is this: There is only diversion and this is one. A spectacle for our entertainment. It's an attraction at Universal Studios." Mel stops to eyeball a lizard hide of a used condom, turns it with his foot. "But the flight imbroglio, what do you suggest?"

"Hole up somewhere comfy-cozy till the fleet pulls out, then head to Manila for a commercial hop."

"That would be preferable, the American way. Hot and cold running indulgence."

"Why not?"

He sighs. "Financial snafu. My paychecks haven't caught up with me. Lost in the cyber-cash trons of some multinational virtual transaction network."

"You're broke."

"I am not liquid."

"You're solid."

"Flat on my ass."

I blurt it without even thinking. "You can stay with us if you want. In town. We threw together for a suite." Rudy's idea. Normally I don't do the squid-bucket communal liberty thing but I'm not so liquid myself and the dives in Olongapo are too divey even for me. Just try getting a TV in this place.

The whole world alters as we pass through the revolving iron porcupine gate from the base to the bridge, that brief limbo between two worlds. I can feel the transition in my ligaments, under my fingernails. A feeling that excites and terrifies me, blood in motion, honing edges in ways I don't have words for. Can you feel things that don't have words?

"What is this?" Mel asks, pointing to the motionless murky, oil-sheeny river.

"Shit River. Guess you can smell why they call it that. Separates the base from the town."

"A moat," he says. "Welcome to the kingdom!"

We stop halfway across the bridge, trellised with razor wire, gaze down at the pretty girls standing balanced in bonka boats offering to flash pubescent tits for coins. The air is damp, rank with bacteria and virus. Mel is taken by the coat-hanger-and-pantyhose nets they cadge the change with, and by the fact of their never really giving up any tit.

"Canny marketing strategy."

"Local spin on bait and switch."

I like how they giggle when they're supposed to pay up so I video. There's one that's real animated, cracking up and mugging — you know she loves getting over on these retreads who think they're Donald Trump just because their fat American pay is twenty times the Philippine national average. When she sees the camera she strikes this Marilyn vamp pose. Or maybe it's a Madonna-doing-Marilyn vamp pose. I zoom her. Then I toss some change. She earned it.

I'm The Donald.

Soon as we're off the bridge and onto Magsaysay we're swarmed by hustlers, beggars and pimps. One guy keeps calling me his "friend" and wants to buy my camcorder. I yank Mel from another badgering him into a poker game at some undisclosed location identified only as "over dere." Then a kid about twelve who wants to arrange a two-on-one with his mother, guaranteed virgin. Olongapo humor. I teach Mel to say *ende*, Tagalog for no, and push on. Then both of us are chopping and waving our arms and *ende*ing all over until another bunch of victims or victimizers or whatever we are comes off the bridge and the hustler-cluster shifts to them. Then past the moneychangers where the girls behind Plexiglas bang combs on steel counters yelling *Best rate here; Change money here; Buy pesos for your honey-ko.*

We tour the town, up Magsaysay to the traffic circle by Jolo's where they show eight-millimeter movies of women getting humped by German shepherds and where old whores pussy-drink beer on stage, then down by Marilyn's where Mama-san hands out business cards reading *Marilyn's — World Famous Blow Jobs.* Still early so the bars are mostly closed and the few that aren't are pretty dead. In one, stinking of puke and a million last-nights' beers, mirror ball hanging dusty and still like a dead planet, the bar girls are sleeping it off, flopped all over duct-taped Naugahyde booths like harbor seals, raccoon-smeared mascara and still done up in their party-girl outfits, glittery petro-fabrics, sad as old wedding cakes.

But what Mel gets off on is the smattering of corporate franchises: Dunkin Donuts, Kentucky Fried Chicken, Shakey's Pizza.

"Logo-virus," he says.

"Yeah, and there's an impressive HIV rate, too."

We get off Magsaysay, up and down alleys and side streets: rattan and wicker, pawnshops, sari-sari stores with live chickens and sagging rice sacks, salted fish, dusty canned goods, Spam, Niblets corn, racks of colorful tabloids, and coolers of San Miguel and Cokes in old-fashioned returnable bottles.

Mel buys a Coke from a dehydrated old guy in cut-off Calvin Kleins.

160

When he drains it he eyeballs the bottom of the greenish bottle, runs his thumb across it like you would an old coin, then shows me. Nome, Alaska, it says in letters swollen from the glass.

On leaving he buys a handful of tabloids, stuffs them in his backpack.

We go deeper, back where the locals own the streets. The suburbs. Clusters of tin-roofed block hovels surrounding a single water-spouting pipe, naked babies crawling in the dust, streams of sewage cutting gullies along path-size streets laid down in WWII-vintage pierced-steel planks, mottled and rusted and half-reclaimed by the jungle. Through glassless windows and doorless doorways you can see bleak bareass interiors, bamboo mats the only furnishing. A teenage girl suckling a baby uses her free hand to sweep with a bundle of palm fronds. She sees us and smiles. I smile back trying not to gawk at her breast. Then I see the black foam of the earphones poke from beneath her hair, the wire snaking down to the black case on her hip, the turning spindles of the cassette.

Mel says, "Why not tape some? Local color."

"No, thanks."

A crowd of toughs grouped near an old busted-axle hulk of a jeepney starts giving us looks. Mel is oblivious. I steer us back for Magsaysay.

"Always remember, men kill. Men kill because of sex. Sexual energy is creative energy is destructive energy. Shiva is the Creator *and* the Destroyer. Yin *and* Yang. But that's mythology and mythology is psychology and psychology is dead as obsidian."

We're sitting in Pizza Hut doing permanent damage to a pitcher of imitation Budweiser while the withered picked-at cadaver of a fake pizza (smothered in fake cheese and a generous topping of the unrealest meat you could imagine) curls and congeals in mockery before us. Mel's doing war talk. I think. He insisted on coming here even though I told him it was horrible and not like a real Pizza Hut. Rudy calls the pizza here an abortion on a cracker, which in my estimation is a compliment.

"Yeah," I say, tracing lines in the condensation on the pitcher. Jungle light slashes the table at oblique angles. "I guess everything's about sex one way or another."

Mel pulls out the tabloids and starts going through them. One is called *Scandals, Gossips And Intrigues*. "Look at this," he says. "Look at the language — an amalgam of Tagalog, English and a smattering of Spanish. *While all the others nga naman from the press seem to sympathize with Kool-Koo-Koo Juices making him appear as the contravida, siguro, the singer feels he ought to be heard. Tamawag kami sa kanilang Cainta residence, kaaalis lang daw ni Boyo (Miguel's nickname).*" He lowers the paper. The pinballs are going. "It's a living semio-historic document. Cultural, economic, political. The whole," he sputters, "colonial and pre-colonial continuum is here."

I'm thinking of videoing the pizza when I'm overwhelmed by this on-slaught of thoughts. They pour down from all sides, from some place I didn't know was in me. Like Mel planted something that just went off. I have to say it, say it all, but it would take twenty mouths to talk it all out. Like the hand-held calculator of my brain was just clunking along when somebody flicked a switch and suddenly it's some huge super-computer processing a zillion data-bits a nanosecond. And all of it just has to come out RIGHT NOW even though there's no way to get it all lined up. It's gotta go.

"It just seems like there's so much *shit.*" I hear myself rant in some-body else's whiney voice, not caring if Mel is listening, not sure Mel is ca-pable of listening. "Not that it's all shit but just that there's so MUCH of it. It's on me all the time. Like everything exists at once, like the whole of everything from time zero, everything that ever existed is in your face ev-ery second of every day. I can't tell it apart. There's *I Love Lucy* and there's *Roseanne* and I can't tell them apart, I can't tell which one's modern and which one's old. I mean I *can* but only on a thinking level, in my gut they're both the same, like there's no time in between them, like all that time is smashed together so they're somehow equalized in history. Like in school and you had those timelines of history and there was the Trojan War and a couple inches later there was King Arthur and a couple inches later the Norman Conquest and a few inches later there was Mozart and then Napoleon and then the American Revolution and the Civil War and World War One and World War Two. It was like a long string and you could see it all at once and where everything fit. This came before that and that after this. It was organized. But now it's like the string is wadded up in a ball that you're trapped inside of and all of this history revolves around your head all the time, like pictures projected inside a ball and there's no order at all. They just exist, all at once, all the time. Like there goes Larry, Moe, and Curly Joe, and there's Eddie Murphy, and there's Walter Cronkite — *And that's the way it is* — and look over there at old Amelia Earhart waving from the cockpit and Khrushchev pounding his shoe and Boy George and butt-ugly Honest Abe and Mary Tyler Moore tossing her hat in the air and Charlie Manson with a swastika between his eyes and Bogart puffing a butt and David Letterman and Mussolini with his funny hat and puppy-eyed Twiggy and four-eyed Buddy Holly and sheet-wrapped Gandhi and Joltin' Joe and Einstein and Hitchcock in porky profile and nerdy Benny Goodman and Sid Vicious and Charlie Chaplin bow-legged with a rubber cane and Neil Armstrong on the moon and Madame Curie and dipshit Gilligan and bulldyke Queen Victoria and Mickey Mouse and Michael Jackson with his stupid glove."

"He makes an appeal to concerned agencies to act with speed kung may mga ganitong pangyayari."

"Used to people just didn't have to deal with all this. Things were discrete. Lines on a gram. You could sort it all out. There's this war thing and that's something to be scared of. But in the old days people went off to war, and they were scared then, too. But at least they didn't know what to be scared *of*. I know what's out there. I know how many troops there are and what equipment they have and how experienced they are. I know where they're dug in. If I wanted I could access satellite intel, see them shitting in their helmets, reading their Korans, eating their yogurt. I know the specs on their weapons, even when they're not OUR weapons. But despite all that, or maybe *because* of all that, I also know I could be vaporized in a micro-second and not know what hit me. The information might not save me. It might be useless. After a point it's not even information. Just stuff. Stuff crowding my head. Random bits without a sequence — no cause and effect. And I'm scared. Now they're talking the GROUND WAR. That's when it all's gonna REALLY break loose. Like *Cover your six, the ground war's a-comin'.* Fuckin-A right I'm scared shitless." Getting really worked up now, dragged along by some whacked momentum. "But I was scared BEFORE. I was scared before there was a war to be scared of."

"Organic fear," says Mel. "It's imbedded in the genetic material. The death of the organic is nigh. The image is the new dominant species. Images replicate without sex. A million years from now images will be asking themselves what cataclysm befell organic life the way we ask what happened to the dinosaurs."

I have to ignore him. I just can't stop. "It's like this big weight we carry around and you see it on everyone else's back but not on yours. You know about THEIR fear but not your own. You don't even know it's *there* let alone how it's working you. Where's it come from? Where's it all come from? And all this data, this information, this SHIT. Why do I have to know about it all? I mean secret sex lives of the stars? Nuclear bombs in South Africa? The Sudan has 1,009 spoken languages? J. Edgar Hoover running around in drag? Some guy in Wyoming jacking off to kiddy porn or Jodie Foster or Barbara Bush? The Japanese have a sanitary napkin named for Anne Frank? Baby M, Baby X, Baby Y, Baby Z. Why do I know this? If a bear shits it's on CNN, if a pop idol buys a shirt it's on *Entertainment Tonight*. I don't need it. I don't need ninety percent of what I know. And it's not like this stuff is sitting around passively, only there when I go looking for it. It's shoved in my face. It's all over. You can't get away from it."

"A study by, quote, a major university exposed a direct correlation between the number of television hours viewed per week and the number of locks on the front door." Mel plucks a turdish bit of non-meat from the non-pizza, examines it, pops it in his mouth. "Who'd ever think there's a market for massacre movie *na noong una'y walang nangahas na gumawa?*"

"It's all there. All the time. Static. Noise. It's too much. Overload. Then there's times I'm *not* afraid. It happens for just a few minutes and it's like my mind, my whole everything just lights up, blossoms, and I know and feel all this stuff I don't normally know and feel. Pictures, smells, faces, feelings. A moment of perfect clarity. This other kind of knowing. The way my mom covered her mouth when she laughed, how Mister Buchanan clapped his hands and sang *Cinco Minutos* in Spanish class, the oil and metal shavings smell of Dad's pickup. Like this whole part of my brain is only accessed when the fear is gone so that most of the time I don't even know this stuff's there. But as long as I'm bombarded with this, this *shit* I can't get to that part of me that's so much bigger than what I normally am. Like being in shock and your body only pumps blood to the vital organs. It's like that, except I'm in it *all the time*. I'm in this kind of overload shock *all the time*." Then this thing comes to me and even though I don't know for certain what it means, I know it's real. "If *everything* exists then *nothing* exists."

Mel swallows, picks another tidbit. "Twenty percent of the American population believe the Holocaust didn't happen. Twenty-five percent believe the moon landing was a hoax. Thirty percent believe President

Kennedy is a vegetable leading a happy, drooling existence in a secret sanitarium in Dallas. Half that believe he never existed. A group of Mormon mystics believe Armageddon took place in 1978, the world was destroyed, and what they now see around them is an elaborate hologram maintained by the surviving Chinese government buried in bunkers peppering Mount Everest."

"And *I'm* part of it. I'm somebody else's information, part of *their* overload. Some satellite paparazzi's aiming at *me*. Whose Nightly News am I on? What Iraqi Barbara Walters is droning on about *my* bowel movements?"

I'm surprised when Mel looks up. I think I have his attention. "There was a time when people, call them the skinny-tie people, watched you, watched me, watched everything and everyone. There was febrile anxiety, life-giving paranoia. These people watched because they wanted something — information, product, money, power. Now the watching is done for its own sake. No desired end, no motive except to watch. It is not even done by people. No purpose, no agent. It is just watching and it is everywhere. It makes us behave, keeps us neutralized as threats. Threats against what? Just threats. Only the watching counts. Not who is or who does. Just the watching."

"And I'm part of it."

"Of course."

Then the horrible thing comes to me. "So if everything exists at the same time and because of that nothing exists then . . . I don't exist."

He scribbles in a little pad, a juicy tidbit about some Filipina movie star. "A famous writer once said, if you're lucky your fiction is life, but whether you like it or not your life's a fiction. *Bakit tila walang halos bumabatikos kay Robbie Tan?!*"

"So then the only thing I've got, the only thing that's real, that I can hold onto, that I can point at and count on and hold in my hand like a stone — the only thing there is, is FEAR. That fear that's everywhere and nowhere, sourceless and pathless like ambient noise in the ocean."

"Ambient fear, yes. Nicely put. Free-floating hyper-anxiety. As true as anything. Here on the inside that is all we have, the amniotic fluid in which we are suspended." He slurps his beer, cranes around unnaturally, eyeballs scooting, then locks onto me. "Isn't that enough?"

I take off my shades, lay them on the plastic checkered tablecloth. Rub my eyes. The light hurts. There are suspicious motes in the air. I re-don my shades.

"*Kesyo naglalarawan ito ng karahasan, kesyo kina-capitalize lang ng mga producer ang mga hapless victims of such violent acts, et cetera, et cetera.*"

Day Eighteen

"KNOW WHY DOGS lick their cocks?"

Rudy's in high spirits. Very entertaining while we wait on our Desert Storm Combos — Patriot burgers and Smart Bomb fries.

"'Cause they can, that's why. Haw-Haw. Tell you I saw a guy who can suck himself off? Bucket woulda loved it."

"Sure it *wasn't* Bucket?"

I'm trying to be normal but it's hard what with Anita's letter burning through my hip pocket. I connived to meet Rudy at this slightly skewed imitation of an American franchised fake-fifties diner just to have a reasonably safe public and non-booze-serving setting so as to give me a possibility of survival after I spring the letter on him. Now I'm having second thoughts.

"Broke my record last night. You oughta be proud to be in my presence." There's a TV on a shelf behind the counter. Local soaps. A girl on a sofa is crying while an evil-looking matron done up like Joan Collins on the skids paces and harangues.

"Yeah? What record's that?" As if I couldn't guess.

"You should be kowtowing to the brown god."

"I should be working on my tan at the Cubi pool."

"You oughta be kissing my ring."

"I oughta be in pictures."

He holds his fat paw up with sausagey fingers spread. "Five! Five short-timers in one night!" Slams the hand on the counter. The cook at the grill in his white hat and greasy Harvard T-shirt jumps, mutters a curse.

"I set a goal, like in leadership training." He recites, "*Goals should *be specific and limited by a time frame. They should be challenging but realistic."* Rudy fans his shirt. I get a noseful of Paco Rabanne.

"Secret to upward mobility."

"I said to myself, Rudy you gotta knock 'em off one every ninety minutes. So I work backwards, all very methodical. Five bitches, hour and a half each. Half-hour for find-and-flatter, hour for fuck-and-forget. That's seven and a half hours."

"With lunch, that's a workday."

"It's tight but challenging. So then I figure I wanna be done by oh-two-hundred so I gotta start at eighteen-thirty, which is what I did. Boom! You shoulda seen me. I was a machine, man, picking off them LBFMs like plink-plink-plink." LBFMs. Little brown fucking machines. "Mama-san calls me the Latin Super Gun."

A commercial for a toothpaste called Tawas that cures cold sores, fever blisters and herpes simplex virus. I try to pay attention to Rudy but this is the first TV I've seen since we pulled in. It's hard to resist.

"You must be hurtin'."

"My dick's fucking carne asada."

The burgers show up and Rudy's is halfway down his throat while I'm still peeling the scary-looking cheese from mine. I mean what could it be? Yak cheese? I scrape off the body-fluidy sauce and toss the green tomato and brown lettuce. Figure I'll compromise and eat the bun and meat-looking patty.

"One hundred percent pure animal meat," reassures Rudy as he sucks grease from his fingertips. Then we start talking about the local bands who all do perfect imitations of American bands and actually play their songs live better than the real bands can.

"They're perfect and you know why? 'Cause they never see the real bands, except maybe on music videos. All they know is the recorded songs, they don't know there's any other way to play 'em. So they play the recordings over and over and get 'em down to a tee. It's bullshit when the real bands play in concert and don't sound like on the radio. I'm sitting there between rounds last night listening to that Styx song, you know, 'Come Sail Away'?"

"I remember it," I'm not proud to say. Sometimes I think we're all just walking archives of forgotten bands. I'm thinking maybe I don't want to spoil Rudy's good time. Maybe I should save it for after we pull out. Maybe I should just chuck it.

"It's a great song." He starts singing a little and I hurry up and say I know it so he'll stop. "So I'm taking a breather between number two and number three and they crank up this tune and Boom! I'm back home in La-La Land. I mean it sounds so perfect I coulda been in my truck cranking KCLX. And I'm seeing Styx, you know, mentally, that lead guy, whatsisname?"

"Oh, yeah, that guy," I lie while trying to bite my burger without looking at the meat stuff.

Rudy sees I'm not eating with gusto. He leans in and whispers, "Y'ever notice you never see any dogs or cats in this town."

Rudy picks up what's left of my burger. "Y'mind?"

"Help yourself." He wipes it in the pile of gook I scraped off and crams it in.

"So I'm jamming to the song, blissing out like I'm back home kicked back with a beer while the old lady's cooking up something good," the words sound-dampened through chewed burger. "When I open my eyes and see these five little long-haired squish-faced gooklets with guitars and shit hanging off 'em and me so stupid from balling and boozing I don't know *where* the fuck I am."

"Mel would call that a psychic rupture."

"That Mel guy, what a fucking twerp."

"He'd probably also say that creation is out and — what's a good Mel word? — *mimesis* is in."

"I'd like to mimeet him in a dark alley."

This is getting nowhere. I mean, when's a good time to boot a grizzly bear in the ass? Do grizzly bears still exist? I pull out Anita's letter and smooth it on the counter, slide it over to Rudy.

"Fucking *professor*, man. I mean what is *that*? What's the guy ever done but talk? Talk a bunch of bullshit. And we're supposed to respect 'em like they're fucking gods and shit. Guy's never done a day's work in his life."

"I think you should read this."

CNN international comes on. Danny Thomas died. Guess they better Make Room For Daddy at Forest Lawn. Three are crushed to death in an AC/DC concert in Salt Lake City. Iraq's still sneaking jets into Iran. About four a day. They fly very low and very fast. A Houston company is accused of arranging for poison gas sales to Hussein. The secretary of defense posing with a Bart Simpson doll dressed out in cammies.

The thirty-sixth Scud hits Israel, injures twenty-six in affluent Tel Aviv suburb.

I reach to put on my shades but they're already on.

I wish I was in a mall, a sprawling, polished, smooth-cornered mall. I like malls. I miss malls. I would ride escalators, watch pretty consumption-crazed girls gawk with desire at empty-faced mannequins, painted fake-gold and contorted in unhuman positions. Listen to the language of shopping, the sexy buzz and whir of credit transactions, penetrate an ATM with my card, watch it ejaculate cash into my waiting hand. I would buy something.

A wadded ball of paper bounces off the counter and onto my plate. Pink paper, blue ink.

The rumble: "This world's a fucking *shit* hole." I look at Rudy and I'm as scared as I've been in my life. He's on his feet and this horrible energy hits me in waves, shock waves off a concussion bomb.

His ears are wine red, big nostrils flaring. I think of my sunglasses pounded into shards, jammed into my eyes. He comes in close and huge, finger in my face like telling me the truest thing he knows, maybe the only thing he knows in the way you can sometimes only know one thing and sometimes not even that. So here he is burning my face like pressed up to a furnace and it rumbles out slow and deliberate and scary, "This-World-Is-A-Fuck-King-*Shit!*-Hole."

Then he flips over his plate on the counter and walks out.

Day Seventeen

DON'T KNOW WHOSE IDEA IT WAS to have a last-blowout-before-the-ground-war party. But by the time I jeepney out to the edge of town and mount the hotel's rickety plantation veranda I can tell it is out of control. I'm met by the manager, a frantic Gumby of a guy with a gold tooth and a very seventies burnt orange polyester suit with contrast stitching and patch pockets.

"You got to say to them to stop!" he half pleads, half demands.

"Stop what?" I'm answered by a wrecking-ball-magnitude crash from upstairs that shakes the whole building.

"That! That! They're wrecking my hotel!"

Closing on the room, it's like I feared. The rumble-tumble and slams gain amplitude. Sounds like all the violence of a Stanley Cup playoff, a Super Bowl and a Nordie's after-Christmas sale all rolled into one and squished into a very small space. I figure after yesterday it's gotta have Rudy at the root.

At the door I hear cheering, hooting, Roy Orbison wailing "Pretty Woman," then another seismic slam. Dust particles drift from the ceiling. More cheering.

Inside I pull a Rob Petrie pratfall on an empty San Miguel bottle. My screech doesn't pierce the stadium roar and nobody notices. The group at the far end of the suite, Nerdy, Bucket, Chief Mattick, a couple of mech-types whose names I don't know, and two bar girls, is parted in two with Rudy in between crouched like a bull. The crowd chants a count and Rudy takes off, head bowed, charging the wall. There's the crash and the building shudders again. Rudy yanks his head from the mortar-sized hole in the plasterboard, shakes off the dust and empties a huge red drink down his vast gullet while they all chant, MO-*JO*, MO-*JO*, MO-*JO!*

I count seven other craters lined up beside Rudy's latest addition.

Chief Mattick, cigarette smoldering from its permanent slip between the livery lips of a skullish, beef-jerky-upholstered face, gives Rudy an ooh-rah back-slap.

"Eight bull's-eyes and not a single stud. This Bud's fer yew!"

And of course he pulls out Rudy's pants and upturns a San Miguel down the waistband, all the time braying like a donkey.

I don't know how much of this Animal-Housey fun and games I can take. But weirdly enough I find that I sort of WANT to be around these genetic mistakes tonight. Seems like the comradely thing. We ARE off to war tomorrow. But there's something old-movie-ish about the whole thing, something Van Johnsony and Spencer Traceyish. Like everyone's trying their damnedest to live out every cliché ever splayed across the little screen in living black and white, some weird pantomime of wartime jocularity that somehow doesn't click.

I get up and test my twisted ankle. Rudy's on me, glad-handing me like a politician. A politician with a beer-soaked crotch that makes him look like the victim of one of those mines that blow off your balls. I'm surprised how cheery he seems, considering yesterday.

He drags over the two bar girls, Zenith and Sabrina, who I mistakenly call Serena.

"No, Sa-*breena*, like on Be-*weetch*. You know." She wiggles her nose. Sabrina has a big shiny forehead and sharp simian teeth.

The other one, Zenith, giggles. Zenith is tiny with deep-set charcoal briquette eyes. Three oversized Swatch watches hoop her pencil wrist. I say hello and she giggles again, covering her mouth.

I ask Sabrina if Zenith does anything but giggle. "Nope. Giggle is all," she says, shaking her head like a kid. Zenith giggles some more. Someone changes the tape to Jimmy Dean doing "Big Bad John."

Rudy wraps around them both, swallows them whole. "We're all playing tuna sandwich tonight, right girls?" he bellows. A squeeze and they both giggle some more like tromped-on baby dolls. "And I'm the tuna. Haw, Haw, Haw."

"Yes! Yes!" pipes Sabrina. "You are the tuna and I am the, um, the, um . . . I am the PICKLES!" A barrage of stomped on baby dolls.

"And Zenith is the, um . . ."

172

Tiny Zenith speaks for the first time. It's an anxious moment. I need to see if she sounds like someone's pulling a string in her back.

"Helper," she squeaks.

Sabrina is poised for another gigglesome outburst but, like me and Rudy, she doesn't get it yet.

Zenith grimaces at our thickness. She crosses her arms under milk chocolate Lycra-wrapped attitudinally adjusted breasts. "*Tuna* Helper," she huffs.

I break off and head for a brew.

I fish a San Magoo from the Igloo cooler. The bottle's sealed in ice, reminds me of the thing in *The Thing,* which is James Arness dressed as a monster which is really a carrot and discovered in the Arctic inside a block of ice. James Arness, I remember, is an actor who played Matt Dillon, who was an Old West marshal and not the other Matt Dillon who is an actor who plays New West disturbed youths. The original Matt Dillon, the one on radio even before the James Arness one, was played by William Conrad who is an actor known for being overweight and playing a television detective named Cannon.

I about rip off half the skin on my palm before realizing the cap isn't a twist-off. Talk about primitive. I'm fishing for an opener when Chief Mattick, who I figure is responsible for the Jimmy Dean (famous for hillbilly yodeling, famous for pork sausage) comes up.

"Try this."

He's got a church-key among the two pounds of keys and Swiss Army knife and tiny screwdrivers on a ring attached to one of those janitor things that zooms in and out like a tape measure.

"Thanks, Chief."

"Don't mention it." Back-zoom.

Suddenly I get a whiff of ganja and considering my proximity to an ate-up-to-the-max boot-licking authority figure I'm thinking I'd like to be elsewhere. I'm not too proud to admit fondness for my two measly chevrons. But Mattick's livery lips curl into what might pass on a reptile as a smile.

"Mmm-*mm*. Guess they're firing up the hemp. That'll give this party a kick-start."

I can't believe this guy.

"Don't worry 'bout me. I'm cool," he says.

I'm trying to picture old Mattick with twenty-five years of alcohol, caffeine and nicotine abuse washed from his parched complexion — a young Mattick draped in love beads and flipping a peace sign. All I get, though, is a skinny redneck with a cowlick and farmer tan, doit-dee-doiting on a tractor seat.

"What about the piss tests?"

He leans in real close. Emission of cigarettes and ingested beer. "Guess who's squadron piss-test security honcho when we pull out?" A sharp elbow jabs my sternum.

"Yup. Your old Chief's a-looking out fer ya. I figger in this time of doom and danger we all oughta have a good blowing out together, comrades in arms, that sorta thing. Hang together and hang low. Might be shitty out there with those sleazy sand niggers. Don't know what's gonna happen. Might get our butts blowed off. Who knows? But I know this; nobody's gonna say, whatever happens, nobody's gonna say any of my boys didn't get as much as they wanted of whatever they wanted irregardless of the UCMJ or right-wing Christian ethos. A man wants what a man wants and there's times he should just have it, no questions asked. Anybody thinks different can piss up a rope. Am I right or am I right?"

He takes a slug off his beer and I'm wondering how he does it without unplugging the cigarette. A neat trick. Then I wonder if he EVER unplugs them, or just lets them smolder in those ghastly lips till they're butts. Pall Malls.

Just then the door opens and my TACCO, Mister Dumchowski, comes in. He scans the room, gives me an unhearty wave, then slips over to join Bucket and the maintenance guys huddled around the source of the herb odor.

The Chief's going on about back before he was in the navy, a tank commander in the army, and how he ran an M-60 into a gully and smashed the barrel in the dirt, but him and the other guys were so fucked up and the Led Zeppelin blasting from the eight track and the heat of battle and all, nobody stopped to check out the damage. So when they got to the other side they let loose a round at the target and the whole barrel blew apart like an exploding cigar (cee-gar). And all the time he's relating this hilarious story of armor-head hi-jinx I'm wondering why he's telling me at all, why this total career guy who treats us like stepping stones to his next promotion is suddenly acting like we're old buddies swapping lies over a brew. I figure I'll squelch my suspicious nature and assume the best, assume he's just being decent and trying to make a little human contact.

"That's funny, Chief," I say, "Like something you'd see on TV." And there's this tick in his eyes, an AA burst over Baghdad.

"It *was,*" he says all proud. "It was *just* like something on TV. Just ex*ack*ly." And he's beaming, flat-out beaming. "As if a benevolent God of the airwaves had reached down and touched us shit-birds in our fifty-ton tank and made us *television.*"

The Chief drones on. Things drift in — a rooster crowing somewhere out in the barrio, Sabrina or Zenith outbursting a titter, a whiff of disinfectant and something fungusy. There's a thick, viscous coat of sweat on my throat that I can't seem to wipe away. I catch voices — *like a cueball, not a fucking hair on it* — any*body goes down,* every*body goes down — call 'em what you want, they're crispy critters when the balloon goes up — these nipples like cigarette butts — says to the waitress,* well, I reckon you've had worse in *your* mouth — *fucking nuke and we all go home — whole muzzle listing ten clicks starboard — chrome offa trailer hitch — blow their legs off or whatever, just go on welfare anyway — never stick in anything smaller'n your elbow.* . . .

The voices slip and slather into a hum ekeing up from behind. Just this hum starting out slow, like ambient noise, but moving up front, gaining amplitude, taking over till there's nothing left but IT. What's it telling me? Thank god for my shades or the Chief would see me fixed on the corner of his mouth which is jawing up and down like a fish, the corner where the white paper of the cigarette is partially soaked brown with spit, the lips glued to it so every time his mouth yawns the stuck skin stretches like a cartoon fly in glue. It's a comforting thing this hum, a thing I know, I'm on personal terms with.

The front door slips open and a nervous looking ball of unruly hair pokes in, does some scoping like checking for the all-clear. It's Mel and I use him as an excuse to dodge out on the Chief.

"Arrrr, Mel," I growl in my best salty-old-dog voice. "Beyond this door thar be monsters."

He waves me over looking surprisingly and profoundly drunk.

"I have a friend with me," he slurs. "Is it inconvenient?"

"You couldn't inconvenience this multicultural gathering with a car bomb."

He slips in towing, I am surprised to see, a stick skinny young thing, maybe eighteen, but more like fourteen passing for sixteen.

"Gee, Mel," I say as they slip in. "Didn't know you had kids over here."

"It is not what you think," he says. "I am interviewing her."

"I believe it. Nothing's ever like I think."

He introduces us with a grand flourish. She flashes a grin that no way belongs on that young face, a grin from a face that's been around the block a few times. A grin with an appetite.

"The din here is too much for our purposes. Would it be rude if we availed ourselves of one of the other rooms?"

"Better hurry. Rudy's got slathering plans for that pair of condiments he's towing around."

I get a fresh beer. Bucket and the two mechs are engaged in fitting Mister Dumchowski into a 'vark with a dope pipe screwed on. Bucket holds a match to the bowl and Dumchowski sucks for all he's worth. Eye-hole cutouts of face vanish behind a cloud.

"Gives new meaning to the term *gas mask*," snickers one of the mechs, a tall gangly guy with a pocked and dangerously stupid complexion.

"'Zat good, Lieutenant?" Bucket wheedles. "'Zat nice? So what about Kelly's asshole. Does she like it licked? Does Jocko lick it?"

The two mechs smirk at each other.

Smoke seeps from under the rubber. Pockface stifles giggles, pokes at Bucket to egg him on. Bucket shooshes him, trying to keep a straight face.

"Take another hit, sir," he prods. "Don't be a wimp."

Dumchowski claws at the mask trying for air. Bucket, eyes shiny slits in that parking lot of face, slaps Dumchowski's hand from the mask.

"I said, don't be a wimp. No wimpiness. Death to all wimps. Us big, bad Fighting Fucking Redtails can take it."

"And we can dish it, too," says Pockface, all fake serious.

Dumchowski takes another monstrous hit then loses it totally, explodes in a coughing fit. The mask comes ripping off and Dumchowski's bent double, hacking like he's about to die, face the color of raw steak. Holding his belly, choking and heaving, he staggers to the window where he frantically tries pushing out the ancient screen which just gives way in a rip. He shreds the thing in a frenzy before hanging out and barfing.

Bucket, laughing, picks up the mask and refills it from a Ziploc bag

176

crammed full. He offers me the bag. Very clean stuff. Says it's local, something they call Manga. I take a long whiff. Wet dirt.

Bucket hands me the 'vark. The laughter's over. Something about the way he offers it is irresistible. Dumchowski took the party mood with him and some kind of solemn thickness settles on our group. The Chief's over my shoulder whispering to go ahead, just go on and have a good time. I know if this is a set-up I'll lose my clearance, my rate and rank. But that's not what I'm scared of. I look from the grey rubber, quivering octopus straps, the anonymous inverted face, greasy with Dumchowski's sweat and spit, to Bucket's face, a leering distortion of the Chief's goading.

With both hands I slide off my shades.

I swab it out with my shirttail. Roll the straps over the front and sink my face in, sucking it snug. Cool and clammy on my chin, comforting tug on my eyes, vision pipe-narrowed. Rubbery smell, sweet wood-smoke residue. On exhale the eye-holes fog, then clear on inhale. I hear my breath. Darth Vader breath. Pull the straps over smooth and easy. Tuck some hair. Textbook. I'm inside.

Someone lifts my chin. A match appears, a flaming projectile. Suck in long and deep. It's not bitter almonds like I expect. The room vanishes behind a cloud of white.

Duct tape. I want duct tape around the seams.

Nothing is spoken. The mask goes around like a ritual. The Chief, then Bucket then the pock-faced mech and his buddy, then Rudy who leaves his dates on the couch to join us. Nerdy, who seems to come out of nowhere, has the final go. Rudy muffs his hair like good-boy.

"Knew you had it in ya, ya corrupt little fuck."

Peripherally I see Dumchowski's got normal. He's sensible enough to leave us alone and take his fat khaki ass over to dick with the tapes and ogle Sabrina and Zenith.

"Yeah, he's a little corrupt, all right," I say.

Nerdy turns on me in a flash. I'm sure he's gonna swing but he pulls back and snarls, "We got some business to clean up, shipmate."

Adrenaline floods my belly and my face is sizzling. The idea of my fist crashing into that smug face suddenly feels therapeutic.

But the moment's wasted when the door busts open and a gaggle of drunken ASWMOD types swarm in led by Maeterlink, whose face is shifted into party-beast mode. A kegger rolls by on a dolly, bar girls bounce in — three, four, five. Someone's waving pitchers of Mojo, a local terminally-boozy fruit punch concoction. Steaming trays of *loompia* and *pancit* float by. More coolers, a hibachi, the coals already smoking, banded clusters of bamboo-skewered monkey meat. It's like some sheikh's caravan hitting town.

Something dissolves. I forget about Nerdy. I break off and melt into it. Time goes soft and gelatin. Everything around me is broad and diffused.

My awareness is in slip-state. Things happen.

A discussion of earwax removal escalates into a yelling match between Maeterlink and Pockface.

One of the bar girls pulls a butterfly knife on her ASWMOD honey-ko. "You want to walk like girl, talk like sparrow? I make you! I make you *good!*"

Chief Mattick's cornered by a girl rubbing on his thigh. His condor face is fire-main red and he's nodding and nodding at her while she subdues him with a non-ending barrage of talk. Tock-tock-tock. I notice something wrong with her, her torso's out of kilter like her spine is bent, half her butt higher than the other. The Chief takes her hand delicately, moves it to his crotch, holds it there. She keeps talking.

Something's let loose in the air. Something's seeped in, yellow and humorless.

The pock-faced mech and his buddy hang out the window. They heat up pesos with a Zippo and flick them at beggar kids in the street.

Rudy rolls a beer bottle across Sabrina's chest while Zenith, shrieking, spins in a circle trying to make her long hair fly out straight.

Nerdy foolishly passes out in a ratty armchair. Bucket, giggly like a kid, digs up an old bottle of Ivory Liquid and does this whisper-whisper yuk-yuk thing with Maeterlink. Maeterlink hides behind the chair. Bucket unzips, pulls out his cock. He poses like he's jacking off in Nerdy's sleeping face. Then Maeterlink, from behind, squirts the white soap into Nerdy's ear and all down his face. Nerdy's eyes jerk wide to find Bucket's cock wagging away and Bucket doing some pretty good post-orgasmic groaning.

I get it all on tape.

Bucket is roaring when Nerdy catches him square in the breadbasket. Nerdy goes for a follow-up but Rudy grabs him by the belt. Nerdy's flailing, arms and legs windmilling, when he mistakenly catches Rudy with a sneaker to the groin. Rudy goes granite. It's instantly clear to everyone, including Nerdy who goes the color of Ivory Liquid, that Nerdy is about to learn the last thing to go through a bug's mind (besides his asshole) when hitting a windshield at seventy.

I am confused. As much as I wouldn't mind witnessing this inevitable act inflicted upon Nerdy's person I don't want it like this. Slaughter. But before I have time to indulge in my usual dance of indecision, a voice rings out, a voice which is a drunken, pale parody of what they call the Command Voice.

"Stop that! Petty Officer Esperanza, I am giving you a direct order to stop that this minute!"

It's Dumchowski, suddenly hallucinating that he's George Patton. He's barely on his feet and looking like somebody, gravity I guess, is trying to pull him down from behind. In one hand is a half-empty bottle of 151 rum and the other a half-eaten *loompia* oozing what looks like mouse entrails. I think of the old commercial, *Weebles wobble but they don't fall down.*

You can just feel this energy or aggression or I don't know what, all this concentrated whatever focused on Rudy and Nerdy, all of it moves in unison, like fire-control moving a missile launcher to a newly acquired target. It locks onto Lieutenant Dumchowski, a throbbing dot on a green scope.

A low utterance from I don't know where. Maybe me.

"Kill the zero."

Nervous tittering. Felonious chuckles. Rudy borrows my beer, takes a long one, sidles over to Dumchowski and drops a paw on his shoulder.

"I didn't catch what you said, Lieutenant."

"You heard me, Petty Officer." Dumchowski takes a nervous swig off the rum. It dribbles down his chin and a couple layers of neck.

"You're a sloppy fuck, Lieutenant. Thought they taught you guys better at knife and fork school. Here, lemme get that for you."

Rudy, casual, stoppers the beer with his thumb and shakes. Dumchowski just stands there, too out of it to see it coming. Then the spritz hits the man. Rudy hoses him good, from top to bottom. "There ya go. That's looking better ya dumb fuck."

The crowd, as they say, goes wild. They're on Dumchowski, dumping drinks, spritzing beers, heaving fistfuls of noodley *pancit*. Somebody appears with an armload of straw brooms. Dumchowski does a duck-

and-cover on the run and they're dogging him, pounding him with the brooms.

I try to keep it steady. Zoom out for the big picture, the establishing shot, then close in, Dumchowski on his knees, blocking blows, dripping *pancit* and soaked to the skin in various boozes.

Bucket appears, wearing his pipe 'vark, belching smoke like a locomotive, brandishing a broom. He parts the crowd, takes a batter stance and nails Dumchowski's ass with a swat that sends my TACCO sprawling, wallowing on his belly like an elephant seal.

A muffled buzzing voice from inside the smoking mask, "You need a *spanking*!" BAP! "You're a bad boy and you need some *dis*ciplining!" BAP! "You need some *pussy*-whipping!" BAP! "I'm Kelly giving you the *what* for!" BAP! "You're loving *this*." BAP!

Then somebody yells, *Bare the butt! Bare the baby's butt!* Dumchowski twists and squirms but Rudy fast sits on his head, pins his arms. Then Pockface straddles Dumchowski's back, yanking down his drenched shorts. Zenith and Sabrina oblige by taking a leg each.

Maeterlink appears in the frame with a dripping pack of frozen wieners. This face is a blown-up version of the dozen other bloodthirsty faces gawking hungry at Dumchowski's wriggling bloat. Maeterlink snaps a hot dog from the pack, shoves the cartoonish red, frozen, dripping thing up to Bucket's eye-holes like it's Excalibur pulled from the stone. Bucket drops the broom, rolls back on his haunches and clasps his hands together like *Thank you God for this most wondrous of gifts.*

Dumchowski's drawers are bunched at his pinned feet, his hairy white pimply ass writhing and trembling. Bucket, kneeling between Dumchowski's legs, brandishes the hot dog with both hands like a bullfighter. Someone starts a low chant, *Mo-JO, Mo-JO, Mo-JO.* Other voices join in. *Mo-JO, Mo-JO, Mo-JO.* Rudy primes the target spot with what's left of my old beer. Dumchowski groans.

Bucket sends the dog home.

Weapons away. Cry havoc. Spindles and gears whir at my ear. The acoustic gram consists of eight octaves of 256 information bins each for a total of 2048 bins which comprise a display area of 10 hertz to 2560 hertz in a logarithmic graduation of declining resolution. True or false? . . . *and touch the face of God*. I thumb the zoom. A motor twists and the display fills with gooseflesh, hair, beer froth, the red meaty nubbin caught out of motion and time. I think, Sea of Tranquillity.

180

Dumchowski squeaks and his whole fat body spasms, launching the wiener on a ballistic trajectory over Bucket's left shoulder. But the real surprise, which shouldn't be a surprise at all, is the spouting magma which follows this eruption, spraying Bucket, Zenith and Sabrina generously about the head and shoulders. Bucket is protected by the 'vark. Zenith and Sabrina are not so lucky.

Amid noises of disgust and horror it's decided to drag my TACCO's fouled remains to the shower.

I decide not to participate and head for a fresh one. The cooler's a lake of melted ice which I gladly plunge my arm into. The freezing water is a nice shock.

I scan around and see the little Gumby manager's worst fears are not only realized but magnified by a factor of ten. The place is trashed.

I sort through the table for an opener, among the dozens of yawning plastic cups, beer bottles — *save the recyclables!* — empty mojo pitchers, mounded ashtrays, cigarette butts ground right into the tabletop, wadded napkins, one with maroon lipstick lips, paper plates of uneaten local pu-pus sealed in red coagulated sweet and sour, a tampon squiggled like a huge bloody tadpole with its head stuffed into a San Miguel bottle, a pair of handcuffs, a set of walking papers for one of the girls stamped with the name of a bar famed for its accelerated evolution of venereal viruses, puddles of red stuff, yellow stuff, bubbly brown stuff, a roach, two roaches, a third counting a cockroach I find squished under a two-liter vodka bottle. Finally I hook the cap on the table edge and give it a smack.

Sabrina and Zenith come over to wash up in the cooler water.

"What's the matter with the bathroom?" I ask.

Sabrina is quivering with disgust and cursing Dumchowski from here to Oman. Zenith eeks every time she finds another drop of the stuff splotted on her. "Some stupid's locked in there," Sabrina says, motioning back with a wet, rapidly shredding bar napkin.

"Not so stupid as that butt guy," squeaks Zenith, daubing at her watches.

"Careful," I say. "That's my TACCO you're talking about. A man I adore and respect and hope some day to grow up and be just like."

They both gape dumbly, then ignore me. Sabrina hisses to Zenith, "We're the stupids. Come here like stupids. Forty bucks easy at the club with short-time boys."

"Sixty buck, easy, " says Sabrina. They lapse into pocky-ticky Tagalog while finishing up their detox.

I hang out the busted-screen window sipping my beer. Warm jungle air full of spores and living things. I can see across the deserted traffic circle down Magsaysay, lit up like a hard luck Las Vegas, poor man's Mardi Gras. It throbs with simulated life.

A commotion yanks my attention back inside.

Violence from the bathroom. Wood splintering. A bellow from Rudy. The bathroom's crammed, door hanging off its hinge. Nerdy, Bucket, Pockface, Maeterlink — who else is in there?

A shriek. A body is pinched from the crowd, a little girl butt-naked but for an oversized gold crucifix piercing her left nipple, skinny, soaked, dripping, hair sleeked back, clutching a wad of clothes. She's halfway to the door before I realize two things: one, she's Mel's juvenile girlfriend, and two, the uncircumcised brown mushroomy thing jutting from her crotch indicates a confusion of sexual identity. At first my beer-soaked awareness, what there is of it, finds this funny. Am I on *Geraldo?* Filipino pre-operative transsexual teenage Catholic prostitutes?

It's Mel of course. The crowd at the bathroom is now a mob, a gang. Mel is dragged out clutching a towel to his waist. Water glistens from his beard and the thick hair covering his scrawny concave chest. He looks suddenly sobered. They chuck him in the same chair Nerdy fell asleep in. Not a lucky chair. He sinks in, swallowed up, not cowered but dazed, resigned to some kind of inevitableness. Rudy launches on me.

"I knew this guy was a fruitcake. He was in there playing hot tub with his benny-boy, weren't you, Professor."

Nerdy pipes in, "That Greg's buddy? Shoulda known. Shoulda known he'd have a cocksucker for a bud."

Mel doesn't look at me. He picks bits of fiber from the towel. Water dribbles from his hair down his cheek. I try to read him but his face is a mask. I hear the buzz and hum.

". . . unnatural acts . . ."

". . . bodily fluids . . ."

". . . chancroids . . ."

". . . *fagma-a-an.*"

". . . don't get none on ya."

There is laughter and tentative prodding of the exotic creature.

Rudy, from behind, drops his fat hands on Mel's clavicles. Mel flinches but doesn't look up. "What's it like, Mel?" Rudy asks all ominous. "I just wanna know. What's the big attraction to sucking cocks?"

Mel says nothing, keeps picking at the towel.

"Nothing to be afraid of here." Rudy squeezing Mel's shoulders, peering down through his skull. "You can trust us. We work for the government."

Maeterlink pulls long from a cup of clear liquid which must be vodka since no one would drink the water. "Watch out for open sores. Fucking oozing shit'll get ya."

"You don't have none of that shit, do you, Professor? Smart guy like you."

Maeterlink drawls, "You can get it from mosquitoes, you know. If they bit someone who's got it."

"Like that lady they were operating on," says Bucket. "When they cut her gut open she exploded from some mystery gas and everyone in the operating room got it."

"It was because she had an electrical transformer outside her bedroom window."

"Shoulda plastered her windows with aluminum foil. Shiny side out."

"You're both fucked in the head," says Rudy, all authoritative. "It was argon gas she got from eating apples all the time. She was a bucolic and all she ate was one apple a day."

"You mean anatropic, like Karen Carpenter. Bucolia is when you barf up everything."

"A corpsman told me the best thing if you fuck something suspicious is to stand in front of the radome for like three minutes. That'll kill anything."

"Scan-convert or raw?"

"The question is," Nerdy interrupts. "What are we gonna do about our friend here?"

"You mean the fagman," says Maeterlink.

"They're called gays," says Nerdy.

"I consider myself the underground railroad of politically incorrect language," drawls Maeterlink. "It is my sacred duty to protect and defend the ways of the oppressed majority."

Nerdy turns on me. "You brought this fungus among us." He says it to rhyme: *fungus amung-gus*. "What'll we do with him?"

The words pull at me from inside. I'm implicated. Part of the tribe.

Nerdy's smart. Either I'm on the inside with them or on the outside with Mel. Lose-lose.

"I guess if sucking dick's a crime you'd be the first one arrested."

Rudy gets a guffaw outta that.

Nerdy's catcalls are cut off when I slam the door behind me.

I feel bad for Mel, like it's my fault. But what's there to do? Why doesn't he get up and walk out? They're not forcing him to stay and be humiliated. It's like he decided to participate, like he wants to be judged by that bunch. Victims and aggressors. I don't get it. Like people choose to be one or the other and that's that, stuck in their roles like sitcom people.

Still I'm feeling guilty trudging down the stairwell on carpet that smells like something's germinating in it. I'm thinking how guilt seems to be the guiding force in my life, the primary emotion, when I stumble across the Chief crumpled up and snoring on a landing. There's a dead butt with a two-inch ash hanging from his grey lips. He's not wearing any pants, which may or may not be considered odd around here. What I find particularly horrible, though, is that he's still wearing his fake-patent-leather Corfams and old man black stretch socks bagged round hairy necrotic ankles.

I dribble icy beer on his thigh which snaps him to.

"Shit," he moans. The ash disengages into his lap. Peppered pubes. "Oh, fucking shit."

"Chief, get upstairs and put some pants on."

"Shit. Oh, fucking shit."

It suddenly hits me that this is my chance. My opportunity for confession and forgiveness. I didn't know how much I needed this. "Hey Chief," I say. "You know that sub-time we had before Hawaii?" As he crawls around I tell him the whole thing, the lost contact, Dumchowski's botched buoy drops, my decision to fake aural contact and manufacture DIFAR points, simulate MAD contact by jolting the magnetometer, the dead buoys I handed off to Nerdy. Everything. He'll forget by tomorrow so why not?

"Whar'd that gimpy little tart get off to with my keys?" he moans.

"I'm ready to take the heat, Chief." I decide to be generous and leave Nerdy out of it.

"What'd she want with my *keys* fer godsake?" He starts pulling up the corner of the carpet, the plucked condor scavenging. I turn away to avoid the sight of his scrawny butt and scrotum hanging halfway to his knees.

184

"I'm telling you I faked a mission, in front of my crew, the squadron, the admiral, God and everyone."

"She coulda hid 'em in here so nobody'd filch 'em off me." He tears back more carpeting. The air fills with brown hairlike dust. Asbestos. Toxic fibers. Cryptosporidium.

Footfalls on the stairs. It's Sabrina and Zenith, still pissed off and chattering away in bitter Tagalog. They stop when they see us. Sabrina gawks at the Chief, spread-eagled, half-naked, clawing at a chunk of smelly carpet. She spits. Rustle of nylon thighs as they pass, cloud of syrupy perfume.

"Malicious and malevolent mutated miscreants."

He gives up on the carpet. Shakes a cigarette from a crumpled pack, feels around where his pants pocket should be. "Muh lighter, too." Looks like he's gonna burst into tears. Turns a hopeful eye on me. I shrug. He heaves a deep sigh, tucks the cigarette behind a Dumbo-esque ear, then tugs off his left shoe. He pulls out a wad of pesos and dollars rubber-banded to his id card. "Least she didn't get my stash." Pulls the shoe back on and I give him a hand to his feet. "Guess the party's over."

"Pretty much."

"Better be gettin' back. We'll need our rest so's to slaughter I-ranians."

"Iraqis."

"Them too. Slaughter 'em all. Rug merchant shits."

He lurches against the wall, knocks loose his cigarette. Stoops painfully to retrieve it but gives up halfway, groaning. "What about the mission," I ask. "Don't you even care?"

Red-veiny eyes move heavy up to mine. "Shuttup," he moans like it's painful. "Nothing happened. Doesn't exist."

I don't know if that's my answer or if he's just muttering. "What are you saying, Chief?"

He looks at me like I'm stupid and he's too tired to deal with it, presses a palm to his head and turns away. Then he climbs the stairs.

I follow figuring he might walk into the wrong room which could have some humorous possibilities but, don't ask why, I'm feeling kind of protective.

The Chief, mumbling something about inferior bloodlines, staggers into the suite, heads for the other room where all the gear is stashed. Doesn't even notice the commotion around Mel who is still undergoing interrogation. Bucket's got his dick out again and is whipping Mel's face with it. Mel is stony, like in a trance.

"This what you want?!" Bucket yells. "Go for it! This is it — the Real Thing! Ain't mine as yum-yum as your benny-boy buddy?"

At the same time, Nerdy and Rudy, who seem to have discovered a special camaraderie in a common enemy, barrage Mel with sneering accusations of all the ills him and his type, whatever that is, have wreaked upon the world.

". . . homosexual couplings, interracial genetic in-breeding . . ."

". . . kiddy porn 900 numbers that take credit cards but aren't really kids . . ."

". . . declining GNP and cars with foreign-sounding nonsense names like Maxima and Starion and Tercel . . ."

". . . morning-after pills so wives can slut around on their husbands . . ."

". . . lack of family values and that old time religion . . ."

". . . alternative rock breeding discontent and neo-Nazism among whiney unemployed youth . . ."

". . . feminism so wives can slut around on their husbands . . ."

They're still going as I pull the door shut. I left my camcorder but screw it. I'll come back later.

I sneak by the front desk but it's okay. Gumby's not around. Outside, down the rickety veranda, around the traffic circle with the busted up statue of Quezon, which is just a name etched at the base of a statue of a guy in a business suit and glasses holding up his arm like *come all ye meek, horny, and dollar-laden*. I hit Magsaysay, which is buzzing like my head. Everything's in motion. Everything's overwhelming: the smells, lights, blasting music radiating from club after club, hookers territorializing me from doorways, mad hawkers wrangling me inside red leather doors. I keep moving, never loitering, trudging pointless vectors, hands stuffed in my pockets, knowing I want something and wondering what it is. I just want.

I try smiling. You can get away with anything if you smile. So I'm cruising, shaking my head at every offer, resisting entrapment, chanting *Ende, Ende*, but smiling all the time. Crossing the street a hooker in yellow spandex stops me. She's real short, maybe four eleven, with thick eyebrows. Says come with her short time. Only twenty pesos. What's twenty pesos in dollars? I'm smiling. I say, show me your tits. Gotta check the merchandise. She obliges, pulls down her scoop top with both hands, grinning proud. Little mice teeth. Her friends are tittering, they think I'm funny. They think she's funny. I don't know what they think is funny. I ask her where the quarter goes, where's the slot? She doesn't understand. Thanks, I say, nice, very nice but not what I'm looking for. Not what I want. *Ende.* She unrolls a brown palm. Five pesos for the sample. Brown people with bombs. I dig out a damp wadded note and give it to her.

Stop at a bar, buy a beer and carry it back outside. The security guy, submachine pistol slung over his shoulder, tells me I can't take the beer with me. I dig out another wadded piece of Monopoly money. He takes it, stuffs it in his belt. Points me out with the pistol. I smile.

What do I want?

Elaine's, Hard Rock Cafe, Spago's, Planet Hollywood.

Fingertips freezing on the wet beer bottle. I think of frostbite, chewing frozen flesh, death. There's a kid selling bundles of red carnations. I lean over to sniff. I don't smell anything. I get in deeper, press my whole face into thick red petals, breathe deep. Nothing.

I don't exist.

Beer isn't what I want. Music isn't either. Couple rounds of Road Warriors? Another disgusting pizza? Hard drugs in some secret back room? I feel hollow and quivery inside. Like nothing will ever fill me, nothing will ever make me feel solid and whole. I will never be a finished thing. I may as well be Mel, trapped in a ratty chair, dick-slapped by Bucket.

I start surveilling. Acquisition mode. Shouldn't be hard, it's a target-rich environment. I'm on wide scan. Maybe a club. They're cleaner there, got their health cards. But there's protocol, drinks, talk, mating activity, negotiate with Mama-san for walking papers. And the noise, the thumping bass, the hum and buzz. Better to stay outside. Take my chances.

It's not long before I spot her. She's in a cluster, four maybe five, grouped at the bottom of a staircase by the theater. *Robocop 2.* She's in back, knees pulled up to her chin. Face a perfect globe, emitting health and freshness. Not too come-onish. Careful but not scared. No easy mark, no cheap grins. She knows she's quite the commodity. In back, where they keep the fresh milk.

She's immaculate.

I can't believe my luck. She's perfect, plump and young. Complexion smooth and polished, almost reflective, like a new car, none of those gaping pores like so many of them.

I give her a fake name. She offers to shake hands. I just look at her. I'm smiling though and somehow that draws her in. In the trike on the way to her place she tries making small talk. I make like the engine's too loud and that's the end of that. I watch through the plastic side curtains. Smell the motorbike exhaust. I sense her discomfort and I like it. At one point the trike driver turns hard and she slides into me. I move away and keep staring out the grimy curtain.

We stop in one of those bleak cinder-block suburbs losing its unarmed struggle against the jungle. I give her money to pay the driver. He guns the trike through a U-ey and he's gone, the down-Doppler of the popping engine's departure fading to salt-and-pepper diffusion, leaving the street silent except for the ambient noise: primordial insects modulating creaking rain-forest time, crazed night-bird squawking. I listen for the message. She leads me by the hand. It's dark as shit and I keep stumbling over roots, ruptures from below, things I can't see.

Finally we get to the door, which is just a doorway with a cloth hung over it. Inside, she lights a hurricane lamp with a Bic lighter. While she screws with the wick I make out the furnishings in the flickery light: a double mattress on the floor draped in mosquito netting, the hurricane lamp and the table it sits on. That's it. Concrete floor, block wall, a window with no glass, another doorway. Luxury adult living.

I tell her I have to piss. "I spell relief P-I-S-S." A blank stare. She takes me through the other doorway, carrying the lamp. A cement cell with another glassless window, a drain in the floor and a plastic bucket. I start peeing in the bucket, steadying myself by leaning into the wall. She smacks me, calls me stupid, points to the drain.

She undresses me and gestures to the bed. I try lifting off her T-shirt — dying for a surveil of those soft, swollen breasts — but she stops me, says all coy that she's gonna pee. I'm suspicious but what can I do? I go around the far side of the mattress, trying to find a way through the netting when I stumble on something. It moves and I shriek. She rushes over with the lamp and I see a bony old body in diapers curled on a bamboo mat.

"My uncle. Don't worry. Is sleeping."

He's ancient, withered. I assess him as no threat.

188

I climb into bed. She takes the light with her. Armor-piercing moonlight arcs in. My watch dial is luminous. Things move on the periphery. I know this mattress is alive with organisms and tiny bugs. Skin mites. Blood pounds my ears. In survival school they taught us how the Vietcong hunted downed aviators by the smell of the good American soap they washed with. I wonder if the old man's nose is dancing with olfactors of Irish Spring. *I like it, tew!* Maybe he's dreaming of the Emerald Isle. Maybe he's coming at me with a straight razor. Maybe I'm back on the boat asleep in my rack.

No TV, no radio, no P.A., no 1MC. No voices from other places.

How would you tape up this place? How would you make it airtight?

"Hey, c'mon," I call, gardening tools scraping my throat. "I'm Cinderella and the night's a-wastin'!"

Shuffling sounds from the other room. Shadows looming on the bedsheet door. Then the lamp goes out. A big beetle crawls up the mosquito netting.

She comes out, nothing but a flat shadowy silhouette, two dimensions. Insubstantial. Outline of hair fanning her shoulders. No face. She's stooped, bent over like guarding a candle flame. She goes down on her knees, burrows beneath the netting. I lean back, close my eyes. Rough, scratchy hands run up my legs, my thighs. I take long slow breaths. I think how my breath must stink from all the booze . . . and will she mind . . . and do I care.

Her tongue tracks inside my thigh, the rim of my pubic hair. I lay my hand on her head, the hair is thick and coarse. She brushes me away. She takes me in her mouth. I think of my Madonna babe neighbor, Anita and her cleavage, Tamara and her scars. Complicated fantasies begin congealing. But NO. I want to see HER, want to be with HER. Right now, right here and now. I sit up to watch but she pushes me back. The heel of her hand is scratchy, coarse. I sit back up and this time catch the outline of the shriveled udders, plank-skinny thighs, sagging belly.

I leap from the mattress, all tangled in the netting, pulling it over my head but it seems like it'll never end. Bang my head against something. "Goddammit!" I yell. "GOD*DAMM*IT!" Where's the lamp? Where's the fucking lamp? Something crashes into my groin. I find the lamp and pat around for the lighter with my other hand. Finally I get it lit and find the little knobby thing that turns up the wick.

When I turn back I see the old man in his diapers huddled up with

189

this naked old woman, this hag, this CREATURE. Their eyes are wide, staring at me, but passively, like two cats, like Mel in the chair.

"Where is she?" I demand.

They keep staring.

"Where is she, goddammit? Tell me or I'll . . . I'll . . ." I search for something good to threaten them with. ". . . I'll *bust* up this place! I'll *tear* this place up! I *mean* it!"

They're just staring, arms around each other, cross-legged. They look like the same person, a male and female version of the same person. Like two Filipino Buster Keatons. I look around to see how much busting up I can inflict. Slim pickings. I could break the lamp, maybe piss on the bed.

"You got thirty seconds to produce her. And that's IT!" I pull on my clothes while counting backwards from thirty. I lose count a couple times and have to start over. Finally I figure time's up.

"All right. Here I go. Kiss your precious little domicile goodbye."

I hoist the lamp up all menacing. They're still just gazing vacantly at me, like watching a little fire that's certain to burn out but just in case you keep an eye on it. Then I realize why they look the same. All these years they've been together. The same forces of their shitty lives working their bodies the same way, shaping and chipping at them the same way so no matter how they started out looking they end up the same. Franchise misery.

This is their business. It's what they do. It's their job. Probably pulling this same scam before I was born. Probably pulled it on my old man when he was on his way to Nam. And they know how to wait me out, know I'll fizzle and walk out of here. Know I don't have any choice. Know you can't threaten someone with nothing to lose.

The old man raises his arm, flaps his hand a couple times like telling me to scoot along now. It's over now. That's it. Curfew. Get along leetle dogie.

I set the lamp back down, take a last look around. I'm about to go but I stop. The old man's atrophied muscles tense, just enough to notice. I am empowered. I take my time. I scrape a tiny scab from the back of my hand, mess with my hair. Then I undo the plastic band of my Casio. Set it beside the lamp. I wave goodbye.

Stumbling along, dog tired, one foot in front of the other, following the rutted moonscape of a road toward the neon glow that is Magsaysay

190

when I come across this weird apparition. The street is empty, not so much as a trike. The moon is high, white as a button. Bugs buzzing all around. Rounding a corner I see this silvery loop throbbing in the road, tall as a man, suspended in the air. I blink and rub my eyes. I'm tired and my head is killing me so I figure now I'm starting to hallucinate. I wipe my greasy face on a shirttail. Move closer for a clearer shot. Then I see it's not silvery itself but something slick and shiny reflecting the moonlight.

It's videotape.

Knotted tape spewed from a busted cartridge, a loop of it lifted into the air and held aloft to make a videotape passageway. Moonlight. Thick living air pressing in all around me. Radiation glow of Magsaysay for a backdrop.

What's encoded on it? What images? What language?

A doorway, an entrance, a gaping hatch. Things get in. A rooster crows crazily. The hovering loop of tape.

I step through it.

Nothing happens.

Back at the hotel the room's deserted. And it stinks like you wouldn't believe. Puke, piss, cigarettes, booze, old food. After all the party noise the place seems creepy quiet, deserted, evacuated. I locate my camcorder. Before jamming I take a scan around. Something about that chair catches me. Set down the camcorder and plop in. Run my fingers along the arms where the fabric is worn smooth, varnished black. The victim chair. Suddenly repelled, I push out.

The camcorder has something sticky on the grip. Some jerk's been screwing with it. The bathroom door hangs half open on its busted hinge. Something stops me from walking right in. Maybe somebody's in there, I don't know. The light's on. Old yellow tile sprouting mildewed grout, sink standing lopsided on spindly chrome legs. I push open the door real slow, scrapes across the deck. The reek of awful human odors. Toilet without a lid on the tank, a plastic pitcher to dip out flushing water. Rust-stained plastic shower curtain, pathetically yellow to match the tile. The floor is wet.

Rinse the grip in the sink below a cancerous mirror. A face I don't much recognize looks back, pulled apart and reassembled wrong. Water drips behind the shower curtain. I dry the grip on my shirttail. An old pair of rubber shower shoes. I kick at one and a roach as big as my thumb runs out. Check the battery meter. Plenty of juice. Another water plop echoes off the tile. Turn off the light and head for the door.

One last scan of the living room. I wonder if someone turned in the key. Dumb thing to worry about considering how much the place resembles downtown Baghdad. I'm about out when I think about that water plopping in the tub. Why's there water in the tub?

When I pull back the curtain I see him. Wearing nothing but the Elvis T-shirt he wore off the boat. His lips dry but swollen almost black. His neck creased and bulged between the layers and layers of Scotch tape wrapped around. Like a cheese, I think, one of those cheeses you see in old-fashioned delis, all wrapped in twine that cuts into them. The tape is wound around and around the shower nozzle. Mel's feet don't quite reach the water standing in the bottom of the tub. Water drips from his big toe.

I can't help it. I settle my eye into the rubber eyecup. I am sick, my mouth fills with bitter spit. Thumb what I know by feel is the red record button. I sense the red through my skin. Gears engage, the motor hums. The tiny black-and-white screen infiltrates my head with light. Photons. Auto-focus trying for purchase on the image, the subject, the object, the target. The flashing word *record.* Finally the image settles, entering me. The swollen black lips, slightly parted, about to say something, eyes closed and for once motionless, the wiry black beard, the nest of wet inky hair. The old prostitute's hair.

He looks real, I think. He looks like a Middle-Easterner. He looks like a terrorist. He looks like an Iraqi.

I'm scared.

I'm running.

Despite the lateness Magsaysay is thick as grease with action. Hellish light radiating from ramshackle clubs and dives and flopjoints. Neon. Incandescent. Fluorescent. Strobe. Photon bombardment. Sharp-edged faces, dark, *negritos,* barking from behind cracked cases of cheap sunglasses and chrome stilettos. Choking on a cloud of hibachi smoke from a monkey meat stand. Gas attack. Where's my 'vark?

Running. A stitch in my side. Run it out. Heart thrumming my ears. An old woman with a cloudy yellow eye pushing fake Marlboros at me. Her life flashes by. Sweet young thing from the provinces shipped off to whore for the sailors, bar to bar till her looks wear out, then the freak bars, pussy-picking pesos from beer bottles, under-table blow jobs for soused boiler techs. *Sucky-fucky Honey-ko?* Disease. No health card. On the streets. The healing shadows. Picking off the luckless drunks. The least discriminating clientele. The meanest. Who's the hero?

It only takes a second, a step. I see it all.

Keep running.

I see everything. I see the thing back at the hotel. Try brushing it away like flies buzzing my head.

I keep running. Nostrils full of uriney smell, ears buffeted by fake speed-metal furnace-blasting from Pizza Hut where I saw Mel yesterday. Mel the fish. Mel in the tub. Bucket's chant: War War War — Kill shoot sex fuck.

Just please get me back to the ship.

A pack of raggedy kids, sidelong glances. Creatures of prey. Aggressors locked on. I'm designated. Triangulated. Try stepping around but they're on me, screeching for pesos. *Ende!* I yell. *ENDE!* Try wading through, full evasive, but they surround me, leaping, snapping jackals. They're patting my pants, my pockets, reaching for the camcorder, all yelping at once. Barking Tagalog and pidgin. Tiny fingers wedge between my butt and wallet. I smack and push and one falls down screaming but I'm out of there and back to a jog, in the street now, feinting and dodging. The street a humming bunker of surrey-topped jeepneys, circus painted, plastic Jesuses on the dash and chrome horses (like the ones I used to win at supermarket carnivals) in formation on the hoods. And trikes, fat-butted motorcycle gnats, dipping and diving and honking and swooping and *pop-pop-pop-popping* in and out and through.

I see that screaming whine fill my display, the thing slicing through black water, closing in on my cavitating ass.

Dodging a careening trike I leap at a puddle but the puddle's a hole and I'm up to my knee in brown gunginess, momentum slamming my shin into a jag of asphalt and my chin into my other knee. My shades fly off, skittering on the filthy street. Lightning pain jolts through me. I'm an object out of motion. I grab and grab, all I know is I gotta have them. The slime sucks at me like quicksand. I'm stuck. Pair of buffed out muscle-droids and their honey-kos getting a good laugh.

Then eye-level: painted toenails extruded from yellow pumps (shower curtain) long nyloned legs, Spandex mini-dress. *You drop these.* Bends over. No tits. Benny-boy.

Almost lose a Nike pulling free. Scraping pebbles from my palm.

No time.

Gotta get up, gotta keep going. They're at my back. Eyes all over me. The danger. The threat. I'm outside it now. Too horrible. Too scary. Get back.

Ankle's screwed up. Damage report. Same one I fucked up at the party. But now it won't work right. Can't run. Just sort of power limping. Check it out later.

Unless they catch me.

But I didn't DO anything. Nothing to be caught FOR. This is what I'm thinking when I get to the main gate, while I stand in line puffing, spasming with it, windpipe a rasp, with the other drunks and losers, the other heroes, waiting to be let onto the base and head back to the ship that pulls out in the morning, taking us all on a ride to a place where people, other people, different people, want to kill us.

I didn't DO anything.

And in the little green Jap cipher of a cab heading over the lightless hill to Subic Bay and my ninety-thousand-ton hometown I'm still chanting to myself. I didn't DO anything.

But that screaming whine that won't leave me. My hand trembles as I run it over my muddy pant leg, trace my ankle swollen to a softball. My whole body conniptions when I bring back that scene, the yellow rust-stained shower curtain, the cheap zoris, the moldy chipped tile. Shiny tape. Plastic tape. Clean tape. It exists. The possibility exists. It's for real.

The cabby, face masked in dashlight green, asks if I'm okay. He falls for it when I tell him I'm just cold, even though it's about eighty degrees and my face is soaked with sweat.

SEVEN

Gulf

Day Sixteen

IT IS LINCOLN'S BIRTHDAY. Who is Lincoln?

Don't know what time it is. After ten hundred, anyway. Lights-out for the day sleepers, an anemic orchestra of sleep breath backing up a deviated-septum solo. Berthing's stenchy and dark but for the red night-lights and the TV hovering in the black corner, emitting like some I-don't-know-what. I'm so tired.

I'm so tired here in the dark, in this plastic chair, feet kicked up on another — petroleum chair, melted-down-raptor chair, prehistoric carnivores stamped into stackable furniture. There's our destiny. Rendered into tallow, grease, oil. Traded on the commodities market. How many bodies per barrel? I lean back on two legs, rock to the sway of the ship. Sway cycle's pretty steep. Making good speed. God speed.

Those with the least chance of survival, known as expectants — expected to die — *will have the letter E written on their foreheads with a grease pencil and will be set aside in favor of casualties with a better chance.*

Channels, channels, channels. What a treat. A new satellite dish to complement our array of exotic transmitters and receivers.

I would be remiss, the president remarked, if I didn't reassure the American people that this war is being fought with high technology.

But where are the Brilliant Pebbles? Where are the Cocoa Pebbles?

The Disaster Channel. Headline News. I oscillate between them, the remote tethered to the set with safety wire. I know I will be doing this all day if they will let me, if they leave me alone. The Hindenburg's about to touch down when it bursts into flames. That's what they say, *bursts into flames.* Stick people run around on the ground. Shadows. Traces. The airship tilts this way then that. A body leaps out. There's no sound but I know the announcer is screaming, weeping, what a tragedy, what a tragedy. I know the guy who jumps is some kind of acrobat or something. Seen it a zillion times. One of the great accomplishments of all time. The cutting edge of airship technology. Wave of the future.

U.S. hints at three-prong attack.

Bush vows no let-up in bombs.

Iraqi army considered world's fourth largest.

Why use my eyes? Why can't I plug it straight into my head? The senses are *so-o-o* retro.

Compartment cleaner whisper-singing a verse from "Duke of Earl" while pushing a broom in the almost dark. Slow motion. With a better remote I could rewind him, move him backwards into the timespace he came from while I stay here in my timespace, which is newer, better.

Southwest Airlines jet has a midair, smashes down in San Diego suburb. Smoldering homes, chunks of fuselage, sooty weeping faces.

The kid with the broom comes closer. I can hear what he's singing:

Nuke, Nuke, Nuke

Nuke I-rack, rack, rack. . . .

Weather enables allies to carry out nearly three thousand bomb runs in twenty-four hours.

I tell him to quit singing and fetch me a flight schedule. He tells me to suck old red meat.

Sears cuts 33,000 jobs nationwide.

I feel like I will never move again. No energy. Ashes. Ashes fill my mouth. They will find me here like this, in my unzipped wrinkled flight suit, no skivvies, no socks, boots unlaced. I tug the Velcro from my sleeve. Enjoy, if that's the word, the ripping sound, like maybe what it sounds like ripping raw tendon from bone. I re-attach it, matching up the woolly synthetic patches perfect as possible, then rip it quick and clean. Is that what it sounds like? When it tears through your skull?

A B-25 slams into the Empire State Building, lodged between the seventy-eighth and seventy-ninth floors. Thirteen killed. View from a helicopter or little plane — circling the skyscraper, ancient symbol of modern things. The fuselage of the bomber pokes out perpendicular, like a dagger plunged into the body of the building.

Will they be able to I.D. him? Did anybody know he was here? Any family, friends? Is there anybody to miss him, to care?

Lithuania declares independence from the Soviet Union. Gorbachev expected to send in troops.

Gorbachev is an expectant.

I will shut off the TV. I will stand up to do this. I will pull my feet off the chair. I will go back to my rack and Velcro the curtains tight. I will wad the pillow up under my head, smell my smells. I will sleep. Soon as I get the energy, I will sleep. If I can get that thing out of my head, I will sleep.

Day Fifteen

I SAW IT. I saw it with my own eyes. I saw it with my EYES.

Therefore it's real. Isn't that how it goes? If you see it with your own eyes, in the same time and space as you're in, then it's real. If/then. Causality. That's it, right? It wasn't relayed or bounced or fiber-optic transmitted, modulated or written or echoed, encoded, encrypted or ciphered, projected through celluloid, optically etched on silver halide, simulated by ordering the polarities of magnetized ferrous atoms, facsimile'd, thermal, laser or holographically imaged, analog or digitally processed, scan-converted, manipulated, synthesized, distorted, Animatronicized, equalized, morphed, tweaked, computer-enhanced, duped, dubbed, multiplexed or multitracked, photocopied, mimeographed or inkjet printed, colorized, SurroundSounded, Dolby-ized, virtually-realized, or electron-energized on the back of a CRT.

The black lips, the tub, the water plops, the toilet without a top. I saw them all. No filters, no intermediary, no question of interpretation. Authentic, three-dimensional. Hard-wired. In my face. The stink of death.

Never seen it before, not so much as an open-casket wake. Dogs, cats, possums, skunks, roadkill, even a cow on a highway in Texas once, but never like this, never a person. TV, sure, movies, books, magazines, thousands, millions, ZILLIONS. Armageddon and beer. Who hasn't? The staple food of the American entertainment diet.

But that smell.

It changes you. What you watch, what you see. You change it and it changes you. I should have known. Somewhere down the line it's always about death. Well, now there's death. I saw it. Meat puppet on a string.

Does that mean it's a story now? It wasn't before but now it is? If story equals death, does death equal story? The uncertainty of the uncertainty. Soylent green is people.

What do I need to know? Do I have a need-to-know? Am I cleared for this? If this was a movie I'd want to know who killed Mel. I'd want to know the cause of this effect. I would collect clues, evidence, analyze lines on the gram, match the pattern to a matrix, a target matrix, a perpetrator matrix. Pattern recognition ability is the opposable thumb of the human intellect. Hunt for the perp. I would garrote the mystery with logic till it coughed up its secrets. There would be intrigue, courtroom drama.

While shaving I imagine my lips black and swollen. I imagine my heart stopped, my eyes milky white, feet fat with pooled blood. Shit and piss. Roasted. Hanging in the window of a Chinese market. Covered by a white sheet, wheeled out on a gurney, or strapped to a rescue basket, an unwieldy load for two paramedics struggling up the hillside. Mini-cams, reporters, the words *tragedy, murder, unknown, name withheld pending notification of loved ones.* That image, me, piercing their taped-up rooms, seeping in through coiled cable, spiked antennas, the antiseptic dish, glowing like neon, a sign, burning, inside their homes. I lay the razor, the Gillette Sensor, to my jaw, cut a wide swath through the foam all the way up to my ear.

Day Fourteen

A REPORTER talking up survivors of a Scud attack. Women in black weeping, wailing, bearded Orthodox guys, black-hatted heads bobbing, dangling hair curlicues — Rudy calls 'em lox locks. The broadcast is interrupted with a live report from L.A. A woman, one of those professionally-famous-for-no-particular-reason types, former Miss America now sidekick on a network morning talkshow, is a fugitive. Richard Kimball.

The modulated talking head summarizes the events leading up to this home video of the fugitive at the wheel of a convertible the angle such that we are looking up at her tanned and sunglassed and perfect and familiarly beautiful face, hair wrapped in a long scarf billowing behind, blue sky hurtling past, the occasional phone pole or tree top. It is clear the videocam is in the passenger seat, propped there, the woman is alone in the convertible videoing herself. The talking head voiceover, just the perfect hint of shock melting the iced fake-objective edges, tells a story of the former beauty queen, cover girl, poster girl, spokesperson for Nabisco Graham Crackers, The Milk Advisory Board, and other wholesome concerns, movie of the week actress and personal profile reporter, a woman whose face gleams from the slicks: *Redbook, Good Housekeeping, Shape,* who volunteers for battered wives, gun control, and the Special Olympics, who was selected *Time* magazine's Woman of the Year for posing with starving Afghani infants, making death photogenic, whose book *You Can Be Like Me* was on the *Times* bestseller list for fifty-six weeks, who has her own personal hypo-allergenic animal-safe cosmetics line as well as a full cranial prosthetic hairpiece line which she founded shortly after her battle with breast cancer (chronicled by a weekly segment on

Entertainment Tonight) and the ensuing radiation-caused hair loss, and was even considered once for a space shuttle mission, that this woman allegedly tracked her husband, billionaire publisher and America's Cup contender Bosch Kiev, accompanied by his alleged extramarital partner former Playmate of the Year Cindi Myerson, into an exclusive Rodeo Drive interior-design showcase and, while onlookers stood by in horror, shot them both to death with a German-made nine-millimeter semi-automatic handgun legally purchased fifteen days ago from a popular Hollywood self-defense boutique with whom she had recently negotiated an infomercial contract.

"Boy," says Rudy. "Happy fucking Valentine's Day."

Her actions were calm and methodical. She reloaded the weapon and fatally shot the owner of the shop, an assistant and one other customer, after which she returned to her Malibu estate where she polished off her three children, neatly, each with a round through the temple, the bodies left artfully arranged in chairs and on a sofa in the living room of the mansion, though at least one had been shot outside (blood on the Playskool jungle gym) then carried or dragged inside. They have already dubbed it the Medea murders.

"That's what they'll call the miniseries," says Rudy.

"Bet she plays herself," says Nerdy.

"Damn shame," says Bucket. "Always wanted to dog her. Since I was a kid."

She is driving the freeways and highways in her pearl Le Baron convertible. She has other cars, Mercedes, Rolls, Jaguar, but she chose to drive American. She is in contact with her media people via cellular, schedules drop points for her videotaped messages to the world. LAPD has issued an arrest-on-sight, she is considered armed and dangerous. Police switchboards are jammed with calls reporting sightings: she is in Barstow, San Luis Obispo, Huntington Beach, Las Vegas, La Jolla, a carwash in Silverlake, drive-through ATM in Santa Barbara, the mission at San Juan Capistrano lighting candles for the troops. Simultaneous news conferences by the DA, chief of police, L.A.'s mayor, her attorney, the chairman of Chrysler Corporation announcing a new Le Baron leasing plan in anticipation of increased demand, perhaps a special signature edition. Talks are under way. The president, a distant relation, has issued a plea for her surrender. Random House is running a special commemorative edition of her book.

The Chief is weeping real tears. "Such a brilliant woman. Such a brilliant, brilliant woman."

The woman is known to me. I grew up with her pin-ups, commercials, fluff pieces, shitty movies. She's like a relation from a branch of the family that looks down on you. She always talked to me but I could never talk back. I didn't like her but she was always around, you couldn't avoid her, friendly, in a fake way, promising something that we both knew would never happen. I don't know what she promised, same thing she promised everyone else, but I gave up waiting a long time back.

Cut to the video of the famous woman driving, blotting tears from beneath big shades, daintily, always the pro, keeping that makeup intact. It's hard to hear with the wind, but she is considerate of us, her audience, leaning toward the mike despite the danger and difficulty of driving in this bent posture. She wants us, her fans, to understand, not to forgive (but you can tell that's just what she wants) but to understand. She is sucked dry, she says, sucked dry by the cameras. She is a victim, a casualty, as sure as we are all victims. They have eaten her like popcorn. She realizes now that she has become pornography, the cameras have made an obscenity of her. "They would have it so the last time you saw me would be led away in shackles and handcuffs. I won't allow it. That's why I'm leaving behind for you these last moments with me. Our last moments together before I vaporize into the collective unconscious. I have a gun. I know how to use it. The media killed my family. The media is death. Now it's time to break to our affiliates."

All forward motion has stopped. All life is halted. I know every television on the carrier is tuned to this. Every station we receive is covering it. The famous woman's image is reproduced around the world on a hundred million TVs, two hundred million. Who knows. The war is interrupted. It doesn't exist while all electron gun assets are reassigned to this image. This is bigger than war. Realer than real, more famous than famous. Probably calling back the strike aircraft so the pilots won't miss out, hooking up the generators in what's left of Baghdad, watching through gas masks in Riyadh and Tel Aviv. This is sensation. This is spectacle. We are grateful.

"Think they'll kill her?"

"They can't kill her. She's a celebrity."

"She's innocent," whimpers the Chief. "There's not a bad bone in her body."

"*I* got a bone for her."

They roll a second videotape. This one dropped at a secret location known only to the network who has her contract. "I chose the Le Baron because it is American like you and me. It is white for purity. It is a convertible in homage to the great American outdoors which I love. I chose this simple Donna Karan sundress, an inexpensive knock-off of which will appear in my spring line, because of the simplicity of my childlike soul. The Hermès scarf is both a classic accessory and a symbol of my sisterhood with battered women everywhere. I am with you all. I am pro-life. Support our troops."

Cut to a live shot, aerial, a newscopter hovering over an immense crowd, forty, fifty, a hundred thousand people, colored dots on the screen, a half mile across. White car in the center, sluggishly propelling the whole organism. We are anxious. We know this is critical but we need words, we need explanation, we need context. The commentator is confused, probably screwing in her earphone, making obscene gestures to the booth, echoes of chaos, of randomized order. All we get is *standby, standby, we have a new development.* Finally the voice has the information. The famous woman is spotted in Anaheim. At Disneyland. We are live. Disney security, a circle of Keystone Kops, escorts her through the mobs into the Magic Kingdom. She is no longer driving but perched atop the back seat, waving like in a parade. There's no sound but you can tell people are cheering, leaping to see, climbing over one another, holding up signs, radiating the senseless joy of the fanatically faithful.

"Who are those people?" says Nerdy. "Don't they know she's a killer? Don't they know she's a fugitive? Don't they know she's got a fucking nine-millimeter and is likely premenopausal?"

"Maybe security confiscated her heater. Don't they have metal detectors at the ticket booth?"

The Chief's on his feet, flapping his arms, wailing. "They know she's innocent. That woman's an American legend. She was abused and she stood up for herself. She's a hero. They know it. They all know it. The woman's an h-e-r-o hero."

I know why they're there. I'd be there too. They're there because they can be, because they were invited. She beckoned, they came. The talking head is approachable. The talking head is accessible. She has broken the pact that keeps her safe and removed, on display behind the glass. She has become less than television, invalidated. The famous woman is a criminal like the rest of us, dirty like us. Bloodstains on her white dress. They are celebrating her fall. It's a bad joke, a lie, a misinterpretation of the signals. They think she's fulfilled the promise, that she's opened the door to them, to us, the rabble, the unwashed, that she has provided access, that they won't have to suffer their smothering anonymity any longer, that they too can occupy her germless electronic space. But they are wrong. Interpreting the signs all wrong. She is on the outside now, locked out for good, and if the poisoned airless atmosphere doesn't get her the crowd will. Soon as they discover that she hasn't carried them all inside they will turn on her. That she can't redesignate them, but only redesignate herself. They will eat her perfect aromatherapied flesh, served up in Styrofoam with ketchup packets and a parsley sprig.

New angle. At the ragged fringes of the crowd are dozens, hundreds, of police vehicles disgorging riot-geared cops, bullet-proof shields, bullhorns, riot masks, flak jackets, assault weapons. Blue dots and khaki dots assaulting the multicolored perimeter of the amoeba, pushing through, infiltrating the mass of the organism. Virus going for the heart. They squiggle and snake, seeking the path of least resistance. It will take forever to achieve the center.

Reports of people crushed in the throng, asphyxiation, trampling. A police source leaks a rumor that the whole fugitive thing was orchestrated, a ploy to distort opinion, pollute the juror pool. Innuendo the videotapes were scripted. The network legal expert calls it police spin-doctoring. The cops fear public sympathy. It's election year for the DA. Murky forces pulling strings. It is clear that nobody knows anything except what they're seeing and that nobody really knows exactly what THAT is or if they're really seeing it. They have contact but they can't classify, can't resolve the ambiguity.

Cut to a reporter working his way to the car, squeezed in the mob, weaving and bobbing, buoyed on the whitecaps of controlled hysteria. Network star trying to make contact but the reporter in the crowd can't hear, looking scared for his life. Local talent. Wouldn't happen to someone with a network halo, part like the Red Sea for Uncle Dan. Finally gives up on his scripted spiel, starts yelling, "She's within sight, in our sightline. Reports of disturbance on the fringes. There's trouble. Police are confronting resistance. The mood? The mood here is *terror*, abject terror . . . What?" Then there's pops, like balloons. All heads shock stage right. "One moment, please. One moment." More pops, trilling now, he's tossed in the swells of flesh and sunny spring colors. "It looks like, *Oh God!* The police are *firing,* yes, the police, it's the police. This is all unconfirmed. They're *firing,* they're mowing them down, they are mowing down bystanders, firing on the crowd, the, *Oh Jesus on a cross!* Sir, your elbow, get your god*dam. . . . Incoming!* Get Down! Everybody Down! They're firing, they're firing, *oh, Jesus God.*" Shot goes out of focus, jerking all over, blue sky, helicopters, the sun. The audio's out, then the picture breaks.

Rudy crosses beefy arms. "Sure count on the cops to fuck things up."

"I ever, God forbid," says Nerdy, "decide not to re-up I think I'd be a cop."

Bucket pauses from playing with his new nipple clamps. "Me too," he chirps. "I'd love to be a cop. Shoot all those shitheads. I hate people. Shoot 'em all, fuck their women."

Back to the aerial shot. Her car inching along Main Street, Keystone Kop chaffeuring, her still waving, dress demurely thigh-tucked, legs Lady-Norelco locked and angled. The albumen crowd's leading edge oozing past cheery Gay Nineties facades, pointillist dots filling every crack and niche, trailing back through the main gates, under the monorail tracks, through familiar turnstiles, bulging huge and humming in the great plains of the parking lot where the shapeless organism's form is rimmed by flashing emergency vehicles of every description and dozens of dish-topped media vans.

A crane appears, a cherry-picker with a basket holding Mickey Mouse, waving with those big white gloves. The crowd goes ballistic, cheering. Mickey descends in his basket to the car where he steps out to join her. They hug and, arm in arm, wave to the crowd in that grotesque flat-handed crowd-pleaser wave, the polished and perfect image of American womanhood, that smile, that complexion as flawless and buffed as the Le Baron's gleaming hood, as an espresso machine fresh from the box, arm-in-arm with some sweaty underemployed actor dressed as an anthropomorphized cartoon rodent.

"You can tell that's not the real Mickey. The real Mickey only has four fingers. Mousetrap tragedy from the old days, 'fore he made it big."

A police spokesthing at a press conference. "You there. Yes. Yes. Crowd control is being handled on-site from the armored mobile command-control unit. There have been disturbances, yes, reports of agitators. These are being handled on a case-by-case basis. It is not my job to second-guess the officers in the field. No. *No.* That's all on that subject. Yes, you back there. The official host of the Magic Kingdom *has* joined the fugitive, that's right. Because she *is* a fugitive, that's why. Of course I support the troops. We refer to all fugitives as fugitives, that's policy. That's all you need to know. We are coordinating with the Disney people. Mickey will attempt to negotiate a surrender. That's what he's paid for. Our prime concern is to save lives. That's all I'm allowed to say at this time. Thank you all. No, that's all. I mean it. *No!* Adios and goodbye."

Back to the network newsroom set. No more aerial shots. The police ordered all newscopters to clear the scene. Meantime the drama has ended tragically. Mickey was of course a police plant. He was wearing a wire. There was a scuffle. A gun or guns were produced. The famous woman was shot dead as she tried to gun down Mickey. Mickey was wounded. He is *serious* but not *critical.*

The Chief, crying hysterically, runs from the shop, slamming the hatch behind him.

Rudy says, "Bad omen compadres. The killing's started."

"I'd still dog her," says Bucket. "Long's they didn't mess her up too much. I don't do facial wounds. Even I'm not *that* twisted." He looks up, deep in thought. "Or if her body's riddled with bullets. Something clean like a single round through the heart, that'd be okay."

"Good," says Nerdy. "It's God's will. Save the taxpayers a few mil for the trial." Then he stretches and yawns. "I'm just glad it's over. What else is on? Any war? I could watch a little war."

Day Thirteen

RUDY'S RIGHT. The killing's started. I've been waiting for a chance to get him alone. I try planning what to say but none of it comes out right. I play out our potential conversations like a chess match, anticipating all the countermoves in advance. But I never get very far before hitting a stalemate. So when I come across him in the shop I take a random uncommitted confrontational approach.

"What do you know about Mel?"

"Mel who?"

"Mel, the professor guy."

"That jerk-off child-molester homo New Age twerp. What about him?"

"Don't you know?"

"Know what? What's to know?"

"About what happened to him."

"What are you talking about? At the party? Hell he prob'ly liked it, prob'ly got off on it, prob'ly pounding his queer little pud right now dreaming of Bucket's cock bouncing off his jawbone."

"So you don't know."

"Don't know what?"

"What happened after the party."

"What happened after the party?"

"He's dead."

"You're kidding."

"Nope."

"Totally dead?"

"Completely."

"*Chingado.*"

"Aren't you curious how it happened?"

"Does it matter? The guy's dead, the guy's dead."

"There were suspicious circumstances."

"Like what?"

I tell him how I found him. He takes it in, rolls it around, then shrugs.

"Prob'ly offed himself. I would too."

"So you think he *should* be dead?"

"If I was a wimpy rump-bumper caught in the act and humiliated by a bunch of normal guys I'd think about doing the number."

"So you think all gay people should die?"

"Everybody dies."

"But are you tormented with rage about homosexual activity, this rage possibly channeled from your rage about the Anita thing or maybe even smoldering rage over an early childhood incident, the memory of which you have repressed over the years and would only come out in grueling heartbreaking hypno-memory-recovering psychiatric sessions involving psychotropic drugs and anatomically correct dolls?"

"Sure I'm pissed off at Anita. I'll rip the tits off the bitch when I get home. But that other stuff — I don't think I was ever molested or nothin'."

"How would you know if it was repressed?"

"Guess I wouldn't."

"Did you have any suspicious relationships with male authority figures? An uncle? Family friend? Teacher? Coach? Ice cream man? Anybody dressed as a clown? Think."

"Nah, nothing like that."

"A nursery school teacher who mutilated rabbits? A priest who kept toys under his cassock? Was your father a strict disciplinarian? Maybe too lax? An absent father? Around too much? A baby-sitter with hydro-encephalitis? Did you collect animal cadavers as a child? Torture insects? Draw cartoon characters with genitalia? Ever see a pentagram? Hang a Christmas tree upside down? Dip a crucifix in urine? Dad have a black cloak in the closet?"

"Naw, we were Catholics but not that kind."

"Grampa like you to sit on his lap? Camp counselor who liked to spank? Gym coach who snapped towels? Dentist who used a general when he could've used a local? Did your father kiss you goodnight? Did he linger? Your brother crawl under the covers on stormy nights? Did you play doctor with Bessie Sue in the garage, the playground, the clubhouse or any other covert location? Do you know the difference between good touch and bad touch? Do you dream about pre-adult barnyard animals or rocket ships? Have you ever had an erection in a locker room shower? Do you wash it too vigorously? Have you ever had homoerotic thoughts about shipmates real or imaginary? Did you ever or do you now have titillating fantasies about Valerie Bertinelli or any other actress who resembles a young boy? Do you wince at the word fruitcake? Or take unreasonable pleasure in saying it? Why am I talking like this? Why are we both talking like this? What is it we're talking *like*?"

"You're the one talking. But go on. Maybe you're getting at something."

"Three childhood traits common to the criminal profile are arson, bedwetting, and cruelty to animals. Sound familiar?"

"You really think I could have some of these repressed memories?"

"It's a possibility crying for exploration. Probably with professionals. I'm not an analyst but I play one on TV. Or rather I am an analyst. An acoustic analyst."

"So am I."

"But I'm better at it."

"So you think I killed Mel."

"I think we've proven the possibility of repressed childhood trauma and if that is so then it's easy to see how those feelings of anger and terror could manifest in adulthood as a rabid homophobia that could turn violent and/or deadly at the drop of a hat. It's understandable. Anita dumped you, you were drinking, war stress. Hispanic males are statistically proven to be violence prone and sexually repressed. Your hairy body indicates an overabundance of testosterone and other suspicious male hormonal agents. You were at the scene, you made offensive comments about him, you jeered and taunted. I'd say it looks very bad."

"No jury would convict me on that."

"Except in California."

"But I'll get off if I can prove I was a victim of some trauma."

"Right, the trauma means you did it while simultaneously being your excuse for doing it. I don't think you really need to prove anything per se, the possibility is enough. Reasonable doubt. But you'll still sit in jail for two years during the trial. You can kiss off your navy career, your family'll be hounded by rude tabloid reporters with British accents, you'll lose your privacy, your identity as an anonymous cipher, other valuable things."

"What, like I'm not in jail now? Look around. It's just jail with the possibility of drowning."

"And two hundred other different kinds of exotic and instantaneous or slow and excruciating death."

Something comes over Rudy's face. A glow, a relaxation of long-tensed muscles, like a rumpled sheet smoothed flat.

"This is perfect."

"What is?"

The 1MC crackles and we both freeze like retrievers: *All interested parties now assemble for estate planning and will writing at AIMD with JAG officer Lieutenant Kineally.*

The announcement is received, analyzed, dismissed as irrelevant. Rudy goes on.

"Like hittin' the lottery. Like Ed MacMahon showin' up on your doorstep."

"Oka-a-ay. . . ."

"Tabloids'll lap it up like dogs and vomit. There'll be bidding wars. Film options. Appearances. Interviews. *Geraldo, Current Affair, Hard Copy, The Enquirer,* Spielberg, Oliver Stone. I'll have a fax in my cell. *Desert Storm hero murders* — no, *slays.* Slays is better. . . No, *EXECUTES — executes degenerate in fit of moral outrage.* See, that's the hook, the fact that I'm one of the troops that everyone is working out all their collective guilt over Vietnam about and the fact that I'm not ashamed of having killed him, that I'm taking a moral stand. I did it and I'm not ashamed, see. It needed to be done, just like killing all these Iraqis. I'm saving the world for traditional values. I'll be the darling of the Christian right, bigger than Ollie fucking North. This is a gold mine. It's my chance to be a victim."

"There's cash in victimhood."

"Think they'll ship me home?"

"Might ship you to a P.I. prison."

"Yeah, extradition. Have to look into that. What about the ethnic angle, good or bad?"

"Could go either way. Ethnic's good for lawsuits — discrimination guilt — and it's good for anything to do with government-sponsored

212

stuff — non-profits, scholarships, SBA loans, city-level elected office. I don't know how it flies with scandal. I think the public prefers its scandals on white bread."

"Racist motherfuckers."

"The way of the world."

"Still, there's the hero angle, and the moral outrage. Good hooks. A good hook can overcome anything."

"If you can't be white you should at least be middle class. That gives you an aura of naive honesty, of good old American values that probably never existed, a hopeless and childish integrity, in short, credibility."

"I'd have to get back with Anita."

"White picket fence, wife at home sewing yellow ribbons, darning socks for the troops, whatever darning means."

"It was my heroic act that brought us back together."

"The murder, you mean."

"That's for media consumption. In reality it'd be for the money."

"Think she'd go along?"

"She's dumb but she's not stupid."

"I take it this means you did it."

"Did what?"

"That you offed Mel, you murdered him in cold blood, ended a vital and productive life in midstream."

"I haven't decided yet. I'll need to think about it, send out feelers. But one thing you have to promise me."

"Yeah."

"This is between you and me. I don't want no one else muscling in. Opportunities like this only come along once in a lifetime." He puts his arm on my shoulder. "And don't worry, I'll take care of you."

"But there's another issue."

"What?"

"I was kinda interested in finding out whodunnit."

"Why?"

"I haven't worked that out yet. It just seems like the thing to do, like there's a moral imperative or something."

"He's dead. You think he's gonna feel better if you know? Look, don't piss this away for me." Then after consideration he says, "Maybe *executes* is too much. Whaddaya think?"

"Go with *slays*."

After Rudy leaves I don my 'vark. I think better that way. The insulation, smell of rubber and sweat, my wheezing inhalations and exhalations which don't let me forget I'm breathing. Maybe something like those sensory-deprivation tanks back when I was a kid. But it's not sensory-*deprivation* I need. I have plenty of that already, the dulling down, the simulation of deadness. I need sensory amplification. I need to be reminded that I am alive. Or at least alive-ish. And maybe that's a dim reflection of the Mel thing. Maybe while Mel's death remains a mystery, DEATH itself remains something murky and arbitrary, something poised to spring from a dark place, anywhere, anytime, selecting victims randomly. In a world of random death, death watches all the time. Maybe when you find out — or not exactly *find out,* maybe when you devise a reason or reasons for, create a cause for this dreaded effect, assign a source for this discrete event that stands out bold against the salt-and-pepper background of ambient noise — maybe when you make THAT happen it lets you put off the horrible inevitability. Find the cause. Like IF this specific (not arbitrary) dreadful thing happened to Mel by this motivated (not randomly activated) perpetrator (even if it's self-perpetrated) THEN I am not in danger, I am not threatened because I am not riding on that same timespace line of cause and effect. It's not my vector. I'm on a zillion other vectors but not that ugly one that leads to death. I can relax. I can put it off another day. I can feel safe.

Is that why murders are *solved*? Solution as salvation? The other reasons they give: justice, retribution, crime, vengeance, I don't know what those words mean. I mean I DO NOT KNOW what they mean. TV words. What I do know is fear and fear is ALWAYS fear of death. Death is real but is fear-of-death real? Mel said it's the only real thing. Ambient fear. Maybe what Mel said about psychology, that psychology is dead. Maybe what he meant was that psychology was invented to explain people's actions so there'd be explanations for killing so we could rationalize the whole stinking thing away. Maybe psychology is/was just another way to avoid the horrible randomness of actions. Maybe it was all fake. Maybe psychology was just a rationalization for behavior which is really random and chaotic. Maybe I can't kid myself anymore. Shit DOES happen. Wake up and smell the formaldehyde.

I take off the 'vark, wipe it up with a paper towel from the coffee mess and put it away.

Day Twelve

"CHIEF, I'M NOT FLYING ANYMORE."

I don't know when I decided this. I was heading to Ship's Admin to misappropriate some copies when I saw the Chief out here on the sponson, leaning over the rail, gazing out across the electric blue plain to where the sky seams on. I stop to watch him, looking so lonely, bent, older than his years, hitting off a cupped illegal cigarette, smoke whipped away in the steaming wind. Before I know it I'm through the hatch, dizzied by the churning water peeling off the hull below, a vertigo like stepping onto one of those moving walkways at airports. The words roll out and I know they're right.

He spits a tobacco shred and turns that leather face my way, looking even worse than that time in the stairwell.

"I'm not gonna fly. I don't want to die. I'm just telling you, I'm not asking for special treatment."

"Funny, I was just thinking 'bout being dead."

"There's too much I don't understand. Rudy says it's bad ju-ju, whatever that means. I don't know. I don't know anything. I just know that plane is gonna kill me. I've never been afraid before. Cold cats, single-engine recoveries, generator failures, hydraulic failures, all that. What do you do? What *can* you do? Stow your tray and assume the position. Either you make it or you don't. Why even worry? Trust the bird, that's what they tell you. I always did. But now I know the bird is out to get me. Something's changed. Don't ask me what."

"Maybe the approach of this little skirmish?"

"Could be."

He looks away, preoccupied with something else, or too tired to listen, or both.

"Lookee here at this ship." A taste of impending parable in his oats-and-barley drawl. "In all these years it still amazes me they float. Ninety thousand tons of steel and the thing floats. Damn. This here is one of the great accomplishments of our species. Never been nothing like it and won't ever be again. It's all coming apart. You pups don't know it yet, but this is the endgame."

"I don't care if they send me mess-cranking for the cruise. I don't care what they do, I'm just not flying anymore."

"The center's not holding. You know what the center is?"

"I won't do it."

"Twenty-nine years I been doing airborne ASW. Didja know I flew P-2s? Yup. Learned Jezebel when the damn *word* was still secret. No joke. Couldn't mention it in mixed company. Three syllables. Did op-tests on the first air-launched sonobuoys. We invented all these tracking and triangulation tactics. Di-Tac, Tri-Tac, we were the ones. No computers, not even calculators, we had slide rules and sound-velocity profiles and stopwatches. Directional listening and null processing. And we found submarines. They said passive acoustics was voodoo, it'd never work. Said we'd never find their nukes 'cause there weren't any diesel engines and they never had to surface but we found 'em and tracked 'em. I flew on the first Deltas and Yankees, boomers, city snuffers, out of Petro."

"Must've been exciting."

"Soviets built 'em faster'n we could name 'em: Echos, Echo IIs, Victors, Papas, Delta IIs, IIIs, IVs, Oscars, Sierras, Alfas — a beautiful boat that Alfa." He lets out a little whistle. "Titanium hulled, liquid metal reactor, deepest diving, fastest, outrun any of our torpedoes, outdive 'em too. So secret it had an all-officer crew, scared the pants offa Congress. We didn't even have the technology to *weld* titanium back then, let alone build a forty-knot hull and prime-mover. Scared 'em *shitless*. They were throwing money at us, *heaving* it, you couldn't take a step without tripping over some new program: P-3 Bravos, Charlies, Charlie updates, Charlie update IIs, the S-3A Viking, bedrock transmission technology, satellite thermal imaging, SOSUS — *SOSUS*, *there* was a piece-a-work. Just think of it, the enormity, the genius, arrays of hard-wired receivers on the ocean floor from Alaska to Mexico, from Maine to Florida. *We bugged the continental shelf.* And every time we built a better way to listen, they built bigger, scarier, quieter subs. Reciprocal paranoia. Fear is the motherfucker of invention. We had a saying, Insecurity means job security."

"Must've been great."

"They built the space shuttle for us."

"You're kidding."

"It was the gravy days," he sighs.

The Chief looks out wistfully, lights another cigarette with his wind-proof Zippo.

"Yup, them days are gone. Soviets ain't got two kopeks to rub together. It's all falling apart. You keeping up with the intel? They're tying up their boats. Brand spanking new Typhoons rusting at the docks in Vlad. Those magnificent Deathstars. Long as two football fields, half the displacement of a Midway class carrier, twenty SSN-20s, all MIRVed. You could take out every city in North America with one of those things."

"Real shame."

"Dual Hoggener stern. Poetry in design."

"I've seen the satellite photos. Pretty hull."

"My golden parachute into the twenty-first century. They'da just hung on another few years, I'da retired full pension, lip-smacking eighty grand a year consulting job at Lockheed. Featherbed all the way through my rocking chair years. Now I'll prob'ly end up in Saudi fucking Arabia or Abu fucking Dhabi dowsing for oil, swatting sand fleas. ASW's dead and so am I. Thirty years' work, I know more than any man alive about twenty-seven different classes of Soviet submarines and who cares. Be better off speaking fluent Aramaic. I'll be like in that movie, that one where all the book people walk around recitin' the books they memorized after all the books were burned. Form a retreat, a cult of over-specialized cold warriors like me. Recite the blue pubs, the yellow pubs, the red pubs, the black pubs. Muttering men keeping the data alive."

"In case they need you again?"

"Who cares if they need us again," he snaps. "Prob'ly never needed us to begin with. Just keep the data alive, that's all. It's knowledge. It's language. It's what I am. You can't just let knowledge die. Ten years hence who's gonna know that Yankee hull number four had a turbine casualty that made that funny little birdlike whine at speeds exceeding twelve knots? Somebody's gotta remember. Somebody's gotta keep it alive, goddammit."

"Why then? Why keep it alive?"

He looks genuinely confused, like he never thought about it. "I dunno. I guess to remember what got us here, what got us to standing here on the sponson of history's greatest warship. The center's not holding. The center's the Soviet Union. Every great technological marvel America's come up with since WWII was in response to the Soviets. Ever thought a that? Most important man in the twentieth century, after Hitler and Elvis, was Stalin. Wasn't for him kicking us in the ass we wouldn't have this phenomenal aircraft carrier, those beautiful birds we fly in. Why'd we get to the moon? The Soviets. Do you know we couldn't get to the moon now if we tried? Forgot the technology. Why? Because the Soviets stopped threatening to do us one better. If the Soviets had'a kept going we'd have colonies on Mars by now. But they didn't. They gave up so we gave up. And all the spin-offs. You can thank the Evil Empire for your VCR, for your PC, for your auto-focus, for your microwave oven, for your fiber-optics, for your Concorde, for your digital watch. So now they're getting out of the offensive military business. Where's that leave us? Sittin' on our duffs, fat, dumb and happy. A society bent on entertaining itself to death. Twenty years from now we won't be able to build another of these magnificent ships. Hundreds, thousands of men died to perfect catapult-launch/arresting-gear-recovery aircraft carriers. Soviets tried for forty years to imitate 'em and couldn't. I mean COULD NOT. All their resources, all their know-how — mostly stolen from us — they could not build a ship like this one. This is the acme of human technological development. You and me, we're here at the peak. If the Soviets go, there won't be nothing bigger, nothing better. They'll look back at this moment and wonder how it was all done and what happened to humans that it can't be done again. The Egyptians built the pyramids and nobody can figger how. They'll look back on these mighty warships and think aliens built 'em. Suspect divine guidance. And you wonder if I care whether you fly? I say good. Get out while you're young. ASW's a dead end. Do something with a future. Information management, holistic medicine, family counseling."

"You mean you don't care?"

"I mean I personally do not give a fat flying fuck at a bunghole." I guess this moment of comradeliness is finished since he suddenly dons his chiefly face. "However, as your chief, it is incumbent upon me to cognize you to the fact that this is wartime and your choice will be construed as dereliction of duty which will surely land you in the face with a court-martial and all the malodorous side-effects therein."

He spits, flicks the butt away, grins at me and pats my shoulder. Then ducks through the hatch, leaving me outside. Here. In the elements.

Day Eleven

THERE ARE THREE GENERAL TYPES of gas used by military forces: blood agents, blister agents, nerve agents.

Armed with a straw from the chowhall, I fill a basin with hot water. Then I fill the straw with hot water and, a finger plugging the top end, tilt my head and sluice the scalding fluid into my ear. At first it hurts like hell, but after the second, then third time, it's not so bad. I repeat the procedure with my other ear until they both throb at the same tempo.

The clap line runs out the sickbay hatch and snakes along the passageway. A lot of crossed thighs and grimacing. I hear one guy whine that he's pissing battery acid, but mostly it's quiet, solemn, choked with fear. Probably something to do with the HIV posters taped up the length of the passageway. One says *If You Get AIDS You Will Die* superimposed over a skull and crossbones.

I push past into sickbay to sign up for regular sick call. Since I'm flight crew I get head-of-line and the corpsman slips me right into a tiny examination cubicle. Anatomical charts and a travel poster for Hawaii. I take a seat on a castered stool and notice another image taped to the bulkhead, a grainy multigenerational photocopy of a nude cutie prone on a bed, sucking off a porkster in a sombrero. The poor composition betrays it as amateur. Looking closer I see the narrow piggy eyes under the dingle-ball brim, the brick-like nose and mean lips. It's Dumchowski.

The flight surgeon's plastic nameplate is etched Daneeka. Brisk and bustling, boomy and intimidating in a way that makes you feel like a liar and malingerer, which I am, he tells me to drop my pants. I tell him I'm here for a head cold. He nods, glancing through my record, ignoring me, and gestures to drop my pants anyway. While I'm unbuckling he takes the stool and starts scooting around, first over to mess with some stuff in a drawer, then to drop my record in an in-box, then to the counter where he pulls plastic gloves like foodservers wear from a dispenser box then, slipping them on, back to me. He's holding my shrunken, frightened balls and hmmm-ing.

"Had any suspicious contact?" A sarcastic chortle.

I flash back to the old lady and further back to Tamara both of whom certainly qualify as suspicious in about twenty-five different ways but likely not in the way he's interested in which I assume is having this body part placed inside the warm wet viral and fungusy interior of someone else's body. I think of telling him that THIS is the most suspicious contact I've had but the guy's had a sense-of-humorectomy. I ask if a blow job counts.

"You're telling me you didn't have intercourse during the portcall?"

"Nope."

"Never? Not once? You're certain? No exchange of fluids? There's no reason to lie. I'm not the chaplain."

"Just some not-very-good fellatio, and not much of that."

"If that's true," he snorts, "then you must be this ship's only bona fide saint."

"I don't trust their hygienic habits," I say lamely. He wears a green smock over khakis, a silver oakleaf on one collar and a medical corps designator, another kind of leaf, on the other. What's with the leaves? What's the secret signification, the code? Tree of life, tree surgeon, roots, dirt, branches, birds. I don't get it. And why do doctors always make me feel like a dishonest child?

"Don't be smug," he barks. "Herpes can incubate for years, decades. So can HIV. Chlamydia has no obvious symptoms, did you know that?

Claw-Media, I think.

"If it has no symptoms, why do I care about it?"

"It doesn't matter. What's important is that we can test for it. Are you suddenly recalling suspicious contacts? Hopped-up prostitutes with tattoos? Dirty little liaisons with foul-mouthed bleached blondes? Overweight girls with low self-esteem who put out after a wine cooler primer? Don't think you're safe because you're *not*." He moves his face close to my puny, vulnerable genitals. He fondles each testicle between plastic-wrapped fingers. In a less accusatory voice he purrs, apparently to my balls, "Excuse my saucy language. I want my sentences to rumble with authority and unspoken meaning."

He turns on me suddenly disgusted, making the casters squeak, but not letting go. "Why don't you men ever learn? Do you know what it costs to run these tests for disgusting ailments that could be avoided with a little willpower, a little caution, a little redirecting of your sleazy sexual desire?" He gives my balls a punishing squeeze. I wince.

"I'm just here for a head cold, sir."

"This time, maybe. And I mean *maybe*." His eyes go narrow like he knows my secret. "But next time it'll be your weeping chancres, your cold sweats, your pustulant sores oozing gonococci, herpes simplex, spirochetes."

"I can't clear my ears is all. I just need a down-chit."

"Mmm-hmmm." He clears his throat making this strange gargling sound. "Are you a doctor now, too? What, may I ask, petty officer [emphasis on the *petty*], qualifies you to self-diagnose?"

"Well, it is *my* body. Aren't I supposed to know when I'm sick?"

"Don't trust your senses. We have instruments, new tools, special tools. Do you know what keratoacanthoma is? Of course you don't. But I do and that's the point."

A bolt of pain is transmitted through my groin. I give out a little yelp. He slapped my penis.

"Get your drawers up. I'm done with you."

"But what about . . . ?"

"Yes, I heard you. You think you have a cold. That's a diagnosis. Haven't we already established that you are not the diagnostician here?"

"Yes, sir."

"Tell me symptoms, give me your complaint. Be specific but stay within the realm of your experience and expertise."

"Stuffy nose, light-headed, can't clear my ears."

"And you are afraid. You think if your inner ear is swollen, perhaps your sinuses, you worry that should you fly in a variably pressurized environment you will suffer discomfort, tormenting pressure, agonizing pain."

"Something like that."

"Or in extremis, an emergency depressurization say, caused by a birdstrike or, God forbid, *enemy fire*, projectiles piercing your canopy, a catastrophic drop in air pressure causing instantaneous expansion of

222

gaseous bubbles in your skull. Result? A burst sinus, ruptured eardrum, deadly brain embolism, that sort of thing?"

"Right."

"Let's have a look then." He peels off the gloves and flings them into the lidded stainless-steel receptacle. While he probes my ear he whispers sadistically, "Does *this* hurt? What about *this*?" He twists the shiny tool like scraping rust from a pipe. "Don't you ever clean in here? Valsalva for me now, please."

I hold my nose and blow, but not hard enough to pop my ears like he's looking for. When he's done he shoots the probe tip into the wastebasket like Stallone ejecting an empty clip.

"Slight redness, minor swelling. No flight duties for three days." He dangles a slip of paper with coded information. "Take this to the corpsman and come back in three days. Goodbye."

The line at the window goes on forever. Even though I'm flight crew they won't give head-of-line unless I'm in a flight suit which I guess proves I have something important to do or else pacifies everyone else in line by making them think I'm an officer, emblazoned with a fate that supersedes theirs. So I go don my flight suit.

"Weren't you just here?" The dispensary clerk is a whiny self-important pasty-faced creature who looks fresh from a test tube.

"You said I needed a flight suit. Now I'm in my flight suit."

There's an immediate crackling animosity between us that's typical between enlisted aircrew and enlisted medical corps types. It's a matter of disguise and status. AWs get a little residual respect because we dress like pilots. Corpsmen get the same for dressing like doctors. Pretty soon you get to thinking you *are* a pilot or a doctor and you sure don't like coming across someone who knows one, that you're a fake and two, that you're getting perks you don't deserve.

"Are you flying *right now*? Are you rushing off to your warbird to confront the enemy?"

"You didn't say I needed a flight. You said I needed a flight *suit*."

"Are you in a flight status? Isn't that a down-chit I see in your hand which would indicate a temporary removal from flight status? And if you are not currently in a flight status is there some reason I should not assume that you have no flight to be rushing off to and therefore do not deserve to waltz in front of these sick and needy men waiting patiently for the medicine they need to stave off their ailments or at least mute the symptoms so they can get back to work keeping the sea-lanes open for decent freedom-loving merchants to move their wares as they please while you in your down status lie around sucking up scarce resources and contribute nothing?"

"The rule says I need a flight suit. I'm in a flight suit. Just fill the prescription so we can all move along."

"I'd love to get you in a triage environment."

"How long can it take? It's just head cold stuff. What could it be, aspirin? Tylenol? Advil? I know he wouldn't give me anything good, anything that might be effective since anything that's effective is abusable and an individual can't be trusted with anything abusable."

"Our suite of pharmocological compounds has been augmented for the war environment. All new agents."

"What, you mean you don't have aspirin? Why would you replace aspirin?"

"Everything is specially synthesized taking into account the local bacteriological environment, anticipated elevated radiation levels, electromagnetic distortion, aboriginal virology, residual offensive biochemical presence, and ozone depletion allowance. Let me see your prescription. Hmmm, yes, the Commander made a wise choice. He has a way in these matters. A deft touch."

"What is it?"

"Of course I can't say. But your allergies and past history of reactions has been taken into account."

"Am I risking stomach upset?"

"I can say that it's a spartistycin blocker with neoclemyotone enhancers. And that's telling you more than I should."

"Will it have a child-proof cap? I'm afraid I have to insist on a child-proof cap."

"Of course."

"Side effects?"

"I'm not going to worry about side effects."

"What I really need to know is whether this is traceable in the system. I'm coming back in three days. Will the flight surgeon know whether or not I've taken this stuff?"

"There are tests, procedures, systems involving samples of painfully extracted fluids. He can look you in the eye and ask for the truth. He can make you swear. Are you planning some subterfuge? Is there sneakiness going on here?"

The pills come in amber plastic along with a lengthy sheet of restrictions. It's called something unpronounceable which could be Latin or Greek or an acronym or the name of a Korean car. While I'm reading how I shouldn't take these with dairy products or virtually any other food or when the outside air temperature exceeds 68 or falls below 59 or if I have a history of almost any kind of illness, another guy comes away with a similar bottle. I stop him and we compare. The bottles and labels are identical except for our names, both of which are misspelled. I ask him what his is for. Ringworm, he says.

It seems silly that I hesitate to throw them away. I don't have a cold. I don't need them. But a prescription is like something bequeathed to you, a blessing, a validation, a cure inscribed onto stone tablets. Heap big medicine. There's magic in a prescription, it comes from a higher authority, there are incantations, secret languages, mystical symbols etched onto the pills, crosses, little circles, squiggly lines, foreign looking abbreviations. From the gods of the mount: Squibb, Parke-Davis, Ortho, Merck. The bottle you keep with you, wear like an amulet to ward off evil things you can't see touch or feel. I wrestle with the cap, finally bite it off, the pliable plastic, so clean. Six tablets, flat, surprisingly large, beveled, sparkling white with a sandwiched layer of high-tech yellow. *One tablet twice daily* is the commandment, authoritative, anonymous, possibly arbitrary. I swallow them all. I will take the bottle to my locker and store it there. Every morning when I open my locker I will gaze at it, be reminded of the medicine coursing through my veins, my vital organs, my brain, reminded that I am inoculated. I suddenly notice I have an erection. Why do I have an erection?

Day Ten

THREE DAYS SAFE. That'll get me to the Strait of Hormuz. After that?

Ground war talk all over. It could start any time. Any minute. Shit's heading for the fan at warp drive, boy. Maybe it already started and I just don't know yet. A million Iraqi troops. The deadly Republican Guard. Suicide attacks, they could come in low, below the radars. Or a barrage that'd overwhelm our layered defenses. I'm riding on the High Value Unit. Almost as scary as being home. Still, it's safer than the plane. One heat-seeker's all it'd take for one of those hogs. Whoop. Whoop. Splash one whistling shitcan. I keep my copy of the down chit in my pocket, touch it at strategic moments throughout the day. Already the time is slipping away. Today, tomorrow, the day after. Does yesterday count? How much of today is left?

Goin' ri-i-ight in-to the danger zone.

Five more months of this cruise, barring extended deployment or other non-deadly cataclysms. How can I stay out of that plane for five months? I'll break my arm, drop a safe on my foot, simulate insanity. THAT shouldn't be hard.

Iraqis claim we bombed a bomb shelter. Home-video-quality tape of a child's charred body, arm aloft, fingers splayed, pushing it, something scary, back. The remains of women, other children. A man, presumably a relative, maybe a spouse, maybe an actor, maybe the meter-reader for all I know, on his knees amid the rubble, concrete and bent rebar, weeping and slapping the dust. The army counterclaims it was a communications bunker. There is evidence pro and con. Nothing's real except the bodies. Some at the Pentagon, "sources," suspect *they* are not real.

Bucket gets up and changes the channel.

"Hey," I say. "I was watching that."

"There's something better on. You're really gonna like it."

I have paper grams spread out on the desk, an assortment of colored pens, harmonic dividers and my calculator, all in deference to our training obligation to analyze thirty practice-grams a week. I do all mine in one sitting, takes maybe forty-five minutes since I know by sight every gram in the acoustic library. I'm verging on my reward gram, my favorite. I always take the last one and give it a plausible classification that I know is not the one in the answer guide. I mark every line, every blot of noise. I use many colored markers, measure the frequencies to a tenth of a hertz. Then me and Nerdy argue and I PROVE my analysis is correct and the answer book is wrong. I pile on obscure facts and made-up knowledge, include reference sources, often also made up. Once I had him convinced that a Soviet SSBN doing crazy-Ivan turn patterns was really the raised and rebuilt Civil War ironclad *Monitor* during a reenactment of its battle with the *Merrimack* at Hampton Roads, Virginia.

The image on the screen is immediately recognizable as a department store surveillance video. Elevated angle, black and white, low contrast. Looks like a perfume counter, young girl spritzing an old lady's wrist.

"Oh boy," I say. "Another reality show."

"But with a difference."

"A cop show with real live cop footage combined with dramatically enhanced reenactments? America's Funniest Store Dicks? Very original."

"Better. Shh. Keep watching."

I'm waiting for the authoritative voiceover of a has-been actor vaguely associated with law and order. Someone to shape the images into a story which may or may not adhere to what really happened but will satisfy our supposed need for beginning, middle, end, for elevated tension followed by release, for reinforcement of our quaint faith in the world as a place of good battling evil.

The old woman shakes her head, asks the girl something, then shakes her head again. The girl searches under the counter for something, messes with some boxes in the display case, straightens back up and says something to the woman. The woman pulls something from her purse, a slip of paper, shows it to the girl, who nods. The girl walks off.

"The old lady's not falling for that perfume-of-the-week crap," says Bucket.

"There's something she wants, something specific."

"Probably some old lady scent. White Shoulders."

"Chanel Number Five. That's what my gramma wore."

"Maybe it's a diversion, maybe she wanted the girl out of there."

Fresh tension. What DOES the old woman want? What's in the big bag over her arm? What's scribbled on the note? Will she use a credit card? Check? Cash? Will she BUY anything? She puts the note back in her wallet, tucks it away carefully like something important, something she might use again. A man in a long coat and sneakers walks past. Dark skin, sunglasses. Suspicious. Terrorist, bomber, raper, cross-dresser, foot fetishist. She takes an atomizer from a crowded oval tray. The tray is bordered with a metallic filigree. These are details which seem relevant if not quite critical, should be noted, recorded, filed away. She waves the bottle beneath her nose, her face gives away nothing, then sprays the inside of her elbow and sniffs. She pauses then sniffs again. The bottle lingers in her hand.

"She's taking it."

"Think so?"

"She's awash in criminal intent."

She reads the label, or at least appears to read the label. Who knows what she's really up to. She wears white slacks and a quilted Asian-looking jacket with half length sleeves, some satiny material, glossy, a scarf tied under her chin, big hat, maybe black, maybe velvet, suggestively tony.

"She's a has-been movie star gone klepto."

"She showers her children and young lovers with expensive gifts."

"Lifted, of course."

"She lost it all to a crooked business manager."

"Who ran off with everything to Belize."

"All she has is the mansion and a couple of rapidly aging exotic cars."

"She lives on Kraft Macaroni and Cheese."

"Buys clothes at the Beverly Hills Goodwill."

"You're right. I like this."

"It's the V Channel."

"V for . . . ?"

"Voyeur, video, vagina, I don't know. Who cares? Department store spy cameras, Nordie's, Saks, Robinson's-May, Neiman Marcus, live, un-cut, twenty-four hours a day. It's hot."

"That's it? That's all they play?"

"Is that cool? It makes me horny, you know, people touching stuff, wanting things, buying merchandise, swiping credit cards in those little swiper things."

He's got something. Or this has something. People shopping, all their coded movements, all the messages they send or try not to send. It's raw, unfiltered. Nobody's forced story onto it, a shapeless narration, an erector set of meaning. You can make it mean whatever you want. It's wonderful.

"But where are the frantic video effects? The abrupt transitions? The shock cuts and unsteady cameras? The half-toning, the jerk-motion, the uncentered framing? All the devices required to retain our technologically truncated attention spans?"

"Got none."

"And what about the music score by Prince or Sting or Springsteen or Billy Joel or the Beatles carefully selected according to the age group of the target audience in order to manipulate our nostalgia for lost adolescence, that time of hope, cynicism and untested potential and to associate the sponsor's product with symbols of trust and the spirit of the outlaw?"

"I told you, radical stuff."

"Or even the old-fashioned emotion-cueing soundtrack, the relentless sharps for tension, melodious strings for resolution, that sort of thing?"

"None of it. Think of the beauty. No production costs. *And* no commercials."

"How do they make money?"

"Maybe the shoppers pay to be on it."

"Vicarious, vinyl, viewer, victim. . . ."

"Vice, vibrator, vicious. . . . You can be a star while you're shopping."

"I thought that's *why* you shopped. It's the natural order of capital T Things, the secret vibrating living core of Things. Acquisition equals power, exaggerated sexual access, stardom, clear complexions. And to be watched, to be on, witnessed, as you touch, caress, pick and choose among the reliquaries of potent Things, the catacombs of merchandise, flourish the magic jin of your gold card — with no pre-set limit — a confined omnipotence, eternal life, special dispensation from American Express, *if* you qualify. No death! Perpetual stardom!"

"Yeah, but now it's for real. New and improved. You can go home and watch yourself do it."

"And others can watch you, can witness and know your awesome power."

"Yeah, awesome."

"Vestige, vertigo, vermicular, veracity, ventriloquist, velocity. . . ."

"Venereal, vampire, *veni vidi vici*. . . ."

"What's that?"

"Latin, dead language. It's on Marlboro packs."

"What's it mean?"

"Who cares. Dead language. Dead like in gone. Dead like in dead. Shuttup and watch the show."

Later I'm in line for chow when I hear a familiar voice booming behind. It's Rudy and he's all jazzed about something, waving and yelling for me to join him, which I do.

"Look at this! Look at this! I'm on my way, buddy, thanks to you. And don't think I'm gonna forget you 'cause I'm not."

He's waving around a sheet of paper, doing a little dance there in the chow line. Other guys are moving back and scrunching against the bulkhead afraid for their lives. I've never seen him so happy. The new Rudy.

"Your laundry came back? You located the lost tomb of the clean shitter?"

"I just got back from the MARS station. Took three hours but I finally got through and you won't believe it. I talked to the MAN himself."

"What man? What are you talking about?"

"Does the name Orestes Michigan flog a familiar dolphin?"

It does but I can't remember from where. Somebody famous for something.

"Michigan . . . Michigan. . . . That guy who had his girlfriend kill his wife and bring him her ear for proof then made the girl eat the ear and only got caught because she got sick and went to the hospital where they pumped her stomach and found the ear and she confessed and ratted him?"

"Naw, you're talking about that guy from Silicone Valley. Wrote speech synthesis software for quadraplegics like that physicist guy."

"Steven Hockney. Only he's not a quadraplegic. He's got some baseball player disease."

"Ted Williams Disease."

"Something like that."

"Michigan's a famous lawyer. He maybe represented that guy though."

"Ted Williams?"

"The ear whacker. He did the Tucson Mangler, the Tremolo Brothers, and that guy who ran the Satanic Church of the Everlasting Modem. Got 'em all off, too. I just talked to the man personally. I mean *personally*. I mean mano a mano."

"By personally you mean via shortwave radio to some wirehead in god-knows-where who patched you into a probably illegally accessed phone circuit, bouncing digitized facsimiles of your voice from geo-synchronous satellites, et cetera, et cetera."

"Right. . . ."

"But isn't that a security breach? A flaunting of emitter silence exposing our position, compromising the clandestine nature of our mission and putting all our lives in jeopardy?"

"This ain't exactly a sneak attack. Now just shuttup and listen, will ya? He's interested in the case."

"Case? Case? What case is that?"

"MY case. My murder case."

That turns the heads of about five guys.

"Hey, did you hear, I'm not flying anymore. I hab a nasty code."

"Yeah I heard. Congrats. This goes through and I'm home watching you guys on Headline News."

"Thought you were undecided about your participation in the dirty deed."

"He's deciding *for* me. Sending out feelers, book interest, hardcover, softcover, foreign distribution, TV movie, talk shows, tabloids. He figures if we can round up two mil in commitments we run with it. Then I incorporate and you know what that means."

"It means you become a non-human currency distribution entity."

"It means I get a fax. What do you think of the Panasonic KX-F90?"

The line moves forward. I'm standing on the top step of the ladder leading down to the messdeck. That horrible institutional canned-corn-and-steamer-trays chowhall smell gusts through the hatch.

"Why's it always smell the same," he asks, "no matter what they're cooking?"

"White smell, like white noise, all smells and no smell. Olfactory entropy. It's standard."

"And if white's the combination of all the colors then why isn't shit white?"

"Mel could tell you but you killed him."

"Not till the contracts are signed. Michigan says it doesn't matter anyway so long as they can't prove I *didn't* do him. I'm getting back with him *mañana*. We'll know better then." We move down the ladder to the messdeck passageway. Grab trays. The stink and steam are overwhelming. "So what do you think," he says. "Thermal or plain-paper?"

That night I go out on the forward catwalk. No flight-ops tonight and the deck is pretty quiet but for plane handlers moving a Whale, a Korean War vintage airframe originally designated the A-3D and nicknamed the All Three Dead for its dipshit egress system that ejected the crew out the bottom for certain death on the flight deck. The dark-continent lowing of the diesel tractor, towbars clanking and tiedown chains clattering to the deck. A brownshirt sitting cross-legged staring into the red beam of his flashlight like some muttering religious man.

The stiff moist Indian Ocean wind hollers past my ears turning my sweat viscous and varnishy. I wipe my face on my sleeve. It leaves a dirty smudge. The sky is opened up like only happens in the middle of the ocean and I wish for one of those star charts from the mall to make out the mythical archers, bulls and bison, crabs and armed warriors. I see three shooting stars within a minute of each other and each time I think of a body hurtling through the atmosphere, toasted.

Day Nine

LIEUTENANT SIMPSON'S WEATHER BRIEFINGS have become impossibly dark and inaccessible. But even so he's developed a following that overflows the ready room at each flight brief. The crews fight for seats near the CVIC monitor. The rest are taken by senior officers while the aisles are standing-room-only with JOs and those enlisted clean and presentable enough to be tolerated here in the power vortex of the squadron. Simpson's early mainstays were dead-on satires of war characters — a particularly good Menachem Begin as a Hasidic Toulouse-Lautrec lobbing nuclear tomatoes at Arab leaders dancing a can-can on a map of Israel — with dark hysterical overtones of what some suspect was a rotten liberal core of pacifism. But soon the briefings took on a new air of solemn and abstract obscenity. The idea of a message, of meaning, becoming more obscure, murkier and less likely. Mutilated dolls and body parts dangled from his uniform. He read passages from the Koran, the Old Testament, Nostradamus, the Physician's Desk Reference, Max Brand novels, the ship's damage control guide, all with the same suggestive intensity, a theatrical fervor hinting at deeper meanings or the bleak absence of deeper meanings. I couldn't tell which. These readings he punctuated with farting sounds, screamed obscenities, photos of fecal matter superimposed atop weather maps and isobaric charts. Shucking any residual husk of meaning, of imparting information, data, he successfully evolved into a pure and unsettling entertainment. His ramblings veered toward the chaotic. Way beyond eccentric. Only his ability to entertain spared him being yanked off. His audience of faithful has been shaped and molded from the merely amused to fans and devotees and now to zealots and disciples. Pimpled and pasty yeomen "do

Simpson" spontaneously in passageways and workspaces. Others have memorized whole bits and quote lines back and forth in secret coded exchanges. When something obscure and erratic occurs, when events take an arbitrary and demented twist, the situation is said to have achieved Simpsonicity. The ordinary and obvious when uttered murkily is considered Simpsonian. He has achieved a hyper-persona, a meta-existence. Beyond stardom. No discussion of Simpson alludes to his life outside the monitors. No mention of an "in person" existence. Not even mythic rumors of a hybernating drooling madman living off sardines and Oreos in the broadcast booth. Nothing. It's as if his followers don't want to admit even the possibility of a corporeal form, any residue of humanness. They are protecting the image. Or maybe they really don't believe anything exists behind or beyond the image. Maybe they think the image of Simpson exists independently of a creator, that Simpson on the CVIC monitor just is.

When I open the ready room door the place is already packed. The knob gets someone in the back. I squeeze in and find myself behind Napoleon scrunched over the ASDO desk, pressed in from all sides. There's an image under the Plexiglas desktop, a photocopy of a photo. It's Dumchowski's fiancée, topless and sucking lewdly on her own left breast. I give Napoleon a tap and say hi. Without turning he says, "*When the Screaming Stops.* 1973. Tony Kendall, Helga Line, Sylvia Tortosa. Color, eighty-six minutes, rated R. A she-monster ruling a kingdom below the Rhine river by day turns fiend by night, cutting the hearts from young women in a village. Gore, special effects, flashes of T and/or A."

I grab his shoulders and shake until he looks up.

"Oh, it's you," he says, one tired puppy. "I'll sure be glad when this is over."

Just then Dumchowski, livid, muscles in, pawing at the Plexiglas until he gets to the photocopy of his fiancée which he rips into pieces.

"I know you're the one doing this," he snarls at me, shaking the pieces in his fist. "And I'm not taking this shit anymore. I'm tired of being the escapegoat around here!" He stomps off.

"Damn," says Napoleon. "Guess he doesn't like porno."

"It's his girlfriend."

"Oh. No wonder all the O's were snickering so much. I thought it was just generic. They're all over the ship."

"You know who's doing it?"

234

"It was just here this morning when I logged in."

"Looks like a good turnout for the Mister Simpson Show."

"I don't know why. I can't understand half the shit he says."

"Maybe you're not supposed to understand."

"Well if that's the case, then I'm doing just fine."

"Why so glum?" I ask.

"I dunno. There's something in the air. Something weird I can't shake. You know what it makes me think of?"

"What?"

"This is really weird. You'll think I'm certifiable."

"I already do."

"When I was a kid, a little thing, maybe seven, I had a cat, a good mouser. Fred was her name. She used to sleep with me, follow me around, hiss at folks who got too close to me. Well she got pregnant before she was ready, hardly more'n a kitten herself, and she got real big and that was okay. So one day I come home from school and she's curled up in my bed having her litter. That's how much she liked me, nested right in my own bed. That's rare for a cat, they're usually not that faithful. But there she was and me never seeing anything like it."

"I thought you were raised on a farm or something?"

"This is before we got the farm. So anyway she has the litter, squirted out like five of the things, little ratlike hairless things. And I'm stroking her and talking and scared half to death for her 'cause I could tell she was in pain. And anyway they were all dead. But I didn't know that, see. I thought they were supposed to be like that. So I'm happy as can be. Five new kittens! You know how kids get. So then she starts licking off the afterbirth and such and takes one of the little heads in her mouth and bites it right off and swallows it. Just bit it off. I couldn't believe it. I didn't know what to do. There wasn't anyone in the house but me, no one to explain it. So I just started bawling and begging her not to do it. But she went on and bit off each head, one by one, like it was just a regular thing. Except even through my bawling I could tell she was hurting. I was screaming and pounding my fists on the floor. I covered my head and cried all afternoon till my folks got home. It was the most horrible thing I ever saw. And lately I can't stop thinking about it. Four or five times a day and at night too. I see those five gray headless kittens. What do you think it means?"

"What makes you think it means anything?"

235

He looks at me with disappointment, like he already regrets telling me this thing. I guess I can't blame him.

"I dunno," he says. "I guess you're right. Whulp, looks like it's showtime."

The monitors have cut to the standby sign. The ready room roar immediately ceases. Cut again to Simpson in dress blues, ribbons, Ray-Bans. At attention in front of a white backdrop. There's something artificial about him, some makeup maybe that makes him look mannequinlike, painted plaster. At the same time, dressed so normally, at least comparatively, he looks as if he's returned to some prior form, journeyed through arduous morphological stages and come out as this pristine original. There is a small table with a digital travel alarm. Nothing else. Simpson doesn't move, doesn't say a thing, ten seconds, twenty seconds, people shifting uneasily in their seats, stifled coughs. Thirty seconds and still nothing. A full agonizing minute. Finally a voice, one of those electronically synthesized voices like on utility company call-routers: A-larm – A-larm – Now – Is – Six – For-ty-five – A. – M. A-larm – A-larm – Now – Is – Six – For-ty-six – A. – M. This goes on for another minute or five minutes or all day. Who knows. No one moves, says a word. Finally the screen cuts to the winds-aloft chart.

There is a certain pride in having known someone who has escaped the surly bonds of the body, of shit and piss and sweat and spit, achieved an immaculate existence on a plane vibrating at a higher frequency than our own. I am beginning to understand this.

Day Eight

IT'S JUST BEFORE TAPS when I bump into Buckethead in the passageway outside the ASWMOD. He's done up in flight gear, just out of his debrief for a mission with my crew in my absence. He's bursting with jolliness, that big head bobbing like a balloon with a painted-on face.

"Boy, that TACCO of yours, what a twenty kiloton dip of gullibility."

"That would be Dumchowski, yeah."

We head down to the paraloft so Bucket can drop off his gear.

"So, what'd you pull on my cherished whacko-TACCO?"

"It was beautiful. Bay-yootiful! Whitman started it in the brief. Since we're down by the Strait of Malacca he suggests zooming down to the equator to fuck with the nav."

"We're at the Strait?"

"Yeah, where's your head. Up topside you can see the lights of Singapore."

"You're kidding."

"No, go look. What, you don't know where you are?"

No, I think, I don't know where I am. "I guess it didn't occur to me we were really moving, you know, that there was any in-between."

Bucket makes a space-case noise and waves his hands around. It's surprising to think of us in motion. It just seems like you walk on this thing like climbing into a chamber and when you walk off you're someplace else, your destination. Embark, disembark. Everything else is just waiting. Movement, motion, progress. What an idea.

"So old Whitman starts talking about how the currents north of the equator rotate clockwise and south of the equator they rotate counterclockwise."

"The Coriolus Effect. A phenomenon of the Earth's rotation causing an object flying in a straight line to appear to have a curved trajectory when observed from the planet's surface. The classic model of which is a baseball pitch where one observer rides the baseball from which vantage the ball appears to fly in a straight line, while the other observer on the ground which is itself in motion sees the ball curve to the left or right depending on whether the ball is traveling north to south or south to north and which hemisphere it occurs in. It causes the currents and also great circle navigation utilized by airlines and other long-haul air travelers."

"That's pretty good. Remember that from A-School oceanography?"

"*Jeopardy!*"

"Right, so he's yam-yamming Dumchowski there's this weird thing that happens at the equator because of the friction of the northern water heading west while the southern water heads east and he's giving me the big eye like *check out this fool* and Dumchowski's totally sucked in. And I'm doing all this *yes, sir, that's right, sir* shit and shit. . . . Oh, wait."

We're by the Ship's Operations bulletin board and Bucket stops to fumble through his helmet bag. He pulls out a sheet of paper and push-pins it to the board. It's another photocopy of a photo of Dumchowski's fiancée. This time she's alone on a pool table doing herself with a rocket-shaped dildo.

"So you're the one. I'm shocked."

"You gotta keep sane."

"He's blaming me, thought he was gonna rip my head off in the ready room yesterday."

"It's not only me. I'm just one small but dedicated cog in a global distribution network."

"Global?"

"CVIC guys scanned a bunch into the system. They're navywide, worldwide. Pentagon, all the ships at sea, everywhere. Max distribution. Released into the air."

"Like spores."

"He oughta be proud. She's famous. That's gotta be worth something."

We head back down the passageway in tandem. "She's surprisingly not ugly."

"I know. She must be retarded. So speaking of retarded, Whitman

238

goes *The bioluminescent plankton there under a constant state of agitation glow so that from the air you can see the line of the equator glowing from horizon to horizon, isn't that so petty officer?* And I'm like, duh, I thought everyone knew that."

"You have planted an image in his gurgling mind. This is called the set-up."

"Right, he's all set up. Visions of a glowing plankton belt girdling the planet."

"I'm with you. I love this. So you take him up in the plane. . . ."

"So we take him up and we're watching the INS count down the latitude till just before we get to zero-zero. . . ."

"And the pilot starts yelling that he sees a glow."

"And Whitman's going, *Yeah, I see it too. Thar she glows.*"

"And Dumchowski's about to wet his pants trying to see it."

"Yes! Yes!" In his excitement Bucket nearly slams into a JG carrying a video-cam. It's a JVC Super VHS-C HI-FI. Nice. "So we bank starboard to give him a good view and everyone's pretending like they see it clear as neon. . . ."

"And he's like *where? where? I can't see it.*"

"Hey, *my* story. You mind?"

"And Dumchowski after a moment of self-conscious, slightly hysterical hesitation says he sees it, too."

"Yeah, no shit! I can't believe this guy. He's got his camera out and snapping all these shots of nothing. Just pure, black nothing. How'd you know?"

I shrug. "I'm his SENSO. SENSO knows."

I don't know why but suddenly it seems kind of shitty to pull that on old Dumchowski. He's too easy a target. Not that I wouldn't of done it myself. But still. I wouldn't wish escapegoat status on anyone, not even my best enemy. But in the end we're all easy targets, the vulnerability is painful. Dumchowski is just a reminder. I feel the electromagnetic waves swirl around me like dust devils, tracking me, keeping me inside their sphere of influence. We're all surrounded by it and the only thing that changes is our awareness and the awareness of others. There is a glowing symbol superimposed over the outline of my return. I am fixed, we are fixed. I decide to hit the rack.

On my way I stop at the shop. Rudy is there alone, pressing a dungaree shirt on Nerdie's desk.

"Big date?" I ask.

"The biggest."

"Michigan?"

A pause, a vibration, a high approaching whine overhead. The muscles on the back of my hand flinch. They are called tensors. Then the crashdown, jet roar, piercing whiz of arresting cable playing out. The fan cage hums sympathetically. I bristle dully but there's a joyful serenity about Rudy as he whistles and attends to his ironing. A bouquet of calm, of rapture. I already feel left behind.

"My man came through. It's a lock-up. Done deal."

"You're going through with it?"

"They are, his words, very enthusiastic about the project."

"They?"

"My new agent at ICM's got Fox Entertainment signed on, Touchstone's begging for an option and about twenty other side deals, all pending my arrest and the official pressing of charges of course. Which happens tomorrow."

"You're turning yourself in?"

"Michigan's on his way to Sri Lanka as we speak. On his private jet I might point out. Helos onboard tomorrow night."

"Here? He's coming here? To this warship? On its way to war?"

"Right here, babe. Tooo-morrow." He chuckles smug, flips over the shirt, mists it with a plastic bottle designed to atomize window cleaner. An offhand motion. So easy, I think. Atomizing fluid with hardly a thought. "This guy," he says, "is better connected than God."

"Bringing along the usual retinue, I presume."

"Network, regional, print, buttsuckers and bodyguards. Ho-hum."

"I'm very impressed. You'll miss the war."

"You'll have to carry on without me as best you can."

"I don't know what to say."

The 1MC comes over with *Taps. Taps. Lights out. All men return to your own rack. Now taps.* I peer around me at the bulkhead seams taped up with duct tape, the coat rack full of canvas-bagged 'varks. A blade of fear. I pull open the bottom drawer of the safe, grab my camcorder and plop into a chair. Switch on the power and it hums to life.

"No video, pal. I think I'm copyrighted."

"Maybe I should pay a user fee for talking to you."

"Always use a couple bucks."

"Where you're going you could use a bodyguard and a chastity belt."

"I been in County before. Doubt the brig's any worse. Easier'n boot camp anyway."

"So, now you gonna tell me the truth?"

"What truth?"

A reverberation, *There is no truth.* I shake it off. "The whodunnit angle."

His thick hairy fingers make the iron look like a toy, the image of some grotesque domestic perversion. "It truly breaks my heart to say this to a friend . . ."

"We're not friends, merely military acquaintances."

". . . but on the advice of counsel I cannot discuss the details of the case."

"I knew you were gonna to say that."

"So why ask?"

"Just exactly what I've been wondering myself."

"There's probably not much to tell anyway. I'm pretty sure I repressed most of the gore and good stuff."

"On Michigan's sage advice, one would assume."

"Right. And what I didn't repress you'll hear on Court TV. Stay tuned."

That night I don't sleep well. I wake up what must be about every hour. In the pitch I reach out for the boundaries: the top of the rack, cool sheet metal, the side, the head, my rack light's skinny fluorescent tube, the taut rack curtain. When I sleep I slip into the same dream about me and Nerdy and Rudy being scheduled for a hop to the moon. It's prestigious duty and I am happy. I have with me a canvas sack of nickels. I don't know why but in dream awareness I know it's something to do with that scene from *The Right Stuff* where Gus Grissom takes along rolls of coins and space toys to bring back for souvenirs. I know my reason for bringing the nickels is not the same but I also know that everyone has seen that movie and will think I'm making souvenirs. And when I drop the bag on the deck of the gantry elevator on the way to the hatch of the rocket-mounted S-3 I am humiliated, found out. Rudy doesn't notice but Nerdy gives me a look, a smart-ass half grin that tells it all. I want to tell him there is more important work for the nickels. More important than he thinks. But the fact is I don't know what that work is or could be.

Day Seven

WHEN I GET TO THE SHOP Nerdy's waiting on me.

"We need to talk," he says from behind his Lockheed Viking coffee mug.

"I need some coffee. This stuff drinkable?" I dump yesterday's dregs into the slush bucket and wipe the cup with a paper towel.

"You have to go flying," he says sounding all dramatically rehearsed, which I know he is. Even so it still achieves the desired reaction, an adrenaline firecracker in my gut.

"We out of Cremora again?"

"Your down-chit expires in about an hour. I expect you to be hale and hearty and the picture of glowing health for your triple-SC hop tonight."

"Who's in charge of the coffee mess? Isn't that an ALPO function? What do I pay dues for?"

"We un-rep tomorrow. Cremora galore. I'm glad we had this chance to exchange ideas and communicate our needs and desires. Compromise is the key to problem-solving. Your brief's at eight. Be there or be written up."

I kick my feet up and peruse the POD. Lasagna for lunch, tossed green salad, seasoned vegetables, hot buttered buns. Deborah Norville reports a speech by Saddam, *The mother of all battles will be our battle of victory and martyrdom. There is no path except the path we have chosen.* It occurs to me that I am in love with Deborah Norville. I sip my coffee, slight taste of fuel. Nerdy's lips are parted, tentative, expectant. *Expectants,* I think.

"Let you know after sick call. Dese dahn head codes ah hahd to shake."

"I already talked to the Chief. I know all about your malingering bullshit." Then he puts on this fraudulent concern. "Maybe you'd like to share these feelings of yellow-dog cowardice you've suddenly developed. We can work through them together. Psychodrama, primal screaming, release the coward within. Your ALPO is here for you."

"My ALPO is a dog penis. Achoo. Achoo. Sniffle-sniffle."

"You think this is funny. We're talking about war, good versus evil, a peaceful people held hostage by a madman terrorist Hitler. He builds nukes to blackmail the West. He sponsors terrorism, kills innocent people. He uses chemical weapons on his own citizens and on his enemies. Sworn to destroy Israel. Holds power through fear, intimidation, assassination. He is another Hitler. There's only one way to deal with a Hitler. He must be destroyed. We must destroy him. It's our duty."

"There aren't any other Hitlers. There was only the one. This is someone else."

"Look at those oil fires, an ecological disaster. It could take years to put them out. I'm talking smoke and soot blocking ultraviolet rays, collecting in giant clouds moving around the planet. A new ice age."

"A clever solution to global warming."

"These are facts. It's in the papers, on TV. Evidence. Hard evidence. It's all around you. You're in denial. Get out of denial."

"Indications, probabilities, likelihoods, echoes and shadows, shaped and formed, massaged and sculpted. For all I KNOW he's the *Monitor* and we're steaming to Hampton Roads. Which reminds me, you correct my gram packet yet? Wanna argue about the *QE II* classification?"

"All right, don't think of humanity, don't think of anyone else. That's your style. Then think of this, shithead; court-martial, prison, dishonorable discharge, never again being allowed to vote, acquire a federal firearm license, take a civil service exam. Think of that. You'll never work for the post office."

"I'm not needed here. We're not doing sub-ops. My expertise has no purpose here. I am superfluous."

"We have other tasks, support tasks."

"What, tanking? They don't need back-seaters for tanking."

"Surface plotting, open ocean surveillance. We've got one of the best radars in the air."

"Achoo."

"What are you afraid of? Half their air force is in Iran. The other half barely flies."

"What am I afraid of? What am I afraid of?" I set down my coffee and lean into him, face to face, American Fighting Man to American Fighting Man, techno warrior to techno warrior, Ground Control to Major Tom. He wants to know, I'll tell him. "I'm afraid of everything. You think war scares me? Is that what you think? Well, it does, it scares the shit out of me. And so does that airplane. That airplane scares me. And nuclear winter scares me. And fallout from Chernobyl mutating Finnish reindeer. And toxic fibers in my uniform. And Legionnaires' Disease, that scares me. And Killer Bees. And drive-by shootings. And poisoned Tylenol. And crude nuclear devices. And strip-mining, and the vanishing rain forests and AIDS and the Rose Canyon Fault and Japanese investors and rising interest rates and falling interest rates and people with accents and Third World population growth and the coming millennium and liquefied natural gas and cable TV and microwave ovens and botulism and *E. coli* and unnamed deadly Amazonian viruses and the little petro-skin floating on my coffee. I'm afraid of my ignorance. I'm afraid of things I can't see, things I don't even have words for. I could go on and on. But the main thing that frightens me is fear. Fear of fear, that's what I'm suffering from. I'm afraid of YOUR fear. I'm afraid of this boat's fear. This boat is jammed with it, it's oozing out the hatches, we leave a snail trail of it in our wake. Oozing, oozing, oozing."

"It's easy to rationalize cowardice. Courage requires faith."

"I like to think facing a court-martial is a courageous act."

"That's cowardly courage."

"Sniffle, sniffle."

Nerdy makes a disgusted grunt and, our pathetic debate stalemated, looks away. I turn to the TV. Willard Scott talking snow. Uncomfortable moments pass. A static interlude. Then from behind me Nerdy says, "Did you hear about Simpson?"

"What about him?"

"He's missing since last night."

"Missing? How is one missing on a ship? It's a finite area, a closed system."

"Didn't come back to his stateroom. Didn't show up for work. They call that missing. I see this as a symptom of a greater reality. Things are happening. Systems are breaking down. I know you don't care but those of us who do are concerned. If you see him turn him in."

"Turn him into what?"

Nerdy's right. Things ARE breaking down. Hot buttered buns with lasagna? Makes no sense. Should be garlic bread.

After parboiling my ears again I head down to sick call. The flight surgeon gives me another three-day down chit but he makes his skepticism clear. There won't be another one. My balls are aching as I swallow my new and unmarked tablets.

That night I'm heading back from the gym in my shorts, T-shirt and tennies. I'm cutting across the hangar bay when I see a commotion. It's the ship's Captain and a bunch of suits and reporter guys with mini-cams, all escorted by marines wielding major firepower. They're moving in a tight cluster, drawing a lot of attention. Motion, color, light. The Captain stands out like a movie star, one of those huge and strangely drawing faces that broadcast for a hundred yards. There's another media face in the clump, some big old cowboy type with long silver General Custer hair, a fringed leather jacket and some kind of endangered species cowboy boots. His face is all tanning-booth tan and unreally healthy looking. Makes the rest of us look like hospice clients. The phrase bigger-than-life comes to mind. A guy with power, smarts, who knows the worth of an image. Like some apparition all bathed in heavenly whiter-than-white video light glinting, refracting from silver and turquoise. He's talking loud, boisterous, jocular, cracking up the reporters.

They approach, an event, an organism, layered: the marines, the suits with fat and pricey briefcases, the video guys, and the glowing, light-sucking core: the cowboy guy, the Captain, and someone in between who I now see is Rudy.

Rudy in the light.

Dumb, happy, proud, grinning from this world to the next. Like he died and went to network. I yell to him and wave but he doesn't see me, blinded by the light. (Springsteen. Manfred Mann's Earth Band.) They come closer and I yell again, jump up and wave. I'm ignored, like I don't exist. The Captain and the cowboy have him hemmed in, carrying him forward by each elbow, propelling him along, part of the organism, like the famous woman's car in the crowd. Rudy doesn't see me, can't hear me, like he's on some other plane of existence, some other dimension that I can see and hear but can't access. I yell one more time but I'm brought down mid-yell by a rifle butt crashing down on my shoulder. I'm flat on my ass, rubbing my shoulder, watching the organism make its way. I can't believe it. Rudy the rock. Rudy so real. And now he's gone.

Day Six

WHILE SHOWERING I notice this big bruise on my thigh. But un-like the jarhead-inflicted one on my shoulder I don't know where this came from, can't remember banging into anything. I press the green-purpleness and feel nothing. Then I remember the other day leaning my palm on a huffer exhaust in the hangar bay and not noticing the burn till I saw the seared arc of flesh. At breakfast I balance an ice cube on the back of my wrist and watch it melt. I feel something but not what you're supposed to feel.

When I stop by the ready room Napoleon asks if I heard about Mr. Simpson.

"Still missing?" I ask.

"They're figuring he's dead. I overheard it from the XO. Found his ID card stuck inside a gas mask hanging off the pitot tube of an F-14. There was tiedown chains missing off the F-14 so they figure he wrapped him-self up and jumped. This is confidential. Don't let it get around. A morale thing."

"No witnesses?"

"Watch says he didn't hear or see nothing."

"Usually you hear the plop when they jump."

"You heard of this happening before?"

"The method's textbook, practically a cliché. Wrap yourself in tiedown chains and take a long walk on a short deck. Usually it's some heartsick non-rate, though, the quiet sensitive type who discovers his hooker is acting like a whore while he's out guarding the sea-lanes. Happens about once a cruise."

"He doesn't seem like the type."

"What type is he? I mean was he?"

"Dunno, never saw him except on the monitor."

"Come to think, me neither."

"Maybe he never really existed."

"May be. That might explain why I don't feel anything."

"You neither?"

The rest of the day I spend in the shop with Nerdy, the Chief, and Bucket hypnotized by Rudy's image on news program after news program. NBC, ABC, CBS, Fox, CNN, Headline News, AFRTS, BBC, PBS, he's everywhere simultaneously. The same empty flat vision of Rudy in custody, flanked by the Captain and Michigan and marine guards. A scene I witnessed firsthand but which looks foreign to me now. I had to learn or re-learn that the figure in the center, so much more humbled and diminished by the tape, all the shades of expression and color just slightly askew, drained of his exuberance, his bearish power, yet simultaneously enlarged in some mysterious way, bloated, that this image was indeed Rudy. But over the course of the day, after repeated viewings of the same footage, this image, this new videoized Rudy rushed along through Michigan's orchestrated media gauntlet, digital and unrelenting in its faithful memory and replay, has begun to replace that Rudy that lived in my squishy porous meat memory.

"It reminds me of that famous picture," says Bucket. "That picture of the guy who shot the President."

"Hinckley?"

"The one that looked like Pee-wee Herman. The one that shot Kennedy. You know, that picture where the Pee-wee Herman guy gets shot and there's the cowboy on one side and the other guy on the other? I don't know the names but I know the picture. That's what Rudy looks like."

Bucket's right. The angle, the crowd, Rudy propelled between the two, Michigan's Dallas caricature. I'm annoyed. Now I'll always associate the two images, some tiny wire of a neurotransmitter will forever tie the two pictures. Oswald and Ruby. Oswald and Rudy. Ruby and Rudy. Synaptic commingling. Another footing for the virus penetrating my memory, the host body, eating away. A further step in Rudy's dissolution into the image world.

248

"Now we're down to four," says Nerdy. Then, glancing my way acid-eyed, "And one's on the sick-list."

"Ye-up," says the Chief. "Funny, though, it's like he's right here with us, old Rudy. I don't feel like he's gone at all."

"He's better than here," says Bucket.

I video some of the broadcasts, making sure to get the network banners. Everyone's wearing their flight suits except me. I should feel guilty but I'm not. I'm not feeling much of anything. Except time slipping away. I feel the oily motion of time.

Day Five

WE PASS THE DAYS in meals, the weeks in mailcalls, the months in paychecks. Only eleven days since leaving the P.I. and it seems like a lifetime since I last stepped off the brow. I try walking off my restlessness. Back home I used to jog the circumference of the island which is divided almost equally between the airbase and an upscale burb that tries to pretend the airbase isn't there. I would start on Ocean Boulevard, lined with lush waterfront mansions of no consistent period or design — Basque fortress beside Tudor castle beside sixties low-slung techno sleek — and jog down the beach to the old Hotel del Coronado where they filmed *Some Like It Hot* and a lot of other movies and TV shows and whose Victorian turrets and conical roof Mel once described as an architectural cross between the Kremlin and Barnum and Bailey's big top. Then I would cross over from the ocean to the bay side and run the shore by the golf course down to the other big hotel, The Meridien, new and low and vaguely malevolent like Dr. No's yacht or a pharmaceutical company, then on down by the waterfront theme mall, T-shirt shops and giant cookie franchises, to First Avenue and the big bayside homes, old retired captains and admirals in million-plus houses they bought cheap in the sixties and seventies, natty old guys in bright double-knits puttering in geometrical gardens or polishing showroom clean '73 Buick Skylarks or Olds Cutlasses. Then down to the air station back gate where I flash my ID and jog past the quaywall where the carriers loom six stories high, then around the bend, still along the water, to the helo aprons, H-3s, SH-60s, CH-53s, 46s swarmed like sleeping wasps on the tarmac, past the fishing pier then around the runways where jaunty white-hulled sportfishers with joke names like Fortuna or Kwitchurbitchin head out to sea alongside terrifying black humpy attack subs. Then back to the ocean side along the Sea And Air's back nine, more natty old white guys and Clark Kent lieutenants, to where that beach is separated from the civilian beach by razorwire and chain link running down the shore and vanishing beneath the surf, then out the gate and back down mansion-lined Ocean Boulevard to where I started. A seven-mile circle. I could jog it in an hour, complete the circle of my daily existence, hem in the geography of my life.

But here on the boat there are no circles, no arcs, no bends. Only straight lines, vectors, channels, the left-brain incomplete reality of ninety-degree angles. Dead ends. And the third dimension of the ship's geography: height, elevation, altitude. Up and down ladders. No single discrete edge rimming in the whole. I walk it anyway, unsatisfied, frustrated by the constant obstacles impeding my forward movement, the lack of a center and a traceable periphery. I am a sound wave in an anechoic chamber, diffracted, diffused, my energy dissipated, attenuated. But still I walk. Each step a second, sixty steps a minute, thirty-six hundred steps an hour, making the most of my time.

Day Four

THE GROUND WAR HAS BEGUN.

The first video of Gulf War ground fighting shows bewildered and terrified Iraqi infantrymen shot to pieces in the dark by U.S. attack helicopters. One by one they were cut down in the middle of the night by an enemy they could not see. Some were blown to bits by bursts of exploding cannon shells. Others jarred from sleep and disoriented fled their bunkers under a firestorm.

They have carried the war to the Iraqis with their powerful Apache attack helicopters, which only strike at night and are designed to destroy men and tanks with cannons and laser-guided missiles using infrared optics.

"A truck blows up to the right, the ground blows up to the left," a returning pilot is quoted as saying. "They had no idea where we were or what was hitting them. When I got back I sat there on the wing and I was laughing. I wasn't laughing at the Iraqis. I was thinking of the training, the anticipation . . . I was probably laughing at myself. . . . Sneaking up there and blowing this up and blowing that up."

"There is a systematic campaign of executions of people they've tortured before . . . they are grabbing people and summarily executing them," Marine Brig. Gen. Richard Neal, chief spokesman for the U.S. command, told a news briefing in the Saudi capital, Riyadh. "This is terrorism at its finest hour," Neal said.

A Newsweek poll reports three out of five Americans support a ground war to humiliate Saddam Hussein. The alternative of letting Saddam save

252

face to avoid a bloody ground war appealed to thirty percent compared to sixty-two percent who favored humiliating Saddam.

The U.S. navy man accused of slaying a gay peace activist in the Philippines has issued a statement saying he is glad he did it. It needed to be done. And he only regrets losing the chance to defend his country. The navy man was assigned to a warship steaming for the Gulf War when he allegedly discovered the gay peace activist in the act of molesting a child.

Violin maestro Isaac Stern played alone on stage to an audience in gas masks during an Iraqi missile attack near Jerusalem Saturday night. As air raid sirens sounded, hundreds of music lovers bent beneath their seats to retrieve their masks. The Israeli Philharmonic Orchestra left the stage. But the seventy-one-year-old Stern returned without a gas mask and played a Mozart solo to the packed concert hall. It was ten minutes before the all-clear sounded and the audience, which included Defense Minister Moshe Arens, removed their masks.

Today's forecast for Iraq is for continuing and variable strong winds whipping up sand, and cloudy, rainy weather with warm temperatures.

Day Three

I HAVE TO ASK DIRECTIONS three different times before finding the MAA shack. It's through a battered black hatch off the hangar bay and down a shaft of ladders that seem destined for nowhere. I can't believe there's somewhere on this ship I haven't seen before. Virgin territory. Inside is a counter with a bell, two bulkhead-mounted TVs radiating porn from jutting angle-iron platforms, hand-lettered signs all over advertising soft drinks and microwavable sandwiches and video rentals. Beta format is half price. Dumchowski's fiancée is taped to the countertop, preserved beneath acetate, posed like Wonder Woman, totally buff except for a huge rubber schlong strapped to her loins. I ring the bell.

Out waddles my old buddy the porn Chief, clutching a half-eaten burrito with the wrapper peeled back like a banana.

"It's you, you crazy fock," he says ripping into the burrito.

"Yo, Chief. Still mad at me?"

"Maybe yes maybe no. What you doin' here?"

"Got a favor to ask."

"You gonna buy sumtin'?"

"Yeah, I'll take, um, a Coke."

"Diet, cherry, no caffeine, Classic . . ."

"Regular's okay."

He sets down the can, makes change from a real cash register that spits out a real receipt.

"I need to talk to my buddy, Rudy. You know, the one in the brig?"

He gets all excited. "Dat guy who killed the child molester? Dat's your bud?"

"He's from my shop."

254

"Oh, yeah. I hear he was an AW aviation fock like you. Dat locky fock. He's all over the news, all over everything. He's one famous sumbitch." He's about to take another bite, looks at the burrito innards and throws it in the shitcan.

"I need to see him. Can you get me in?"

"Focking thing's still frozen inside." He smears burrito residue on his pants. "You can't get in dere. Dat's Mar-Det. Jarheads ain't gonna let you see him."

"No way, huh?"

"No focking way."

"Thought you might know someone or something, you know, have a little pull."

"Sure, I know dose guys. I know all dose guys. But dey're not letting you in dere. He's a celebrity now, the locky fock. I could maybe get a message to him, though. But it'll cost you."

"I was kinda hoping to talk with him. But I guess . . . What's the price?"

He hands me a bunch of flyers from a stack on the counter.

"One of dese in all your squadron spaces."

"Not the line shack," I mock plead. "Don't make me go into the line shack."

"Especially da line shack."

I scrawl a quick how-ya-doing note and give it to the Chief. He tucks it in his pocket and says he'll be right back.

"Mind da store."

I sip my Coke and flip through a porn rag called *Jugs*. A green shirt drops off a video. I just finish my Coke and toss the can into the recyclable bag when the Chief gets back. He hands me a note.

"Don't forget," shaking a pudgy digit. "Da line shack, too."

The note says, Fax me at 0576. Rudy.

Maeterlink charges me twenty bucks to rent his PC. But it's the only one I know with a fax modem so I pay. Who needs a fax on a ship? The computer's set up in a black-curtained cubicle in the back of the cold humming bunker of the ASW Module. Takes an hour to wire into the ship's antique phone system, numb fingers tied up in knots, but finally I get it all up.

I click on the fax program and type in a message asking whether Rudy still thinks it's worth it. While waiting for a response I bundle up tighter in the borrowed parka and try to squeeze my fingers warm. I swear I don't know how these guys work in this cryo-storage twelve hours a day. I imagine my words scrolling out on shiny curled paper somewhere in the bowels of the ship, the mystical quality of the fax. Thermal parchment. Finally the computer beeps and a cue tells me a fax has been received. I click to display and there's Rudy's surprisingly neat and feminine Catholic school script. A representation, I think, a facsimile.

You kidding? Worth it? I'm happier than I ever been in my life. I'm in jail. I'm going on trial. I'm famous and on the inside. You see me on Brokaw? Christiane Amanpour's piece on CNN? What a stern babe. I want her for my dominatrix. Think I could wangle an intro? I now know all the rest of my life was preparation for this moment, this event. It's what I was meant for. I'm in this cage but the world comes to me here. You should see the letters. Michigan, the reporters and flunkies, they talk to me, show me respect. Michigan's handling everything, shows me how to talk, what to expect, what to say and how to gracefully dodge blabbing other stuff, how to frame and merchandise. I'm a product, he says, and I need the proper packaging. Package me, I tell him. Ha! He's got a whole separate demographics department. He's negotiating with Anita to come back. The media beast is stirring, going for the bait. The jarheads treat me like a sage, seek my counsel, ask for my autograph. One guy offered me a hundred bucks for a stenciled dungaree shirt. I'm collectable! They think I have secret knowledge, like I'm plugged into God or something. It's better than fucking. Almost. Ha-ha. Fax back.

I blow into my cupped hands. Tap out a response.

Something I want to ask you about. Maybe like your marine friends I think that since you've departed this plane you've achieved access to some wisdom or something. Maybe that's crazy and maybe not. I don't know. But you know my down-chit expires today and they'll be making me fly tomorrow and I don't want to. In fact I'm petrified. Of course this is partially your fault since by deserting us for killer/victim fame and fortune there's one less body here and the pressure's doubly on me to mount the deathbird. I could break my leg or something but I'm too chicken to hurt myself to avoid getting hurt. Even though getting hurt is better than getting dead in the short and long run. There's no shortage of things to be afraid of but I can't put my finger on one thing. I know I don't want to fly but I can just as easy get killed right here in my rack (like I just heard happened to twenty-eight soldiers in their Scudded barracks in Dahran) so why I draw the line at flying I can't say. Except that I think, I KNOW, the plane is trying to kill me. It's the technology that's out to get me. It's turned on me. If I just refuse the Chief says they'll court-martial me and in wartime that's sure to mean prison and despite your lofty example of success with incarceration I'd just as soon pass thank you oh so much. So tell me great wizard but please make it brief, is it a sharp stick in the eye or a swift kick in the ass?

It takes a long time for Rudy to answer so while I'm waiting I break Maeterlink's pathetic security access code and re-format it so when he punches in his password he'll get a series of interrogatives like Are you a butt-sucking, shit-eating herpetic mongrel dog? or Is your mother a subsidized low-income rental unit? all of which he will have to answer in the affirmative in order to log on. Small things amuse small minds. Finally the fax beeps.

I am no longer of your measly world or its puny concerns. I have con-tracts to sign, meetings to meet, deals to cut. I'm supposed to be prac-ticing my non-regional media elocution so I can speak TV-talk which is supposed to sound like you're not from anyplace. God, I love this. But I'll tell you what I learned so far. And that's this, everybody knows too much about everything to know anything. And somehow that turns into everyone thinking everything is probably the opposite of what it is, or maybe not the opposite, but something else anyway. Everything you al-ways thought is always proved wrong so the only way to act is against whatever you think. Michigan says truth is vapor, it's dog farts. Once it happens it disappears into the air and you can't get it back. I don't know what he means but I know he makes a shitload saying stuff like that. He also says the bucks justify the bullshit. I know what *that* means. I got two things to say here. Whatever you think is true and reasonable and nor-mal probably *isn't* so do something else. And if you're gonna trash your navy career (ha-ha) then you better have a good hook 'cause otherwise ain't nobody's gonna care and you'll end up cooling your ass in a cold place for a long long time. And they won't give you a fax machine let alone elocution lessons. Gotta go. My audience awaits. Barbara Walters' people want a one-on-one and I gotta practice making real tears come out on cue. Fair winds and following seas. Your Buddy, Rudy.

Nothing is true. There is no truth. I think I'm beginning to under-stand. Like when a submarine gives off a turbine whine, that message of its existence. The truth of the message. It's all there at first but as it moves farther from the receiver things assault it, try to damage it, chip away at it, other sounds, fish and surf, other ships, then there's physical deterioration, refraction and absorption, the energy being consumed as it passes from molecule to molecule in whatever medium, salt water or telephone lines or human transmission paths. Assaults from everywhere. All this warfare waged against the message until there's almost nothing left of it by the time I hear it, by the time it gets to the listener, the receiver. Almost nothing, a shadow of the original message, bits and pieces, a trace. Or maybe it's been totally degraded, maybe it's been so worked over by the time you get it that it's something else altogether, a completely new message that makes you believe you're listening to the *QEII* when it's really a Soviet cruiser or a Madonna babe in a window. Maybe your feelings make mistakes, maybe my fear has misclassified its source. Maybe it's not the airplane. Maybe I'm afraid because I don't know what I'm afraid of.

I close the fax program and power down Maeterlink's PC. I look around the dark claustrophobic module for Maeterlink's outline. All the green scopes and dim lights and banks of flashing CPUs and processors and scanners and backlit plotting boards. The hum. Data in motion. Ones and zeroes. Tick-tick-tick. Garbage in, garbage out. No Maeterlink. I don't localize his form. No trace or residue. I find myself standing, in my loaned parka, behind a tech monitoring a scope. Glowing radar sweep rotating. Viruslike blips, contacts, returns, messages, irradiated, light, throbbing with each sweep.

Preparation H stops the itch and pain of hemorrhoidal flare-up.

I tape one of the Chief's flyers to a plotting board, dump the parka in a chair and leave.

After I go by medical for my up-chit I drop by the shop. No one's around. I leave the up-chit in Nerdy's in box with a note. I'm up. Fly me.

Day Two

"WHAT DO YOU MEAN I'm not flying? What kind of bullshit is this?" I can't believe it. I'm holding the flight schedule, hot off the antique reproduction device they call a mimeograph. We're heading into the Gulf, passing through the Strait of Hormuz. It's choke point ops and the squadron's been tasked with laying sonobuoy barriers ahead of the task group, searching for lurking subs lying in wait in the shallows. Real anti-submarine warfare. REAL ASW. The thing I've been training and simulating for all these years.

Nerdy's smirking. "You said you didn't want to fly, you're not flying. What's the big deal?"

"My down-chit expired yesterday. I'm up. I'm supposed to be flying. It's my yob, man. I love my yob."

"I can't read minds. How'd I know you'd have a change of heart? The other day it was achoo-achoo. Now it's wah-wah, why can't I fly? Why don't you get your shit in one sock?"

"You knew I was up. You knew this was real ASW. And you knew I'd want to fly."

"I didn't know shit."

"Gimme one of your flights. You don't need two flights. What about crew rest?"

"Fuck that. This is real ASW. Live torps. If there's badguys to be got, I'm gettin' 'em."

"Where's the Chief. I'm taking this to the Chief."

"Too late. He launched an hour ago."

"I'm going to skeds. I'll talk to Whitman."

"Go ahead. It's too late, schmuckhead. The flight sked's etched in stone. Why not relax, do some training grams. You could do to log a little training time."

We're on modified general quarters all day long, which means we don't have to wear our 'varks but we do have to stay at battle stations. This translates to me sitting in the shop twiddling my thumbs with not even TV to look at while the Chief, Bucket and Nerdy rotate on and off their flights. So it's me with my mask, which I wear anyway, and my fear. I'm dying to get in the plane. I don't really care all that much about the ASW shit. I do but I don't. Mainly I just didn't want Nerdy knowing my real need. I'm eating myself up with all this and it just seems like facing the plane will bring something to a head. It's not like *confront your fears and everything will be swell.* Not that at all. Or maybe it is. I don't know. I don't know anything. But I know that sitting here soaked in this malignant festering fear is unbearable. If getting in that plane might change this then let me at it. I'll try anything. It's getting so I'd almost rather be dead than be afraid. Maybe this is what happened to Simpson. Maybe he just saw it all around him, maybe he was reading the signals in his own way and couldn't make them mean anything but dread and horror. Maybe he realized that even if the bombs and gas and fuel-air explosives and missiles and the war and everything, just everything went away, maybe if all of this turned out to be a big nothing, a total zero, maybe he knew that even if that happened the fear would remain. Who wouldn't jump with a thought like that rolling around in your head?

That night after flight ops and everyone's racked out I go down to skeds to see tomorrow's flight schedule rough. I've got a brief for a surveillance hop at eleven hundred. We're in the Persian Gulf. Hallelujah. I'm flyin' or I'm dyin'.

Day One

AFTER THE BRIEF I'm heading for the paraloft. It's a surface search and surveillance mission, vectored around by the E-2 to ID surface contacts. Radar run-ins, drilling holes in the sky. Eye in the sky. Watching them watching us watching them watching us watching them. . . . Piece of cake with microwave frosting. Anybody wants me I'll be radiating.

But this is a REAL mission. It's not ASW, not the sexy stuff like the fighter guys but still my very first REAL mission with a war and an enemy and guns and missiles and deadly intent. They are out there, making a target of me, I am becoming a blip in need of classification, their microwaves will pierce my body, agitate me at the molecular level, which they already do anyway but this time it won't be just watching. Or at least the intent is not just watching.

This war is being fought with high technology.

I am less than assured.

But at least I'm flying. The joy of sweating black balls of terror.

In the paraloft I lace claustrophobic through rows of metal racks hung with droopy green-hide flight gear to the back, the riggers call it the AW ghetto, and the hook where my name is scrawled in felt-tip on lime masking tape. I go through my survival vest, clockwise from the right top where I check my flashlight, the battery in my Prick-90 radio, signal mirror, strobe light with the Velcro patch for helmet mounting. I check the CO_2 bottles at the waist. I check my pencil flares making sure no PR ripped 'em for shooting off at pool parties. I go all the way around, zippers and snaps, enjoying the ritual, drawing comfort from my economy of motion, the drilled-in sameness and completeness of the inspection, a downy numbness overtaking me. Whistle, shroud-line cutter, sea dye marker, knife and whetstone. Each in its own pocket, each secured by a jungle-green lanyard.

Discuss the parachute landing techniques for the following: land, water, night, day, tree.

Man, hero, mission, fear, death. Potent words which have no surface. I can't grip them. Too slippery for meaning. Old books and movies full of those words, back when there was substance to them. My father in Nam, Grampa in the South Pacific. Now it's NOW. The only thing I know is that I don't know anything.

I check my helmet bag, pocket my gouge book (with its subject tabs made from blue Dymo label tapes: COMMS, ESM, RDR, RECCO, SUBS, NAV, DTALNK; I have the best collection of checklists, gouge cards and cheat sheets of anybody, a fact that normally gives me no end of joy) next to my blue NATOPS in-flight-emergency pocket-rocket. Swap a dark visor onto my helmet and polish it with its flannel bag. Check for my O_2 mask and its long snaky hose that always reminds me of those joke snakes that sprout from cans. Finally I stuff in my 'vark. Zip up.

I step into my torso harness, pull the leg straps up around my thighs and crotch, unbunch my longjohns and adjust my balls, pull over the shoulder straps, careful not to catch the left one on my shoulder pocket full of pens and Rolaids, thread the strap through the chest buckle, *threading the needle,* hopping from foot to foot while yanking it tight, making sure everything constricts around me, squeezing my ribs, sternum, clavicles, compressing my spine, the python that squeezes you safe, the tighter the better. In an ejection slack maims, slack kills. I don my survival vest, zip it, snap it, clip it. I savor the heft, the bulk. Eyes closed I move my hands to the beaded lanyards connected to levers that pierce CO_2 cartridges and inflate the flotation bladders. I do it again, three times, until I find them without fumbling. It's supposed to be salt water activated but you never know.

One last go-over. Snapped, zipped, strapped, feeling the authority of bulk. Give a buff to the toes of my boots on the back of each leg. Dressed to kill.

I pass Dumchowski cursing and futzing with his kneeboard, one of the dumbest, most over-engineered pieces of flight equipment a subcontractor ever put his kids through law school on. I threw mine away the day they issued it.

"What's up, Lieutenant?"

262

"This fucking thing. . . ."

It's a writing pad you strap to your knee, contoured, built-in night light, clip for paper, pen wired on, all in high-tech matte black. He's banging on the light.

"Fucking light won't work."

"If that's news, sir, then you might want to know that the pens never work and the thing's too bulky to wear under your INCOS tray anyway."

"They work okay. I just gotta . . . *shit!*"

He drops the batteries and all trussed up like we are the idea of bending over is pretty dreadful. He's taking deep breaths and his face goes maroon, kneeboard hand trembling. Then he makes this gurgling anguished noise and slams the kneeboard against the iron piping of the rack. Not just once but over and over, bits of plastic flying, pen on its lanyard whipping everywhere, screaming, *you fuck-king THING, you fuck-king THING!*

Last thing before heading topside is to drop by the module for the TTC and ATR, which I always save to last since the two weigh about twenty pounds and along with the other twenty pounds of flight gear and survival stuff and me wearing my fire-retardant thermals in this tropical steambath, you do much running around and you're chasing heat stroke.

I sign the log and Maeterlink hands over the red bag with the ATR and TTC.

"You scared?" he asks.

I have to think for a minute while tucking away the load cue sheet and shouldering the bag. "No more than usual, I guess."

"I'm scared," he says. "Seeing you geared up and heading out there makes me scared."

"It's just surface search and surveil."

"I know. There's no reason for it. I think it's like an opportunity to be scared. Like I always wanted an excuse for being afraid and this is it and I don't want to waste it. Here we are in the Persian Gulp, Injun territory, my chance to bask in justifiable fear. I want to celebrate, rejoice, wear a T-shirt that says, I AM AFRAID."

"You look like you're handling it pretty well."

"Never happier in my life."

I notice something's different about the Mod. The yellow brick road is gone, so's the OZMod on the door. It's all back to standard issue. "What happened to your motif?"

"Time for a change. Now we're doing a war theme. Like it?"

Down the passageway, over kneeknockers, squeezing through traffic, strap from the ATR/TTC bag slicing my shoulder, sweat breaking out on my forehead, backs of my hands, armpits slick with it when I hit a dead-end. Non-rate's got a passageway taped off for buffing. I try bluffing like I'm a zero. "Mind if I come through, son? I'm in a hurry." But the kid doesn't fall for it. Just shrugs a big negative. "Sorry, sir, closed for field day." Keeps pushing that humming buffer around like it's attached to him, an extension, a fifth rotating extremity. I consider ripping down the tape, charging through, screaming at the kid, *This is WAR you little shithead! WAR WAR WAR!* but in the end I'm not up to it. Instead I cut across the beam, more kneeknockers, dead-end in a fighter squadron maintenance space, then around and back to the ladder that leads up through the island where I take a breather before stepping out into the mayhem of the flight deck. Two brownshirts in cranials and goggles are squatting, haggard and beat in their grimy flight-deck vests. One says something and I pull my helmet away to hear. He has to yell over the jet roar outside.

"Going out to blow up A-rabs, sir?"

"I'm no 'sir', " I yell back. "I knew *my* father." A standard line for which I am rewarded by a weak smile.

"Helos? SAR swimmer? Flying plane guard?" He makes swim stroke motions, slicing the air in greasy gloves with snipped fingertips.

"S-3s."

"Oh." He looks a little baffled. "Guess you guys don't do anything."

"Nothing I know of."

I grin (*mirthlessly,* I think, *sardonically*) and wave, snap my chinstrap, drop my visor, do a last check of me and my gear, making sure all the zippers are secured, FOD flaps, nothing loose to be sucked up intakes. Pat my ankle pocket for my supply of piddle packs and barf bags. Normally before a man-up I'm feeling pretty jazzed about now, clomping around in my flight boots, big and bulky and manly, about to embark on a mission where no man has gone before. All that. I'd never admit it but I kinda got off on that *Top Gun* myth-of-the-flying-warrior stuff. But not today. Today I feel like I've been set up, like I'm the victim on *Murder, She Wrote,* the guy who dies before the first commercial. People are watching while that heavy-handed about-to-be-murdered music plays and I'm walking sappy-dopey right into the claws of my betrayer.

Out on the flight deck my senses are overwhelmed, it's a flat-top antfarm. The usual flight-ops pandemonium but there's something new, something sweeping up in waves like heat from the non-skid, something wrapping, glazing the sensory onslaught of engines turning, planes taxiing, yellow gear zooming, exhaust clouds, furnace wind, prop wash and jet blast buffeting from every direction, vested and cranialed men who holler and dart, burdened, like me, with the accessories of technology, the men dogging ordnance carts stacked high with Sidewinders, HARMs, Harpoons, five-hundred-pounders, thousand-pounders, lugging electronics boxes, tiedown chains, dragging towbars, the plane guard helos launching, the amplified bellowing of the Air Boss trying to coerce some order on the whole mess. Something holds all this in a kind of suspension and I don't know if it's me or if it's something real and loose in the outside world.

I head aft to find the bird, dodging a turning E-2, careful not to trip over the arresting wires, insulated in my gear, the roar and 360-degree threat of flight-ops dulled down, blunted, but still there, an arm-length away. I find 702 wedged between a couple F/A-18s, Commander Whitman already doing the walkaround with the pilot. Looks like they're arguing about something, the pilot pointing and poking in the wheel well, Whitman listening, hands on hips. I wave and he gives me a distracted thumbs up. Before I climb in the hatch I peek around the intake for number two, sometimes you can't tell an engine's turning even if you're standing right beside it. Lost an AT troubleshooter that way last cruise. Coming in to swap out an IRC, sucked up before he knew what hit him, fan blades sliced him into baloney. Pink spray from the exhaust.

I hoist in the ATR/TTC bag and toss my helmet bag after, then climb in just far enough to make certain all four headknockers are down. Seats aren't safetied I don't go in. That's the name of *that* tune. Ejection seat took out an AME couple years back. Bent over an unsafetied seat when something, who knows what, goes shitty. Rocket fires, seat launches, he's shot through the canopy and two hundred feet across the tarmac skipping like a stone. I saw the replay on the security tapes.

Inside's an oven. I pull off my helmet and toss it in my seat, then hang my helmet bag on the hook thing that holds up the INCOS tray. You're not supposed to hang stuff from it but everyone does. Thermometer on the computer is pegged at one twenty-three Fahrenheit. I mop my face on my jersey sleeve and start pre-flighting.

I climb aft and start with the starboard circuit breaker panel. Run my fingers along rows and rows of black buttons, making sure none are popped. Most guys just eyeball 'em, but the only way to be certain is to touch. When I'm satisfied I go back to the bottom row and pull the two Search Stores breakers; always leave those out till after we launch. Don't want to be jettisoning buoys on deck. Air Boss frowns on that.

Next the starboard avionics shelves. First I check all the knurl-knobs, twist them tight, make certain the boxes are secured and seated right, won't become missile-hazards during launch or recovery, won't be unseating, disabling a system right when we need it. Then I check the comm-boxes which have their own circuit breakers and the Integrated Radar Control Unit. After that's done I go back forward and get the KOK card in its little plastic case from my helmet bag. I unscrew the two knobs that lock the door to the KYK-28, the black box that encrypts radio comms for secure-voice, turns voices into blurps and chirps and back again. Voice to noise, noise to voice. I pull down the locking arm and slide in the coded KOK card, an abacus with numbers on one axis and letters on the others and these little beadlike things you slide up and down with a ballpoint pen to set the code-of-the-day. I lock it in with the spring-loaded bar. It's kind of like a hand grenade in that if you let go too soon the whole thing springs open and the card decodes.

The pilot climbs in and hollers back if I'm ready for the APU. I give a thumbs up and he signals to the plane captain outside. The APU whines out and finally catches. Pilot flicks on the generators and suddenly the plane is full of noise and lights and buzz and best of all, air conditioning. I put my face up to the vent letting the cool fog blow over me, drying the sweat, cooling my scalp as I run my fingers through my hair. Ice pellets hit me like bullets. Then I pull out the neck of my drenched steamy jersey letting that frosty air circulate through my flight suit. Nothing in the world feels better. Nothing.

Dumchowski climbs in, broadcasting tension. He yells at me to quit blocking the vent.

"AC's for the computer, not for *you.*"

I push past him for the TTC making sure to elbow his spine acciden-
tally.

I pull the DMTU and ATR circuit breakers, then plug in the TTC,
suddenly realizing that this supposedly high-tech, vacuum-sealed black
box is virtually a mil-spec eight-track tape with the computer program
on it. Dinosaur. Thing weighs five pounds, big as a loaf of bread and
holds about as much software as a twenty-dollar data cartridge on my
PC's tape backup. And the GPDC, the general purpose digital computer,
the *electronic heart of the S-3*, big as a four-drawer file cabinet and about
a hundreth the RAM of a good Macintosh with a processor that moves
like old people fuck. I look around and suddenly all these electronics,
these racks of black or grey boxes, it all looks so old, so primitive.

The acoustic tape recorder pulls out in a steel drawer. I lift the lid
to something from the Radio Shack electronics museum, metal toggle
switches and chromium buttons, fifteen-inch glass reels with inch-wide
magnetic tape threaded through a maze of stainless-steel spindles and
tension arms. Ferrous metals, iron-age electronics. The stuff's old as I
am. It used to seem so exotic and tricked out, so complicated and sophisticated, so NEW. But now . . . looks like the prop room for *Assignment
Outer Space*.

Something yanks at my sleeve. It's Dumchowski giving me this hurry-
up look. I secure the ATR and punch in the circuit breakers, do a quick
pre-flight on my seat, pull on my helmet, plug into the ICS so's to hear
what's going on, and strap in. Whitman's going through the checklist up
front. Dumchowski's loading the computer. The hatch is shut from the
outside, the handle turns and locks. We are sealed in. I get a time hack
from the HF radio and set the time-code-generator. Whitman calls for
headknockers. We all arm our ejection seats and confirm.

"TACCO."

"SENSO."

"Pilot."

"COTAC."

The green self-eject light on my console blinks black. If Whitman
yanks his ejector handle, we all go flying in our rocket-powered seats
which may save us or may kill us depending on posture, luck, angle-of-
attack, altitude, and assorted unquantifiable aerodynamic forces. Pilot
releases the hand brake and we taxi to the shuttle. The theme from *The
High and the Mighty* hums through my head. I slip into my gloves, the

flame-retardant backs to prevent incineration if the TACCO ejects prematurely. Happened to a SENSO back east, barbecued the tendons, kiss off motor skills. The plane jerks with a *thug!* as the launchbar locks into the shuttle. Out my porthole the steam of the catapult gusts by. Men clear the aircraft, jump into the catwalks. I put my tray up and assume the position, feet flat on the deck, calves flush against the seat, arms and elbows tucked, spine straight, head back, tops of my knuckles dancing on the lower ejection handle. We go full throttle, the high-pitch roar, shaking, bucking. Then the stroke and we're hurtling down the deck, slingshot. I'm pinned to the seat, heart in my mouth, my dangling helmet bag flies back horizontal, the rackety-clack roller-coaster giving way to smooth flight as our wheels run out of deck, off the pointy end. Out my window black deck and watching faces turn to blue water as we bank port. Endspeed good? Are we climbing? Is there altitude? Are we alive?

Whitman radioes the tower, "Beefsteak seven-oh-two airborne." We're okay. I relax, drop my tray, remove my gloves. I look over at Dumchowski. He's still in his ejection posture. I tap him on the shoulder and he flinches. I put up my visor and give him an everything-copacetic? look. He fumbles up his own visor, gapes all around, out his window where the ocean is falling away. He lets out the breath he's probably been holding since we were on the cat, turns my way and pretends to wipe sweat from his brow, smiling grimly. For the moment we're buds, grateful survivors of the same potential disaster.

The mission goes easy. You'd never know there's a war. The E-2 assigns us a quadrant to search; I run the radar, Whitman does the nav and the comms, the pilot drives us around. Dumchowski keeps track of the ESM, monitoring all the emitters, of which there are a billion, mostly coming from the coast. Khafji, Kuwait City, Bubiyan, Basra. Fingers of light on the scope, reaching.

Each time I get a new radar contact I pass a vector up front. We fly by for a viz then I fill out the contact parameters tableau, assign a contact number and pass it to the E-2 via data-link. Cookbook. Takes about three hours to sweep our sector, ship's name, nationality, course and speed. It's mostly oil tankers, dozens of them. Might seem like business would slow down with one of the locals getting bombed into oblivion by the largest multinational force assembled since World War II but the commercial lanes are jammed. Guess war's not so hard on the oil biz.

"You kidding," says Dumchowski. "They love it. Drives up oil prices. Those OPEC camel jockeys got together and told Saddam (he says Sad*da-a-am,* like the President) to invade just so this'd happen. Kuwaiti oil stops pumping, Iraqi oil stops pumping, instant oil shortage. Everyone else doubles the price on crude and Omar's cuz gets a new Rolls."

"Yeah," says the pilot, "but how'd they know we'd get involved?"

"Texaco, Gulf, Aramco, they're all in on it. Guaranteed the A-rabs they'd get Washington to come ball-busting in. They jack the prices on refined stuff they bought at pre-war prices and make billions. National security."

"National *Social* Security."

"What's good for Shell Oil . . ."

"They're Dutch."

"Oil companies don't have nationalities."

"Shit, oil companies *are* nationalities. This plane oughta say EXXON on the side instead of U.S. Navy."

Whitman slips into a pretty decent sarcastic redneck drawl. "Shit, yew tew boahs soun' lahk a coupl'a commies all that multinashnal eekonomic cornspiracy tawk."

"I ain't no commie. Commie's just a guy with a gun who can't buy bullets. I just know who butters my toast is all. Oil prices might go up in the short run but when it's all over we're gonna own Saudi Arabia, Kuwait *and* Iraq. We'll be floating in cheap oil for the next fifty years. I say *that's* worth fighting for."

Whitman gives an unconvinced uh-huh then, "SENSO, what do you think it's about?"

I'm doing some housekeeping, organizing contacts for the data extraction. "Dunno, sir. I guess I really don't think too much about oil companies or politics or economics or whatever this is. I'm more interested in just keeping my skinny little ass intact."

"Attaboy. The wisdom of the common man. Guess that puts us all in our place." Then with concern, "Well god*dam.*"

I can see the caution panels up front where a red warning light is lit but I can't tell which one. Whitman says, suddenly serious, "Fire light, number two engine. Pull out your pocket rockets."

"Mother*fuck*er!" screams Dumchowski, showering his CRT with spit, "I'll jettison the buoys." He's going for the Sono Control Panel.

"Standby TACCO," Whitman barks. "Let's go through the checklist."

"I can punch 'em at the same time."

"I said STAND*B*Y!"

"But sir. . . ."

"We're not dumping thirty grand of buoys till we know what's going on."

I pull out my pocket checklist and turn to the engine fire section. Whitman reads the steps and doublechecks that the pilot does each one right. *Pull the overhead fire T-handle for the affected engine.* I follow along while making sure I'm strapped in right and stowing all the loose shit that might screw me up during ejection. BEST case is a single-engine approach. That's IF the fire goes out after shutting down number two. Death comes if you bolter and there's not enough end speed to fly off the pointy end and come around for another try. Splash. But, I reassure myself, we've got a lot of wing area, only need a hundred twenty knots to fly. I do some ballpark calculations: for an emergency approach they'll crank up the carrier, that gives us about thirty knots of wind, plus being turned into the wind, add maybe ten knots, that's forty knots of free air. We'll only need another eighty to be flying when we run out of deck. But there's windshear, that'd kill us. Wrong attitude. Arresting gear failure, snapped cable. Dead air. Hydraulic failure. Propulsion casualty on the carrier. Blown tire. Generator failure. Frozen flaps.

Worst case is if the fire doesn't go out, then it's eject-eject-eject. No questions. I'm going through vivid recreations of low-level ejection scenarios, wondering if the seat will work and, if it does, what it'll feel like to get blasted through the canopy like riding on the cone of a Delta rocket. I'm seeing videoscapes of guys ejecting in the wrong posture, arms ripped off, spines snapped, faces barbecued by rocket blast. Or the plane too low, attitude screwed up, casualties of attitude, fired straight into the water, a bullet shot into a pond, or splatted into the flight deck, or the island structure like that guy on the *Coral Sea*. Or surviving the ejection okay only to be run down by the boat, meat-grindered by the props. Or tangled in the chute, it filling with water and dragging you down, down like the giant sea anchor it becomes. That's the worst vision, the conscious victim sinking to the bottom, watching the light above turn to murk and vanish while falling through the sonic layer, the thermocline, the deep sound channel, maybe even getting some breath from the O_2 mask so to watch yourself die, screaming a scream that shows up as a small dark spot, a trace, on some analyst's display, an insignificant and unnoticed blurb, a bit of ambient noise, part of the background clutter. Noise. A message ignored. Fanmail from some flounder.

Number two is shut down. A layer of vibration vanishes, its absence filling me with anxiety.

"It's out," he says. I exhale a breath I didn't know I was holding. Whitman radioes in, explaining the sit. The pilot's dumping fuel and Dumchowski's dumping sonobuoys, happy to be getting his way. For lack of anything constructive to do I've got the Nav Parameters Tableau up, keeping an eye on our altitude and airspeed. The computer is worthless to me now. All the sensors, MAD, ESM, RADAR, FLIR, worthless. My sonobuoys, sixty of them, thrown away like bags of sand, junk. All those hydrophones and no one to listen. There's nothing for me to watch, nothing to surveil, nothing to listen to. I'm a rock on a sled. All I've got is the old Mark One Mod O window out of which I see the carrier, black trapezoidal outline floating against vast blue, like the earth pictures the moonguys took, and I think of what Mel said about getting outside the Machine, and how now I AM outside the Machine, but looking at it from up here isn't telling me ANYTHING. There's nothing exposed, nothing revealed. Mel was a fake.

When I snap to I realize something's up. There's an edge to Whitman's voice when he talks to the pilot and now that I think of it I haven't heard the pilot much lately. I look over at Dumchowski since he can see the pilot and I can't. I motion up front and shrug like what's up. Dumchowski looks scared.

"Hey Pilot," he says. "Everything okay up there?"

But instead of the pilot, Whitman answers. "We're fine, everything's fine, just a little busy. We're commencing approach. Let's start the landing checklist."

We descend into some overcast. He reads from the checklist on the overhead console, tracing each step with a gloved finger. "Trays stowed, headknockers up, harnesses locked. . . ." I go through the motions like always except this time with a crystalline concentration, a clarity. After donning our O2 masks, Whitman sounds 'varked through a walkie-talkie. "Flaps to take-off, gear down." He radioes in, "Beefsteak seven-oh-two commencing."

Roger Beefsteak seven-oh-two, we have you, five miles.

It's unusually quiet with only one engine. Dumchowski shuts down the computer and assumes the position. There's nothing for us to do but cross our fingers and wait. I tell myself everything's okay. I've done this before and it's not all that dangerous. My fears are irrational. There isn't any bad ju-ju.

"The gear's not down," the pilot says.

"It's down," reassures Whitman. "Three down and locked. All set in back?"

Me and Dumchowski both grunt a roger.

"Doesn't feel right," says the pilot. "I don't think they're down."

"It's sluggish 'cause of the engine," says Whitman. "Indications are three down and locked."

"Doesn't feel right, goddammit."

"All right," says Whitman. "Let's cycle the gear."

I look at Dumchowski. He looks at me, reaches for his upper ejection handle and makes like he's yanking it.

"There, Bob," says Whitman. "Three down and locked."

"Don't call me Bob. I'm the goddammed pilot. Call me Pilot."

Beefsteak seven-oh-two come right two degrees. Four miles.

"The deck's pitching."

"How can you tell? I can't even *see* the deck."

"I said the fucking deck's pitching. And this fucking LSO doesn't know what he's talking about. We're too high."

"He says we're on the glide slope."

"We're too fucking high. It's a rookie. I know his voice."

"Just pay attention, Pilot."

Beefsteak seven-oh-two you are below glide slope. Three-quarter mile, call the ball.

"Give us some power, Pilot."

Pilot radioes in, "Roger. Viking ball." Then snarly, "*I'll* fly the plane, COTAC!"

Beefsteak seven-oh-two, apply power. Power! POWER!

"Listen to the power calls, Pilot."

"Shuttup. Would you just *shut up!*"

"Wave it off, Pilot. That's an ORDER! Wave it OFF!"

Power, seven-oh-two, POWER! — WAVE OFF! WAVE OFF! WAVE OFF!

Somebody mutters, *Aw, fuck you.*

I just get a glimpse of the ramp, the tower, rotating lights, when the whole world turns to shit. The slam-down pounds the breath from me, whips my head like a fist crashing into my jaw. Anguished metal screes and yaws. Dumchowski's tray comes slamming down. Opposing forces pull, push, suck and jerk me from my seat. I fight to retain ejection position. Every muscle is clenched. Outside, deck, planes and people whip by. Postures of terror. *Hurtling,* I think, we are *hurtling* down the deck. We are skidding, sliding, at crazy angles, totally out of control. Someone's screaming to eject and someone else is just screaming. Debris from the overheads is flying all over, strut pins and first aid supplies, the APU handle, piddle packs, a helmet bag. Dumchowski wrestles with his tray. My canopy cracks, light knifes through. Semi-monocoque construction. The screeching twisting roar.

Then silence, a sudden terrifying silence, and outside all is blue. I yank my handle with all my might. I can't believe how far it comes out. I never thought it came out so far.

I am wrapped in thickest smoke. Hot. It is hot. Tremendous weights press on my head, my lungs, my lower lip feels like someone is hanging from it, my face is pulled from my skull. My eyes are collapsing, compressing, squished beneath a rubber boot. My vision narrows to a slit. I fight but I can't keep my eyes open. Where is the beckoning lady? The tunnel and the white light? It all goes narrow pink, then red, then purple, then black.

I've pissed myself. I'm waking up because I pissed myself. My crotch is wet and warm. I've pissed myself and my sheets are soaked and I'll have to air my mattress and everyone will know. I can't believe it. I sigh deep. Water catches in my throat, choking me. I try for another breath and get more water. Coughing, coughing. I panic. I slap at my face. It's my O_2 mask, water's in my O_2 mask. Get the mask off, get the fucking mask off. I'm still coughing, fighting for breath. Claw for the releases, finally the mask falls away. There's air. Thank God there's air. I inhale deep but slow to stave off another fit, avoiding the water lapping at my chin. Water pulses at my helmet. My body suspended in warm fluid. I hear wind and see crisp-edged sunrays glinting in the droplets huddled on my visor. I taste salt and rubber. Sky revolves above me. The droning of the airplane is gone. The humming of the ship is gone. No buzz and hum. Tranquil is a word, I think. Calm is a word.

I am alive. I feel wonderful, high on something, warmth surging up.

I am happy, as happy as I have ever been. *Joyous,* I think, the word is *joyous.* I lift my hand and hold it over me, watch water drape from my glove and matted sleeve. I wipe my visor, smearing, marveling at the designs made by sun and water, hydrogen bonded, forming shapes, skirting the plastic. I am alive, but better, I am not afraid. For the first time since I can remember I am not afraid. I want to mouth religious things, I want to believe something unprovable. Shit happened. And I am alive. Fuckin'-A. I laugh out loud.

Practical thinking creeps in. Slivers of my deep water survival training reminding me that I have simulated doing this before. But this time it is real. I am doing something real. Not processed, not digitized or simulated. Real. And so simple. So simple to be alive. There are complicated mnemonics for recalling survival tasks, acronyms for procedures, but of course I can't remember them. I check for my parachute but it's already detached. Detach from my seat pan and sink my raft. Won't be needing those. I'm floating kind of crooked, tilted over. The neck bladder on my flotation vest isn't fully deployed. I blow into the rubber tube, scrunch the bladders around until it evens out and I'm floating straight, kind of on my back. The swells are big but gentle and I rise and fall from trough to peak without effort. I push up my visor and scan for the ship. It feels like I'm alone out here, solitary, until I kick around and see the looming underside of the flight deck not two hundred yards off, dead in the water. Massive steel jutting. The size of the thing from this vantage shocks me. It's monstrous. And the people. Hundreds, thousands lining the decks, the sponsons, the elevators, every inch of rail occupied by a body pointing, leaning, straining, hollering. I realize they are afraid. Petrified. Terrified. I'm confused. What's to fear? They're throwing stuff in. Flight deck vests are hitting the water, somebody launches a twelve man life-raft, one of the hundreds lining the deck edge, then another goes, and another. They're all over the place. These guys are nuts, they're crazy, they're hysterical. Their voices drift across to me, high wails and squeals like small animals being attacked. Maybe they can't see me, I think, maybe if they saw me they'd see I'm safe. So I pull off my gloves and start feeling around for my rescue strobe and stick it to my helmet's Velcro patch. I wave my arms over my head and yell I'M OKAY, I'M OKAY. But still they launch more rafts and heave in more vests. Then I realize what they're doing, why they're all so crazy and panicked. My thinking is clear. A crystal transparency of events. They're watching ME but SEEING themselves. They're witnessing the possibility of their own deaths in me. They're crazy doing anything to keep death away. I'm the Madonna babe of death here with my little white light flashing them a message, a message from the chaos. I'm on the outside and they're looking to me for the message, the interpretation, for the way the story comes out. And the story is death. It ends in death. All that fear, all that fear of dying, the constant buzzing proximity of it, the ever-denied and buried and disguised REALNESS of it. Keep the story going, they're saying, don't let the story end because we all know how it ends, keep watching, change the channels, find another story. Don't let it end. Keep us behind the glass. Keep IT behind the glass. They are watching me like on a screen, like a naked woman behind a shade, they have traded places with me and become the object of their own gaze. They are me and they are terrified of their own intentions.

The plane guard helo rises to view, a hovering droning insect. I scope around for my crewmates. Between the swells I catch sight of one helmet bobbing and waving and then to the left another doing the same. That's three of us. I twist around and around looking for the last, replaying the horrible possibilities. Finally on the side of me opposite from the others I spot some color between the waves. I wait for the next swell to lift me and push myself up as far as I can. For sure it's a helmet but there's no motion, something's wrong, it's facing down. That's why they're still howling, why they're still petrified. It's not me it's him. It's him they're scared about. There's nothing to do but wait for the helo.

The slope of the swells. I am lifted up one side and ride gently down the other, then up again and down. I ride the waves. Sine waves. Molecular transmission paths. Compression and rarefaction. Ebb and flow. Vibration. Vibration is motion, motion is action, action is life. We ride the waves. I am the message modulated onto an oceanic carrier wave. All of us, all four of us are the message. The helo is a tuner scanning the ocean of frequencies, tuning us in, oceanic demodulator seeking to pluck us from the waves, decode us, unscramble us, amplify us, broadcast us. What is the message?

The helo circles, moving downwind into position, on line with my side of the carrier. I keep my eye on the helmet. No movement. The helo dips down about deck level and starts forward, running the length of the carrier, heading for the helmet behind me. The blades whip the water below and I'm standing by for the pelting rotorwash, all the time keeping an eye on the helmet.

But something happens, the helo stops closing. I look up in time to see one of the twelve-man life rafts spinning on the surface, caught in the helo's vortex. The raft turns and rises up on one end, twirling like some weird ballet, then it leaves the water and goes straight into the helo's tail rotor. The rotor shreds the thing and flings it aft. The helo turns, tilts, then dips and settles slowly and gracefully into the water. At first I am surprised. I didn't know H-3s could land in the water. But then the white body tilts starboard and the rotors hit the water like gunshots. BLAM! BLAM! BLAMBLAMBLAM! The rotors and the gearbox blow apart sending shrapnel flying. The crew, all four of them, come bailing out the side hatch, the last one just as the thing rolls over and fills with water, electronics sparking off inside like fireworks.

I can't believe my eyes. It's like a war zone but with no bad guys. Eight men in the water, thousands on deck screaming hysterically, life vests and rafts all over, fifty million in airplanes, in *high technology*, trashed in the drink. It IS war, I think, war against the fear of war. That's the enemy, that's the bad guy. Fear. Where's the threat? There is no threat, real or simulated. Yet still we're losing.

But the helmet. It'll take ten minutes to turn around another helo. I go on my side and start kicking. This is something I can do. Those faces up there, begging, pleading. I can do this. I can go to my crewmate. My arms are impossibly heavy. There's something wrong with my thigh, the muscle feels bruised and swollen tight so I kick with one leg and pull myself with my arms, somewhere between a side stroke and a back stroke, turning every few strokes to relocate my target, update my fix, refine my vector. I am lifted and dropped by the swells, transmitted. It seems like I'm making no progress, like I'm not closing on the target of interest. Like it'll take forever to achieve the center. But motion is relative. The speed of sound in water depends on three factors: temperature, salinity, and pressure. What's the waveheight? The wavelength? The frequency? Every movement is such an effort, everything weighs so much, flight boots like dumbbells strapped to my feet. But it's action, I tell myself, I am taking action. I see the faces on deck, like the whole ship, the whole world in some grueling, gut-wrenching, breath-held moment. I rise and I fall. I skim the waves. This is a real thing. When I turn now I see more detail, the lieutenant bars sewn white into the shoulders of his flight suit. The water takes on a pinkish tinge. Sea dye marker I think, and continue thinking it even though I know those are Day-Glo green.

When I get to him I lift his arm but the sleeve is empty, hanging like seaweed in my hand. The water's red with arterial blood, the sleeve drenched with it. *Sharks,* I think, *Get away.* I drop it quick, not for that but because I know they've got binoculars on me, magnifying the details. I know the salt taste in my mouth is part him. I want to get sick but there's no time so I swallow the bile and spit. I don't want to be this close. Oh God, I think. Oh God. The faces, all those faces. I turn him so his back is to the ship so they can't see what I already know. I see the crack snaking the helmet's perimeter, the edges of the white reflective tape covering his helmet tinted pink. I lift the helmet from the water. The front half is busted clean off, no visor, no O2 mask. Shards of tape, jagged plastic, polystyrene. There is no jaw or mouth or nose, only a hole of dangly fleshy material drained gray, slack, not rubbery like in movies. Not like in movies, I think. But the eyes, thankfully closed, swollen closed, black and bloated, are Dumchowski's.

I can't hold it back any longer. A rope yanks tight around my gut and the puke erupts past my salt-swollen throat and tongue in a single heave. I cough and catch my breath. Floating bits of food and spit and bile and blood oscillate between us. I know what I have to do. I know what they want. I take a deep breath, let it out and take another. I hold his head so it won't droop and with my other hand peel off what's left of the helmet, all the time keeping his back, his good side, to them. Then I take him and hug him to me, letting that part that used to be face nestle between my cheek and shoulder. Something pokes my neck and I don't imagine what it is or what it might transmit. Then, hugging him close like this I gaze up at the ship, at those thousands of needy, watching eyes. That grand sweep of ship and its sad humanity, the fear, the anguish, the hope. I see the pattern that tells the story. I have, finally, like Mel said, the perspective, to take it all in. I can give them what they want. I can unscramble the message from the noise and chaos. I AM the message. I lift my free arm from the water as high as I can and give it to them, the old thumbs up. I lie to them. I tell them it's all right, the message is that death has not come today. I lie. I simulate life. I am a hero. The crowd goes wild.

When the swimmer comes I am still holding Dumchowski. The roar, the blinding rotor wash. I don't want to give him up. I won't give him up. I didn't like Dumchowski when he was alive, I never liked him. But now he is mine and I won't let him go. I clutch to his waist, hug him to my body,

277

coddle his head like you would an infant's. It doesn't bother me that he is dead. I think he is better off dead. His life has no meaning for me. The beating barrage from the helo pummels us with rock hard water pellets. It's hard to breathe. I miss the calm of twenty minutes ago and know I will not have that again for a long, long time. But somehow that's all right.

The swimmer has assessed the situation and wants me to go up first. He keeps a few feet's distance because he knows I might be panicked, might grab him and pull us both down. I might want to kill us. But I am not panicked. I am calm. I will not give up Dumchowski. I tell the swimmer so, hollering over the roar. He argues but I am adamant. While waiting for the hook to winch down the swimmer keeps his cautionary distance, treading water, visor hiding his features, as unreadable as a trout float. I keep my grip on Dumchowski, my hand on his back under the SV-2. My other hand on the back of his neck, the stubble of his bad haircut. I feel the concavity of his spine, the flesh and muscle like cold stiff dough. I smell his odors. When the hook comes I smooth his hair before lifting him from my shoulder. The swimmer lets the hook ground out in the water then brings it over. He turns away when he sees the hole that used to be Dumchowski's face. With the rotorwash and the swells and spray and the the hook and cable jerking all over it's a struggle hooking us both on but I finally manage and they reel us up, away from the swimmer, they reel us from one context through another, from water through air, hugging, revolving, and finally into the body of that hovering, beating, grey-bellied machine.

When the crewman pulls us inside I am too exhausted to do anything but lie there, shivering, convulsing, watching water run in the grooves of the helo's steel deck. I am helped into a canvas jumpseat. My slouching body resonates with the vibrations of the thing. I will accompany him down to sickbay or wherever they take him. I will stay with him as long as I can, as long as they will let me. I pull the strobe from my helmet, stare at it in my hand, count the seconds between flashes which make purple ovals inside my eyelids. Hematomas. Dumchowski is in the back, laid out and covered with a blue plastic sheet. I shut off the strobe and stow it in my wet pocket, fumble with the snap. I want things organized.

"The War's Over!" It's the swimmer, plopped down beside me and yelling over the engine noise as we vector to the carrier. "Didja hear?!"

Out the side door, framed by it like a movie camera panning by, I see the flight deck covered in white foam and crash trucks, men in all manner of safety wear, fire crews in silver suits, others in black rubber OBAs, still others in their 'varks cleaning up the debris from our crash, and past that another helo plucking crewmen from the water littered with lifeboats, bodies, vests, and the first helo's inverted carcass.

But behind and above and beyond all this manicness and mayhem, this portrait of fear and death, making it all seem puny in proportion, is the most amazing sunset I've ever seen. The sun a huge pulsing red disk hovering over a horizon of thick purple, red, pink and yellow bands, stacked scarves made of the pulp of exotic fruits, that star, menacing, the unblinking eye of the beast, glowing through, obscene, vibrating, lewd, unbelievably big, red as the light in my viewfinder, the light on her stereo.

"It's the oil fires," he yells. "The smoke from the oil fires makes 'em like that."

I nod, still dazzled by that sunset, the throbbing eye. Then it registers what the swimmer said.

"The War?" I yell.

"We're ordered to suspend combat attacks. I guess that means it's over."

What's over? There wasn't any war. Nothing's over. I think of Mel, of Lieutenant Simpson, and now Dumchowski. I mumble to myself, *war war war.* Then to him I yell, *"WAR! WAR! WAR!"* and he looks at me like I'm crazy but I feel pretty good, like that kid's game where you repeat a word over and over until it's gibberish, until the meaning melts away, so I holler it again, as loud as I can, I howl it . . . *WAR-WAR-WAR-WAR-WHOR-WHOR-WHOR-WHOR-ROR-ROR-ROR-ROR* . . . until it becomes a chant, a vibration, a hum I modulate and distort, a transmutation, a transmission, *WAH-WAH, WAH-WAH, WAH-WAH.* . . . An old and basic thing, a proto voice, a throbbing human hum resonating through my skull, my lungs, my bones in counterpoint to the ambient buzz of the helo, wanting to appropriate my vibration, slave me into synch, its motors and engines and whirling gyros, the invisible network of trons and fluids, the zeroes and ones, the ons and offs. My thrum in opposition, in conflict, in action, the reverberations, the molecular penetration.

My howl. My name. Discrete. I feel it. Perfect pitch. Real and true.